THE VANISHING ZONE

THE FIRST TIME: GLASTONBURY, ENGLAND—An ancient and picturesque town, filled with houses, churches . . . and people. Until a demon darkness swept down from the heavens. Then there was nothing but a marshland beneath a murky sky. . . .

THE SECOND TIME: STONEHENGE—Popular tourist spot, crowded with spectators visiting the old Druid stones. Then the black pillar covered it all . . . and everything vanished but the disembodied voices of the people lost forever, until they, too, faded away. Then there was nothing at all. . . .

THE TIMES BEYOND: All the oldest places of the Earth would become vanishing zones—a doorway to oblivion . . . a gateway to terror, or to . . .

Eden

Eden

W. A. Harbinson

A DELL BOOK

Published by
Dell Publishing Co., Inc.
1 Dag Hammarskjold Plaza
New York, New York 10017

For Leslie

Dell ® TM 681510, Dell Publishing Co., Inc.

ISBN: 0-440-12212-0

Printed in the United States of America

May 1987

10 9 8 7 6 5 4 3 2 1

WFH

Book
I

The Past

Prologue

The magnetic forces of water and air tugged Miles Ashcombe out of his restless sleep. Opening his eyes but still held in the web of his dream, he stared into the darkness, briefly frozen by his fear. He took a deep breath and sat upright, sensing a presence in the room, then swung his legs off the bed and walked to the window.

He looked out. The sun was rising slowly over the dark Mendip Hills, surrounding the black cone of Glastonbury Tor with a thin rim of crimson light. The light expanded as the sun climbed higher, erasing the stars above the clouds, turning the dawn darkness into a pale, shifting yellow that lent definition to the still landscape and let a solitary tower emerge from the night to dominate the legendary hill.

The sun was a crescent-shaped, silver-limned fire forming an arch over the conical Tor. It continued rising, growing bigger and brighter, and eventually took the shape of a perfectly round, phosphorescent globe partially eclipsed by the parapeted tower on the silhouetted hill's summit over five hundred feet above sea level.

Now a heavenly halo around the majestic Tor, the sun also shone through the arch-shaped doorways of the tower and looked, from where Miles Ashcombe was standing, like a single, very brilliant eye, focused directly upon him.

Later, when the sun had been defeated by advancing mist, Miles Ashcombe drove from his home just west of Glastonbury, parked his car on the narrow, stone-walled road by Chalice

Well, and walked up the steep slopes of the Tor. He stood on the summit by the base of the hollow tower, which was all that remained of the fourteenth-century church of St. Michael.

Standing on that windswept summit, shivering with cold and fear, he thought of St. Michael, the Archangel, that flaming, winged creature who floated between heaven and hell. He felt the tug of air and water, a magic portent deep within. He gazed all around at the remarkably smooth, sloping green fields, thinking of what this place represented: the Land of the Dead; a center for Great Goddess fertility rites and celebrations; a Druid initiation center; a magic mountain; the Arthurian hill fort or Grail castle of Avalon; a ley-line crossroads and magnetic power-point over which flying saucers were often seen.

He looked around him and shivered, whipped by wind, chilled by fear. He felt the forces of air and water tugging at him, draining his mind, then he rubbed his weary eyes and stared southwest, across the sublimely curving, emerald-green Bushy Coombe to where the red-roofed modern houses of the ancient town seemed to float in the drifting mist.

Glastonbury had once been an island—an ancient Celtic burial ground, the Isle of Glass—and now, with the mist drifting around numerous patches of green, it eerily resembled that primal, watery marshland out of which it had originally been formed.

Ashcombe was frightened. The landscape seemed unreal. He stared across Bushy Coombe at the town thrusting up through the mist, and saw a cube-shaped patch of darkness materializing magically over the slender spire of St. John's Church.

He blinked and looked again, wondering what he was staring at. He saw the darkness growing spectrally in the morning's gray light: an incorporeal mass that had formed out of nothing —like a ghost or mirage. It seemed to float in thin air, immense, slightly transparent, and pulsating oddly. It was about half a mile wide, its height slightly more than that, inching southward as it descended vertically and very slowly, its nearest side forming a shifting wall that stretched across most of the town center.

Though unable to believe his own eyes, Miles Ashcombe now found himself staring at an enormous, perpendicular rectangle of darkness that was slowly covering the whole town center and, just as slowly, advancing south toward the hill upon which he was standing.

First stunned, then terrified, Ashcombe watched that faintly transparent, mysterious mass as it expanded in all directions, growing taller and wider, its nearest side now hovering just over the lower slopes of Chalice Hill, before the darkness fell over the entire town like the funnel of a great, cosmic chimney.

The town started to disappear.

That awesome dark mass kept advancing. Ashcombe raised his hands to his face and stepped back onto gravel, trying desperately to cling to his sanity. He backed through the arched doorway of the fourteenth-century tower and only then did the fear force his eyes shut.

It was colder inside the tower. The ground started to shake beneath him. He heard noise, then realized it was the ancient stones reverberating and shaking violently. He opened his eyes and looked directly above him.

His body went numb first, but then his mind also froze. An iciness clamped around him and he lost more of himself when he saw an incorporeal darkness sliding across the tower's open roof to block out the sky.

Whimpering like a child, he lowered his head and closed his eyes, terror rooting him to the spot. The ground shook beneath his feet and he heard distant noises all around him: a bass rumbling . . . strange growlings . . . a sharp squawk and beating wings . . . the rushing of wind, falling rain, volcanic explosions, and splitting earth.

He opened his eyes again, glancing wildly around him. He saw the ancient walls shaking and spitting dust—then he ran from the tower.

Once outside on the lofty summit of the ancient Tor, he found himself at the edge of a great wall of darkness that had obviously passed over the town center, over the slopes of Chalice Hill, and was now inching south like a dense mist dissolving into dawn light.

That mist swirled around him, an icy, freezing shroud, as he stared down at Glastonbury and saw, instead of the town, a broad swath of steaming marshlands, water gleaming between green grass, prehistoric beasts moving along well-trampled, muddy banks. Beyond them, where the lush Mendip Hills should have been, a volcanic mountain belched purple fire and black smoke over a glittering mosaic of waterways, lagoons, and tree-filled, steaming swamps.

He heard beating wings. His dazed eyes turned toward the sky. A prehistoric pteranodon flew overhead, its enormous beak pointing down in his direction, its wings of skin beating awkwardly.

Miles Ashcombe started screaming. He sensed that someone was coming toward him. He kept screaming in the hope that that someone would disappear with the rest of it.

His own screaming finished him.

"DISAPPEARED," Frances said, turning her head to stare at Laurence, who was driving them along the desert road, his red hair whipped by the wind that was also sweeping the dust in dense clouds across the path of the shuddering jeep. "Most of Glastonbury. It just disappeared overnight."

Laurence nodded, his lean face caked in dust. "Unbelievable," he replied, speaking loudly against the wind. "Completely out of this world. The scientists can't find a rational explanation for it."

Frances, a medical doctor herself, could not accept it and still felt very shaken. She had been in her apartment in Ashar, in Basra, relaxing on her patio and gazing out over the Shatt-al-Arab river, when the news, spoken in Arabic, had come over the radio. Staring beyond the palm-fringed bank of the broad, muddy river, her gaze lazily following the colorful spectacle of large-sailed trading boats, primitive canoes, circular rafts, paddle steamers, motor launches, and oceangoing steamers, she had thought at first that she had misinterpreted the broadcast, her Arabic not being all that good. But when she had changed to an English-language channel and heard the same news, she had felt herself slipping into dazed disbelief.

The ancient town of Glastonbury and its unfortunate inhabitants had disappeared inexplicably from the face of the earth, leaving only lush marshlands where the town center had formerly stood and a few hysterical witnesses from the immediate vicinity. All of them had insisted that the town had been "swallowed" by an immense pillar of darkness. On television they showed the actual site of the miraculous event: a perfectly linear square mile of lush green, watery marshland, surrounded by a military cordon of soldiers.

Frances stared at Laurence, hardly aware she was doing so. Beyond him, the desert of dry, seasonal marsh was like the landscape of a dream, the dust billowing and swirling above a featureless, flat terrain that ran out in all directions until it dissolved into the murky sky. More dust-swept desolation. An achromatic terrain. The jeep passed a palm grove, then bounced over a pothole, causing the medicine chests, one on top of the other, to squeak and rattle in protest. Frances twisted around in her seat to push them closer together, and by the time she had turned back to the front the strong wind was weakening.

"It's just too incredible to believe," Laurence said, shaking his head.

Frances shivered. She tried in vain to visualize what had happened. "I can't think clearly about it," she said. "I don't even want to try. So let's not talk about it anymore. Let's talk about work."

"Are we getting close?"

"Yes, we'll soon be there."

"Hallelujah for work," Laurence said. "At least it keeps us distracted."

"A stiff gin and tonic," Frances replied. "That, sir, is what *I* need for distraction."

"As a Christian let me state that I'm glad we're not carrying booze with us."

"You don't have to sound so pleased," Frances said.

Laurence grinned. "I'll try not to."

The landscape was still desolate but gradually, the late afternoon light returned, started burning through the haze, and revealed what at first seemed like a mirage in the desert: the glint of distant water, swaying bulrushes and fig trees, then reed houses springing out of the flatlands as Laurence drove straight toward them.

It was not a mirage, but it did seem incongruous since suddenly there, where the desert should have been, was a broad swath of marshlands, water gleaming between green banks, the tall bulrushes swaying against a ripening, crimson sky while the reed houses of the marsh Arabs shifted rapidly into black silhouette.

Frances brushed strands of dark hair from her mouth as Laurence slowed down, drove past some reed houses that were nestling under dusty fig palms, and braked to a halt where the first of the bridges led across the irrigation ditches to the center of the somnolent village. Laurence wiped dust from his face, glanced around him as the first Arab children approached, then threw Frances a teasing grin.

"This is *it?*" he asked.

"Yes," Frances replied as they both climbed down from the jeep, "this is it. You're about halfway between biblical Babylon and Ur—the Tigris river to the east, the Euphrates to the west —and this is the home of the Ma'dan—the marsh Arabs. Between the two great rivers are the marshes; beyond them, the desert."

"Mesopotamia," Laurence murmured, gazing dreamily about him. "The cradle of civilization . . . Lord, I can't believe I'm here."

Frances was amused by Laurence's reverential tone. "Don't get too romantic about it," she said. "It's not the place you imagine. It's no more magical than Glastonbury was—and Glastonbury, my mystical friend, was just another small market town."

"It *was,*" Laurence emphasized. "Before it disappeared without cause. That strikes *me* as magical."

Wishing that she hadn't mentioned the missing town, Frances looked down as the Arab children surrounded her, their eyes large and shy, the strings of beads dangling from their restless fingers being clicked rhythmically. A few of them were naked, holding spears or poisoned fish bait, but most were wearing the customary headcloth, the *keffiyeh,* draped over their head and shoulders, as well as the *dish-disha,* a long, unadorned shirt reaching from the throat to the feet, usually plain, sometimes striped in modest colors.

She greeted the children in her very basic Arabic, smiling at those she recognized from previous visits to the village, then introduced Laurence as her "new friend," though he was, in reality, only her new assistant.

Laurence, having spent most of his first six weeks in Iraq locked up in the mission house in Baghdad, was now visiting the marsh Arabs for the first time. He was instantly intoxicated when he took in the surrounding reed houses and, beyond them, the dimly glittering mosaic of watery marsh and lagoons fed by the two great rivers that became one near Basra and, as the Shatt-al-Arab, flowed on into the Persian Gulf.

He managed to tear his gaze from the scenery around him, glanced down at the milling children, then grinned again at Frances and followed her onto the bridge that crossed a water-filled ditch and led them into the heart of the village and, more specifically, to the *mudhif,* or guesthouse, of the sheikh.

The *mudhif,* shaped rather like an immense jelly roll and much larger than any of the houses surrounding it, had been constructed out of a series of arches that had been woven, like the smaller village houses, from the giant reeds that grew in the marshes. Frances and Laurence, approaching the flat end that was turned toward Mecca, were greeted by one of the sheikh's servants. After kicking off their shoes, they were led through the low, arched entrance into the *mudhif*'s dimly lit interior.

With its thirteen high arches, elaborate roof, and flickering, dim lighting, the *mudhif* resembled a spartan, gloomy cathedral. It contained no furniture, but the servants had spread woven rugs on the floor of reed matting, and Sheikh Hamaid was already sitting there, legs crossed in the customary fashion, beside the coffee hearth with its exotic row of brass and copper pots. The light from the flames of an open fire in the hearth blended with that of the hurricane lamps, which swayed dangerously on the walls of the *mudhif* and gave off an acrid smoke. They illuminated the inquisitive eyes of the many villagers who had crowded inside to observe the ritualistic socializing of their sheikh and his guests.

Frances greeted the sheikh by shaking his hand and then placing her own hand over her heart. "Peace be with you," she said in Arabic, before stepping back to let Laurence do the same. "On you be peace," the sheikh replied, also in Arabic, waving one hand to indicate that they should sit in front of him. Frances sat on the woven rugs, curling her legs under her and tugging the hem of her gray dress down over her knees. Laurence, close beside her, sat cross-legged, as all men were supposed to. The reed fire, crackling beyond him, filled the air with spiraling smoke, casting flickering shadows and light over his lean, pleasant face.

Sheikh Hamaid was not the handsome Bedouin warrior so beloved to the Western imagination, but an unshaven, hollow-cheeked man with skin so sun-scorched and wrinkled that his true age was impossible to determine. With black hair sprouting from his nostrils, meeting like the fine wires of an old shoebrush over the bridge of his Semitic nose, and similar hair sprouting thickly over the brown eyes that were shadowed by the *keffia* covering his head and shoulders, he looked like a sly old trader, or one of the marshland's cutthroat bandits, rather than a linear descendant of Mohammed, which he and a great many other marsh Arabs claimed to be. This first impression of primitive slyness was, however, soon belied by the lively intelligence of his steady gaze, and by the quiet arrogance of his full, sensual-lipped smile and good-natured mockery.

"It is most pleasant to see you again, Dr. Devereux," he said, speaking in excellent, if slightly formal, English. "My people always appreciate your kind attentions—and I, of course, enjoy the pleasure of your company."

His eyes moved questioningly toward Laurence, and Frances, anticipating him, said, "This is my new medical assistant, Laurence Gilbride, presently a student at the Friends to Christ mission in Baghdad. Naturally, like most of the students in that mission, Laurence is studying medicine as well as theology."

The sheikh nodded, examining Laurence in a candid manner, then, noting his embarrassment, turned back toward Frances.

"Ah, yes," he said. "That *is* a good thing. Since we believe in Mohammed, where you Christians do not, it is better that you concentrate on our physical ailments and let us be the shepherds of our own souls." He smiled, placing his hands beneath his unshaven chin. "Of course you, Dr. Devereux, are not religious at all, so it is odd that you should have religious assistants."

"Not odd," Frances replied. "The hospital in Baghdad is desperately short of trained staff. So, in return for their assistance in running the wards, we give free training to the students of the mission."

"A fair trade, Dr. Devereux. We Arabs understand such arrangements. As for yourself, instead of living in the comforts of England, you come to this bleak place to help the Ma'dan—so you must, in your secret heart, be a religious person . . . or at least a truly spiritual woman."

Frances smiled with amusement. "I'm not a spiritual woman," she said. "Quite the opposite, in fact. Now Laurence, here, *he's* a spiritual person—and deep down disapproves of me."

The sheikh raised one eyebrow and stared quizzically at Laurence. "This is true?" he asked.

"No," Laurence replied, shaking his head, his grin open. "I *do* have some concern for Dr. Devereux's soul, but I think highly of her."

The sheikh thoughtfully studied Laurence, eventually nodded and smiled, then turned toward the servants and clapped his hands lightly, thus indicating that the food should be served.

One of the servants emerged quickly and silently from the smoky, lamplit gloom near the cushion-lined wall of the *mudhif* to pass around the small bowl in which they could rinse their fingers. Even as they did this the other servants were busily setting bowls of mutton, chicken, and gravy—all placed around a mound of rice—on the floor between the sheikh and his guests, while an extremely old man, sitting cross-legged not far away, struck up a tune on his 78-stringed *al-qanoun,* the musical instrument most loved by the Arabs after the lute.

As was customary with the Ma'dan, the food was eaten quickly if awkwardly, the rice being soaked in the gravy and then scooped up with the right hand and forced by the thumb out of the palm and into the mouth. It was a messy way to eat and was clearly causing Laurence some problems, since he kept spilling handfuls of rice down his shirtfront and onto his crossed legs, much to the silent mirth of the perceptive sheikh.

Laurence, physically awkward at the best of times, was becoming more so under the amused scrutiny of the sheikh and his chattering villagers, but was saved from humiliation by his ability to laugh at himself. Nonetheless, he was obviously relieved when the meal ended and the plates were removed, the village children swooping in to grab the uneaten food, the servants expertly clearing away the bones and rice littering the mats.

"The Arabs believe in quantity rather than quality," the sheikh explained to him, "and what to the Western observer might be an unpleasant mess, is to the Arab but a sign of satisfaction."

Frances, who prior to this field trip had known Laurence

only through her monthly visits to the mission in Baghdad, and who had found him to be an attractively good-humored American, now took a mischievous pleasure from his discomfort and, as she again rinsed her fingers in the bowl proffered by a bowing servant, could not resist smiling wickedly at him. Laurence grinned back and brushed his red hair from his face, then gave his attention to the music being played on the ancient instrument. The sheikh, after glancing around the crowded tent, gave his attention to Frances.

"The food was to your satisfaction?"

"Yes, thank you. It was fine."

"You will share coffee with me?"

"Of course."

"Then we can have entertainment."

While they had been eating, a servant, having prepared the coffee, was pouring it from one pot into another where they stood close together. The sheikh sniffed, as if testing the aroma of the coffee fumes, then clapped his hands to call for the entertainment to commence. The first performance was by an amateur singing group: four young men who provided high-pitched, nasal, dramatically quavering laments of the most alien and inexplicable poignancy. Shortly after this performance started the servant rose from the smoldering coffee hearth and approached the matted area to offer Frances and Laurence each a tiny cup into which he poured steaming coffee. It was hot, aromatic, and exceptionally strong, and when Frances, too distracted and moved by the singing, was handing her cup back to the servant after her third drink, she shook it to indicate that she wanted no more.

"They sing of the pleasures of the flesh," the sheikh explained, "and of how all those pleasures come to dust when payment is due."

"Must the pleasures always be paid for?"

"If not materially, then spiritually."

"That sounds very depressing," Frances said.

"It is natural and proper."

Frances gazed at the sheikh and saw his smile through swirling smoke. He was having his little joke at her expense, but also sexually challenging her.

The smoke stung her eyes; the heat was increasing and making her sweat; the noise, ricocheting in the crowded *mudhif,* was making her dizzy. She started to imagine that she was melting and dripping down through her own core, but was jolted back to reality by the sudden ending of the last, aching song.

Before the abrupt silence could take command, some professional dancers stepped forward and began to dance in the flickering light from the hurricane lamps. All young men, but with their hair long and loose, they first mimed a few stories of misfortunes and triumphs, but all too quickly moved on to some graphically explicit sexual pantomime. There could be no doubting what was being enacted by those sinuously swaying and shuddering boys, and Frances, though she had seen it all before, was helplessly aroused by it.

The boys writhed in the swirling smoke, their lithe bodies glistening with sweat, hips swaying and groins thrusting rhythmically. Frances couldn't help herself: she wanted to reach out and touch them, to let her fingers slide over their knotted muscles and then have them envelop her.

She glanced across at Laurence, saw him shifting uncomfortably, and then looked to the front to catch the searching gaze of Sheikh Hamaid.

"The dancing is to your liking, Dr. Devereux?"

"Its strangeness is interesting."

The sheikh smiled at that, his gaze very steady upon her, then eventually, after nodding in a judicious manner, returned his gaze to the dancers.

The entertainment went on a long time, the villagers shouting constant encouragement, and eventually the tent became very hot and filled with the smoke from the cigarettes, pipes, and hurricane lamps. At once exhausted and sexually aroused, feeling the sweat soaking her clothing, Frances was glad when it finally ended and the villagers, all chattering excitedly, filed out of the tent.

When the villagers had departed, leaving silence behind them, the sheikh called for tea, which was served by the servants in minute glasses half filled with sugar. While Frances was sipping at her tea, the sheikh gave instructions to the remaining servants, who quickly tidied up the *mudhif* and then discreetly disappeared, leaving Frances, Laurence, and the sheikh in a silence broken only by the soft snapping of the still burning fire, and by the wind that was starting to moan across the marshes beyond the walls of the *mudhif.* The sheikh, apparently cool in his roped headcloth and robes, sighed and stared thoughtfully at Frances.

"You must be tired," he said.

"I am."

"Then I must take my leave."

However, instead of leaving, he merely glanced at the silent Laurence, offering him a neutral smile, then again stared very directly at Frances.

"Please let me say, Dr. Devereux, as I am sure I have said before, that I greatly admire your courage in continuing to visit my people throughout these dangerous times."

"It was never dangerous for me," Frances replied. "And the war is finally over."

"Yes, Dr. Devereux, the war is over at last—Iraq and Iran are now at peace—nevertheless, you continued to visit us while the war raged in these marshlands, as well as in Basra where you live. I think that was courageous."

Even as he spoke, the sheikh was staring at Frances with a calm and candid sexual interest, his gaze flickering from her eyes to her body in open inspection. Frances was not offended—in fact, she found his attentions pleasing—but she kept her gaze steady and gravely attentive, as if unaware of his silent invitation.

"It was a very bad war," she said, "and I'm glad that it's over. I wasn't frightened when the shells were exploding, but I didn't like what I saw."

"Death bothers you?"

"Yes."

"To the Arabs it is natural. The desert has no mercy on the weak, so it is they who fall first."

"That may well be true. Nonetheless, I am delighted that the destruction and killing have ended."

"And do you think that this peace, which so delights you, will last forever?"

"Nothing lasts forever," Frances replied, "but I hope it lasts for a long time."

Laurence, obviously keen to involve himself in the conversation, leaned forward and coughed into his clenched fist.

"It should at least last for a reasonable period," he said. "Most Iranians have had enough of the old ways, so it's unlikely that another war with Iraq is on their current agenda."

The sheikh raised both his hands in a histrionic gesture. "But the dead are still rotting in the desert and marshes," he said, "and that is something many Iraqis cannot forget. . . . So, it might start again." He lowered his hands, letting them rest on his thighs, then offered a loud sigh. "The horrors of war are repugnant to the Western mind," he said, "but to us they are as natural as the wind—and like the wind, will not cease. War is not a mystery, nor an aberration or sickness—though there *are* certain mysteries that even this humble Arab cannot explain."

Frances remembered what had happened the day before in Glastonbury, but the very thought of that awesome event sent a chill down her spine.

"Such as?" she asked.

The sheikh shrugged his shoulders in a gesture of bewilderment, then uncrossed his legs and stood up.

"Come," he said, addressing them both. "Stand up. Let me show you."

Frances and Laurence did as they were bid and then followed the surprisingly small, ungainly sheikh along the gloomy *mudhif,* walking under the thirteen high, woven arches until they arrived at the very far end. There, lying flat on his back on blankets spread out on the reed matting, was an apparently sleeping, lightly bearded man dressed in blue denims and jacket, a soiled rucksack propped up not far from his head. Frances studied him, wondering how he could sleep so stiffly, then turned back to the sheikh.

The sheikh shrugged again, almost forlornly. "It is not normal sleep," he explained. "He has been unconscious for a long time. A fisherman found him this morning, lying on the riverbank near the mouth of the Shatt-al-Arab. Seeing that he was unharmed, the fisherman tried in vain to revive him—then, not knowing what else to do, brought him back here. He is healthy —yet no one here can waken him, which seems very strange. I am hoping that you, with your medical experience, can do what we cannot."

Frances and Laurence automatically stared at each other, then Frances knelt down to examine the man on the floor. The sheikh took a step backward, letting his shadow fall away from the unconscious man, and at that moment, when Frances saw the man's face properly, she felt something lurching within her, as if in surprised—and fearful—recognition.

Instantly confused, trying to ignore her racing heart, and wondering why she should imagine that she knew this perfect stranger, Frances blinked and studied him more intently.

Looking down at his lamplit face, which was unshaven, middle-aged, slightly brutal, and possibly corrupt, she shivered and hastily averted her gaze, shocked to realize that she simultaneously felt repelled by him and attracted to him, for reasons that lay somewhere just out of her reach.

She shivered again, suddenly aware of the moaning wind, her head filled with a vision of the marshlands outside, the lagoons black and glittering beneath the stars in that cold, frightening darkness. Then, filled with inexplicable repugnance and desire, she bent low to press her ear to the stranger's chest and hear his healthy heart beating—a distant drum calling to her.

2

CHERYL had never been noted for her punctuality, and her father, Michael, who had arrived only five minutes early, was well into his second glass of white wine before he saw her standing in the doorway, silhouetted in the summery London light outside. Her head moved left and right as she scanned the packed, noisy restaurant, then she saw him, waved, and moved toward him. She wended her way skillfully between the many tables crowded with young men and women who had already managed to make Michael feel much older than his forty-three years.

Moving away from the sunlight and advancing through the smoky haze, Cheryl eventually reached his table and stood in front of him, that inner radiance which she threw out with the calm assurance of her twenty years instantly obliterating his lingering aggravation at being forced to sit alone in this rather fashionable art deco restaurant, being stared at, often far too frankly, by expensively dressed, attractive young ladies who were roughly the same age as his daughter.

"Hi!" Cheryl exclaimed, raising her right hand in the air. "Sorry I'm late."

"I just arrived a few minutes ago," Michael lied, delighted to see her. "And I've really enjoyed being surrounded by these lovely young creatures."

"You should have come to the dance studio," Cheryl said. "They're even prettier there."

A modeling agency's dream of casual elegance, she was wearing a dark blue cotton shirt with embroidered front and cotton jodhpurs that, tucked into high canvas boots with buckled sides, emphasized the long legs supporting her slim body. A dark alpaca wool shawl had been dangling with calculated care-lessness from her shoulders, and now, as she pulled the bamboo chair back and sat opposite Michael, she let the shawl slip from her and fall across the back of the chair as if placed there by an invisible waiter.

"My handsome father!" she said. "What a treat! And he's all mine for lunch!"

"The pleasure is all mine," Michael replied. "And well worth the wait."

"You *were* early. That was a sly reprimand. A drink will buy you forgiveness."

She placed her small tan suede shoulder bag on the table by her left hand, leaned forward to kiss him lightly on the cheek, then, cupping her perfectly proportioned, suntanned face in her hands, stared very directly at him, her ravishingly blue, rather too open eyes, emphasized by the slightly boyish fringe of blond hair that fell down from the slanting brim of her men's wide felt hat.

"Just call the waiter. *I'll* order it. You wouldn't know where to start."

Michael was not offended by his charming daughter's brash impertinence. Getting the miniskirted and peaked-capped wait-ress to their table with surprising speed, he insisted on sticking to white wine, whereas Cheryl, after perusing the list at consid-erable length, ordered a very exotic cocktail.

The waitress, who had been growing visibly impatient with Cheryl's procrastination, gladly departed back through the crowded tables, her tight miniskirt and very high heels making her long legs look delectable.

"Stop thinking about it," Cheryl said. "A man like you should know better. As a clinical psychologist, you know per-fectly well what happens during the male menopause. And, apart from being too young for you, she's also too dumb."

"How do you know that? Is she a friend?"

"No. I just know the type."

"And I suppose you know your father's type as well. The male menopause type."

"Oh, *mein Papa*, that was just a joke!"

She lowered her head slightly to let her eyes widen, her broad smile puffing out her golden cheeks in an irresistible manner. Michael returned her smile, amused and warmed by her, but was uncomfortably reminded of how much like her mother she looked. After the waitress had brought their drinks, he studied her thoughtfully.

"Well," he said, "you *are* looking beautiful."

"I'm glad," she replied. "That's why I suffer so much in that so-called dance studio. It's not the dancing that makes me lose pounds, it's the aerobics—so I'm glad you approve."

"You're more suntanned every time I see you."

"It's all the traveling. I've been doing a lot of it recently, as you know. And if you're interested, I've just returned from the south of France."

"Cannes?"

"No. Nice. We're shooting a low-budget feature film in the old city, and the producer had to check on soaring costs, so he dragged me along. We were there for five hectic days—and every one was a scorcher."

Michael sighed enviously at the thought of his daughter's life-style. Although still only twenty, Cheryl had already traveled extensively as the personal assistant to the top executive of one of the few thriving film-producing companies left in London. When not at a film festival in Cannes, Los Angeles, Berlin, or Manila, she was visiting locations in such tax-advantageous countries as southern Spain, the Philippines, Israel, and the Far East. His envy of her constant traveling, and his gratitude that she had such a good job in these days of high unemployment was tempered by his occasional unease at the effects of her way of life on her personality. Most of these doubts had arisen during the infrequent film previews or publicity parties to which she had invited him. Extreme extroversion, casual promiscuity, and a ruthless desire to succeed at any cost appeared to be the prevalent traits of most of those whom Michael had met at such gatherings, and it sometimes made him apprehensive to think that Cheryl—who was in many ways still immature—might fall under their spell.

"You don't supplement that tan with a sun lamp, do you?" he asked her.

Cheryl actually blushed. "Now, Daddy, don't—"

"You do, don't you?"

"Not often, but sometimes. It prevents me from getting too burned when I have to suddenly fly off to some sunny spot."

"Nonsense," Michael said, quietly despairing of her childish vanity. "You only do it because you can't bear the thought of stepping out in front of your fancy friends with too pale skin."

"Well, what's the matter with that?" Cheryl responded, smiling at him, but with a hint of defiance brightening her blue eyes.

"You know damned well what's the matter with it. I've told you a thousand times—that sun lamp will eventually ruin your skin."

"Oh, tosh! Let's order."

With pouting lips and a theatrical toss of her head, she picked up the large menu and buried her nose in it. Michael wearily shook his own head and then likewise picked up a menu, letting his gaze run down a list of dishes that were mostly of the American fast-food variety but embellished with currently popular Tex-Mex trimmings such as enchiladas and chili.

"You *eat* this stuff?" he asked.

"When I'm in a casual mood."

"Now I know why you're attending aerobics classes. You're working off what you eat."

Cheryl giggled at that and Michael called the waitress. Cheryl was still undecided, so Michael ordered his own meal—an unappealing combination of hamburger, french fries, chili dressing, and green beans—and then waited while Cheryl made up her mind. Every table in the restaurant was now taken and the exotically costumed, blond waitress was obviously under some pressure to attend to them, but she managed to roll her eyes good-humoredly at Michael and give him a sardonic grin while Cheryl kept changing her mind. Michael was just about to lose patience, when Cheryl finally gave her order. As she watched the waitress hurry away she folded her hands under her chin and leaned slightly toward her father, her radiant smile erasing his temper.

"Don't think I didn't notice you and that waitress," she said. "I'd be offended, except I'm so proud that my father's still so attractive."

"I don't know what you're talking about," Michael replied, amused by her cheek.

"You were giving each other the eye."

"Nonsense. She was rolling her eyes because you were taking

so long to decide what to order. Her eyes suggested no more than the frustration that comes from dealing with customers such as yourself. Not, I fear, a case of sexual yearning."

"You found her attractive, didn't you?"

"I find a lot of the young ladies in this place attractive. That doesn't mean much."

"You're still a womanizer, Daddy."

"I retain a fondness for women, true. However, I *do* tend to stick to my own age-group, so don't play any games, girl."

"When are you going to stop playing the bachelor and settle down like a decent man?"

"I *am* a decent man. I'm just not settled. And what's wrong with that?"

"I think Mother still misses you."

"It's been *eight years,* Cheryl."

"Time means nothing to a woman in love. You should bear that in mind."

Michael killed that subject by glancing around the crowded room. Arc lights flashed off silver railings and ornate art deco mirrors, illuminating in different colors the many bizarre hairstyles and the equally strange clothing of the privileged youth, most of whom were drinking cocktails or champagne. He wondered if they were aware of the extraordinary event of that morning, and if so, how they could all look so unconcerned. It was difficult to accept that *he* could actually sit here with his daughter, given the inexplicable, terrifying disappearance of Glastonbury.

"Did you get a paper this morning?" he asked Cheryl.

"No," she replied. "I always watch the news on telly."

"So you know about Glastonbury?"

"Oh, God, yes," she said, her glowing smile disappearing. "I still can't believe that it's actually happened. I don't think anyone can."

"Frightening," Michael said.

"Yes, frightening. Let's not talk about it."

"A whole town disappears," Michael said, ignoring her plea. "So do most of its inhabitants. Where a great Tor once dominated the landscape there is now only marshland, still steaming and flat. It just doesn't seem possible."

Cheryl shivered. "It makes me feel unreal, as if I'm dreaming. Everyone I've talked to feels the same way. I don't want to think about it. Let's talk about something else."

Noting how disturbed she was, Michael decided to drop the subject, but could not resist looking around him again at the packed, noisy restaurant. He thought of the scenes on television —of the weeping and hysteria—and could scarcely credit that here, in the middle of Covent Garden, London, life continued as if nothing had happened.

"And how is your mother?" he asked her. "No problems, I hope."

"Oh, she's fine," Cheryl replied, clearly relieved at the change of subject. "She just gets a bit lonely now and then."

"We *all* get that way now and then. It's part of the human condition."

"You don't, Daddy. You *like* living alone. You're a natural bachelor."

"Yes, I am. But your mother has always refused to believe that. She mistakes my need for independence as a lack of paternal instincts. In other words, she thinks I don't care enough about you."

"I know you care."

"Well, that's good. Because I care very deeply."

It was an unusually emotional confession, which left them both a little embarrassed, so the arrival of their lunch was a welcome distraction. Soon regaining her ebullience, Cheryl kept up a lively stream of conversation during the meal, mostly about her experiences in the very unstable but colorful film industry. Michael was enjoying himself, taking pleasure from her youthful optimism. At times it was difficult to believe that this beautiful young woman was his daughter.

He had married Cheryl's mother, Janet, at the age of twenty-four, two years before Cheryl's birth and just after he had gained his medical degree and was starting as house physician in psychiatry at the Maudsley Hospital in London. He and Janet, who was then also in psychiatry, had been deeply attracted to each other, and the marriage during its earliest years was, if not particularly passionate, emotionally satisfying. However, with increasing maturity and a self-knowledge gleaned from his further work in clinical psychology, Michael had gradually come to accept the truth of his own nature. Not a particularly passionate man, he nonetheless enjoyed sex; not a particularly emotional man, he still had the need to experience many different women and, beyond that, to live a life unrestrained by domestic trivia. It was a combination of these factors that had led to his divorce from Janet eight years ago. Only in recent months, however, had he come to realize that if he had been able to go through with the divorce with minimum damage to himself, he had certainly caused some damage not only to his former wife but to Cheryl, an only child, who had been a sensitive twelve-year-old at the time.

As he studied his lovely daughter, he wondered if the pain he had caused her years ago still lurked in the back of her mind. Cheryl was attractive, well-educated, and adored, but a part of her refused to grow up, a trait that tended to make her highly impressionable and too dependent on others. Michael wondered if his divorce had caused that insecurity, and dreaded the thought that sooner or later someone, most likely from the film world, would sense it and ruthlessly exploit it.

It was possibly that concern which prompted him, while drinking his Irish coffee, to ask her casually about her love life.

Her reply began with a careless shrug of her shoulders. "Oh," she said, "it comes and goes."

"No one special at the moment?"

"They *all* seem special during the initial heady encounters. Unfortunately—or fortunately—that feeling never lasts for too long."

"I think fortunately," Michael said. "I'd rather you have more experience before you settle down. One of the most damaging aspects of marrying young is that one tends to still have too many desires and ambitions unfulfilled—desires and ambitions that marriage simply cannot permit."

"Such as?"

"Oh, travel—not the kind you're presently doing as part of your work, but the kind one chooses for oneself and does independently. That, and perhaps a more ambitious career—one requiring free time and a minimum of other commitments."

"I *have* a career, Daddy."

"You have a *job,* Cheryl. I would hardly call a secretary's job a career. More a stopgap."

"I'm a very responsible assistant to a movie producer. And he's a very talented, attractive one at that. So I'm quite happy, thanks."

"Sounds like you're doting on this fellow."

"I'm not doting on him. I just feel very lucky to be working with him."

"Handsome?"

"Correct."

"About your age?"

"Not correct. He's in his late thirties and is happily married with two kids. He's just my *boss,* Daddy."

Michael smiled at that. "I still think you should stay free as long as possible—to give yourself time to think out what you really want to do. And, of course, to learn more about men and what kind you could seriously live with."

"That's a very logical attitude to life, Daddy."

"I'm a very logical man."

"Maybe. And maybe you're simply justifying your reasons for leaving Mother. *You're* a practicing psychologist, but we can't all apply that kind of objectivity to our personal lives."

Michael finished his coffee and sat back in his chair, surprised at Cheryl's display of self-awareness.

"Well, well," he said eventually. "For a highly impressionable young lady you can be quite hardheaded."

"I get that from you." She flashed him a dazzling smile, her blue eyes bright with mischief, and he realized once more, with a mixture of pride and trepidation, just how attractive she would surely be to most men.

"You still share that flat in Bayswater with those three other girls?"

"Yes," Cheryl replied. "And go home to Mother every weekend, which I think keeps her happy. So, what about *your* love life? What's happening there?"

"I have to get back to the hospital," Michael replied, "so let's pay up and leave."

"Well, *that's* a neat cop-out!"

Cheryl chuckled triumphantly while Michael waved to indicate that he wanted to go. When the bill eventually arrived, he paid with cash and tipped generously, thus receiving a warm smile from the waitress. Cheryl watched the girl weaving her way between the tables, then gave her father a knowing glance before letting him take her by the elbow and lead her out.

"Well," he said when they had both stepped into the bright light of Henrietta Street, "that's a relief."

"You didn't like my choice of restaurant?"

"The company at my table was wonderful," he replied, "but I felt a little out of place with that music and all those pretty young women. I was starting to feel very *old.*"

"I prefer more mature gentlemen like you," Cheryl said. "Tall, broad, and handsome. Distinguished academic career. Now principal clinical psychologist of the psychiatric wing of a leading hospital in upper-middle-class Hampstead. A real catch to any bitch with foul intentions—but all mine for lunch."

"Dear daughter, you make me feel so young—as Frank Sinatra once sang."

"That *does* age you, Daddy."

Nodding his agreement, Michael took her by the elbow and led her along the street into the Central Piazza. In the square in front of the Tuscan columns of St. Paul's Church, a crowd was gathering around two men dressed up as clowns. The first clown, juggling a balloon painted to look like the globe, comically tried to avoid the second clown, who was balletically attempting to prick the balloon with a giant hatpin. The attack and retreat of the two clowns was performed as a sort of mimed pantomime, by turns comic and threatening; but as the performance drew to its climax, the mood edged away from comedy altogether and closer to something distinctly macabre, until eventually, with a demonic shriek of triumph, the clown brandishing the giant hatpin managed to prick the balloon, thus causing the globe of the earth to explode.

"What's the matter?" Cheryl asked her father as they walked away. "You suddenly look *terribly* thoughtful."

"It was the clowns' pantomime," Michael replied. "They were mocking the millennium. Yet their actions seemed strangely prophetic in light of Glastonbury."

"Well," Cheryl said, "it is a frightening business—and no doubt that until we know what really happened, we'll all be frightened by the thought of what it might mean."

They passed the people dining at the tables outside the Hard Rock Cafe, walked up the crowded pavement of James Street, and eventually stood facing each other outside the entrance to Covent Garden underground station in Long Acre, beside the racks of newspapers, the front pages of which were dominated by the disappearance of Glastonbury.

Michael glanced only briefly at the newspapers, then distracted himself by studying his daughter's face. Cheryl was no longer a child and he, who had held her on his knee not long ago, was now the middle-aged father of a very desirable young woman. Touched by a fleeting paternal anxiety, he leaned down and kissed her on the cheek and then straightened up again.

"Take care," he said. "And don't forget to call me when you feel like another free lunch."

"Don't worry. I won't."

She stood on tiptoe to return his kiss, then turned away and plunged into the swarming crowd, her wide hat bobbing like a boat before disappearing behind a sea of heads.

Michael stood there for some time, filled with love and concern, then eventually went into the station to catch the train back to work.

"**D**ID you have a good sleep?" Laurence asked, setting down his glass of sweet tea and picking up a piece of thin, golden-colored bread. He was sitting cross-legged at the other side of the coffee hearth, directly facing Frances, his face hazed by the smoke from the small fire upon which the coffee was heating.

"No," Frances replied. "I hardly slept a wink. I kept thinking of Glastonbury and that man lying beside us, and finally I just gave up and went out for a walk. Naturally, because of all their bloody dogs, I didn't get very far."

"Yes, I've noticed that they've all got vicious dogs."

"*Lots* of them," Frances emphasized. "All large and un-friendly and *noisy,* barking all day and night."

She shook her head with a weary gesture. First awakened by that relentless barking, then kept awake by haunting thoughts, she had risen in the cold, gray dawn, crept quietly from the *mudhif* still wearing the clothes she had lain down in, and crossed a couple of the narrow, scum-covered ditches that threaded the village until she passed through some palm groves and emerged at the bank of the Euphrates river. There had been no boats on the river, making it seem oddly ominous, and be-yond it, on the flat and barren horizon, had been a featureless dark strip that she knew to be the densely reeded perimeter of the permanent marshes. All in all, a desolate sight, devoid of color and warmth.

"You sound angry," Laurence said. "I get the impression that you don't like it here—and yet you've chosen to work here of your own accord."

"I'm not angry," Frances replied, sipping her coffee and wincing. "I'm just irritable because I'm tired. I don't like their vicious dogs at the best of times, and when I'm tired, I could kill them."

"We're all God's creatures, Frances."

"You're entitled to that belief."

Laurence smiled. "You're a very tough woman. I wouldn't like to cross swords with you."

"Oh, I'm not really *that* tough," Frances said, returning his smile. "*My* bark's worse than my bite."

The sheikh's servant was kneeling at the tall coffeepot in the smoldering hearth, and Frances stared past him, through the lazily coiling smoke, at the man lying at the far end of the *mudhif.* He was still unconscious, breathing deeply and evenly, lying flat on his back with that slightly unnatural stiffness. The hurricane lamp strung from a post just above him painted his face with wavering lines of yellow and black.

The very sight of him frightened Frances. In truth, it was not the dogs that had kept her awake, but the sound of that stranger's breathing: a rhythmic rising and falling of air that had eventually taken hold of her and convinced her that her heart, which had been racing, was in fact beating mysteriously in time with his.

She had seen his face throughout that night—visualizing it behind her closed eyes—and had felt her body tingling with desire and inexplicable revulsion.

"It's not natural," she said thoughtfully, still staring along the gloomy *mudhif.* "I can't find a thing wrong with that man, and yet he won't wake up."

Laurence shrugged and raised his hands in bewilderment. "Some sort of coma," he said. "We just don't know what caused it."

"Some sort of coma, yes. But no kind that *I* know about. He wasn't *knocked* unconscious—there's no sign of bruising—and his heartbeat, pulse and skin tone are perfectly normal, just like those of a sleeping man. So, whatever kind of coma it is, it's a mystery to me."

"Shivery," Laurence said.

"Yes," Frances replied. "Just like the disappearance of Glastonbury. . . . And *that* kept me awake as well."

She glanced once more along the gloomy *mudhif,* saw the shadows flickering over the stranger where he lay on his back on the reed matting, then turned back to Laurence.

"No matter," she said. "It's a new day today and we've got our work to do. Let's attend to the Arabs and then, when we're finished, we can take that unconscious man back to Basra and put him into the hospital for observation. Let *them* deal with the mystery."

Standing up together, they went outside to find the gray morning giving way to brilliant sunlight. Frances instructed two of the villagers to bring the medical chests from the jeep parked at the other side of the palm-log bridges. While many of the Arabs started gathering around expectantly, she saw Laurence surveying the village, his gaze taking in the scum-covered water drifting around the stilts of the reed houses that were poised precariously over the mudbanked ditches.

A light wind was blowing, picking up dust, sand, and small fragments of reed, then sweeping them together in a cloud that spiraled lazily around the gathering Arabs. Beyond the village, the horizon was flat and featureless, but here, by the river, the tall bulrushes parted noisily as the fishermen pushed them aside and moved in their long, thin canoes out onto the broad, calm lagoons. Smoke poured out of the reed houses, dogs barked, chickens squawked, and the smell of coffee and baked bread filled the warming air, briefly defeating the unpleasant stench of the crisscrossing ditches.

"It's not like I imagined it," Laurence said. "It's not nearly as exotic as I thought it would be. . . . In fact it's all fairly colorless."

"That's what extensive traveling does for you," Frances replied. "It strips the most exotic places of their glamour and forces you to realize that what on a postcard is local color, is in reality just poverty. And most of the places we think of as exotic are in fact simply *poor.*"

"You don't have any illusions about it, do you?"

"No," Frances replied, watching a group of young males struggling across one of the palm-log bridges with her two medicine chests rocking between them.

"Then why are you practicing medicine here instead of back in the comforts of England?"

"Because I like my independence. Because here, in Iraq, I can live my own life without worrying about what people will think of me."

"And why would people worry about that?"

"Oh," Frances replied, shrugging, hardly aware of what she was saying, "I like total freedom—to do what I like with whom I want—and here they just assume that all white women behave that way naturally. Back home, in London, my behavior can be offensive; but here, in Basra or Baghdad, I can quietly do what I want. I'm an exotic flower to the Moslems—to be discussed but not touched—and since most of the European men are just passing through, I have few complications."

A very large, long table was carried out and set down in front of the *mudhif,* the medicine chests were placed on the table and opened, then the expectant villagers—most of whom, when they were not seriously ill, treated the clinic as a marketplace where they could bargain and plead for the tablets and medicines they so loved—were lined up in an orderly fashion to be examined and treated.

The marsh Arabs were riddled with many acutely infectious diseases, and as Frances examined them, and diagnosed the various cases of dysentery, yaws, ringworm, hookworm and bilharzia, she thoughtlessly barked her instructions at Laurence, who, starting to sweat in the brightening sunlight and growing heat, swabbed weals, infectious cuts, and cataracted eyes, lanced suppurating boils and rashes, took blood and urine samples, administered various injections, stitched a wide variety of revolting wounds, and handed out a few hundred of the pills that the Arabs loved as a child loves its candy.

Sweating more with each passing minute, his eyes squinting against the brightening glare, and obviously trying to adjust to the sight of the often appalling wounds and disfigurements of the Arabs, Laurence eventually distracted himself by asking Frances how long she had been visiting the villages of the marshlands.

"Two years," Frances replied. "I spend three days a week visiting the various villages, work another two days a week in the hospital in Basra, and spend my weekends either in Basra or Baghdad."

"Then you must know Sheikh Hamaid fairly well," Laurence said, holding his hypodermic up to check it.

Frances glanced at him, then smiled to herself. "Yes," she said, "I know him fairly well. Why do you ask?"

"Oh," Laurence replied, sounding casual, almost abstracted, "I just thought he was a bit of a character . . . and was obviously making some kind of pass at you."

"Don't be so coy," Frances replied. "He *was* making a pass. And he does so every time I visit this village."

"You didn't seem to mind," Laurence said. "In fact, you seemed to enjoy it."

"That's right—I enjoyed it."

Still holding the wrist of the Arab whose bitten hand she had been examining, Frances stared at Laurence, keeping her eyes on him as he expertly slid the needle of his hypodermic into an upraised rump.

"And why shouldn't I enjoy it?" she asked rhetorically. "I've always been attracted to strong-willed men. I don't go much for coyness."

Laurence slapped the naked rump and allowed his patient to straighten up, waving one hand to indicate that the man could leave.

"Coyness," he said mischievously, "seems more applicable to women than to men."

"Not to *this* woman."

"I *have* noticed that," Laurence said with a chuckle. "Am I allowed to ask why you never married?"

"I'm still unmarried because I don't want children, I don't want to be a housewife, I don't want to be dependent on the whims of any man—and, most crucially, because I like sex but don't want to have to pay for it with domestic slavery. Would you like to know what *kind* of sex I like? Or can I keep that a secret?"

Laurence blushed and smiled, taking pleasure from his Christian shock, then avoided Frances's gentle mockery by simply giving his undivided attention to his next expectant patient, an old woman with a boil as big as an egg disfiguring her withered face. The old woman handed Laurence the treatment instructions that had been scribbled down by Frances, and as he read them, his face turned slightly sideways, he said, "Well, that's a fairly straight reply to an impertinent question."

Frances, enjoying their banter, kept talking while attending to her next patient, one of the many villagers suffering from dysentery after drinking the excrement-filled water that lapped against the walls of his reed house.

"Let's change the subject, Laurence. Let's talk about you instead. How's *your* love life?"

"I think you know perfectly well, Frances, that I—"

"You don't have a love life—I know. It's not approved outside of marriage. But that must be very difficult, Laurence, for someone of your age."

"All right, Frances," Laurence said as he spread some ointment on lint and prepared to clean the old woman's boil. "I think this conversation's gone far enough. Let's change the subject again."

"No," Frances replied. "I'm enjoying this. Tell me how you stay celibate. Celibacy, like coyness, is something that only women are meant to practice—so how do you manage it?"

"Perhaps I don't want it as much as you do," Laurence said, applying the lint to the enormous boil and making the nervous woman groan audibly. "We're not all that desperate, you know."

"You're not, eh?" Frances smiled maliciously at him, then lowered her head to the desk while she scribbled a prescription for her dysentery sufferer. "So, let's indeed change the subject. What did you think of the Arab dancing last night?"

"Interesting," Laurence murmured.

"It was highly erotic," Frances said.

"Yes, I suppose it was."

"In fact," Frances insisted, exhilarated by Laurence's discomfort, "it was about as sexually explicit as you can get without actually doing it."

Now truly embarrassed, the celibate Laurence threw his piece of used lint into the rubbish bag beside the table, brought a smile to the face of the suffering Arab woman by giving her a handful of tablets, and then stared directly at Frances for the first time.

"Okay, Frances," he said, placing his hands on his hips, "it was explicit and I found it embarrassing. Does that thought amuse you?"

"You weren't *just* embarrassed," Frances said. "Admit it: you found it exciting—and *that's* what made you uncomfortable."

The dysentery sufferer left Frances and, with his prescription in his shaking hand, joined the end of the line facing Laurence. Snatching Frances's written instructions from his next patient, Laurence studied them with more intensity than they warranted, then, after taking a deep breath, spoke again while rummaging through one of the medicine chests to find the tablets he needed.

"You're a very attractive lady," he said, "but you're also a ruthless one. To protect my mortal pride, I'm refusing to discuss this matter any more."

"That might be wise, Laurence."

Smiling, she glanced at him, amused to see him blush as he handed out more pills and prepared to swab an ugly boar-bite. He caught her glance and grinned back at her, accepting defeat with grace, then returned his attention to the wound, while Frances, having dispensed with her last patient, called to a servant to prepare a pot of tea.

At that moment, Sheikh Hamaid, who had obviously been watching her from the doorway of his house, and had waited until she was finished with her patients (though Laurence was still attending to the diminishing line of those waiting to be treated), walked across the clearing toward her, his dark robes and headcloth fluttering lightly in the breeze, sunlight glinting off the studs and buckles of his webbed belts and straps. When he reached Frances, he bent down to pat the heads of the smaller, mostly naked children, after which he straightened up, glanced at the working Laurence, then finally offered Frances his slow, full-lipped, sensual smile.

"So," he said, raising his hands in a benediction, "again you have cured the ills of my suffering people. You are our angel of mercy."

"You're very generous with your compliments, Sheikh Hamaid, but I'm just doing my job and you know it, which means that you're teasing me."

"Women like to be teased," the sheikh replied. "It is part of their nature."

Frances smiled at that, but didn't offer a reply, knowing just how far to go with this man who could normally get what he wanted. She glanced past him, across the village, saw the buffaloes in the river, a line of Arabs standing upright in their canoes, all with forked spears in their hands, their eyes fixed on the fish swimming below them. Beyond the Arabs, the lagoons formed a glittering tapestry of light and shadow that was bordered by the thin dark line of the reeds which marked the visible edge of the permanent marshes. The sky above was bright and very blue, but filling up with white clouds.

"And how is the man in the *mudhif?*" the sheikh asked her.

"Still the same," Frances replied, the simple mention of the stranger making her feel that she had been slapped. "He didn't move all night. He's still in his coma, but otherwise seems perfectly normal. It's a mystery to me."

"You will take him back with you to Basra this morning?"

"Yes."

"I am relieved to hear that."

"Why?"

The sheikh shrugged and waved a languid right hand to indicate the crowd of milling villagers. "My people are superstitious," he said, "and think this man is bad luck."

"Because he is a mystery?"

"Yes . . . and as such he could possibly be an evil omen."

"As you said, that is pure superstition."

"Perhaps," the sheikh said. "Perhaps not. There are still unanswered questions. . . . How did that man come to be lying unconscious on the riverbank with not a mark on him—and with no footprints at all in the mud around him? And why, if he is physically perfectly normal, can he not be awakened . . . ? No, there are certain riddles here—and my people whisper of magic."

"Magic can sometimes be good."

"It is more often frightening."

Strangely haunted by that unconscious man, and feeling more uneasy each minute, Frances glanced across at Laurence and noted that he had dispensed with the last patient and was starting to clear up the cluttered table by putting bottles and instruments back into the medicine chests in preparation for their departure from the village.

"A good day's work?" she asked him.

"Yes," Laurence replied. "Fascinating. And I'm amazed at how many patients we got through in that short time—probably because so few of them ask questions."

"That's exactly right," Frances said.

They smiled at each other, then Frances returned her gaze to the sheikh, who was staring steadily at her.

"Don't worry," she said. "We'll take him away for you. He'll be in a hospital in Basra by this afternoon, and then you'll have no further cause for concern."

The sheikh nodded and smiled, his gaze steady and flirtatious. "I think that will be best for all concerned," he said. "And, of course, my personal *tarada* will be at your disposal."

"My thanks."

"My *pleasure.*"

"You sound as if you would like to get rid of me, Sheikh Hamaid."

The sheikh immediately put his hands to his own lips, indicating that Frances was speaking a kind of blasphemy.

"No, no!" he exclaimed. "That is definitely not true! It always gladdens my heart to see you coming here—not only because you tend to my people, but also because of the personal pleasure your company gives me. However, what is also true is that I would, on a personal level, prefer the pleasure of your company in Basra, in less public circumstances."

"Whatever do you mean by that, Sheikh Hamaid?"

"Whatever you *want* it to mean."

Frances could never resist such sexual boldness and this instance proved to be no exception. Immediately suffused with warmth, her head teeming with fleeting images of clandestine trysts with the wealthy sheikh, she was nonetheless aware of the basic foolishness of her imaginings even as she experienced them. Feeling helpless at her own weakness, but also exhilarated, she almost broke her own rule about not getting involved with Arab chieftains. But then she stopped herself and let silence return her to common sense.

A little while later, obviously recovered from his long and inexplicable sleep, the unknown man, wearing the denim jacket, trousers, and leather boots he had had on when he was discovered, was standing in front of the *mudhif,* gazing around him in growing surprise.

He raised his left hand, scratched his head, rubbed his forehead, then stared across the busy clearing at the squatting women and naked children, at the canoes and buffaloes in the river, at the glittering lagoons and swaying bulrushes along the marshes—then at Sheikh Hamaid, Laurence, and Frances.

The man studied Frances thoughtfully, as if trying to place her face. Eventually, his lips curved into a thin, oddly frightening smile.

Bewildered by her rising panic, Frances glanced at a puzzled Laurence and at the surprised, staring sheikh. Then, controlling herself, she returned her gaze to the man standing in the clearing and saw the steel in his smile.

He waved his left hand in greeting.

4

"WHAT the hell . . . ?" the stranger said, spreading his
hands in bewilderment. "Am I dreaming? Is this some kind of
trick? Just where the hell *am* I?"

"Not far from where we found you," the sheikh replied. "Just
a few miles upriver."

Still obviously confused, but surprisingly unshaken, the
stranger stared directly at Sheikh Hamaid with no great sign of
warmth.

"Up*river?*" he said. "*What* river? There *was* no river! I was in
the middle of the goddamned English countryside!"

He glanced around him again, trying to take in what he was
seeing, then lowered his hands to his sides and shook his head
in perplexity, before staring with unsettling boldness at Frances.

"So," he said, "what the hell's going *down* here?"

Frances observed him up close in the sunlit clarity of the
morning. He had a thin, hawklike face, a tall, lanky body; his
hollow, unshaven cheeks framing a patrician nose and thin lips.
He was in his late thirties and his brown hair was tinged with
gray, his eyes seemingly opaque.

"Am I dreaming—or what?" he asked aggressively.

"You were found lying unconscious by the river," Frances
explained. "Don't you remember being there?"

"*What* river?" the man repeated with growing impatience.
"And what's with this goddamned Arab village? I mean, where
the hell *am* I?"

"You were found on the bank of the Shatt-al-Arab river," Frances said. "You're in southern Iraq."

The man's impenetrable brown eyes stared steadily at Frances for some time, then, as his brow furrowed, moved briefly left and right, taking in Sheikh Hamaid, Laurence, and the milling Arabs, then the glittering expanse of the nearest lagoon and the thin, dark line of the distant marshes.

"I'm going crazy," he said, sounding absolutely sane. "The last thing I remember is falling asleep on a bench in Glastonbury, in England. I *can't* be in . . . *Iraq?*"

He offered a tentative grin and Frances took a deep breath, feeling her shock turn into fear at what all this might mean.

Glastonbury, in England—the town that vanished overnight . . . the town whose disappearance had haunted her dreams with remarkable intensity. . . . She looked at the man in front of her, trying to keep her senses together, aware of how unnatural his calmness was, given what had occurred.

"I'm afraid you *are* in Iraq," Laurence said. "Do you know *who* you are?"

"Yeah . . . yeah, I do." The man studied Laurence at length, as if measuring his possible worth, then grinned in a quietly contemptuous manner and turned his gaze on Sheikh Hamaid.

"Jack Schul," he said. "From Atlantic City, New Jersey. I'm not married, I live in a crappy apartment located conveniently near the racetrack in Pleasantville, and I work the casinos, scamming the tourists."

He grinned tightly at Sheikh Hamaid, whose painfully polite attentiveness could not hide the distaste he was obviously feeling in the presence of this crude intruder. Then he turned his head and stared directly at Frances, his eyes moving up and down her body in immodest appraisal.

"No," he said, "no doubts about who I am. I remember everything that happened until I fell asleep in England—and woke up in *this* country. Jesus, I still can't believe it! Are you gonna tell me what happened? I mean, how long have I been sleeping, for chrissakes? And who brought me here?"

"I think you better sit down," Frances said. "Let's all have some tea."

"Tea? I could do with a fucking beer."

"We only have tea," Frances said.

Laurence and Sheikh Hamaid were both obviously offended
by Schul's obscenity, but neither said anything, the sheikh
merely nodding at Frances and then leading them all into the
mudhif, where, after they had removed their shoes, they sat
cross-legged in a circle near the hearth and were served tea in
tiny cups by the waiting servants.

Schul reached out for his first cup with his left hand, but was
prevented from taking it by Frances, who quietly told him that
he must use his right. Schul did not apologize, but merely
grinned and explained that he was left-handed, after which he
had his first sip of tea and visibly winced. Then, after everyone
had been introduced to him, and as the ritualistic tea-sipping
continued, he told them how he had ended up in Glastonbury.

"I didn't know nothin' about Glastonbury when I went
there," he explained. "I had no special interest in it. It's just
that I like to kick around a lot and I had this old friend who
used to drive a cab in Atlantic City and then married this English broad and went back to live with her in Glastonbury,
where she had come from. Anyways, he tol' me to come see him
if I ever got to England, so when I scraped up a little money
and got bored, I decided to hitchhike around England and also
pay him a visit, if only for the free bed and breakfast. I spent a
day and night with him in Glastonbury, hung one on, forgot
what I was doing, made a play for his old woman, and got
thrown out. This, you understand, was in the middle of the
night, so I decided to sleep on a bench and then try for a lift
when the traffic started to flow. Just before dawn, I found a
bench on that great fucking hill with the old church on top of it,
was still drunk enough to fall asleep pretty fast, had really
weird dreams about prehistoric days . . . and then woke up
here, thinking that I was still dreamin'—'cause the marshes
here look just like the marshes that I saw in my dreams."

Remembering the television films of the lush, watery marshlands where the town of Glastonbury had formerly stood, Frances felt a cold chill going through her.

"And that's all you remember?" she asked him.

"Yeah," he replied. "I fell asleep on that hill in Glastonbury,
had some pretty weird dreams, then woke up in this Arab hut
in Iraq. I mean, who *brought* me here?"

He stared quizzically at each of them in turn, then eventually let his gaze rest on Frances. She felt the hardness in him—the calculation and aggression.

"We can't answer that question," Laurence said. "It's a mystery to us. However, what we *do* know is that the whole town of Glastonbury disappeared without trace a few hours before the Arabs found you on that riverbank near Al-Qurna, where the Tigris and Euphrates come together."

Now Schul turned his head to stare at Laurence, his expression frankly amazed. "The whole town . . . *disappeared?*"

"That's right," Laurence said. "It vanished, and no one knows how . . . or where it has gone."

"It wasn't *destroyed?* It just *vanished?*"

"Yes. It obviously vanished when you were lying on that hill —and now, here you are."

There was a brief, uncomfortable silence during which Schul, his dark eyes alert and hard, gazed around the large, smoke-filled *mudhif,* stared at the village outside, thoughtfully surveyed the sunlit marshes beyond the lagoons, and then concentrated his attention on Sheikh Hamaid, who at that very moment was gazing at Frances with open admiration. Schul grinned knowingly, then turned the same grin upon Frances, his eyes brightening suggestively.

"Are you hungry?" Frances asked, observing Schul's expression and aware of what it meant.

"Yeah," Schul replied, "I'm hungry. And I'm thirsty as hell."

"Have some more tea."

"I was thinking of something stronger than that."

"You can have something stronger when we get to Basra and you've been medically examined."

"Basra?"

"It's the second biggest city in Iraq, on the bank of the Shatt-al-Arab river, down south, not too far from the Persian Gulf. It's about an hour from here by car, but we won't get there till nightfall, since Laurence and I have to attend to some more villages near Al-Qurna and also we'll be making the rest of the journey by boat. If you're hungry, stay here and have some bread while we put our things in the boat. We'll be leaving in fifteen minutes or half an hour. Okay?"

"And what happens when I've been examined in Basra?"

"Do you still have your passport?"

"Yeah. Everything's still intact in my rucksack."

"Then we'll get the American Embassy to fly you from Basra to Baghdad, and from there on back to New York."

"I could sell this fucking story to the papers."

"That's right. You could do that."

Offended by Schul's arrogance, greed, and crass indifference to the miraculous nature of his appearance here in Iraq, but also uncomfortably aware that she was drawn to his particular type, Frances tried to control her facial expression. She stood up, thanked the sheikh for his hospitality, then led Laurence out of the *mudhif.*

It was late in the afternoon when they completed their work in the last village near Al-Qurna and reboarded Sheikh Hamaid's large war canoe to be rowed along the river to Basra. The *tarada* was nearly forty feet long and no more than four feet at its widest beam, thus forcing Frances, Laurence, and Jack Schul to sit on separate plank seats. Laurence was near the stern, between Frances and the two Arab oarsmen; Frances was in front of him, her back turned toward him, sitting face-to-face with Jack Schul, who had more or less insisted on that position. Schul's knees were almost touching Frances's, and his head was framed by the high, slender prow that curved up toward the sky like a gigantic, inverted bird's beak.

From Frances's position, in the middle of the long canoe, she was forced to stare either directly at Schul (which she knew had been his intention) or beyond the high prow, and a third Arab oarsman who stood beside it, at the banks of the narrow, reed-lined tributary they were moving through.

While the oarsmen at the stern did the actual rowing, the oarsman standing beside the prow was expertly controlling the canoe's course with a long pole reaching down to the bed of the river. Frances studied him as much as possible, not only out of genuine interest but also to avoid the increasing insinuation and challenge in Jack Schul's conversation.

Already torn between her attraction to sexually aggressive men and her self-loathing for that apparent weakness, she was soon feeling drained by the constant effort of trying to remain distant. Schul, throughout the long day, kept up a relentless monologue composed of bad jokes, obscenities, and an exhausting amount of sexual innuendo aimed directly at her.

To make matters worse, it quickly became apparent that

there could be no bridging of the distance between the religious, sexually naive Laurence and his widely experienced and amoral American counterpart. Indeed, as the hours passed and as Laurence became increasingly exhausted from treating the Arabs in the villages they stopped at, his patience with Schul visibly deteriorated and gave way to anger at the crude manner in which he was trying to capture Frances's attention.

Even as the sun sank lower over the marshes and the canoe brushed past some beds of tall bulrushes, and while Laurence sat in sullen silence behind her, Frances could not avoid talking to Schul.

"—always found it easy to pick up a broad, especially the married ones. A woman's hottest when she's cheatin', which is one of life's harsh facts."

"I wouldn't know," Frances said.

"No?"

"I'm not married."

"But not without the odd man in your life, right?"

"That's none of your business."

Schul simply grinned and then glanced over her shoulder at Laurence, as if measuring his silence.

"He's got the hots for you," he said.

"Please keep your voice down."

"That's why he doesn't like me talking to you," Schul continued, unperturbed. "That kid, your religious virgin, is secretly carrying a torch for his boss. He's jerking off in his mind."

Frances tried to put Schul down with her silent contempt, then, failing, glanced past him to see the darkening azure sky moving over the tall prow. The standing oarsman was silhouetted, his body leaning across the pole, giant palm leaves brushing against his head as the canoe grazed the nearest bank. Here the water was muddy, the grass like bamboo; there were dark clouds of mosquitoes around the reeds that thrust up from the water.

"I don't understand you," she said, hardly aware of her own voice. "You fall asleep in England, the whole town disappears, then you wake up in southern Iraq—and you don't seem to be bothered. That experience would frighten most people; at the very least, it would bother them."

"Why should I be bothered?" Schul replied. "I can't do nothing about it. It's weird—I'm willin' to admit that—but what's done has been done."

"And that's all you think about it?"

"What else *is* there to think? Something weird made that town and everyone in it disappear, and somehow I ended up here. So, fuck it. I'm still alive and unharmed. I don't give a shit about the others. I'm alive and feel great."

"The mystery doesn't intrigue you?"

"Sure it does. I'd like to know what happened as much as you—but that's as far as it goes. Maybe the town will reappear and maybe it won't; but either way there's nothing I can do—and I'm not about to lose sleep over *that* fact."

Frances lowered her eyes to look at Schul. He was a brute—unfeeling and self-serving—but to her shame, it was his callous aggression that drew her toward him.

Frances shivered, feeling confused. She distracted herself by studying the riverside village they were passing. Smoke rose from the reed houses; dogs barked and snapped above the tall grass; the women and children silently watched the canoe go by while enormous and hairy buffaloes drank the muddy water below them, their shadows stretching farther across the river as the sun kept on sinking. Frances felt Schul's eyes crawling up her legs.

"You're a real attractive woman," he said, grinning lecherously. "I can't understand why you're not married. You must be pretty popular."

"Popularity," Frances replied, "has got nothing to do with it. I've just never fancied living with any man."

"Why? Your dad used to beat your mom when you were a kid?"

"No," Frances replied levelly, ignoring his sarcasm. "My dad *died* when I was a kid. As for my mother, she and I are very close—and in fact I still live with her when I'm at home."

"What about your love life?" Schul asked bluntly.

"What about it?" Frances replied.

"Do you have one?"

"Yes. Intermittently. With any man that I fancy."

"And you don't hold yourself cheap for that?"

"I hold *the men* cheap."

Schul snorted at that. "You're some sweetheart," he said.

The canoe was now taking them past the smoke of burning

reed beds. More small villages were planted untidily above the muddy water and dripping, humpbacked buffaloes were silhouetted in crimson as the sun started sinking behind the flat horizon and spread its light across the distant marshes. Eventually, when the sun had been replaced by an enormous moon and brilliant stars, they were assailed by the crying of geese, the croaking of frogs, and the rise and fall of ghostly voices that came from the torchlit darkness above the rustling wind-tossed reeds of the riverbank. Here a brief burst of laughter, there children calling to children, now a boy singing beautifully, his voice first quavering out of nowhere, then his face materializing in flickering firelight in a dark village clearing. Frances stared at him, entranced, letting his lonely voice stroke her heart, then his face disappeared abruptly, lost behind a line of fig palms as the canoe moved along a gradually broadening stretch of river and came to a glittering lake that appeared to be about three-quarters of a mile wide.

"There is no sign of wind," said the Arab standing upright. "I think it will be safe to cross the lake."

The lakes had always frightened Frances, and this one was no exception. As a child she had frequently dreamed of getting lost in a place like this and drifting forever through eternal night; and, as she stared past Schul's head at that immense body of water, black, striped with moonlight, the fear took hold and refused to release her.

"It's all right," she heard her own voice saying, "but let's get across quickly."

The oarsman at the prow nodded, dipped his long pole into the water, and pushed the canoe out into the lake. Frances glanced back over her shoulder to see Laurence's thin face, his gaze obviously fixed resentfully on Schul. She turned back to the front, but could not avoid Schul's knees when they deliberately pressed against her own.

Again, she distracted herself by studying her surroundings. She saw a flock of ducks, disturbed by the canoe, winging into the starry sky. The silence was complete and pervasive, almost palpable.

"Weird," Schul suddenly muttered, glancing around him. "Something odd about this place . . ."

His voice trailed off into the silence and he continued staring around him, his brow furrowed in concentration, his eyes moving left and right in searching motions, taking in the whole lake. Frances did likewise, wondering what he was trying to find, and saw nothing but the dark, limpid water and a broad stretch of starry sky.

"What do you mean?" she asked him. "What are you looking for?"

"I'm not sure," Schul replied, still scanning the surrounding night, "but I seem to be losing my sense of direction." He pointed with one finger. "See that bank we're heading for? It doesn't seem to have moved at all. I mean, we've been moving toward it for ten minutes, yet it doesn't seem to be any closer. . . . And the stars . . . I don't recognize the stars. I looked up at the stars and I recognized them all; then I looked at you and looked up again—and the stars had all changed. I *know* the stars, lady. I *know* them . . . but not those stars up there."

Frances, who knew nothing about the stars, saw nothing unusual. She stared hard at Schul, *felt* the silence, shivered slightly, then looked all around her at that broad expanse of black water, then at the darker strip of land toward which they were heading. The canoe kept moving forward but the land drew no closer; then, when the Arab who was standing muttered something, Frances saw him wiping sweat from his brow as his eyes widened fearfully.

"He's right," she heard Laurence say behind her. "Those aren't the stars that are normally in this sky. There's something strange going on. . . ."

Like Schul, Laurence let his voice trail off into the silence while he tried to take in what was happening. The oarsmen behind him had stopped rowing and were muttering to one another, their heads bobbing in a conspiratorial manner, their voices sounding hysterical. The Arab standing at the prow had raised his long pole out of the water and was staring wildly about him, his eyes growing larger as he realized that the land was no closer than it had been five minutes ago.

"Oh, my God, have mercy upon us!" he whispered. "Oh, my God, lead the way!"

At that moment the wind rose, whipping lightly across the water, making its placid surface ripple in low waves that shook the canoe. The standing Arab yelped in panic and let go of his pole; he watched it sliding down into the lake and then, groaning audibly, sat down behind Schul and covered his face with his hands.

The wind blew more strongly, whipping up higher waves, then the canoe was carried sideways into a darkness that filled Frances with dread.

She gripped the sides of the boat, then blinked and examined the darkness into which they were moving.

"What the hell . . . ?" she heard Schul say.

The three Arab oarsmen were now groaning and muttering prayers while the wind, growing unnaturally fierce, pushed the canoe well off course, away from the distant strip of land to which they had been heading and deeper into the great darkness that seemed to be even more unnatural than the wind.

Staring into the darkness made Frances feel disoriented, her stomach lurching as she tried to work out why. The wind howled and whipped the waves up, making the boat rise and fall, and Frances, holding her seat with one hand, rubbed her eyes with the other. She kept staring into the darkness, trying to make out what it was, and then felt that she was being sucked into it, as if into the vortex of a whirlpool that was turned on its side.

"That's what's wrong!" Schul suddenly exclaimed. *"There are no stars out there!"*

The sound of Schul's voice screaming against the wind made Frances study the night more fully and, to her horror, see that Schul was right—that the darkness into which they were being forced contained no moon or stars.

Even more disoriented, feeling as if she were actually falling, she gripped the side of the now violently rocking canoe and tried to make sense of what she was seeing.

There were stars to the west, and to the north and south; but to the east there was only a great wall of unnatural darkness with roughly vertical edges that, limned with silvery light and pulsating rhythmically, had eclipsed the stars encompassed by her field of vision.

Stunned, Frances still managed to tear her gaze away. Glancing up in an attempt to gauge how high that darkness rose, she saw the stars shining all around it where it merged with the sky. It was shaped like a great pillar, almost certainly rectangular, about half a mile wide on each side, its peak lost in the clouds. It was darker than the night, yet oddly transparent, displaying what appeared to be a faint line of forest beyond its light-flecked, rhythmically pulsating base.

Frances struggled to define what it was that she was seeing, gripping the boat, breathing deeply, trying to calm her racing heart; but she struggled in vain, her senses confused and deceitful, then collapsed into the well of a terror that made her feel naked.

"What—?" Schul started to ask.

"God have mercy!" an Arab cried.

"We're not being *pushed* off course!" Laurence screamed. *"That thing's sucking us in!"*

The wind howled around the boat, which was being sucked into that strange mass, and it was drawn forward on the water as it swirled and splashed over them. Frances was drenched and almost choked; she heard the water drumming against the boat's hull and then she looked up again. Schul was reaching out to grab her. She felt his demanding fingers. The Arab at the prow stood up, babbling wildly and waving his hands; he swayed dangerously as the boat surged high on the swirling waves and then, his arms flapping like wings, threw himself overboard.

Frances saw him disappearing, a foaming wave washing over him; then another wave, much bigger, a surfer's roaring peak, curled high above the boat, briefly forming a tunnel around it, blotting out the moon and stars and that distant stretch of land, then smashed down with the force of a giant hammer as Schul fell upon her.

She was battered and deafened, then numbed by the cold. She saw a swath of stars tilting, a spinning cloud, a shifting moon, then was sucked down into the watery depths again and swept through streaming darkness.

Not pushed: *sucked.* She would remember that all her life. She was sucked in and surrounded by the darkness, then hurled into oblivion.

5

RENDERED pleasantly drowsy by another wine-bar lunch, and reminded of the hour he had spent a week ago with his daughter, Michael was jerked out of his reverie by the buzzing of the telephone on his desk.

Glancing out of his fourth-floor window at the rolling slopes of Hampstead Heath, he picked up the telephone and listened more alertly while his secretary informed him that a Mr. Lionel Sampson, from the Ministry of Defence, had arrived for his three-thirty appointment. Michael told the girl to show the visitor in, then sat back in his chair and again felt the confusion he had experienced when Mr. Sampson had phoned that morning, saying that he had to see him urgently, that it was government business, and that Michael was to tell no one that he was coming.

Not knowing Mr. Sampson, or anyone else in government circles, Michael clasped his hands under his chair and raised his eyes expectantly to the opening door.

The man whom Michael's secretary ushered into the office was short, well-fed, rosy-cheeked, and slightly bald, his waistcoat buttoned tightly over a protruding belly, his pinstriped suit immaculate. Once the introductions had been completed, Michael's secretary left the office, closing the door quietly behind her, and Michael indicated that Mr. Sampson should take a seat at the opposite side of his desk. Setting the black leather pilot case he had been carrying on the floor beside him, Sampson crossed his legs and carefully smoothed out his trouser creases as he offered a cheerful smile.

"It's very good of you to see me at such short notice," he said. "I assure you, my department appreciates it."

"And what department would that be?" Michael asked.

"Sorry. I'm the chief projects officer for the Department of Atmospherics and Meteorological Phenomena."

"At the Ministry of Defence?"

"Correct."

"Atmospherics and meteorological phenomena?" Michael said. "I'm intrigued. What on earth have you come to see *me* for?"

Sampson grinned, as if amused by Michael's bewilderment. "Well," he said, "it's obviously a bit unusual—but we do have our reasons."

"Which are?"

"Well, according to our information, you, Dr. Phillips, are heading the most advanced experimental clinic in the country regarding psychological disorders or traumas induced by extreme shock."

"In layman's terms, that's correct."

"In your field I *am* a layman, Dr. Phillips."

"Of course. I didn't mean to be facetious."

Sampson smiled again, crossed his legs the other way, then patted the bald patch on his head as if searching for hair. "The function of my department," he said, "is to monitor, analyze, and assess ambiguous or inexplicable atmospheric or meteorological phenomena, including comets, meteors, plasmoid and corona discharges, ball lightning, temperature inversions, all manner of unidentified flying objects, and unusual electromagnetic and other atmospheric disturbances—such as those which may relate to the remarkable disappearance of Glastonbury. So, that's why I'm here." He leaned forward and gazed more intently at Michael, his basically cheerful face solemn. "Presumably," he said, "you *know* what happened at Glastonbury?"

Michael instantly recalled the two clowns in Covent Garden, the darkening expression on Cheryl's face when he had mentioned that very same subject.

"Of course," he said. "But whatever occurred, it would seem to be a scientific matter—hardly a psychological one."

"Not necessarily," Sampson replied. "This is, after all, an

unprecedented event—and one with the most terrible conse-
quences and implications. *People* are involved, Dr. Phillips—
not only those who disappeared with most of the town, but
those in the surrounding area, many of whom have been very
seriously disturbed by what has happened, whether or not they
had relatives involved. There is also the fact that at least *one* of
those who *should* have disappeared was found—alive if rather
crazed—near the critical radius."

"The what?"

"The critical radius. It's . . ." Mr. Sampson stopped talking,
nodded and smiled ruefully. "I'm sorry," he said. "I'm running
ahead too fast. Please, listen to this."

So saying, he picked up his black leather pilot case, placed it
on his knee, opened it, and produced a miniature cassette-re-
corder. He set this down on the desk, pushed it halfway to
Michael, pressed the play-button, and sat back in his chair
when the tape started turning.

At first there was only the sound of the winding tape, then
the hissing of static, then eventually the very audible groanings
of an obviously tormented human being.

Michael leaned forward to listen more intently as the groaning became louder and increasingly fearful in tone, then eventually turned into a babble of hysterical words. Initially incoher-
ent, but gradually making a kind of sense, the words soon
formed a litany that expressed some kind of vivid imagining—
or nightmarish experience—in which there were repeated fearful references to an icy coldness, steaming swamps where Glastonbury should have been, then prehistoric birds, dinosaurs,
other unrecognizable animals, then the threatening advance of
what the voice obviously thought were ape-men. His demented
speech went on a long time, repeating the same bizarre words,
eventually managing to paint a picture of a prehistoric world
that seemed more real in his mind than the real world.

The more he talked, the quicker he talked, until he was simply babbling, rendered senseless as he repeated that an icy coldness had enveloped him, that the landscape was *changing,* and
that an ape-man was advancing threateningly upon him. At
that point his shrieked words trailed off into tormented moaning, which in turn faded away into static and a click as the tape
stopped.

Sampson leaned forward and switched off the machine, then

stared steadily at Michael. "Now you know why I've come here," he said. "We need someone to treat that man."

"Who is he?" Michael asked.

"Miles Ashcombe. A well-known writer and resident of Glastonbury. The army found him when they moved in to cordon off the area. He was lying unconscious by the edge of the marshes, just about where Glastonbury Tor had formerly stood —on the perimeter, as it were, of what we already refer to as the 'vanishing zone,' and what might well be the dark mass's critical radius."

"Ah," Michael said, "that phrase again!"

"We'll get back to it in a moment," Sampson replied. "The point is that Ashcombe was discovered at what was almost certainly the outer edge of the area that disappeared. He might even have been slightly inside it. Maybe, because of that, he escaped. I repeat: he was unconscious when the army found him. But then, as soon as he awakened, he started screaming and babbling, most of which was exactly the same as we have on that tape."

"He's still hysterical?"

"Yes. But if you can bring him back to a reasonable level of normality, he might tell us much more about what happened to him inside that dark mass."

"What do *you* think happened to him?"

Sampson shrugged. "We've no idea. We only know that he's probably screaming about what drove him crazy."

"Are you trying to tell me that you think he might have *seen* what he's babbling about?"

Sampson very deliberately returned Michael's steady gaze. "I know it sounds crazy," he said, "but he *has* been through an extraordinary, theoretically impossible experience, and all he can talk about, delirious or not, is what he describes on that tape."

"He's traumatized," Michael said. "He has to have something to cling to—something with which he can identify and claim as reality."

"A *prehistoric* world?" Sampson said with blunt skepticism. "Surely that would be the most *remote* thing he could possibly cling to. What about the world he vanished from? The world that he *knew?*"

"You think that what he experienced was *real?*"

Sampson shrugged. "Who knows?" he said. "All *we* know is that what happened at Glastonbury has happened elsewhere. Not in this country—I can't say where—but it's happened before."

Now Michael, for all his pragmatism, experienced a shock of disbelief out of which arose, like smoke from burning tinder, the gray breath of fear. For the first time he was being compelled to face the impossible, and it threatened everything he believed in.

"You mean that man disappeared with Glastonbury, but then reappeared again?"

"Yes," Mr. Sampson said. "And we want to know if what he experienced was real or imagined."

"Imagined, surely," Michael said, startled that Sampson should seriously suggest otherwise.

"We can't be too sure of that," Sampson replied. "We can't be too sure at all. Do you mind if I smoke?"

"No," Michael said. "I smoke myself. Here, have one of mine."

He removed a packet of cigarettes from a drawer in his desk, gave one to Sampson, took one himself, then let Sampson give him a light.

Sampson blew a smoke ring in the air, then squinted through it. "Tell me," he said. "Have you *any* idea what *actually* happened at Glastonbury?"

"Only that it disappeared in an impossible manner. That's *all* I know."

"Right, Dr. Phillips, it disappeared. No explosion, no earthquake, no flood—it just disappeared."

Sampson stood up, went to the window, and stared out at the rolling hills of Hampstead Heath. He stood there for some time, lost in thought, then turned back to Michael.

"Do you know what a black hole is?" he asked.

"I've a very rough idea," Michael replied, "but I didn't think—"

"That's right." Sampson quickly intervened, anticipating Michael's train of thought. "It *wasn't* a black hole. If it had been, we wouldn't be here right now—the *whole world* would have disappeared. However, we *are* receiving reports that it was a great dark mass that more or less *swallowed* Glastonbury."

Michael said nothing, patiently waiting to hear more, automatically behaving as he did with most of his patients. Mr.

Sampson, scratching one ruddy cheek, offered another bemused smile.

"Let me explain," he said. "The whole area of Glastonbury has been cordoned off by the army and is presently being surveyed by my department with a variety of scientific instruments." He patted the bald spot on his head and sat in his chair again. "Already we've ascertained that, one, it contains an unusually high density of electromagnetic radiation and, two, it has an exceptionally strong, though gradually weakening, gravitational pull. In other words, if we're not dealing with a legitimate black hole, we certainly seem to be dealing with something that greatly *resembles* such a phenomenon."

"And whatever it was, that man you recorded, Miles Ashcombe, was also swallowed by the dark mass, but then, instead of disappearing for good like the rest of them, mysteriously materialized back on earth."

"Correct. We don't know what that dark mass is, and it certainly defies all known knowledge, so let's use the black hole as a convenient analogy."

Sampson inhaled on his cigarette, blew some more smoke rings, watched them grow larger and disappear, then turned back to Michael.

"Theoretically speaking, a black hole represents the ultimately compressed state of matter. Because of its immeasurable gravitational field, the black hole permanently traps light and all other forms of electromagnetic radiation—including infra, ultraviolet, and radio X rays—inside it. Because light cannot escape, the objects are termed 'black holes,' but this term refers to a physical condition rather than a true color, since in theory black holes have *no* color."

"Which suggests the dark mass that covered Glastonbury," Michael said.

"Right," Sampson replied. "Most of the witnesses who viewed the dark mass from a distance were in agreement that although it *seemed* dark, it also appeared to be incorporeal and *colorless* in some way they could not quite define. So, in that sense, it's a *kind* of black hole."

"So, how did it make Glastonbury disappear?"

"Well, accepting our black hole hypothesis, it is possible that the dark mass—our so-called black hole—*sucked* Glastonbury in past its critical radius, either to crush it out of existence or to spew it out somewhere else—as a black hole might do."

"The critical radius," Michael said. "That's the phrase you used before . . ."

"Ah, yes," Sampson replied, nodding and smiling almost apologetically. "The *critical radius*—more widely known as the *event horizon*—marks the point beyond which there is no escape from the black hole."

"Which rather destroys your analogy," Michael said. "Since, if there is no escape from the black hole, your Miles Ashcombe should not have escaped from the dark mass."

"Clever," Sampson said, "but not quite right. Our investigations have already raised the possibility that the dark mass that swallowed Glastonbury, and other places I cannot name, might possess a similar critical radius—but one that waxes and wanes in strength, refusing for the most part to release what it sucks in, but *occasionally,* perhaps when its strength lessens, allowing some object, or person, to escape—as in the case of Miles Ashcombe."

"Fine," Michael said. "I'm with you so far. I'm accepting your black hole analogy for the dark mass. So, what do you think happened *inside* it? Since, as you said, what gets sucked into a black hole is probably crushed out of existence."

"That's true of a *stationary* black hole," Sampson replied without pause. "However, it is a widely held scientific belief that since stars spin, black holes must spin also. Ergo, if this is true, an object heading into a spinning black hole could follow a course that does *not* take it to the obliterating center of the black hole—the singularity of its core—which in turn leads to the theory that if the aforesaid object does *not* get crushed out of existence, yet cannot reemerge to its own universe, then it must end up somewhere else—which could be a distant region of our universe or, just as likely, given the remarkable distortions of time that must exist within the black hole, in some *other* time, after a journey through instantaneous interstellar travel."

Michael took a deep breath and stared steadily at Mr. Sampson. Had it not been for the fact that he was from the Ministry of Defence, Michael would have thought of this bizarre conversation as some kind of insane joke.

"Some kind of *time* machine?" he asked disbelievingly.

Sampson shrugged. "I know it sounds ridiculous, but it's possible that the dark mass, in a manner *similar* to that of a black hole, distorts time and space inside its critical radius. Or—perhaps less remarkable and therefore more conceivable—actually *traps* time in some way and holds it forever. Certainly, theoretically speaking, a black hole would do that."

"You mean that Miles Ashcombe, when he was rendered invisible, actually *witnessed* the past?"

Sampson glanced at his dwindling cigarette, shrugged and stubbed it out in an ashtray, then crossed his legs again.

"If we accept the possibility that black holes do exist, we must then accept that they can distort and ultimately *freeze* time. The notion of time travel also contains the hidden supposition that there are thousands of parallel universes, each a mere fraction of a second ahead or behind this one time, each with its own past and future—and, if this is so, and if those parallel worlds exist within the black hole, then some similar phenomenon might exist beyond the critical radius of the dark mass that spirited Glastonbury away."

"Are you trying to tell me that Ashcombe may not only have *witnessed* the past, but actually *lived* it?"

"What can I say, Dr. Phillips? We only know that that dark mass was an extraordinary phenomenon—one that defies all our scientific knowledge—and that Miles Ashcombe, in his delirium, but also under hypnosis, has forced us to consider every possibility."

Michael glanced out the window, then realized what he was doing: he was trying to focus his attention on something real . . . the tangible world.

"I'm confused," he confessed. "Even accepting your rather mind-boggling hypothesis, surely if Ashcombe was sucked into, or spirited away to, some other time and place, he must have ceased existing in *this* time. And even if he had been somehow lost in history, to return he would have to travel *forward* in time, which is just inconceivable."

Sampson sighed, gazed down at his own crossed legs, picked a piece of lint off his trousers and let it fall to the carpet. "I have sleepless nights thinking about it," he said, "but *all* things are possible."

"Two-way *time* travel?" Michael said skeptically, hardly able to credit that he, a sane man, was actually tolerating this conversation.

Sampson sighed again and raised his gaze from his striped trousers. "Beyond the black hole," he said, "time and space are distorted. Theoretically speaking, for someone traveling through a black hole time would gradually slow down and eventually cease altogether—though our hypothetical person, completely unaware of it, would continue to live his normal life in some kind of bizarre, eternal present. Given this, Miles Ashcombe *could* have briefly regressed through his other selves and then, in some equally remarkable manner, returned to his present self."

"And all the others? The ones who didn't come back?"

Sampson shrugged and uncrossed his legs. "The point of no return. Who knows *where* they are?"

Now it was Michael's turn to stand up and go to the window, to stare down at the green hills of Hampstead Heath and reassure himself that he actually existed and was not simply dreaming. If what he had just heard had come from the lips of anyone else, he would surely have thought them mad, but when he turned away from the window, and looked down at the still seated Mr. Sampson, he knew that he was dealing with a very experienced, level-headed civil servant.

Sighing, he sat down again, folding his hands on his desk.

"This is all too unbelievable," he said. "It's simply too much to grasp."

Mr. Sampson smiled and spread his hands in a rueful gesture. "It's too much for *us* to grasp," he said, "but we're having to deal with it."

"I don't think *I* can deal with it," Michael said. "My head's reeling already."

"You're a psychologist," Mr. Sampson said. "That *should* be a help."

Michael smiled at that, drummed a pencil on the desk, became aware of what he was doing, dropped the pencil and looked up.

"I take it," he said, "that you want me to attend to this Miles Ashcombe and, if possible, ascertain just where imagination ends and reality begins."

"That's it. Precisely."

"He'll be brought to the hospital?"

"Yes—without papers. We believe you have private wards for special people and we want him in one of those. A room well barred and guarded. No name on the door. We'll deliver him with false identification, then it's all up to you. So, will you do it?"

Michael stared around his office, shook his head as if to clear it of cobwebs, and then sighed disbelievingly.

"It's the case of the century," he said. "It's one I simply can't miss."

Sampson removed the cassette tape from the recorder, left the tape on the desk, slipped the recorder back into his pilot case. Then he stood up and pointed at the tape, his smile brightening his ruddy cheeks.

"You can keep the tape," he said. "I'm sure you'll play it often. I'll phone later to make arrangements for the delivery of your patient. The best of luck, Dr. Phillips."

He turned away and walked out, closing the door quietly behind him, leaving Michael sitting there in the chilling silence of the afternoon's deepening gloom.

6

FRANCES blinked against a bright haze, licked her lips, rubbed her eyes, moved her head experimentally from left to right, then took a deep breath. How long had she been unconscious? Had she broken any bones? Perhaps she had actually died in that darkness and was now *imagining* her body. She took another deep breath, touched herself, *felt* herself, then raised herself onto her right hip, her hand pressed to the damp grass. She was wet and steaming slightly as the heat dried her clothes. She shook her head, squinted through the bright haze, and saw Laurence watching her.

"You've been unconscious all night," Laurence said. "You were knocked about a fair bit."

Frances sat upright, feeling feverish and dizzy, shivered and studied Laurence again. His hair was untidy, he badly needed a shave, his eyes seemed slightly dazed and bloodshot. He was covered in dirt, and his clothing, also wet, was disheveled.

"God," she said, "you look a mess."

"So do you," he replied.

"Then I must look exactly as I feel."

"You're not alone," Laurence said.

The great lake was behind him, its surface vitreous in the morning light, but when Frances tried to ascertain the exact position of the sun, she was almost blinded by the constant, brilliant haze.

"I've been unconscious all night?" she asked, hardly recognizing her own voice.

"Yes," Laurence replied. He was holding a gnarled stick in his right hand, scoring rings in a small patch of mud surrounded by shiny stones. "You were hammered repeatedly into the bank before Schul and I managed to drag you out of the water. Naturally, by the time we got you out, you'd been knocked unconscious."

Frances ran her hand experimentally over her head and limbs. "No serious damage," she said eventually, "so it must have been shock."

"Yes, maybe so."

"And the others?"

Laurence shrugged. "The canoe was smashed to pieces against the bank of the lake, Schul and I managed between us to drag you ashore, and the Arab oarsmen seem to have vanished with the remains of the boat."

Squinting into the brilliant haze, Frances saw that she was in a clearing by the lake, in what seemed like a natural garden of orange and lemon trees, fig palms, and a lush profusion of buttercups, boxthorn, saltbrush, tall rushes, and uncommonly rich, untended green grass. She felt very strange when she studied it, but she didn't know why.

"The Arabs must have drowned," Laurence said. "There's no sign of them anywhere."

"And Schul?"

Laurence languidly waved his hand to indicate the forest behind Frances. "He's somewhere in there," he said. "He's been wandering about all night, trying to get some help, but so far he hasn't found a soul."

"That's not particularly unusual: he's not likely to find anyone between here and Al-Qurna—and he probably doesn't know where that is."

"Let's hope that's been his only problem." Laurence raised his short, gnarled stick and plunged it into the patch of muddy earth, scoring coils and circles abstractedly, but with suppressed nervous violence. "Do you remember anything else about last night?" he asked.

"Just that darkness . . ."

"That's right." Laurence threw the stick onto the ground, rubbed his dirt-smeared hands on his trousers, then wiped his lips with the back of one hand. "That great wall of darkness," he said. "There wasn't anything natural about it: that thing was real strange. It had a definite shape. It was rectangular and very high. It blotted out the stars, but it seemed slightly transparent and had flecks of light darting about inside it. I don't know what it was, but it was frightening. It wasn't natural at all."

Frances remembered and knew just what Laurence meant. She closed her eyes and saw that great mass towering above as its pulsating darkness drew the canoe in on the turbulent water.

"Yes," she said, wiping sweat from her forehead. "And that thing sucked us into it."

Laurence stood up and walked to the water's edge, his body framed by the glittering surface of the lake, his feet close to a mass of bulrushes that swayed by the muddy bank.

"Yes," he said, "but into *what?* The only thing that Schul and I can remember is that the stars disappeared. There was darkness—a terrible darkness—and flecks of light were darting around us. It was cold—*freezing* cold—then it grew warmer as the darkness faded away. The stars returned, but they weren't the stars we knew: they were the same stars that suddenly appeared just before last night's storm. It was a different sky, Frances—a *different* sky—but we don't know *what* sky."

Frances hardly knew herself. She had never felt so strange. Staring across the forest clearing, trying not to breathe too quickly, she saw Laurence as a black silhouette framed by rippling, silvery light.

The lake, she thought. *It's only the lake. I must not start imagining things . . .*

"Please, Laurence," she said. "Do me a favor. Don't talk with your back to me."

Laurence sighed audibly, walked toward her, and stopped a few feet away.

"While I watched you," he said, "Schul went looking for help —but each time he went into that forest, he lost his sense of direction."

"Schul doesn't know the area, Laurence. What's strange about that?"

"Do *you* know where we are, Frances?"

"Yes. We're just a couple of miles north of Al-Qurna. We could walk there in no time."

"That's what *I* thought," Laurence said. "But Schul couldn't find Al-Qurna—or anywhere else."

Already disoriented, Frances now felt more confused, her

thoughts writhing in the thickets of that darkness which had swallowed her senses.

"He can't find Al-Qurna. He can't find a living soul. He went looking three times during the night—and he's looking right now."

"I repeat," Frances said, aware of the strain in her own voice, "Schul doesn't know the area. He's probably just—"

"No, Frances, it's something other than that. Schul's a Vietnam veteran, well trained and possessing a compass, and could normally find his way anywhere. I told him where Al-Qurna was, but no matter how far along the bank he walked, he ended up right back here. He can't figure it out—and neither can I. It's as if we're on some kind of island . . . except it *isn't* an island."

Frances was exhausted, drained by the fierce humidity; when she stood up, rising awkwardly, she realized just how badly she had been bruised when thrown out of the boat.

She placed her hands above her head, stretched herself, loosening up, then looked around the clearing again, surprised by its beauty. The grass was remarkably lush, the green splashed with yellow buttercups, the trees rich with oranges, lemons, and figs; the foliage resplendent with wild flowers.

Schul's rucksack was on the ground, lying under one of the trees, opened, its flap hanging down to the grass.

"Does he have any food in that rucksack?" she asked.

"I don't think so," Laurence said.

"Perhaps he can find us some," Frances said.

She walked past Laurence and stopped at the muddy bank, looking out over the limpid water, into that strange, dazzling haze.

Why strange? She wasn't sure. She rubbed her eyes and kept staring. The rippling silvery water gradually merged with the shimmering white sky, revealing no land at the far side, no dark line of bulrushes.

She shivered and turned away, hearing birdsong from the trees, but aware that that singing was encased in a great dome of silence. Laurence was still standing there, his gaze intense and a little frightened, then she heard snapping twigs, shifting foliage, and looked to her right.

It was Schul. He was emerging from the forest and coming toward her, stripped to the waist, denims rolled up to his knees, carrying a makeshift fishing pole across one well-muscled shoulder, with three or four fish in the small net dangling from his left hand. His naked torso was suntanned, badly scarred, hard with muscle; and even his walk, Frances noted immediately, was clearly aggressive.

He stopped just in front of her, took a deep breath, wiped sweat from his brow.

"So," he said, "you're awake at last."

"Yes," Frances replied.

"Oh, man, that was some sleep you had. . . . First me and then you."

"I don't think there's a connection."

"Maybe, maybe not. There's odd things going on here." He held his small net up high, displaying the freshwater fish. "You like 'em?" he asked. "I caught 'em in a pool back there. There's no shortage of food in this place—and we might need a lot of it."

"You kept that net in your rucksack?"

"That's right, lady," Schul replied. "*And* a compass, matches, an all-purpose knife and lots more. I'm a sensible traveler."

He sneered at Laurence, then threw the fish at his feet. "Do you know how to light a fire, kid? If so, we can eat."

Laurence looked down at the fish, the blush on his cheeks displaying anger. "No," he said. "I can't light an open fire. I was never in the Boy Scouts."

Schul laughed at that, slapping one hand on his hip. "Shit," he said. "The Boy Scouts! *That's* a good one. I didn't pick it up *there,* kid."

"We *know* you've been to Vietnam," Laurence said with quiet sarcasm.

"Fuckin' right, kid. And learned a lot." As if dismissing a minion, Schul waved his left hand. "To hell with it," he said. "I'll light the fire myself—*and* I'll cook the damned fish."

He turned away from Laurence to fix his attention on Frances; she noticed the sweat trickling down brown skin and making his hard muscles shine.

"We've been shipwrecked," he said, his lips curling into that crooked grin. "We're gonna have to fend for ourselves."

"It shouldn't be too long," Frances said, speaking more hopefully than she felt. "If I'm not back at Basra by tonight the hospital will contact the sheikh—and if he tells them we left his village yesterday, they'll send a helicopter to search for us."

"Oh, yeah?"

"Yes."

Schul grinned sarcastically, nodded contemptuously at Laurence, and said, "Do you know the situation we're in? Do you know what's going on?"

"He told me that we seem to be lost," Frances said, "but I'm sure there's a rational explanation."

"And what's your rational explanation for what we saw last night?"

"I don't have one."

"Right, you don't have one. And do you have a rational explanation for why I can't find that town your friend here sent me to?"

"Obviously—"

"Shit," Schul said brutally. "I could find my way anywhere just by tracking the stars, but those stars we saw last night don't conform to any stars that we know. As for the town, Al-Qurna, that's supposed to be south of here . . . well, let me tell you, there's *nothing* south of here—nothing at all. As a matter of fact, lady, if you follow the water's edge you just end up right back here—which at first made me think this was an island. But then, when I cut straight across this island, I ended up right back here *again.* Here there's no north or south. There's no east or west. Believe me, you walk in any direction and you'll end up right here."

"That's impossible," Frances said.

"Impossible?" Schul replied, then, rubbing a hand across his bronzed, hairy chest, nodded again, this time indicating the sky. "Look up there," he said, "and tell me what you see . . . or what you *don't* see."

Frances shaded her eyes with one hand and looked up, squinting painfully. "I . . . Just the light. It's very bright."

"Yeah," Schul said, "it's *too* bright. And where's the sun? Tell me *that,* doctor lady! *There's no sun in that sky!"*

The light flashed in front of Frances, making Schul seem unreal, but she blinked until her vision returned and brought with it the mystery: the lake merging with the sky, the sky sunless, air hazy, Laurence framed by a rippling silvery light behind Schul who, in his inexplicable arrogance and lack of fear, had himself given shape to this dream by springing out of nowhere.

Frances wiped sweat from her brow, feeling hot, yet shivering. She rubbed her eyes and tried to make real this unnatural garden. No north or south, no east or west; just a peculiar, brilliant haze that made everything seem even more unreal.

"Christ," Schul said. "Let's get to work. Let's think it out while we eat."

But before they ate, Schul decided to prepare for a long stay by the lake and took pleasure in showing them how to survive in the wilds. From what had seemed like a fairly normal rucksack, he unpacked a two-man mountain tent, a five-pound down sleeping bag, a methylated stove comprising an aluminum cooking set with two large frying pans and pot lifter, a lightweight canteen including cooking and eating utensils for two, a first-aid kit, a flashlight, some Brillo pads, toilet paper, spare clothing, and a pack of waterproof matches.

"I've also got some emergency rations," he said, grinning maliciously. "Glucose tablets, chocolate, dried fruit, and other shit—but that'll stay in the rucksack until we're desperate—or, to be more precise, until *I'm* desperate. You people, you don't come prepared, you deserve what you get."

Frances felt as sheepish as Laurence looked while Schul, frequently casting them mocking glances, gathered some brush and made a fire, which he lit with his fire-starter tablets and a large, waterproof match. He sliced the head and tail off the fish with a five-inch sheath knife, expertly removed its bones, fried it in a pan heated on the stove, and served it with relish.

"I've got some salt in the rucksack," he said, "but we might need it later."

Frances ate her meal in silence, using a fork and nervous fingers, slightly nauseated by the dry, unsalted fish but grateful to have it. She was aware of Schul watching her, his lips curled in a licentious grin, and although she felt removed from herself, her warming flesh captured her. *What's happening?* she wondered. *Where are we? Is this real?* She dissolved into a realm of confusion, feeling time slipping past her.

"Here," Schul said huskily. "Have some Scotch. I always carry this hip flask."

Frances accepted the offer, letting the drink anesthetize her, turning away from Laurence's reproachful stare and offering

Schul a small smile. The Scotch burned quickly through her, illuminating her dazed mind, pushing time even farther away and making the dream more acceptable.

"It's getting colder," she finally murmured.

"Yeah," Schul said. "That's right. It's afternoon already— Jesus Christ!—and the sun's goin' down."

"There *is* no sun," Laurence said.

"Christ, man, I forgot that! Still, it's gettin' colder and darker. . . . *Too* cold . . . And too quickly."

Frances noticed that the hazy brilliance had turned gray, though was still oddly unreal. She stared across the wide lake, trying to see the marshes beyond, but saw only a slowly shifting mist where glittering water met darkening sky.

"Cold," she murmured. "It's turning much, much too cold."

"Yeah," Schul replied, sounding almost hoarse, "and it's gonna get worse."

"It shouldn't," Frances said. "It never gets that cold here. I don't know why it should be that way now—nor, for that matter, why it should be turning so dark this early."

"What the hell *is* the time?" Schul asked. He studied his wristwatch, furrowed his brow in surprise, shook the watch close to his ear, and then registered more surprise.

"It's stopped," he said. "It's never done that before."

Frances and Laurence both checked their own wristwatches and discovered that they, too, had stopped.

"The same," Laurence said. "They stopped at the same time. That's approximately when it started getting dark."

"But that was only two-thirty in the *afternoon*," Schul replied, "so it shouldn't be dark *or* cold right now."

Laurence coughed into his fist, his gazing wandering back to Frances. "That struck me last night," he said, speaking directly to her. "One minute we were out there in the warmth of the lake, the next we were inside that dark mass where the cold nearly froze us. You were unconscious through it all, but believe me, you were shivering all night."

Frances yawned, no longer frightened, feeling drunk, and saw that the grayness was deepening into a strange, swimming darkness. She raised her head but saw no stars, examined the sky but saw no sun, placed her right hand, fingers outspread, on the grass and felt the cold earth.

"Christ," Schul said, "I'm drunk."

"So am I," Frances replied.

"I've never got drunk so fast before. I think I'll have to lie down."

"You're not drunk," Laurence said. "Neither of you is drunk. I didn't have anything to drink and yet I feel the same way."

"It's this darkness," Frances said, rubbing her forehead. "It's making *all* of us tired."

There was no sun in the sky, but it kept growing darker as Schul jumped to his feet and then, swaying a little, started putting up his two-man tent. Frances watched him, amused, more so because of Laurence, impelled perversely by his visible anger to move closer to Schul.

There was something weird here. Schul knew it and would protect her. Like a lot of men—or at least like most of those she had known—he was driven by a brutish, selfish ego that would not let him rest. What he wanted, he must have—she understood that, having known it—and if the impulse often made her feel revulsion, it just as often made her surrender to her need for oblivion.

He's a brute, she thought. *Look at him: flexing his muscles and smirking.*

And yet, even realizing that, she felt her flesh aroused by him.

"Okay," Schul said, "the tent's ready. . . . And I've got room for one more."

His grin had two sides, inviting Frances, mocking Laurence. He put his hands up in the air, palms turned toward the sky.

"It's *my* tent," he said. "So that means I can use it. That leaves space for one of you two—and ladies come first."

"You and I can sleep out here," Laurence said. "Frances can sleep in the tent."

"It's *my* tent," Schul repeated.

"That's hardly the issue," Laurence replied.

"It doesn't matter," Frances interrupted. "I'd rather sleep outside."

Schul threw her his wolfish grin. "What's the matter? You don't like me? You're gonna freeze your ass out here, lady, so why not share the tent?"

"And what about Laurence?"

"Where he sleeps is his problem."

"To hell with you," Frances said contemptuously. "I'll sleep out here with Laurence."

Schul stopped grinning, then took a deep breath, the lake and marshes beyond him dissolving rapidly into the strange dusk. Frances returned his hard stare, trying to keep her face blank, not daring to show him what she felt, knowing how he would use it.

Then Schul shook his head, very slowly, in mock despair. "Okay," he said, "stay out here. You'll come crawling in soon enough."

He shivered, spat, and crawled into his tent. Frances smiled nervously at Laurence, received a grateful smile in return, then glanced at the darkening forest around her and out to the lake.

Something was wrong: it was too early to be dark. And the darkness itself had a quality she couldn't pinpoint. She studied the lake and felt peculiar. It didn't seem to be dark out there. The darkness was gathering here, wrapping its chilly wings around her, but out there, beyond the darkness, was what seemed to be normal daylight.

In fact, studying the lake and marshes, Frances had the distinct impression that she was looking through a sheet of tinted glass. The darkness was *here,* gathering around her, but it wasn't out there.

She glanced at Schul's tent, remembering his well-muscled, sweating torso, then stood up and walked across to the lemon tree and sat down beside Laurence.

"God," she said, "it's cold."

"Yes," Laurence replied. "You better swallow your pride and share Schul's tent."

"No, thanks," Frances said.

It was now as dark as night, but Laurence's face was illuminated by numerous darting lights that first in their hundreds, then in their thousands, were pulsating as they drifted to and fro. The lights multiplied constantly, streaking the gloom with their shifting brilliance, resembling shoals of luminous, silvery minnows in the depths of a river.

Frances felt drugged and sleepy, but she stretched out her hand, spreading her fingers to catch one of the sparkling lights and see what it was. The lights passed through her hand, through her arm, then through her head, so she closed her eyes and let herself drift through a spiraling galaxy.

"What's *happening?*" Laurence whispered. "Is this *real?*"

He stared at Frances with wide eyes, his face a quiltwork of light and shadow, then automatically placed his arms around her and drew her close to him. When he did so, Frances heard a mechanical whirring sound in her ear, and looked down to see the hands on Laurence's wristwatch spinning into a blur.

Startled, she jerked her head back and pulled his wrist away; she examined the spinning hands on his watch and then looked at her own. When she saw that it was doing the same, she felt the breath of insanity.

"Hold me, Laurence!" she whispered. "Just *hold* me! I have to know this is *real!*"

They took warmth from each other, soothing their fear in togetherness, and then Frances squinted through that darkness filled with drifting, sparkling lights to see a series of completely different landscapes taking shape magically.

The scenery moved. It changed. It was never the same for long. First volcanoes and fire, then boiling water and sprouting greenery, then bizarre creatures flapping their wings overhead while large plants bloomed and died. Seasons came and went, dissolving into one another, and the landscape changed from molten rock to desert, from that to lush foliage and wild flowers. It was real, but obscured, as if viewed through tinted glass; and the thousands, perhaps millions, of tiny sparkling lights darted to and fro, and drifted up and down, cascading in mysterious, dreamlike grandeur before her dazed eyes.

Frances felt drugged and sleepy. Her body was very heavy. She felt that she was turning into stone and sinking into the ground. The earth was pulling her down. Gravity had clearly grown much stronger. She glanced at Laurence and saw that he was sleeping, and that made her smile. She breathed deeply and looked above her, but the sky was unfamiliar. She lowered her head and closed her weary eyes and fell asleep almost instantly.

She dreamed about humming lights. She dreamed that someone was coming toward her. She stayed silent in the hope that that someone would disappear with the rest of it.

7

FRANCES awakened to a ghostly chorus of frogs, geese, birds, and mosquitoes. Opening her eyes, she squinted into morning sunlight and saw Schul at the center of the clearing, lighting a fire. Stiff with cold, she moved painfully, sitting up and stretching herself, then stared across the glassy, placid lake at the marshes beyond. Everything seemed normal, making her wonder if she had been dreaming. Then Laurence, sitting beside her, also yawned and faced the new day.

"Is it normal?"

"Yes," Frances said.

"Thank God for that."

Laurence sat up, rubbing his eyes, shaking his head, distastefully took note of Schul working, then glanced up at the sky.

"Look," he said, pointing. "We've even got the sun back."

It was true. The familiar sun had returned and the morning light seemed natural, blazing down on the water and earth to burn the coldness away. Schul struck a match and set fire to his pile of twigs; when the flames burst into life, he threw Frances and Laurence a crooked grin.

"You look frozen," he said.

"We *are* frozen," Frances replied.

"You had your chance, lady," Schul said. "It was real cozy inside that tent, and you could have been with me."

Frances didn't bother replying, but she and Laurence stood up together, then walked over to the fire as Schul heaped larger sticks on the burning twigs. They both knelt down by the fire, opened their frozen hands to the flames, and shuddered as the warmth filtered into them.

"I think we should try to get out of here," Schul said, "while everything's okay. You want coffee?"

"Yes."

Schul had filled a metal pot with water from the river; now he dropped a couple of purifying tablets into the water, then put the pot onto the fire to boil. While he rinsed out his two tin cups, then put coffee and sugar into them, Frances took comfort from the fire and thought of her strange night.

She remembered the streaming darkness, the thousands of darting lights, the scenery that changed as the hands on her watch spun in a blur. She had grown very weighty, as if turning to stone; then, while the scenery kept changing, she had fallen asleep.

What had she dreamed about? She now struggled to remember. The dreams had been so vivid at the time, but now she couldn't recall them. She remembered humming lights, perhaps someone coming toward her, her silent prayer that that "someone" would disappear with everything else.

"I hope you two appreciate what I'm doing for you," Schul said. "First I catch and fry the fish, now I'm giving you my coffee. You don't seem too grateful for my efforts."

"Why be grateful?" Frances replied. "You're getting satisfaction out of it. It gives you a sense of power to have us so completely dependent on you. It makes you feel you're in charge."

"I *am* in charge, lady. That's automatic in this case. I'm in charge because I'm the one most capable of getting us out of here. I make the decisions and you do as I say."

"God," Frances replied, "you're obnoxious. You really *do* need to be in charge and lay down your orders."

"You know that because you understand the type. Deep down I'm the kind you like, lady. I know what you want."

"I just want your coffee."

The conversation had embarrassed Laurence, but Schul just grinned maliciously. "Anyway," he said, "it looks like everything here is back to normal, so we might be able to find our way to that town. That weird darkness has been and gone, but it might come back again, and I want us to get out of here while the going is good."

"Did you sleep all night?" Frances asked him.

"Yeah. Like a bird."

"Then you didn't see what happened after you left us?"

"No, not a thing."

Frances summarized what she and Laurence had witnessed, but Schul, though he wrinkled his brow, still seemed unafraid.

"Weird," he murmured. "Real weird . . . And I slept through it all."

He examined the pot on the fire, saw that the water was boiling, made the coffee and handed each of them a cup. While they sipped he made himself another in the hollow lid of the pot. He drank some, then glanced across the lake, raising his eyes to the sun.

"Well," he said, "we've still got the sun and everything else seems normal, so we better try to get out of here as soon as possible. Maybe what happened last night was just an odd happening, but just in case it wasn't—in case it comes back—we better forget breakfast and try to get as far away from here as possible before anything happens."

"Let's try to get to Al-Qurna," Frances said.

"Sure," Schul said. *"Anywhere."*

While Schul doused the fire and Laurence simply looked on grimly, Frances washed the tin cups in the lake, then gave them to Schul. He expertly dismantled his tent and packed it in the rucksack, then glanced at the sun, checked his compass, and led them out of the clearing.

Since it would naturally lead to the continuation of the river, they stuck to the muddy bank of the lagoon, Schul walking out ahead, Frances just behind him, and with Laurence as the last link in the chain. The sun was high in the sky, making the lagoon look like glass, and the heat had an unrelenting ferocity that drained them of strength. Mosquitoes buzzed all around them, attracted to their running sweat, swarming up from the trampled grass and bulrushes and darkening the bright light.

Frances wiped sweat from her forehead, licked it from her upper lip, felt it trickling from under her armpits, down her neck to her breasts. Exhaustion claimed her quickly, making her sag and draining her mind, and she sank into the well of her senses, hardly aware of her own thoughts.

Schul had removed his shirt again and had it flapping from his rucksack; Frances followed that whipping flag like a donkey after a carrot, then tried to gather her scattered thoughts together by lowering her gaze. Schul had also removed his trousers and was now wearing only shorts. Frances saw his deeply tanned, hairy legs moving under the rucksack.

She kept staring at those legs, mesmerized by their hard muscle, her gaze following a line of glistening sweat that wound through his dark hairs.

"A couple of miles?" Schul asked, looking back over his shoulder. "Al-Qurna's only a couple of miles from here? Is that what you said?"

"That's right," Frances replied. "It's not far. Another few minutes should do it."

Yet even as she spoke she sensed that something was wrong, her gaze taking in the sweep of the great lagoon but not recognizing it. They should have passed the lagoon by now—it should have narrowed down to become the river—but instead the opposite side was as far away as ever, the marshes dissolving in a haze that grew brighter each minute.

"Oh, God," Frances murmured.

She realized what was happening, jerked her eyes up to confirm it, and saw, where the sun should have been, only a sweeping white haze.

"Oh, God!" she repeated, this time loudly. "The sun's disappeared again!"

Schul stopped walking and glanced at the sky, shading his eyes with his hands and shaking his head.

"Oh, shit," he whispered.

"That means it's starting again," Laurence said. "That's what happened yesterday."

Schul glanced at his wristwatch. "It's stopped again," he said. Frances and Laurence both checked their own wristwatches and found the same thing. "Fuck it," Schul said, "let's keep going anyway. We're probably out of the range of that thing and might get to Al-Qurna. Let's move it. *Right now!*"

Remaining close together, they continued along the muddy bank, almost blinded by the dazzling white haze that covered sky and lagoon. Frances glanced across the water, trying to see the far side, saw only that same blinding haze, and then turned to her left. She was passing orange and lemon trees, the fruit packed close together, but their coloring had been washed out completely and the trees were mere shadows. She wiped tears from her stinging eyes, then focused on the ground; the bulrushes were swaying by the bank as a breeze rippled through them.

"Oh, God," she said, far too loudly, "that wind is returning!"

The heavy rucksack bounced in front of her, then, as a shifting shadow, his features erased by the swimming haze, Schul was turning toward her to grab her hand and pull her close to him. She felt his arm against her own, his skin sweat-slicked and electric, then he dragged her along the muddy bank, trying to make her go faster. She thought about Laurence behind her, wondered if they would lose him, then forgot him when she noticed that the fierce haze was starting to darken.

"Shit!" Schul hissed. "Too late!"

As he tugged even more urgently at Frances's hand, the wind rose dramatically, sweeping violently across them, almost forcing them into the trees, which were bending and rustling. Frances stifled a sob, squinting into the changing light, knowing that they should have reached Al-Qurna by now and hoping to see it.

What she saw destroyed that hope, plunging her spirit into despair: The great darkness was returning, materializing magically from nothing, blocking out the sun's light and warmth as it deepened inexorably.

"Where is it?" Schul shouted. *"Where's Al-Qurna?"*

"I don't know!" Frances cried.

The darkness had taken command, turning the day into night, and it forced them to stop and take shelter beneath the shivering trees. They huddled together for some time, but then the wind suddenly ceased; and too bewildered for words they all looked across the lake to see what appeared to be normal daylight beyond the unnatural darkness.

Frances couldn't believe her eyes and felt increasingly unreal as she took in that daylight at the other side of the darkness, then focused on the bank where it curved away from her and disappeared into light-flecked gloom.

She shivered with cold, wrapped her arms around her raised knees, blinked, and squinted into the sparkling gloom to see the lights multiplying. They were tiny pulsating lights, first in their hundreds, then their thousands, bursting out of the distant darkness and suddenly swirling about her, then moving to and fro, up and down, in loops and circles, forming cartwheels and winding streams of silver that dazzled the eyes.

"Oh, dear God," she heard Laurence whisper. "What *are* they? *Where* are we?"

Schul muttered something, then stretched out his left hand, fingers spread like a net to catch the darting lights.

"Damn!" he hissed. "They just pass right through me. I must be losing my mind!"

Frances raised her own hands, watched the lights passing through them, examined her body and legs, saw the same thing.

The darkness kept growing brighter, throwing the lake into clear perspective, but the marshes at the other side of the water started melting, then growing. First the dark line of reeds, then low dunes and windswept sand . . . then the dunes dissolved and turned into hills that were sun-scorched and barren.

Frances heard beating wings and turned her gaze toward the sky. There was no sun up there, but the sky was very bright, and a prehistoric pteranodon flew overhead, its wings of skin beating awkwardly. It grew hazy as it approached her, disappeared in a flash of light, emerged as a great golden eagle that passed silently overhead. Then the darkness faded completely and the trees changed some more, the greenery too lush, the bark toasted a deep mahogany, the figs, oranges, and lemons in dense clusters, the branches shedding white pollen.

"It's hot again," Schul said, staring at Frances. "And the sun's disappeared again."

"No north or south," Laurence murmured. "No east or west . . ."

The light-flecked darkness was no more, but a sunless sky arched over them, bathing the landscape in a heat haze of dazzling intensity. The land beyond the lake was different, a series of sun-scorched, ragged hills, while around them the trees seemed familiar, though subtly altered.

"It all looks like stage scenery," Laurence said. "Or scenery painted by God . . ."

Schul snorted without mirth. "Don't give me God," he said. "We're all going nuts in this heat—and that's all there is to it."

Frances studied the two men, trying to take comfort from them, hoping that the reality of their presence would keep her senses together. They looked strange in that bizarre light, their skin as white as marble, their eyes gleaming with a brilliance that made them seem glassy and mad.

"Let's keep walking," Schul said. "Let's try it one more time. Let's move while the going is good and see where we end up."

"It's hopeless," Laurence replied. "You tried before and got nowhere. You always ended up in that same clearing, so we'd be wasting our time."

"And what do we gain by staying here? Not a goddamned thing, kid. We don't know what time it is or where we are or what's happening, and staying here won't help a goddamned bit. I say we keep moving. I say give it another shot. What the hell? We've got nothing to lose, so let's get off our asses."

Laurence reached down to help Frances to her feet, and as he did so she saw that his face was pale with anger, his lips forming a grim line. She tried to smile at him, but singularly failed to do so, and she covered her embarrassment by turning away and falling in behind Schul.

Schul twisted back toward her, revealing his unshaven chin, his grin sardonic and his eyes bright with a humor that sprang out of arrogance. Frances was glad when he straightened up, his head cut off by the rucksack, but she felt an obscure, nagging desire as she marched close behind him.

They marched a long time, through that blinding, sunless haze, forced to rely on pure chance since the compass was useless. Their wristwatches raced wildly, stopped, raced again, while the flowers blossomed only to die and be instantly renewed. Time shifted back and forth, changed the scenery, changed it back, encircled them and scattered their thoughts into a common delirium. Schul started to laugh hysterically, then stopped and stared at them; he leered invitingly at Frances, then glared at Laurence and marched forward again. The sky remained sunless. Snowy-white clouds moved across it. Frances noticed that the light, though intense, produced no shadows at all.

No sun: no shadows. The light had no fixed direction. She heard her own sigh as she turned her head lethargically to see Laurence stumbling close behind her, clearly dazed and exhausted. She wanted to sympathize but felt drained of all emotion, so instead she wiped the sweat from her stinging eyes and concentrated on walking.

They walked a long time, but did not find Al-Qurna. They

kept following the muddy bank until they returned to the original clearing; then, at Schul's insistence, they cut straight across the "island" and, after another arduous walk, arrived at what seemed to be the very same clearing. The dark mass did not return; nor did the normal sun. They followed the shoreline again, gave up and went inland, but always arrived back at the same place and eventually accepted defeat.

"Okay," Schul said magnanimously to Laurence, "you were right. We're trapped here."

"We'll stay here?" Laurence replied.

"We don't seem to have a choice. But don't give me that goddamned smirk, kid. You ain't that fucking smart."

Schul's gaze was very direct and now more patently aggressive. He stared Laurence down, snorted triumphantly when he turned away; then he turned his attention on Frances, his grin sexually challenging.

"Let's hope that that helicopter actually comes," he said. "Otherwise we're gonna be trapped here forever."

"It'll come," Frances replied, wearily sitting down on the grass, leaning her back against the trunk of a fig palm, taking deep, even breaths. "However, since we can't seem to find Al-Qurna anymore, how's the helicopter going to find *us?*"

"Oh, Christ, that's right."

Obviously frustrated, Schul angrily kicked some grass, then stared thoughtfully out over the placid lake. His shirt was tied around his neck, leaving him bare to the waist; Frances saw the sweat trickling down his chest, over his hard, sun-tanned belly.

"It's getting darker," Laurence said. "I don't know how, but it's getting darker. Not that dark mass, but more like a normal darkness—though I still can't see a sun in the sky."

"Evening," Frances replied. "This place has its own kind of evening. My watch has started working again—at more or less normal speed."

"*And* mine," Schul said. "Time seems to stop and start here, runs too fast, runs too slow, and sometimes it even seems to be normal. What the hell's going on?" He took a deep breath, then shrugged as if defeated. "Well," he said, "no matter what it is, we're gonna have to stay here a while. I better catch us something to eat before the light disappears; after that, we might as well try to sleep—or at least say our prayers."

With that parting shot at Laurence, he walked away from

them, stooping briefly to slip under the nearest trees and vanish behind them. When he had gone, Laurence sighed and sat beside Frances, not touching her but very close to her, his breathing uneven. They were silent for some time, neither knowing what to say, but eventually, and with a certain reluctance, Laurence sighed and spoke softly.

"I can't help it," he said. "I just can't stand that Schul."

"Don't look at him," Frances replied.

"I can't help it," Laurence said. "He's hardly stopped talking since we met him—and he's full of sarcasm and innuendo."

"He's a bit aggressive, I know."

"He's more than that," Laurence insisted. "There's something evil about him—and something unnatural."

"Unnatural?"

"Yes, unnatural," Laurence insisted. "How did he get from England to here? And why is he not even disturbed? He seems normal, but he's missing something—natural nervousness, fear, a sense of wonder at what has already happened to him and is happening to us right now—and that missing part of him convinces me that he's somehow abnormal."

Frances studied Laurence thoughtfully, seeing only his shadowed profile, then she let her gaze roam across the darkening lake and back to the clearing.

The clearing was crescent-shaped, its straight edge the muddy bank; the bank had originally run from east to west, though that was now problematical. Frances and Laurence were under a tree, both facing east, and down there, at the far end of the clearing, was a natural arch of more fig palms.

Laurence sighed loudly and shook his head from side to side. "What with Schul and all these magical events, I think I'm losing my senses. Either that, or we're actually in Purgatory—and will remain here forever."

"No," Frances said. "Not Purgatory . . . Maybe somewhere more magical."

She leaned forward a little, studying the clearing more intently, feeling a distinct surge of excitement at what she was thinking. The light was still fading, turning the air a pale crimson, giving everything a strange, dreamlike quality, as if viewed through fine gauze. Unseen birds were singing in the trees; leaves rustled, twigs snapped. Frances sensed the great silence over all, coming down with the darkness.

"Presuming we no longer know *exactly* where we are," she said, "we *do* know that when the storm blew up we were nearing Al-Qurna."

"That's right," Laurence replied. "No question about it. Al-Qurna should be somewhere in this area, but it's mysteriously disappeared."

"And what's in Al-Qurna?"

"I don't know. Surprise me."

"The possible site of the Garden of Eden."

She looked expectantly at Laurence, her excitement tinged with fear, and saw his eyes glittering in the shadow that was falling down over him.

"You know the story," she said, hardly aware of her own voice, only conscious of the light in Laurence's eyes where they shone in the gathering gloom. "According to Genesis, Eden is east of Israel, in an area out of which flowed a river that then divided into four others. Those rivers were the Gihon, which may have been the Nile; the Pison, which was most likely in the Persian Gulf, just south of here; and, of course, the Tigris and the Euphrates. The latter two rivers meet near Al-Qurna, where they form the Shatt-al-Arab river, which actually flows down into the Persian Gulf. So, the most widely accepted location of the Garden of Eden is Mesopotamia—or, to be more precise, Al-Qurna."

"But Al-Qurna has disappeared," Laurence said.

"To *where?*" Frances asked him.

Laurence did not reply immediately, but Frances knew what he was thinking: that the place they had been seeking might be right here—all around them . . . unseen.

"Oh, Lord," Laurence whispered eventually. "I just can't believe this."

Feeling remote from herself, her skin tingling with an odd excitement, Frances squinted through the growing darkness at the natural arch of trees that stood on the eastern corner of the clearing. She stared at it a long time, almost hypnotized by it, then let her gaze fall on the very large fig palm that stood alone in the center of the clearing.

Looking at that particular tree, at its fat, clustered figs, she thought of the walled-in tree in Al-Qurna—and of the sign placed beside it. *In this holy spot, where Tigris meets Euphrates, this holy tree of our Father Adam grew, symbolizing the Garden*

of Eden on Earth . . . Frances closed her eyes, saw that site in
her mind's eye, wondered where it was right now . . . or
where she and the others had been transported by this bizarre,
timeless zone.

"This *could* be it," she said. "We don't know. Nothing else
makes sense anyway."

"Now it's *you* who's reading too much into things," Laurence replied. "You better watch yourself, Frances."

She opened her eyes to see him smiling, without malice, almost gently, and was touched enough to reach out toward him.
She didn't know what she had intended—perhaps just to shake
him gently—but at that moment the sound of snapping twigs
announced Schul's return.

He emerged from the trees, holding up a dead rabbit, the
darkness hiding the blood that had doubtless drenched his
hands, but not able to dim the triumph in the eyes that were
staring down at them.

"Let's eat," he said.

After the meal, when the darkness had descended, Frances
stretched out near Laurence and watched Schul creeping into
his tent. She ignored his inviting wave, closed her eyes, tried to
sleep, but tossed and turned under her sheet, feeling cold and
tormented.

Laurence was right: there was something evil about Schul.
She thought of him making the campfire, remembered how he
had prepared the rabbit, recalled the relish with which he had
skinned it before roasting it for them. *He's an animal,* she
thought, still tossing and turning, trying to sleep. *There's something primitive and rapacious about him; he thinks little, feels
less* . . . Yet even thinking thus, she felt a certain desire for
him.

She was cold, but felt on fire. The thin sheet was suffocating
her. She glanced through the darkness at Schul's tent, but saw
no movement inside. *He knows,* she thought despairingly. *He
has the instincts of the beast. He knows that sooner or later I'll go
to him.* And so thinking, she almost groaned, biting her lower
lip to stifle it, distracted herself by studying the sky, and saw a
vast, starless darkness.

Frightened, she closed her eyes again, hoping for escape. She
thought of Laurence lying near her, worried about her, caring

for her, then understood that she was attracted not by his decency but by Schul's crude, aggressive lust.

She kept tossing and turning, her skin slippery with sweat, then lay flat on her back and imagined Schul pressing on top of her. He would show little tenderness. He would crush her and subdue her. She groaned softly, then licked her parched lips and let sleep ease her shame. . . .

The experience was very vivid. It might even have been a dream. The ground started shaking beneath her and made her open her eyes. The landscape had changed. The great lake was a cratered plain. An alien word, *Edinu,* was whispered and she knew what it meant. There it was where the lake had been: a great plain like a dust bowl. A savage light was beaming out of the sunless sky and turning the stony earth white.

The ground was still shaking when she sat up and grunted. Not many trees here—just a few between scorched rocks—but she recognized the one bearing strange fruit. Her fear had filled her belly with hunger, but she didn't dare stand up: she just stared at the tree with inchoate longing and thoughtlessly scratched herself. The others were grunting loudly. She understood and shared their feelings. She started making as much noise as she could, though she sensed it was useless.

Within the light more light was growing. The ground trembled and made strange sounds, one of which gradually rose above the others to make her head tighten. She soon lost all her senses, first grunting, then shrieking, finally covering her eyes with her hands and whimpering helplessly.

The brightening light scorched through her fingers, showing the bones beneath the skin. She stared through her hands into the brightness and watched them coming toward her.

She was frozen when they gathered around her to carry her off.

Edinu: plain. The only world that she knew or wanted. They picked her up and carried her from the plain as terror shattered her senses. . . .

Frances awakened, groaning loudly and sobbing. Laurence was placing his hand on her burning forehead and whispering to comfort her. She stared wildly around her, saw the trees in white haze, and beyond them the broad expanse of the lake where the cratered plain had once been.

It was morning and the darkness had departed to leave her back in this mirage.

Gasping, clutching the grass, trying to control her fear, she lay back on the ground and breathed deeply.

"I'm all right," she said.

8

THE voice of Capital Radio informed Michael, as he sat in his
car in a traffic jam in Finchley Road, that the Finchley Road
should be avoided if at all possible. Cursing, Michael switched
to Radio 3 to hear Haydn's Sonata in A flat. Sighing with relief,
he let the music flow around him, inched forward with the
other traffic, and thought pleasurably of the long night he had
just spent with his lover Rebecca.

An occasional lover for the past five years, Rebecca was a
tall, raven-haired Jewish career woman who, in the double bed
in her elegant period house in Golders Green, had told Michael
that his attention was wandering at the very worst time. Now,
remembering that, and well aware of what had caused it, Michael smiled and slipped into the nearside lane to turn up
Frognal Lane.

Driving more freely up the winding tree-lined road past the
houses now inhabited by Third World ambassadors and the
wealthier English, he felt increasing excitement at the thought
of seeing Miles Ashcombe for the first time.

He had in fact received a telephone call from the hospital the
previous evening, just before leaving his own flat in Belsize
Park, telling him that his patient had been delivered to the
hospital; and there could be no doubt that it was his thoughts
about Ashcombe that had made him rather distracted when in
his lover's bed. He had long ago developed to perfection his
ability to separate his work from his private life, and it was a
tribute to the magnitude of this new case, and to his fascination

with the vanished Glastonbury, that he had been unable to keep it out of his mind even when in Rebecca's warm embrace.

It took a considerable amount of time and patience to maneuver the car through the relatively brief length of Hampstead Village, but as he did it he found himself smiling again at the thought of his distracted lovemaking the previous night. Rebecca's laconic criticism would doubtless have amused his daughter, Cheryl, who was fond of teasing him about his bachelor's life. In truth, if he liked women and suffered no shortage of them, his bachelor's life was for the most part devoted to work; and it was, as he often joked, dealing with the insane that kept him sane.

As the sonata washed over him, he studied the dense traffic crawling down Rosslyn Hill and wondered that the world could continue as normal after the awesome disappearance of Glastonbury. Not a day passed without some mystified reappraisal of the event on television, radio or in the newspapers, yet most people were simply going about their business as if nothing had happened. The ability of the human psyche to narrow itself down to its own concerns irrespective of what was going on around it had never ceased to fascinate Michael; but now, even as he smiled ruefully, his rising excitement over the impending meeting with his new patient drove those very thoughts out of his head.

Eventually he turned into Pond Street, then right into the hospital grounds; and when at last he parked his car and entered the large modern building, the weariness caused by the traffic jam was already falling away from him.

His mood of keen anticipation was rudely broken when, having taken the lift up to the fourth floor, he entered his office and found his former wife, Janet, waiting for him in his secretary's reception area.

Standing up to greet him, Janet was almost as tall as Michael, a fact emphasized by her slimness, her high-heeled shoes, and the subdued elegance of her tight-fitting dress and knee-length woolen overcoat. She gave him a fleeting smile and nervously stroked her short blond hair, which reminded him again, as it always did, of how like Cheryl she was.

"Surprise, surprise," Michael said.

"I'm sorry, Michael. I should have phoned . . ."

"It's all right," Michael said, glancing down at his secretary,

Mrs. Beaumont, and noting her shrugging shoulders and rolling
eyes. "Come into my office."

He held the door open to let her walk in, felt her brushing
past him, glanced backward to see Mrs. Beaumont's sardonic
smile, then stepped in himself and closed the door. Janet sighed
as if nervous, her spine visibly straightening, and he walked
around her, indicating that she should sit down. She responded
by merely shaking her head in a negative manner.

"I'd rather stand," she said, her accent pure Cambridge, her
voice still a little smoky and distinctly sensual. "I'm sorry. I
should have called," she repeated. "So, how are you?"

"You don't have to call," Michael replied, secretly wishing
she had. "And I'm fine."

"You disapprove. I can tell."

"Nonsense," Michael lied, wondering what the problem was.
"I'm delighted to see you—and delighted that you're looking so
well."

"Liar."

"Absolutely not."

Janet nodded and smiled, nervously bit her lower lip, then
started pacing to and fro in front of the desk. Watching her,
Michael realized that his automatic compliment was well de-
served; but he also wondered what new problem his former wife
was about to pass on to him.

Although they had been separated for eight years, and actually divorced for five, Janet, who like him had never remarried,
tended to treat him as if their marriage was still intact, depend-
ing upon him to sort out her problems, both material and spiritual. In the sense that this situation had ensured that Cheryl did
not become involved in any emotional tug-of-war between her
parents, Michael thought the effort worthwhile; but there were
times, such as today, when he could not resist feeling resentment at what he felt was an unwarranted intrusion upon his
work. Indeed, his former wife's preoccupation with material
matters and ephemeral concerns was inclined to stretch his patience to the limit, so now, watching her pace up and down in
front of his desk, he sighed and prepared himself for the latest
of her generally trivial concerns.

"Stop pacing the floor," he said levelly, "and just tell me your
problem."

"Problem?" she replied, standing still and staring at him. *"My* problem?"

"Well, I assumed—"

"Not just *my* problem," she said. *"Your* problem as well."

"Oh? Something wrong with the house . . . ?"

It was one of the ironies of their separation that Janet should have retained their spacious, five-bedroom house in Esher, which Michael, who could now only afford a modest apartment in Belsize Park, was still called upon to keep in good repair. It was not a legal obligation but rather one based on Janet's assumption that Michael, until someone else came along, was still the man of the house.

"No," she said firmly, "it's not the house. I wouldn't come here uninvited just for *that.*"

She would and she had, but Michael decided not to say so. Instead, eager to be free to see Miles Ashcombe, he simply said, "So, what *is* it?"

"It's your daughter," Janet said. "Your *beloved* daughter. She's involved with some man."

"That's hardly surprising," Michael said, though he suffered a sinking feeling, some instinct preparing him for bad news. "She's twenty years old, which is certainly old enough for such involvements."

"It's not old enough for this," Janet replied. "She's involved with a *married* man."

She threw him an accusing glance, which did not soothe the shock that jolted through him with unexpected severity. There was a moment of disbelief, a sharp rise and fall of grief, but he managed to hold Janet's gaze and keep his voice steady.

"With a *married* man?" he asked, rather stupidly.

"Yes, Michael, that's what I said."

"Are you *sure?*"

Janet rolled her eyes and stared up at the ceiling. "Oh, God," she said. "Am I *sure?* Why do you think I've *come* here?" It was a purely rhetorical question uttered clearly as a reprimand; she then shuddered and sat in the chair at the other side of the desk. "Yes," she said. "I'm absolutely sure. She's having an affair with her boss."

Feeling a pain that was surprisingly sharp, Michael was forced to accept that for once his wife's concern was not trivial. He glanced down at his desk, closed his eyes and took a deep breath, massaged his eyelids with his fingers, and remembered his lunch with his daughter. . . . *I'm a very responsible assistant to a movie producer. And a very talented, attractive one at that. So I'm quite happy, thanks.* . . . Her praiseworthy words and skittish support for that nameless man now came back to Michael with painful clarity. He had sensed something then, but had chosen to ignore it, and so, as he opened his eyes to take in his former wife, he felt the inexorable rise of a primitive hatred for the man who was possessing his daughter.

Which was not, as he instantly realized, an intelligent response.

"When we had lunch," he said wonderingly, "she joked about how attractive he was. But I didn't really imagine that . . ."

"No. Why should you? You don't live with her."

"Now, Janet, I don't think—"

"If she had a proper father—"

"I hardly think that's the issue. People her age fall in love. That's all there is to it."

"That's *all* there is to it?" Janet's voice quivered with outrage. "Is that what's known as psychological objectivity? Your own daughter can have an affair with a married man—and that's *all* there is to it?"

"That's not what I meant, and you know it," Michael replied, trying to keep his despair out of his voice. "But for God's sake, let's discuss this as calmly as possible. For a start, are you *sure* it's an active affair and not just an infatuation that hasn't yet—?"

"It's an affair," Janet intervened. "I *know* it's an affair. They've just spent a weekend together in a hotel outside Bath—and it's not the first time that they've done so."

"How do you know?"

"I overheard Cheryl talking to that bastard on the telephone."

"You were listening to her *phone* calls?"

"Of course not, Michael. I was going to make a phone call myself from my bedroom—and I picked up the phone and heard them speaking. Naturally, in normal circumstances, I would have hung up instantly; but something in the tone of their voices—something rather conspiratorial—made me listen in. . . . They were discussing their last weekend together, the other times they had spent a weekend in the same hotel, and the fact that they'll be together again when they return to Nice for more location work on that bastard's film."

"He may not be the bastard you think he is."

"He's married and has two adolescent children. I would call that being a bastard."

Janet crossed one leg over the other, took a deep breath, glanced at the window that overlooked Hampstead Heath. She was still a very beautiful lady, though less attractive when angry, and when she turned back toward him, green eyes flashing, she was very angry indeed.

"So," she said, "what are you going to do about it?"

He hardly knew what to think, let alone what to say. For the first time in a long time he was almost lost for words, knowing nothing but the chaos of emotions he had thought were long since buried. He had always been proud of his logic and self-control, but now he could only think of his daughter with a fierce sense of loss. His confusion and pain were palpable, shaking him leaf and bough, shaming him with the knowledge that he was actually struggling to keep himself calm. Love made logic redundant and children out of men; and as he shifted uneasily, aware of his racing heart, he was wounded by the realization that he shared that same weakness.

"I'm not at all sure that there's anything I *can* do about it. I can talk to her, of course, but I doubt that it will be very effective. If she's already *involved* in this affair—"

"She is!"

"—any disapproval on *our* part will only drive her even closer to him."

"You mean we do . . . *nothing?*"

Michael shrugged, still hiding his rage and pain, feeling utterly helpless. "You know what she's like," he said. "She can be very contrary. As I said, if you want I'll talk to her—but that might be the very worst thing to do."

"You can talk to *him,*" Janet said. "You can put an end to it. You can tell him to fire her from her job and not see her again."

"And if he refuses?"

"Threaten to tell his wife."

"I don't think so, Janet."

She uncrossed her long legs, glared at him, then stood up again.

"She's our only child," she said, "and she's having an affair with a *married* man. I won't have her used and then cast aside —which, beyond any shadow of doubt, is what's going to happen."

"Perhaps he's in love with *her.*"

"Oh, Christ!" Janet snapped. "You don't believe that any more than I do. It's just sex, pure and simple."

She blushed and pursed her lips, expressing disdain and shame at once, perhaps remembering that her own life with Michael had been sexually incomplete. Most of Janet's sensuality resided in her voice and had never happily expressed itself in bed. For a long time Michael had thought the failure was his own, but the intervening years had shown the opposite. Before and after his marriage he had enjoyed sex very much, whereas Janet, in a kind of quiet desperation, had led the life of a nun.

"Anyway," she continued, unaware of his line of thought, "that's what *I* believe, so either you talk to our daughter or you talk to her boss. If you don't, *I* will—and if I don't receive a positive response, I'll talk to his wife."

"That would be cruel."

"No worse than what he's doing."

"Let's try to keep his family out of this."

"That's up to you, dear."

Michael sighed. "All right, Janet, I'll talk to Cheryl first. Please don't do anything rash until then. I'll keep you informed."

Janet stared gravely at him, then nodded and turned away; she walked to the window and looked out, as most visitors did.

"Fine," she said eventually. "But when? I can't let this continue."

"I'll ring her tonight," Michael said.

"Good," Janet said. "Excellent."

She turned back to face him, offering a grateful smile; and aware once more of how attractive she still was, Michael felt a familiar spasm of guilt because their marriage had failed.

"I have to get to work now, Janet."

"This isn't a *favor,* Michael."

"I know. It's just that—"

"She is *our* daughter, after all. And if you weren't so casual about your *own* love life, she might not have—"

"Please, Janet, that's unfair, and we've been through all this before."

"And your work comes first. I should have *known* that. I'm leaving right now."

The sarcasm was familiar and had its roots in insecurity; for that reason he did not respond to it, but simply stared at her. She shrugged, as if apologizing, then said, "Well, not the best of circumstances, but it *was* nice to see you."

"And you," he said gently.

He stood up and walked around the desk to give her a kiss on the cheek. It was a rather prim kiss, almost brotherly, in fact, and she responded by sniffing and stepping back to turn away from him. She opened the door, then stopped to stare at him; eventually, with a tremulous smile, she shook her head sadly.

"God protect us from our children," she said softly.

"They're our only future," Michael replied.

Janet nodded and stepped out, closing the door behind her, and Michael simply stood there for a moment, giving her time to depart. In that silence he was exposed to his own very human frailty, stung by the realization that his professional objectivity was useless when it came to personal matters. He remembered his lunch with Cheryl—the concern he had felt for her—then experienced a keen sense of betrayal and smoldering rage. What he had feared had come to pass—his daughter was doubtless being exploited—and unlike a psychologist, but very much like a normal father, he could not help but feel a growing hatred for the man she was involved with.

"Damn!" he whispered. "Why *now?*"

Still badly shaken, he entered Mrs. Beaumont's office, first noting with relief that Janet had actually gone, then seeing the sardonic glint in his secretary's eyes. Raising his hands in mock despair, thus disguising the despair he felt, he walked past her desk and opened the other door and stepped into the corridor. He hurried along it, feeling confused, his stirred emotions in conflict, his excitement at the thought of seeing his patient, Miles Ashcombe, now blending with his feelings of betrayal, anger, and shame.

Why shame? he wondered as he passed through some swinging doors, and sensed, even as the question was raised, what the answer might be. *You don't live with her,* Janet had said. *If she had a proper father . . .* The implication that he had been derelict in his duty had not been made for the first time. No, indeed not. Janet had often implied the same thing, her voice vibrant with the thrill of accusation and a certain self-righteousness. Janet's vanity was soothed by suffering, by the martyrdom of her position, yet Michael knew, even understanding this much, that her accusations were valid. He *was* guilty of selfishness, of placing himself before his family; and thus, as he approached the barred room containing his new patient, he realized that what Cheryl had done was—indirectly and probably unwittingly—pay him back for his betrayal of long ago.

He arrived at a locked door, was admitted by a male nurse, walked along another, shorter corridor to the rooms that were always barred. Saddened by the news of Cheryl, perhaps more by its implications, he was abruptly plunged into a much deeper gloom when he realized that just like his fellow motorists that morning, he, too, was placing his own, relatively petty concerns above the monumental Glastonbury Event.

Further shaken by this awareness, he stopped halfway down the corridor, at a lime-green painted door that had, instead of a normal glass window, a movable panel of wood. He took a deep breath, forced his family from his thoughts, then unlocked the panel, slid it open, and looked into the room.

The new patient, Miles Ashcombe, was stretched out on the bed, staring up at the ceiling and murmuring a constant stream of demented words. He did, however, jerk upright almost as soon as Michael looked in, and stared directly at the peephole with widening, crazed eyes.

Michael was used to madness and its bright, glacial vacancy, but in this case the eyes staring upward mesmerized him, drawing him into a world that lay beyond all known perimeters and for which he had no prior frame of reference.

For the first time in his professional career, Michael actually *felt* terror.

FRANCES continued dreaming while they all lost track of time. The great pillar of darkness would appear without warning, fade away, then return to torment them. During its absence the world would seem perfectly normal, but when it had covered them again, forming a shroud of quiescent beauty, the geography of the stars would be different from what they knew, and the world outside their strange prison, incorporeal and unreal.

The mysterious phenomenon came and went, obeying some law of its own, materializing like smoke from the air and disappearing back into it. It continued playing bizarre tricks—distorting time, changing the scenery—and when it disappeared the world returned to normal . . . or what *seemed* to be normal.

It was the gravity that was different. They all noticed it in the end. Each time they were surrounded by the shifting, light-flecked darkness, they felt heavier, more sluggish, and very sleepy, afflictions that became more pronounced with each passing day.

Yet what was a day now? They could no longer tell. They were measuring their days by the arrival and departure of the phenomenon, but knew in their hearts that this bore little relation to normal time. They slept in the flickering gloom, awakened to the dazzling haze, saw their wristwatches racing crazily, slowing down, gradually stopping, and soon lost all concept of duration and former reality, until eventually the unnatural became natural, the magical, mundane.

"Where's Al-Qurna?" Frances asked. "Where are we at this moment? What time is it? What day or *month* is it? We can't answer such questions anymore—and might be trapped here forever."

That possibility was very real and made them share the breath of fear. Time kept changing before their eyes, though not as rapidly as before, and when the plants bloomed and died to be reborn as different species, when the great lake became a cratered plain filled with dust, when a golden eagle suddenly turned into a flapping pteranodon, the rate of change seemed to be slower, the new landscape more lasting.

Time kept slowing down until it came to a halt, finally leaving them in an oasis that appeared to have sprung miraculously from a former landscape of desolate lakes and mist-covered swamps. They caught fish in the nearest lake, plucked the fruit from the trees, and as the landscape had changed, so they also changed, losing their civilized habits and becoming more primitive.

No one discussed this change, but Frances felt it in herself: her thoughts thickened like mud forced through a pipe while her body grew heavier. She felt awkward, uneasy, divorced from her former vigor, and she stumbled with the new weight of her dead flesh through the dream of an ancient past.

That past eventually became the present and seemed to be here for good: various eons had come and gone to leave only this strange garden whose beauty had a magical, haunting quality that permeated the senses.

The garden was crescent-shaped and ran roughly from east to west; it was hemmed in by a forest whose every path led straight back here, and it lay by the side of the broad, placid lake that, in her dreams, Frances had seen as a great dust-filled plain encircled by mountains.

"We're in the past," she said to Laurence. "Perhaps the original Garden of Eden. But in my dreams I go back even farther—to the dawn of mankind. In those dreams there are always others present, but I can't see them clearly."

Her dreams were so vivid they might have been hallucinations—or real events viewed through the haze of a disarrayed mind. She was always in the same place—right here in Eden—

but in her dreams the landscape changed as time moved back to
an even more distant age.

The great lake would be drained, turning into a dust-filled
plain; and beyond, where once the marshes had been, volcanic
mountains appeared. There was a fierce, sunless sky—or light
so bright that it hazed the sun—and the relentless heat dead-
ened her mind as well as her body.

Yet in that heat, more heat; in that light, a greater light. The
light expanded like an opening eye, became a whirlpool in the
sky, increasing rapidly in size as it descended and spread out
above her. The swirling wind whipped the dust up; the heat
scorched her skin. In her dream she always fell on hands and
knees to hide her face in the dirt.

God was descending to punish or reward her. God, in His
benevolence or wrath, would bring joy or pain. And then the air
was filled with strange noise—the music of the spheres—and
she tore her hair and gnashed aching teeth as voiceless singing
surrounded her.

God roared and pulsated above her, making the very air vibrate, while His angels, rendered featureless in the silvery haze,
looked silently at her. Then a brighter light, more heat, the
swift bite of strange pain, then she usually slipped into a protec-
tive daze until they departed. . . .

The dreams were frightening to recall. Were they dreams or
hallucinations? Were they even, in fact, actual events that she
wished to deny?

Haunted by such questions, Frances passed them on to Laurence. He simply stared oddly at her, then moved off across the
clearing—while Schul, who had been watching them both, offered a mocking grin.

"He thinks you're going crazy," he said. "He's just too embarrassed to say so. He's got the hots for you, but he gets frightened when you say those things to him. He thinks you're losing
your mind."

Schul's presence made things worse, causing more fear and
dissension. His oddly inhuman lack of concern, his unnatural
ability to ignore this miracle, made him seem positively
demoniac—perhaps the dream's sole creator. Also, he was
threatening, growing more aggressive daily, assuming the man-
tle of leadership over them and demanding submission.

It was Schul who caught the food, skinned and gutted the fish and animals, showed them how to light the fire, cook the food, and generally survive in the forest. Given this, they were dependent upon him, and he knew it and abused it, humiliating them with relentless, cruel mockery, and increasing contempt.

"You need me," he said. "You *both* need me. And that makes me the king here."

Surprisingly, given their circumstances, Schul's base concerns remained unchanged; and while Frances suffered her dreams and Laurence retreated into silence, Schul behaved as if their world were perfectly normal and this was merely a camping trip. Untouched by fear or wonder, still wrapped in his former ego, he responded to the situation by merely giving in to his baser appetites. Becoming king of his small domain, he started lusting for further conquests and in his growing hunger for Frances, invited her into his tent.

"Anytime you want," he said to her, "you just crawl right in. . . . And you'll want soon enough."

He had set up the tent near the arch of fig palms and was turning it into a symbol of his authority. Seemingly undisturbed by being trapped in an alien world, he was intent on utilizing it to his personal advantage, and thus, in the shimmering, sunless light of this strange place, he more frequently flaunted the tent to remind them of their dependence upon him.

"You're freezing out there every night," he said to Frances. "Come into my tent and share my sleeping bag. That way we'll *both* keep warm."

He owned everything else and now he wanted her. Frances knew it and was tempted, even despising herself for her weakness, feeling revolted by Schul's crude animalism but wanting what he could give her: the illusion of security, the warmth of the tent each night, a release from personal responsibility during this frightening experience.

All that, and something else—something that Schul knew all about—the temporary obliteration of the self in ephemeral passion. Yes, she saw herself exposed (she wanted to lie down like a whore) and as the days came and went, as the Garden of Eden became more permanent, her sensuality flared out of the growing fear that she might be trapped here forever.

"You want it," Schul said, reducing all emotions to basics. "You're purring like a bitch cat in heat, which is why you can't sleep at nights."

She couldn't sleep because of fear—and the fear increased her sexual desire—because the dreams or hallucinations were becoming more real each night. Now, when she lay on the ground in the darkness, Laurence on one side of her, Schul's tent on the other, she was convinced that she was not really sleeping when the world changed about her. . . .

The eye of God descended as a whirlpool of pure light, freezing her mind and burning her body as His angels surrounded her. Their voiceless singing split the silence, filled her head and dimmed her thoughts, until she slipped into a daze, experienced more strange dreams, and awakened at dawn to see the trees in the Garden of Eden, Laurence still tossing and turning in restless sleep, no visible movement from Schul's tent.

She started yearning for that tent, desperately wanting its protection, then accepted, with the sorrow of the lost, that Schul would soon have her.

Schul knew it as well, and constantly used it on Laurence, humiliating him by sneering at his unrequited passion for Frances. That passion, which was naked, was rapidly growing stronger; and as each day passed and their mutual fear became contagious, Laurence took refuge in the love he could no longer hide. Schul observed him with amusement, took pleasure from mocking him, rarely missed an opportunity to remind him that his love served no purpose.

"You want her," he said, "and you think that's what matters; but what matters is nerve and conviction—and you don't possess those. You think your love will win her—that your respect is enough—but the only thing she wants is sexual heat with someone who knows how to raise it. She may find your innocence touching, kid, but she needs more than that."

"Shut your filthy mouth!" Laurence replied.

He was frightened of Schul and had little defense against him, but his resentment over what was being said was driving him close to the edge. His hatred, now more obvious, was more frequently stated, and Frances sensed that Schul would soon have the confrontation he so obviously longed for.

Schul wanted to crush Laurence, to break his pride and spirit, and combined with his own lust for Frances that need came to obsess him. He was goading Laurence more often, using Frances as his weapon, and she, even knowing how Laurence felt, knew whom she would go to.

She genuinely despised Schul, yet was forced to face the fact that in the end she would be drawn to his strength. Lord knows, she had always needed it (and had often suffered for it) and now, with her fear growing, stirred by thoughts of her unknown future, she wanted even more to submit to another's will, to lose herself in that particular kind of bondage, swept away by her melting flesh.

"You wouldn't do that, would you?" Laurence eventually asked her, his changing voice reduced to a whisper. "Not while *I'm* here?"

"Oh, dear God!" Frances groaned.

Because she knew that she would, that Schul was aware of it, and that nothing would prevent it but the sudden reappearance of the normal world. That was what she was praying for, every day, every hour, but this strange, lovely garden, with its impossible, sunless sky, seemed to have become a permanent feature in an unchanging, alien world.

Apparently they were trapped here, beyond time and space, in a world that bent back upon itself to render former laws meaningless. And as that realization grew, boring through her disbelief, Frances knew that she would only find escape by erasing herself.

Neither dreams nor hallucinations: she was convinced that they were real, that God's angels, when they came in the night, were as real as this garden. The garden itself was ancient history—it existed in times long gone—but the great swirling light that whipped up the dust was doing so in an even earlier time—at the very dawn of mankind. Only she experienced it (Laurence and Schul both slept through it), but she knew with the certainty of the doomed that the visitations were real.

Real and becoming more so—in body as well as spirit. She now lived in dread of the breaking silence of the night, and quivered when that single, staring eye became a bright light expanding. She had lived then and now—in the past and in the present—but when God breathed upon her, scorching her with His breath, she was cooled by the touch of His angels as they silently studied her.

She surrendered to God as she would soon give in to Schul,

neither knowing nor caring what would happen, only wanting
protection. She and Laurence thought Schul a demon, an inexplicable, mysterious visitor, whose bizarre arrival in their midst
had convinced them that he could not be normal. Indeed, they
thought him supernatural—and decidedly evil. And being evil,
he was banal, ignoring miracles, concerned with trivia, his conversation revealing his ignorance of all outside himself.

He wanted total obedience—their physical and moral subju-
gation . . . and one particular evening, when they were huddled around the campfire, as Schul fried some fish and Frances
wearily watched him, he pressed again for the victory he knew
would eventually come to him.

"Not him," he said of Laurence. "Not this dumb kid, here.
You may respect this kid because he's decent, but you know
what you *need*. And what you *need* is the animal that ruts in
your hottest dreams."

Frances ignored the remark, but Laurence, as he usually did
when he could not bear such talk, hurriedly walked away from
the warm fire to kneel by the lake. Frances glanced at him, saw
the slump to his shoulders, then found herself focusing on Schul
with her heart beating fast. He was grinning, his eyes bright
with mockery, as he forked the fish in the frying pan.

"You wanna eat?" he asked her.

"I've lost my appetite," she replied.

"I don't think so," Schul said. "I think that's something
you'll always have. You're a woman who wants everything or
nothing. I specialize in the type."

He forked out some fish while Frances glanced across at Laurence and saw him still kneeling by the water with his back
turned toward her. He was staring out across the lake, into that
darkening, sunless haze, silhouetted where lake and sky were
divided by a thin line of marsh reeds.

The descending night was normal—it was not the magical
dark mass—but it was falling in this long-ago time to bring
dread and confusion. The scenery had stopped changing and
was now their sole environment, dominated by this lush, enchanted garden which should not have existed. The evening
light was fading, its white haze turning gray, and across it flew
brightly colored prehistoric birds whose shadows, gliding along
the earth, fell on other strange animals. Time had moved back

and forth, constantly crossing its own path, but eventually it had slid to a halt at this particular moment.

Here, all ages met and all places became the one, forming a world beyond imagining and trapping them in it. Yet the fruit and fish were edible, the water clear and pure: they could live here forever if they had to . . . though they tried not to think of that.

Tried not to, but did—as Laurence was doing right now, his gaze focused on the marshes beyond the lake that could not be crossed. He was looking for an exit that no longer existed, praying for a sign that would show the way . . . the way out of this purgatory.

Frances returned her gaze to Schul, staring into his hard, bright eyes. "Am I crazy?" she asked him. "Is that it? Am I just going mad?"

Schul handed her a plate of fish. "Here," he said. "Eat. I only like strong, healthy women, so I want you well fed."

Frances accepted the plate but crossed the clearing to give it to Laurence, kneeling beside him by the lake as the graying haze dimmed. Laurence stared at the proffered meal, raised his gaze to her face, took the plate from her with a nod that expressed more than thanks. Then, though he was starving, he picked halfheartedly at the food, but suddenly burst forth with the words that had been locked up inside him.

"What's happening here?" he said. "Are we dreaming or awake? Where are we and how long have we been here and *why* are we here? I ask these questions every day and they're driving me crazy—yet what's driving me even crazier is the thought of you surrendering to Schul. He's not human, Frances. He doesn't feel the way we do. No one human could react as he does to what's happening here. Don't do it, Frances. Promise me that. Not with Schul. Not while *I'm* here."

Frances was touched, but she simply nodded agreement, then stroked his cheek with shivering fingers and hurried back to the campfire. Schul was still there, pouring water on the dying embers; he gave her a crooked grin, then, with a nod, indicated the tent near the fig palms.

Frances simply stared at him, fascinated by his cold, bright gaze, wondering who he was and where he had come from, then feeling dread when she thought of the possible answers. Schul spoke with a forked tongue and derived his pleasure from in-

flicting pain, yet Frances knew, even sinking into shame, that
she would go to him soon.

"Tonight," Schul said. "I feel it in my bones. I'm burning up
just to think of it."

That echo of her own thoughts drove her away from Schul.
She stretched out on the rubber sheet he had lent her and pretended to sleep. *I am burning,* she thought. *My skin is on fire
. . .* She opened her eyes again, looked at the sky, saw the stars
in the new night. She didn't recognize those stars, but otherwise
the sky seemed normal, making her think of her home in London, the view from her bedroom window, the stars cascading
down on Hampstead Heath and the trees draped in mist. Then
her burning turned to pain, to the bitterness of her loss, and she
closed her eyes again to visualize that lost home, hoping to find
in that singular image something to cling to. She almost heard
her mother's music—a soothing violin or piano—and then the
crushing reality of her situation swept her toward sleep. . . .

It was not a dream this time. The ground was definitely shaking beneath her. She let out a soft, frightened moan, then looked
up at the sky. That single eye was descending, growing larger as
it dropped lower, becoming a whirlpool of light with brilliant
stars in its vortex.

She had to look away, dazzled, burning as if with fever, then
she blinked and saw scorched rocks and parched earth where
the forest had been. The great lake had disappeared and was
now a dust-filled plain. Laurence was running toward her out of
an expanding light-haze, his eyes large in the thin wedge of his
face, displaying his panic.

No, it was not a dream. Laurence was obviously seeing it too.
Frances looked the other way, at the arch of fig palms, and saw
Schul's tent as a triangular silhouette in the brightening light.
The flaps of the tent were beating as the wind swept across it.
There was noise—a voiceless singing rising out of bass hum-
ming—but she heard Schul cursing loudly inside the tent,
which was now shaking visibly.

She was blinded by the light, but felt Laurence close beside
her. He grabbed her by the wrist, but she sobbed and jerked
away, then jumped up and ran through the streaming haze, past
the voiceless singing and distorted, silhouetted, human-shaped
figures that were emerging like ghosts from the ether.

Heat. Dazzling radiance. The awareness of beating hearts. The singing was like the music of the spheres, ethereal and magical.

Frances sobbed and fell, moved forward on hands and knees, heard Laurence calling out some kind of plea, and then crawled into Schul's tent. "What the hell . . . ?" Schul began, his bright eyes staring wildly, his hands reaching out to pull her in and hold her close to him. She felt his racing heart, his body's sweat, flesh and bone, then she buried herself in his embrace as the ground shook again.

"Son of a bitch!" Schul exclaimed, holding her tighter, pulling her down. "What the hell *is* that out there? What the fuck's going on?"

Frances did not reply but simply sobbed and held him tighter, her fingers sliding under his shirt and digging into his chest. He was muscle and bone, solid, her one contact with the real world, and when the ground stopped its shaking, when the light disappeared, when the fierce heat was replaced by the cold, she still would not let him go.

Her clothes fell easily from her, littering the ground around her body, then Schul pulled her legs apart with brutal urgency and rolled quickly upon her. He entered her immediately, making her cry out as he pierced her tightness and thrust up inside her.

Someone sobbed outside the tent, and she bit her lip, remembering Laurence. The shame whipped her, but could not make her stop as Schul pressed down upon her. She thought of Laurence outside the tent, and realized that he could not avoid seeing what was going on in here.

Strangely, she saw it too: herself and Schul locked together, two silhouettes, one on top of the other in carnal embrace. She heard Laurence sobbing outside, then a sudden, anguished cursing, then footsteps hurrying away toward the lake, leaving silence behind. Schul was sucking her swollen nipples. She writhed beneath him as his belly rose and fell to slap down on her own. She imagined Laurence kneeling by the lake, adding his tears to the water.

After this, he would hate her. No forgiveness would be forthcoming. His love would understandably turn to poison and make matters worse. *God, forgive me,* she started thinking but, feeling her body, failed to finish, losing her senses as she melted inside her flesh and plunged into sensation.

Schul was pulling her thighs higher and wider, his fingers kneading her aching skin. Whipped by shame, she obliged; defeated by lust, she surrendered. She arched her spine to give him more, gripped him fiercely, pulled him closer; let him gasp and grunt hungrily in her face as they both became animals.

MILES Ashcombe opened his eyes, licked his lips nervously, shuddered, and sat upright on the bed, glancing around him.

"Me no fear," he said, using a primitive form of English. "Me have courage. Go outside."

Obviously thinking he was going outside, he swung his legs off the bed, tested the floor with his toes, then very carefully stood up—or as near to standing as he could manage in his present condition.

"Dark now," he said. "But light coming. Soon sight will clear."

Michael observed him through the peephole, again marveling at what he was seeing, trying to fathom how Ashcombe could have regressed so completely to this primitive state. Ashcombe was not standing properly—he was badly stooped, hands hanging loose. He moved away from the bed, swinging his arms like an ape, his feet barely lifting off the floor, nostrils twitching and sniffing.

Michael was looking at an ape-man. There could be no doubt about it. Miles Ashcombe—reportedly an educated, professional writer, only in his mid-thirties but prematurely gray-haired and aged—had turned into a Neanderthal man in all but physical appearance.

Now, as Michael observed him, he reached the wall opposite the bed, scratched curiously at it, as if trying to ascertain what it was, then in sudden fury hammered upon it with a white-knuckled, clenched fist. He snarled something and turned away, sniffed the air, glanced at the peephole, shambled forward and stared directly at Michael with bright-eyed malevolence.

Looking into those eyes, which were devoid of human feeling, Michael once more experienced fear of the most primitive kind. He tried to hold Ashcombe's gaze—to conquer his fear that way—but those eyes seemed to glow with the chilling light of a strange moon, and Michael turned away, ashamed of himself, his heart racing uncomfortably.

Frank Mullard, the male nurse, had been standing beside him and, holding the door keys in one hand, offered a teasing smile.

"It's okay," he said, "you can enter. He's not violent at all."

"I can tell you don't like me," Michael replied. "That's why you're encouraging me to go in there and get my brains smashed out. Seriously, though, how has he been since yesterday?"

Frank's grin widened, then he shrugged his broad shoulders. "Peaceful," he said. "He really *is* okay. He sometimes hammers the wall with his fist, as you've just seen, but he only does that when he's alone. If you go in there, he'll sniff at you and explore you tentatively with his fingers. He'll even try to make conversation—though he still finds that difficult. I think he's puzzled —he's not too sure of who or *what* we are—and he certainly seems to need space to roam in, which is why the walls bother him."

"He doesn't scare you?" Michael asked.

"I avoid his eyes," Frank replied. "But I know what you mean when you say they bother you—they remind me of my very worst nightmares."

Michael nodded his agreement, thinking of the bad dreams he had suffered since first meeting Ashcombe. The man had more than regressed—he was *inhabiting* the mind and soul of a primitive—and looking into his eyes, with their curiously hard, inhuman brilliance, gave one a feeling of falling into vertiginous depths.

This new Ashcombe was a creature of primal awareness and brute impulse. He had, in fact, become a part of that same primitive world which either he had witnessed or actually *experienced* when inside the dark mass. Thinking of that, Michael shivered again, starting to doubt his own senses.

He turned back toward the barred door and looked through

the peephole. Ashcombe was staring straight at him with alien intensity.

"Hello," Michael said lamely. "I'm your doctor, Mr. Phillips."

There was no spoken response, merely a quickening of Ashcombe's breathing, a visible widening of those oddly luminous, animal eyes. Michael felt the fear again and quickly walked up to the door, slid the wooden panel back across the peephole, then looked at the male nurse.

"Have you heard even *one* sentence in proper English?" he asked.

"No," Frank replied. "I'm pretty certain that he's actually *talking* more, but it's still fairly basic. So, are you going in, Doctor?"

"No," Michael replied. "Not yet. Talking to him just confuses me. I'm going to go back to my office to read my notes and then collapse into madness."

"Sounds like fun," Frank replied.

Michael returned to his office and noticed, when he walked in, that the sun was sinking over the hills of the heath below. Since his office was already darkening, he switched on his desk lamp, then leaned over to study his notes.

Scrawled on a piece of paper tucked under his notes was the single question *"Cheryl?"* Seeing it, Michael remembered that for the past week or so he had been trying in vain to contact his daughter. He reached out for the telephone, thought of Ashcombe's fierce gaze, was stabbed by a shaft of familiar fear, and decided to try Cheryl later.

Lighting a cigarette, which he had sworn not to do today, he inhaled, blew the smoke out, then squinted down through it at his unusually hesitant, confused notes about his patient, Miles Ashcombe.

> Patient is 35 yrs old. Born and raised in Glastonbury, and still resident there until its disappearance. Never married. Well educated. No prior history of mental disorder. Successful author of speculative books on the more mystical aspects of Glastonbury—the Celts and Druids; medieval, Christian, and Arthurian associations; flying saucers, et al.
> Any bearing on present condition?

Even under drugs or hypnosis is convinced he is inhabiting what would seem to be a primitive or prehistoric world. Displays great terror, but speaks normal English. However, when unaffected by drugs or freed from hypnosis, reverts to a very basic form of English, as if only able to express the most simple thoughts—again, perhaps primitive, or even prehistoric.

Possible link between this and subject's literary work? I.e., lifelong obsession with ancient past and mythology manifesting itself as an alternate reality induced by trauma caused by experience inside the dark mass.

A form of schizophrenia? Obviously not in the sense of being a "split personality" but, rather, a withdrawal from reality.

Disassociation? Certainly from the present. Possibly replacing the present with the myths of the past . . .

No. More than that. His new "personality" is too complete and exact for that. He is not "behaving" but actually "living" as this strikingly primitive personality. Has in fact been "taken over" and actually "sees" that other world, whatever it might be.

The world inside the dark mass? Existing outside the known time-scale? Is it actually possible, as Sampson suggested, that Ashcombe "experienced" rather than "witnessed" the past and still thinks he is part of it?

Unacceptable. Not comprehensible. Too removed from known psychological or psychoanalytical theories . . . Yet no positive response to drugs or hypnosis. No sign yet of a reversion to normality.

Present condition: Patient moves and talks like some kind of primitive creature. Possesses certain sensory perceptions lacking in "civilized" human beings—acute hearing and keen sense of smell—and often displays a kind of mental telepathy—just like certain animals . . . or, according to numerous theories, like our primitive ancestors.

What happened inside the dark mass?
Will Ashcombe recover?
Will he tell . . . ?

Having finished reading the notes, Michael continued to stare down at them, not seeing them, but reading them repeatedly in his weary, confused mind. The light outside was growing darker, the day giving way to evening, and he felt that darkness closing in on his thoughts as if threatening to blot them out. He had worked for ten days on this case (it seemed more like ten months) and now was no nearer to curing his patient than he had been at the start.

He tried to put himself into Ashcombe's shoes, to imagine being inside the dark mass, but to do so was to invite a clammy fear and greater incomprehension. He tried to think of it as a black hole, a void beyond space and time, but that only led into a series of concepts which threatened his reasoning. There was no way to treat Ashcombe—since his condition defied psychology. His affliction, if indeed it was such, was beyond rational analysis.

Michael sighed, feeling impotent, surrendering to an old man's tiredness, his handwritten words blurring before his eyes and forming a mist in his brain. He thought of Ashcombe and the dark mass, remembered his own bad dreams, and was just about to slip into a reverie when the telephone rang.

He picked it up automatically, expecting to hear his secretary, but instead heard the voice of his daughter, Cheryl, sounding unusually nervous.

"Daddy?"

"Cheryl!"

The very sound of her voice was enough to bring the past week rushing back—reminding him of his former wife and what she had told him; of the phone calls he had made in vain every day to Cheryl's flat; and of the calls he had *received* every day from her mother, demanding to know if he had spoken to her. Now, with Cheryl actually on the other end of the line, Michael felt his familial responsibilities impinging upon him again.

"Where are you?" he asked. "Back in your apartment?"

"Yes."

"I've been trying to get you all week. Your roommate didn't seem to know when you were due back, so I rang every day."

"I was in France."

"I know that. Your friend did at least know that much. She just didn't know when you were coming back—and you didn't leave a phone number."

"I forgot."

"No, you didn't," Michael said. "She said you *never* leave your number when you go away these days. Why is that?"

"Oh," Cheryl replied, sounding suspicious. "I don't know . . . I just don't think, I suppose . . . So," she continued, as if collecting her thoughts, "what's so urgent?"

"I have to talk to you. I think we should meet."

"Oh, Lord," she said, trying for a note of levity, "that sounds so *serious.*"

"It *is* serious," he replied.

"Is it Mother? Is something wrong?"

"There's nothing wrong with your mother," he assured her quickly, "but she *did* raise the subject."

There was a hesitant silence at the other end of the line, and Michael, closing his eyes, had a clear picture of Cheryl biting her lower lip and nervously stroking her blond hair, sensing that something unpleasant was forthcoming. He thought he heard her breathing, but wasn't sure; then she managed to speak again.

"You mean it's me," she said.

"Yes," he replied, "it's you. Your mother came here to see me."

This time he *did* hear her breathing, or at least giving an audible sigh, but he said nothing, giving her time to think, not wanting to panic her.

"I can't meet you for a few days," she said, "so you might as well tell me."

"You know what it is?"

"I didn't say that. Why don't you tell me?"

At that moment Michael felt the despair of a father who knows he has lost his daughter. There was a sharpening edge to her voice that he could not fail to recognize: she intuitively knew what he was about to say, and was already resisting him.

Feeling like an assassin, Michael took a deep breath. "All right," he said, "I'll get straight to the point. Your mother says you're having an affair with the man you work for—a married man with two children."

There was no cry of outrage, no faltering denial; only a brief silence and the question: "How did she know?"

"Christ!" Michael exclaimed.

"Pardon?"

"So it's true!"

"Yes," Cheryl replied, sounding calm. "So, how *did* she know?"

"She didn't put a detective on to you, if that's what you mean. She simply happened to use the upstairs phone at the very worst time."

"Oh," Cheryl said. "I see."

"Yes," Michael said. "And now that it's out, I think we should meet and discuss it fully."

"I don't *want* to discuss it, Daddy."

"I'm not concerned with what you want. I'm considerably more concerned about your future and what this could do to it."

"For heaven's sake, Daddy—"

"Don't tell me I'm being silly. I want us to have a talk before this goes any further."

"I don't want to meet you. I don't want to talk about it. You're only going to give me a lot of clichés about how wrong it is. Well, right or wrong I'm involved—and I won't be talked out of it."

"Let's meet."

"No."

"Dammit, Cheryl, don't be so silly! I'm your father and I have a right to talk, so don't give me this nonsense!"

Having just warned her not to use the word *silly,* he felt silly at using it himself. God, he sometimes hated emotions—for the lack of common sense they engendered—but when it came to his beloved daughter's welfare, his objectivity failed him.

"I won't meet you," Cheryl said, after what seemed like a long time. "I'll talk to you on this phone anytime—but I'm not going to meet you."

"A married man. Christ, why a *married* man?"

"There *are* no 'whys,' Daddy. These things just happen—which is something you certainly know."

"What does that mean? Is it a reference to my *own* love-life? If so, it's decidedly out of place in this particular context. You're not my age—you're still only twenty—and you're involved with a married man."

"So?"

"Stop sounding petulant. Now tell me: Just how *serious* is this affair?"

"It's serious."

"On his part? Or just on yours?"

"He's serious."

"Has he said that?"

"He doesn't have to. I know it."

"Is he willing to leave his wife and children?"

"Why should he? I haven't asked him to! Oh, for God's sake, this—"

"How serious is it with *you*, then? Tell me that."

"I love him."

"Oh, Christ!"

"I don't expect you to understand."

"I understand that he's married and has two children not much younger than you."

"That isn't fair, Daddy!"

"Where's this affair going to end? How long can you continue to love this man who returns home each night?"

"It's not important at this stage."

"How do you feel when he goes home? Do you wonder what he's like with his wife and children? Do you dream of his leaving them?"

"Oh, Daddy! You *bastard!*"

The line went dead abruptly and he knew she had slammed the phone down. Shocked, he simply stared at his own phone as if examining a bomb. He only did it for a moment, but it seemed a lot longer, then, feeling angry and hurt he dialed her number again.

"Yes," she said, very quickly and nervously.

"Cheryl, it's me again."

"I don't want to—"

"Cheryl, listen to me for a moment. Neither your mother nor I would normally interfere in such a personal matter, but in this case it's clearly very necessary. Your personal life is your own, and in the end you'll have to run it, but you can't expect your mother or me to keep our mouths shut when it comes to something we know is very wrong. No good can come of this, Cheryl. This isn't just another boyfriend. The very fact that you're having an affair with a *married* man is proof that you're serious. I know you, Cheryl. You're very easily impressed and far too dependent on others—and falling for an older man with children is, sad to say, your misguided way of dealing with your own weaknesses. Being older, he gives you a sense of security;

being married, he absolves you from any decisions regarding your future. But it won't work, Cheryl, because your own love will trap you; sooner or later, you'll want him as a permanent fixture in your life—and when you do, you'll probably find that he doesn't want *you*—and that's when the real pain will start. Don't let yourself become his mistress, Cheryl. If you do, you'll be finished."

She was silent for some time and again he imagined seeing her: doubtless leaning against the wall, biting her lower lip, blushing, perhaps stroking the blond hair out of her eyes in her insecure manner. Thus imagining her, he loved her, with a pure, anguished heart, and felt the rising tide of his contempt for the man who was using her.

"All right," she finally said, her voice quivering with nervousness. "You've had your uninterrupted say, and now I'm going to hang up."

"Let's meet."

"No."

"Dammit, Cheryl, just for a *talk!*"

"I don't want to talk about it, Daddy. I want to live my own life."

"I'm not stopping you doing that. I'm just trying to protect you."

"I don't want your protection. I don't need it. I'll deal with this in my own way."

"The only way to do that is to leave your job *and* your boss."

"I won't do that, and that's all there is to it. I'm hanging up now."

"Cheryl, *meet* with me!"

"No."

"Then I'll come to see you."

"No!"

"Damn you, I'll come without an invitation! I won't be put off this way!"

"Don't do that, Daddy! If you do, I'll never speak to you again! Do you understand? *I mean that!*"

"Then when am I next going to see you?"

"When I call. Good night, Daddy."

The line suddenly went dead and he knew she had hung up again. He put his own phone back on its cradle and stared out the window. The sky was dark and cloudy; the streetlamps be-

low were lit. He studied the people in Pond Street, watched cars
and buses pass, then raised his gaze to look at the darkened hills
and the moon high above them.

He shivered, feeling helpless, thinking of Ashcombe and
Cheryl, two problems that now dominated his life and cast their
shadows across him. One problem was very human, brutally
painful yet commonplace; but the other came from outside normal experience and suggested the magical.

Michael felt exhausted, drained by fear and confusion, but his
thoughts kept bouncing back and forth between Cheryl and
Ashcombe. The father in him was hurt, the psychologist rendered impotent, and he grieved that the vanity of man could
transcend even miracles.

Miracles? Yes, the Glastonbury event could be so classified.
And he, a normal father with very human concerns, had to deal
with his personal problems while wrestling at the same time
with the seemingly insoluble riddle of an extraordinary happening.

Still shaking from the vehemence of his beloved daughter's
rejection, Michael sighed, rubbed his eyes, stood up, and
walked from his office. He went straight to the psychiatric wing,
to the door with the sliding panel, opened it, and looked in.

Ashcombe was sitting upright on the bed, returning his stare.

He stared at Michael for a long time, hardly blinking at all.
He was sitting up very straight, his shoulders no longer
slumped; and his eyes, even from where Michael stood, were
still visibly bright.

Michael said nothing. He was waiting for Ashcombe's
speech. He waited for a long time, but Ashcombe said nothing,
so eventually, unlocking the door with his own key, Michael
entered the cell.

"Good evening," he said.

Ashcombe stared at him with diamond-bright, insane eyes,
then offered a slow, macabre smile and climbed to his feet. He
took a deep breath, glanced left and right, sniffed a little, then
gave that frightening smile again and slowly advanced.

Michael shivered instantly, surrendering to fear, even though
he sensed that Ashcombe would not harm him and only wanted
to talk. Nonetheless, the fear gripped him, squeezing the breath
from his lungs, and he felt his senses slipping away to render
him helpless.

He looked into Ashcombe's eyes and saw the unknown in their depths. He stood there, quite numb, his fear giving way to passivity, and only noticed that two hands not his own were being raised in the air. Those hands waved very gently, fingers opening and closing, as if trying to grasp something invisible and crush the life out of it. Then they fell onto his shoulders. He felt the strength of restless fingers. He was shaken and just as quickly released and saw Ashcombe's macabre smile.

"I know you," Ashcombe said. "You have been there as well. Soon, in the near future, you will go back to where you have come from. Me tired now. Me sleep long night."

Ashcombe turned back to the bed, his shoulders slumping again. He fell into a pool of inky shadow and seemed to sleep instantly.

Michael stood there like a man on a gallows—awaiting his doom.

11

GOD did not return to Eden, but other things remained, most notably the daily sunless haze and Schul's merciless dominance. Having possessed Frances, he had stripped Laurence of his will-power, and now used him for labor or sport, with a pharaoh's contempt. Frances saw it and was ashamed, knowing what had broken Laurence. But she now shared Schul's tent on a regular basis and had little to say.

At last they had all accepted that they might be here forever. The dark mass no longer surrounded them, the scenery no longer changed, but since all of them had jointly experienced the last manifestation, they now believed implicitly that they were indeed caught in a nightmare.

Even Schul was frightened, although he refused to show it. The deeper his fear grew, the more autocratic he became. As his secret desperation increased, his attacks on Laurence grew worse.

"She's mine," he said of Frances. "This bitch now belongs to me. She and I share the tent, and you sleep outside, and if I ever catch you looking at her sideways I'll cut your throat with this knife. We're probably here for life, see? We'll probably stay here till we die. So don't think I'm gonna worry about what I do, 'cause laws don't mean shit here."

Laurence did not reply—he rarely did anymore—but he quivered with the rage of the helpless and lowered his gaze. He now lived as a ghost, with the slave's natural invisibility, complying with every demand, shouldering every injustice, but quietly boiling in the vats of his resentment and nurturing his hatred.

Frances knew that when she saw him, but tried to forget it, avoiding his soulful gaze whenever possible and retreating into herself. Just as much a slave as Laurence, she not only shared Schul's bed but suffered the many humiliations heaped upon her, both mental and physical.

"Do it this way," Schul said.

"Oh, Christ," Frances replied. *"Please!"*

"Shut up, you bitch, and do as I say. You'll soon learn to like it."

Frances sought release in dreams, in those visions of descending light, feeling terror, but also yearning for salvation from the hell she was in. When she thought about it, she felt crazy, convinced that there was no hope, and she sensed that she was about to explode out of her steadily mounting dread. She had almost lost her old self, and had actually watched it vanishing, awakening each morning to find less of herself to take hold of. The Garden of Eden was her new home, unchanging, inescapable, and the lake that stretched out to the horizon only led straight back here.

The vegetation was lush and luminous; the water crystal-clear. The whole place was impossibly beautiful—and decidedly unreal. Surrounding her, it drained her, turning her into someone else: a more primal version of the woman she had once been; a creature physically sluggish and mentally dull, hardly knowing her own name. Yet that creature knew fear—a fear of everything outside herself, fear of water and sky, of the demon darkness, of Schul's swift retribution.

"Take your clothes off," he said. "Let's do it now. I want it right here."

"Oh, God, no!" she protested. "Not here. Not in the open. Not with Laurence sitting over there. Even you, Schul . . . not *that!*"

"I want it here and right now."

The first time, when she tried refusing, he ripped her clothes off; the next time she didn't bother trying and scarcely knew what was happening. Nonetheless, she heard Laurence weeping and saw him fleeing into the forest. He was gone a long time— doubtless trying to escape—but returned in despair a few hours later, prepared for his punishment.

Schul had made a whip from marsh reeds and he punished Laurence with it. Laurence bit his lip and whimpered, but made no other sound. And when Schul let him go, he nursed his wounds in the lake's healing water.

Thereafter it became normal practice—Schul enjoyed the open air—and he and Frances fornicated in the clearing while Laurence tried not to look at them. Frances felt like an animal, dull-witted and egoless; but sometimes, with Schul heaving on top of her, she would hear the sky's silent screaming—a lament that actually came from within herself to justify her humanity.

Very much a lost humanity, remembered only in fleeting moments, a question mark flicking at her thoughts as lightly as feathers. Such moments were very bad, giving rise to dark emotions, making her feel that she was looking into an abyss of bottomless darkness. To drop into it would be fatal—she would drown in her own memories—and those memories would drive her into the madness of an utterly vain hope.

"We're on our own now," Schul said. "We're the only three here. I'm lord of the whole goddamned universe, and you two are my people. Laurence is my servant, and my descendants will come from you. The world begins and ends in this place—and my word is law."

That was too much for Laurence and actually made him display some spirit. "That's blasphemy!" he hissed with eyes blazing. "I won't let you say such things!"

This time Schul used his fists, beating Laurence very badly, then kicking him when he finally fell to the ground, gasping with pain. It was a highly professional beating, causing no visible damage, and Frances sensed that Laurence had not really tried to resist.

That was common to her *and* Laurence: They had both lost pride and willpower. The bizarre experience through which they were living had rendered them powerless. It had simply overwhelmed them, destroying confidence and self-esteem, making them retreat into themselves and live for each moment.

Even Schul had been changed—though in quite the opposite way. He had responded to his new world by taking command of it, escaping from his fear and bewilderment by giving vent to his cruelty.

So it was that they existed like savages in paradise, with Frances and Laurence living only to be ruled, Schul to be ruler.

* * *

God did not return, but Frances often looked for Him—on the one hand terrified that He might actually reappear; on the other, yearning desperately for salvation from the hell of her new life.

God was the sunless sky and the light-reflecting lake; he was also the stars that shone at night and the wind in the marsh reeds. God was neither here nor there, but was simply hope and promise, He who could cast out the night to let the dawn break. Schul now thought that *he* was God—and in one sense he was —but to Frances, in the dimness of her reasoning, earth and sky were her masters. He was of the earth and water, and His voice was the wind, but when He came back, which she knew must happen eventually, He would come from the sky.

"Eat!" Schul commanded, tearing white flesh from fish bones, throwing the lesser morsels to Laurence as if feeding a dog. "Eat!" he snarled at Frances, his voice oddly distorted and hollow. "You hardly eat a thing anymore and look like a skeleton. So, eat! I like my women fatter. I want something worth holding."

Laurence now looked like an ape (perhaps she did, as well), but his eyes held the fire of a zealot who was finding his cause. He still believed in God—his original God from remembered times—and he heard Schul's every word as a blasphemy deserving of punishment.

A flicker of will was returning to Laurence. It was the glow of spiritual faith. He was being shaken out of his paralysis by the strength of his outrage. Also, with that, was a primal sexual hunger. Laurence, one of the only two men on earth, wanted the earth's only woman.

"Why him?" he said. "Me!"

Frances stared at him, bewildered. He had not spoken to her for a long time and now his voice sounded different.

"Me?" she asked. "You?"

"Me better," Laurence said.

Frances didn't think it sounded like speech at all, but that's what she heard him say.

"Bad," she replied. "Trouble. No speak. Go now you." And she turned, when he looked blankly at her, and crawled back into Schul's tent.

She was not herself at all, and yet part of her remained. She now lived with the instincts of a primitive, but still recognized human things.

Mostly Laurence and Schul: she knew their names and who they were, knew that Schul had not always owned her and that Laurence now wanted her. Schul and Laurence fought a lot. Or at least Schul beat Laurence. Schul now liked to draw blood from Laurence when he lay in the dirt.

"I kill him," Laurence said, his voice throttled by his leaning shoulders. "Silent I make him. And still. And then God can return."

Frances whimpered and tried to hide, but Schul found her soon enough, roughly rolling her onto her back and pushing her legs apart. She thought of silence as he pushed inside her, tried to visualize him as nothing; but his presence permeated her whole being and made her cling to him. She was then rolled onto her belly and he took her that way also. She felt the earth's heartbeat through her breasts and was touched with the spirit. She saw time passing through her. The fecund garden turned to barren rocks. The glittering lake became a great plain over which dust clouds drifted.

Edinu, meaning "plain." Its whispered name gave it life. She was taken from the rear in the dust while her own kind surrounded her. Neither caring nor looking at her, huddled by firewarmth, shoulders stooped, grunting words that had once made sense to her as he panted behind her. She felt something flooding her insides, making her body shake, then she squealed and crawled away, released from his hungry hands, and gratefully huddled whimpering in the rock hole, filled with food-thoughts and slavering.

She raised her gaze to the sky, which was a dazzling white haze. She was blinded by the light, rubbed her eyes, and saw Schul when she opened them.

"Good," Schul growled. "Feel better. Soon nighttime we hide."

They always hid at nighttime, lying together in the tent, now terrified that God and His angels might come back to rout them. Even Schul, who ruled the earth, feared the dark ones from the sky, and ashamed, he would take it out on Laurence, beating him viciously. Laurence sometimes fought back, but always bled and lost his pride; on other occasions he did not fight at all, but merely stood there and took it.

His bright blood frightened Frances, as did his burning eyes. He stared at her with hunger and rage, then tore the bark from the trees.

"Me weak," he whispered. "He strong. Me need strength in hand."

Dimly aware of what was happening, Frances lived in growing fear, her gaze focused frequently on the sky from which God might descend. The eye of God did not appear, nor did His light or angels, but she prayed that He might intervene before it was too late.

Laurence shuffled to and fro, his shoulders stooped, his gait awkward, and Frances noticed the hunger making his nostrils flare when he came too close to her. Schul saw that also, and usually snarled his resentment; then, if Laurence failed to retreat immediately, he savagely beat him. Laurence often licked his bloody wounds, whimpering under the fig palms; and the bright light, when his eyes moved out of the shadows, illuminated his growing rage.

"Kill!" he hissed. "Need stronger hand. Disappear him. Forever!"

Schul knew what was happening and started beating Laurence more brutally; then, because he knew that Laurence wanted her, he turned his fists on Frances as well. She received the blows silently but in sullen, rising resentment, aware that Laurence was trembling with anger, his fists opening and closing. Later she smiled at him, scarcely knowing what that implied, and he responded by stroking her arm with his enlarged, hairy hand.

"You, me," he whispered. "Soon to be. When his silence is always. Kill him with stronger hand."

He found his strong hand soon enough, in the shape of a thick, gnarled branch, picking it up when his rage flared out of control and he had to give vent to it.

It happened during the great change, when fear tore them all apart, when Schul realized that the change was taking them back to the present—to where he could not have dominion and would be just like other men.

Schul saw his own end in that.

The sunless sky had darkened and night lay upon the lake when Frances, placing her ears to the ground, heard the earth's quickening heartbeat. Startled, she jerked upright, saw Schul's coarse-haired body beside her, heard God's voice whispering on the wind and started to crawl from the tent.

Awakened, Schul grabbed at her, his free hand on his stiffened member, but she kicked him, hardly knowing what she was doing, and hurried into the cold night.

Schul's frustrated snarl pursued her, but was swept away on the wind. Still on hands and knees, Frances looked up and was stunned by the stars.

Stars streaming and cascading, forming waterfalls and pools, curving into immense loops and coils that blended into a brilliant haze.

Frances whimpered and clutched the grass, saw Laurence, eyes skyward, reaching out to pull her close to him. The surrounding land was changing, as was the lake and sky, with alien flowers blooming and dying to be reborn, the distant marshes altering subtly to become more familiar, and the stars, in their multiplicity and brilliance, forming patterns that soon became recognizable as those of the former world.

The ground shook as its heart raced, the darkness glowed and pulsated strangely, then a snarling Schul crawled speedily from his tent and stared around him in wonder.

Lost. All lost. He was losing everything he had gained. As his slightly bestial, snarling face became more human, he glanced up at the changing sky.

He recognized the stars of earth. His shocked expression revealed that much. He saw that time was moving again and returning them to the normal world, but that was something he no longer wanted, nor could possibly deal with.

Schul sat back on his haunches, raised his face to the sky, then howled in the anguish of his loss. He was baying at the moon, letting it know he had seen it, outraged that it should suddenly have returned to that glittering, normal sky. He tore the grass from the soil, shoved it into his shivering lips, spat it out again, then looked at Frances and howled even louder.

His changing form was striped by moonlight. Frances saw his human skin. She felt the sluggishness leaving her own body, and touched her raw, newborn flesh. Laurence sobbed and leaned forward, pressing his forehead to the ground, quivering as he thanked God for this deliverance from the bondage of frozen time.

Schul snarled and vented his rage, swinging his left fist in an arc, the blow slapping Frances's face sideways and making her cry out. Then Schul was upon her, tearing away her flimsy rags, trying to force her unwilling legs apart in order to take her one last time. Frances struggled and screamed in protest, now aware of her true identity, and Laurence, lifting his forehead from the ground, stared at them with startled eyes.

"No!" he cried. *"Not again!"*

It was then, as a snarling Schul turned away from Frances, that Laurence took hold of the thick, gnarled branch that had been lying on the ground beside him, and, with his body arched, silhouetted against the moonlit lake, raised the weapon high above his head. Schul was already halfway through the air, his greedy hands outstretched, when Laurence, with a quavering, high-pitched wailing, brought the branch down on his skull, making Schul careen sideways and roll over on the grass with blood already splashing from his first wound.

It was the first but not the last, since as Schul attempted to rise again, Laurence repeatedly struck him over the head and face with a fury that, accompanied by his peculiar, demented wailing, merely emphasized the extent of his long-buried resentment and anguish.

Frances screamed at Laurence to stop, hardly believing what she was seeing, but Laurence kept striking Schul with that terrible, helpless rage, sobbing even as he was doing it, aware of his guilt. Schul's hands dropped to his sides, revealing a head like a pomegranate, then as Frances finally managed to pull Laurence away, Schul fell onto his side, tried in vain to get up again, shuddered in a long, drawn-out spasm, fell back and was still.

Spent by his own violence, Laurence dropped the bloody branch, sat back on his haunches, and stared at Schul's prostrate body with wide, disbelieving eyes. Frances also stared at Schul, her senses returning to her; she was aware of what that terrible stillness meant, but was reluctant to dwell on it.

She studied Schul's bloody head, then the stars glittering above, then looked out and saw that the lake was the one she had known in former days. The familiar disoriented her, ironically making her feel more unreal, but she managed at last to explore Schul with professional fingers. *I'm a doctor,* she thought wonderingly. *I'm back to being what I was before.* Her experienced fingers examined Schul's bloody skull, then fell on

his naked chest. Schul's heart was still. He was silent. And that
silence was permanent.

"He's dead," she said, speaking in her normal voice.

"Are you sure?"

"Yes. You've killed him."

Laurence had also returned to normal, but he seemed completely dazed, and he covered his face with his hands and
sobbed for what he had done. Frances, in a similar turmoil, her
relief destroyed by shock, went to him, put her arms around
him and held him close to her. He wept like a real person—
returned to consciousness and conscience, to the very human
awareness of his guilt regarding the murder—then, in that same
awareness, he glanced wildly around him, studied the lagoon
for some time, before returning his attention to Frances, breathing into her face.

"We've got to get rid of him!" he said. "And we've got to do
it immediately!"

"The lake," Frances replied, surprised by her own words.
"Let's take the raft and drop him into the lake and then get out
while we can."

"Yes!" Laurence exclaimed gratefully. "Let's do that! *God
forgive us, let's do it!*"

Frances would not forget the next few hours for as long as
she lived. Together, she and Laurence dragged Schul's bloody
remains across the grass to the water's edge, where the crude
raft was swaying gently against the bulrushes, its wooden
planks bathed in moonlight. Schul was very heavy and his head
was a ghastly mess, so Laurence gagged and retched while
Frances sobbed and they dragged the corpse after them. Although the night was cold, they were soon drenched in sweat,
and as they manhandled Schul onto the bobbing raft they were
both gasping painfully.

Frances felt her old self returning and exposing her to guilt,
but as she rested on hands and knees on the rolling, creaking
raft, trying to get back her breath as she leaned over Schul's
body, she gazed out across the lake and almost wept for joy
when she recognized the outline of the far shore, which would
lead to Al-Qurna.

The world had returned to normal, but she still dwelt in fear,
aware that the dark mass could return at any moment and
plunge her back into the same nightmare. Taking a deep breath,

she looked down at Schul's eyes—two dead orbs reflecting the moonlight with wide-open, blind clarity.

Frances jerked upright and turned away quickly. She sat back on her haunches, refusing to believe what was happening, while Laurence, occasionally sobbing, once throwing up on the bank, hacked off lengths of bulrush and tied them around heavy stones, then tied the same stones to the lifeless Schul, some to his wrists and ankles, others around his waist and neck. When Laurence had finished, Schul looked monstrous, a Neanderthal man preserved in stone, and Frances shivered and took another deep breath, trying to swallow her horror.

Moonlight striped the water and lent the ripples a silvery quality as Laurence rowed the raft out into the lake. He seemed calmer now, but his eyes were dazed and disbelieving; and occasionally he wiped tears from his cheeks and glanced down at the dead Schul.

Frances also studied Schul, shivering each time she did so, wondering obsessively who he had been, trying to accept that Laurence had murdered him, and haunted by the knowledge that she was about to become a partner in the crime. She could not believe that this was she—Frances Devereux, of London, England; once a mature, thirty-five-year-old woman and respectable doctor.

Shaken even more, she studied the far shore of the lake, her gaze following the line of marsh reeds where they curved back to rejoin the Shatt-al-Arab river and the rest of the land she knew so well. The sight of the marshes overwhelmed her, filling her with longing; but when she glanced up at the sky and saw familiar stars, she found herself waiting fearfully for them to change and plunge her back into hell.

"God," she murmured, "just let me get out of here. I just want to go home."

"Here!" Laurence snapped. *"Here!"*

He was obviously lost for words, his moonlit face white and strained, his eyes glazed with shock and disbelief. He stared about him like a startled deer, first at Schul, then at the lake; and Frances, following his gaze, saw the water rippling in silvery lines around the sides of the raft. The water was very black, but reflected the large white moon. The moon seemed to be very deep in the water and drawing everything to it.

Laurence pushed Schul's body overboard, so quickly that

Frances missed it. She just heard the splash and looked down to
see the body rolling over with the weight of the stones and
sinking under its own waves. The waves bubbled and gurgled,
turned into a small whirlpool, then became still again.

Frances shuddered and closed her eyes, imagining Schul's
body, wrapped in bulrushes, weighted with stones, sinking silently into the cold, eternal darkness of his watery grave. When
she opened her eyes again, she saw Laurence, bathed in sweat,
his face anguished.

"Are you all right?" she asked him.

"I feel feverish," he replied. *"Oh, dear God!"*

He covered his face with his hands and wept. Eventually,
when he managed to control himself, he took the oar in his
shaking hands and rowed the raft on toward the far bank. Once
there, he followed the shoreline, heading south toward Al-
Qurna, finally leaving the lake behind and heading along the
placid river, between rustling rows of fig palms.

The darkness gave way to light, dawn to bright morning,
while Frances, haunted by what had happened, tried to conquer
her trembling. The sky was a white sheet but no longer sunless,
and she had to shade her eyes to see the clouds drifting over the
treetops. The raft passed waterside villages, humpbacked buffaloes, and other canoes; and gradually, as such familiar scenes
closed in about her, she felt herself returning to sanity and a
certain control.

Then she heard a descending roaring, glanced up and was
dazzled, collapsed into a well of fresh terror as the noise grew
louder above her. She screamed "No!" and was whipped by
wind. The raft rocked and water splashed her. Gusts of hot air
were suddenly whipping around her, then settling down again.

Frances sobbed in despair and fear, imagining God descending upon her. When she thought of what she might have to
endure again, she came close to hysteria.

Then she felt hands on her shoulders. Someone was shaking
her and shouting. Feeling hysterical, she opened her eyes and
saw Laurence in front of her, holding her and shouting to calm
her down. She licked her lips and held on to his shoulders,
letting him know she was all right.

The roaring above was diminishing as God ascended on high
again. Frances glanced up, shading her eyes, and saw the brilliant light shrinking, first flaring out of that roaring mass in

silvery striations, then disappearing back into a duller core beneath large, beating wings.

Not wings: rotor blades. The sunlight was actually flaring out around an ascending dome; and the dome, made of metal and glass, was reflecting the sunlight.

Someone was leaning out of that dome. Frances saw a white hand waving. She gasped in relief, then fell back into Laurence's arms, laughing hysterically in the realization that it was actually a helicopter above her.

The rescue team had arrived.

HOME. Frances Devereux, a mature, thirty-five-year-old woman and respectable doctor wearing a buttoned-up gray trench coat, slacks, and high-heeled leather boots, and looking a little older than her years, stood on the summit of Hampstead Heath and stared abstractedly out over the green hills of the Vale of Health at the spires and concrete towers of distant London. *Home,* she thought. *Thank God. Now it all seems so unreal.* She shuddered as a gust of wind slapped her, then started walking.

The winding, well-trodden path led her away from the sounds of traffic and down into the soothing silence of the Vale of Health. She was further soothed by the birdsong, but not entirely so, since to a passing stranger she would have seemed nervous—blinking too much, her gazing roaming restlessly, her right hand constantly brushing at her hair where it fell on her forehead. *God,* she thought, *I've aged. I'm not the woman I used to be.* She hesitated on the lower slopes, studied the sky that Constable had painted, then made her way into the tiny street named Byron Villas, stopping in front of the home of D. H. Lawrence.

The famous writer had lived here in 1915 with Frieda von Richthofen, the woman who had eloped with him three years earlier. It was, according to Lawrence, the year the old world ended; and Frances, thinking about that in an attempt to forget her own recent experience, was only reminded that her personal "old world" had ended in Mesopotamia. *I cannot forget,* she thought. *The world conspires to remind me of it.* And she trembled again, this time untouched by the wind, then walked away from the dead writer's home to circle the pond.

She could not forget it, although she tried during these walks, breathing deeply of the damp English air and enjoying the grass underfoot. Yet everything reminded her of it—a glint of sunlight, a birdcall, the very grass she enjoyed underfoot—and now as she circled the pond looking down at the English bulrushes, she was reminded of the bulrushes of the marshes in southern Iraq.

They said we were missing for twenty-four hours, but it must have been longer than that. We spent months there. We aged. We changed. . . . Yet they said it was only twenty-four hours.

She continued walking around the pond, distracting herself by trying to visualize this place as it had originally been—not a vale of health, but a very unhealthy swamp that had to be drained before being turned into a second reservoir to the town's water supply. *An unhealthy swamp,* she thought, then remembered the marshes of Eden, the dark line of reeds around the lake where time had played bizarre games.

How long had she been back? A month? Two months? It hardly made any difference to her, since she dreamed of it constantly.

Home, she thought as she cut across East Heath, heading toward the twin pools of Heath Pond. *There is no such place as home anymore . . . and there never will be.* She felt broken in mind and spirit, robbed of her sense of reality, and knew that she would now be aware of time for as long as she lived.

Time—and mortality. The prismatic face of the eternal present. She had gone back in time and returned again, so now had to learn to live as two people. *What time was it that I inhabited? What kind of creature was I then? What dream did I have of God's eye coming down from the heavens?* She felt cold just to remember it, numbed by its awesome nature, realizing that the present, this very moment, was less real than the dream.

She soon passed the two ponds where people were fishing beneath the cypress trees, a scene so unchanging that Constable had painted virtually the same one in the early 1820s.

Unchanging? she thought. *A mere century and a half ago. And the Tudors actually made the ponds with water that came from the River Fleet; and before that, the river was a sea, and before that . . . .*

Dear God. Before that, more changes. And other changes before them. Time moving back to eons yet unknown, to the very birth of the dawnlight. . . .

Frances passed the ponds, trying to stop her nervous blinking, then hurried through the ugly parking lot beyond until she arrived at East Heath Road. Still not used to the city traffic, she glanced left and right, kept doing so for a long time, eventually managed to find a gap between roaring vehicles, and darted across.

She passed the garden of the Freemasons Arms, then the mock-Tudor main building, contemplated going in for a drink, but decided against it. *Too much drinking lately,* she thought. *And it only makes things worse.* Thus determined but feeling deprived, and therefore wanting a drink even more, she walked along the elegant Downshire Hill until she came to her own gate. She put her hand on the latch, started opening it, hesitated. *Home,* she thought. *Think of it that way. It's all you have left now.* Then she pulled the latch down, opened the gate and walked up the garden path.

Home was an elegant Regency villa with elaborately wrought-iron balcony railings around the windows, finely gabled sloping roofs, and gardens profuse with shrubbery, trees, and flowers. Inside, the house had an air of genteel decay, with large, high-ceilinged rooms, a lot of very valuable antique furniture, and white-painted walls covered by paintings and books, most of which were the works of the notably famous Hampstead residents, past and present.

Standing in the hallway, glancing up the charming stairwell, Frances felt like the little girl she had been long ago. There was the sound of music—as there seemed to have been every day of her life—and she instantly recognized Handel's "Largo," played superbly on a good piano. She listened for a moment, then walked along the hall into the music room where her mother was playing.

Her mother was small and slim, with a weatherbeaten, birdlike beauty, her face flushed and webbed with lines, gray hair piled on her head and pinned together with ebony combs of a coloring that perfectly matched her Victorian dress. She was perched on a piano stool and appeared to be an extension of it, her cigarette smoldering in the ashtray on top of the Steinway.

She was playing the "Largo" with great tenderness, leaning forward in a dreamy manner, but she sensed immediately that someone had entered the room, which made her turn toward Frances. Her eyes, unusually large, were as blue as a summer's sky, focusing intently on Frances, but with no great surprise.

"Ah," she said, "my daughter is back. I thought it might be a rapist." She stopped playing and returned Frances's smile as she placed her hands on her lap. "So," she said, "you had another walk."

"Yes," Frances said.

Her mother sighed histrionically. "I don't know how you stand all that bird shit and those men in their gaberdines."

"You don't have to try to shock me, Mother. I'm too old for that now."

"No one's ever too old to be shocked—and it *can* be therapeutic." Mrs. Devereux, who at sixty-one years old was still filled with aggressive energy, raised herself from the piano stool and walked across the room to the liquor cabinet.

"Did you drop into the Freemasons Arms for a drink?" she asked.

"No," Frances replied.

"Then I'll reward you with a little dry sherry."

"You're too generous," Frances said.

Her mother smiled fleetingly, put on a pair of spectacles, then peered owlishly at the well-stocked liquor cabinet. "A little amontillado," she said, picking up one of the bottles. "That should be safe enough." She filled up two glasses and gave one to Frances. "I'm only generous," she said, sampling her drink, "because I had to have one myself—so you needn't feel guilty."

"I don't feel guilty. It's just that you've recently been nagging me about my drinking."

"Naturally, dear, I *nag*. I *nag* because you start drinking at noon and don't stop until bedtime. *Nagging* is what mothers are *for*, dear."

Frances smiled, though she didn't feel good-humored. "I've only been doing that since I returned from Iraq. I never did it before."

"The point, my child, is that you're *doing* it—and I simply won't stand for it."

Frances had a sip of sherry, then, after removing her trench coat, sat in a chair and lit a cigarette.

"My," she said, blowing smoke out, "I *do* love this house."

"Naturally," her mother replied. "Your father had exquisite taste in all things. The name Devereux, after all, is the family name of the viscounts Hereford and though we may not be immediately related, we *are* surely connected, so it's understandable that we should be a family of distinction."

"You're such a snob, Mother."

"Perhaps. Perhaps not. But I *do* wish your father hadn't died so early and left you without a man to look up to."

"Mother!"

"All right! I won't start!"

Mrs. Devereux walked away from Frances and sat on the sofa opposite, her back turned to the French windows that, overlooking the rear garden, framed wisteria and wild flowers. Frances thought of her childhood, fatherless, filled with love, then saw her mother, radiantly beautiful and spoiled, a long time ago. Time moved back and forth, both in memory and speculation, and now, studying her mother, Frances was filled with love and despair. Her mother was beauty ravaged, spirit turned into eccentricity, a lovely creature reaching the end of her life and trying to keep her head high.

"About the drink," Frances said. "I still have bad dreams and I need the drink to relax me . . . to help me forget them."

"Too much drink will only make the dreams worse," her mother replied. "And what you need to make you forget is a decent man—not your usual low types."

"I don't think we should be discussing my taste in men, Mother."

"Why on earth not? I should think that *any* mother would show an interest in her daughter's love life, particularly if it seemed a trifle *bizarre,* as yours surely does."

"Any bizarre traits I must have picked up from you."

"I do not have a love life, and haven't had one for years, so you certainly picked up nothing from me in *that* particular field. You're such an intelligent woman in every other respect—but your men! Dear, oh dear! There's a touch of the masochist in you—of that I am certain."

Frances sipped her sherry, wishing it was something stronger, disturbed by her mother's deduction but forced to accept it. She remembered Ravello in southern Italy, dizzying gorges and corkscrew roads, its Roman steps and arches leading through riotous wild flowers into cool, shaded courtyards of vine and mosaic tiles. She had been bored in Ravello, then she fell in love, surrendering her virtue at seventeen to a man twice her own age. They had made love in the sweltering afternoons in his apartment off the main square, with the bells of the church tolling away the hours. That man had taught her everything, enslaving her en route, before breaking her and leaving her addicted to shameless desires.

Intelligent? Possibly she was . . . but not when it came to sex.

"I refuse to let you bring up Ravello, Mother, which is what you are clearly planning to do. So, just don't try it."

"I just want you to accept—"

"I don't have to accept anything. Least of all something that happened eighteen years ago. What I have to accept, Mother, is what happened in Iraq a few *weeks* ago."

"You still find it hard to believe that it actually happened?"

"First I do, then I don't. It just doesn't seem possible."

"Well, dear, as you know, I am certainly *one* person who believes that *all* things are possible."

"Yes, Mother," Frances said, suddenly weary.

"Please don't adopt that patronizing tone with me. I am simply saying that the story you told me, fantastic or not, could have certain perfectly reasonable explanations."

"There's no way to explain what happened, Mother. No way at all."

Standing at the cabinet, she stared out the window, raising her gaze above the clinging vines and flowers to the gray sky above. She remembered that other sky, the sunless haze above Eden, then the helicopter descending like God's eye to take her away.

"You've been back six weeks," her mother reminded her, "and in all that time you haven't told the real story to anyone but me. I'm sure that if you simply *talked* to someone, you would find sleep much easier, dear."

Frances did not reply. She had told her mother the story—not all of it, but most—and now, as she remembered the rest of it, the horror returned. . . . Schul—and their fornication. Schul's murder—by Laurence's hand. Schul's body sinking into

the lake, weighed down with heavy stones . . . Frances closed
her eyes, let the dread and revulsion whip her, then sighed and
poured another sherry, taking a large drink.

"That's enough," her mother's voice said from behind her.
"That's a very strong drop, dear."

Luckily, after the rescue, when she and Laurence had given
their false, plausible story, there had only been a few questions
asked, most of them perfunctory. And, indeed, who would have
doubted their version of events? According to their rescuers,
they had only been lost for twenty-four hours, and pieces of the
wreckage had confirmed their story about the canoe being
wrecked in a storm. Regarding the fact that their Arab oarsmen
and the American passenger had disappeared—well, given the
wide area over which the boat's debris had been found, it could
reasonably be assumed that they had indeed (as Frances and
Laurence had implied) been swept downriver and drowned.

Subsequently, there being nothing in their story to arouse
undue suspicion, Frances and Laurence had been routinely examined in a hospital in Basra, then flown back to their respec-
tive homes in England and America, leaving the American Embassy the task of ascertaining Schul's proper identity and
informing his nearest relatives, if such existed, of his untimely
death.

It had all been a very bad dream, but at least it was over.

"God," Frances said, "I'm weary. I feel that I haven't really
been awake since I returned from that place."

"The experience certainly aged you," her mother said with
customary candor. "But then I always *did* believe that a little
maturity goes a long way. Youthfulness is such a terrible burden
when one has to live with it."

"Do I look *that* bad?" Frances asked.

"Not *that* bad, dear, just more *lived-in.* And after all, you're
thirty-five years of age, which speaks for itself."

Frances smiled, feeling bleak, aware of time moving constantly, but no longer sure if it moved forward or in both directions. Returning from the liquor cabinet, she sat facing her
mother, studying her weathered, birdlike face for a moment,
then gazing around the room that held so many memories.

Her father had once worked here, composing film music, and
although he had died when she was too young to remember
him, she liked to imagine him sitting here with her, as a child,

on his lap. It was not a very mature thing to do, but it gave her some comfort.

She kept looking around her, still entranced by the room, trying to visualize her father squinting at his sheet music while his wife played the piano for him in that long-ago time. Her childhood had been filled with music—and the emotional resonance it provided—and these days, when her mother played, she often chose her husband's compositions, filling Frances with unutterable longing for the man she could never have.

"Memories," Frances murmured, hardly hearing her own voice. "Everything reminds me of something. Everything haunts me. . . ."

"What was that, dear?" her mother asked sharply, cocking her head to hear more clearly.

Frances blinked and stared at her, as if seeing a ghost, then had another sip of sherry. "Nothing," she said, sighing. "I simply can't believe what happened to me—nor can I forget it."

"You *won't* forget it," her mother replied. "You'll just have to learn to live with it. There's no other way."

"Do *you* believe that what I told you was true?"

Mrs. Devereux shrugged. "Well," she said, "strange things are happening every day, so I'm inclined to accept that something peculiar happened to you. And after all, the whole town of Glastonbury *did* disappear shortly before your own extraordinary adventure. And that American who turned up so mysteriously *did* say he had fallen asleep near the Tor—so there *might* be a connection between those two events. However, I still don't see why you won't talk to someone about it as I've been suggesting. I mean, that nice Dr. Phillips in the Royal Free Hospital, who is working in conjunction with those officially investigating the Glastonbury event, would, I'm sure, be very interested in talking to you."

"He's a shrink."

"You may need him."

"I won't talk about it, Mother. I just can't—and that's all there is to it."

Her mother's brow wrinkled, as if she was wondering just what Frances had left out of her story. Frances knew what she hadn't told her—and could hardly bear to think about: that she had been an unwilling partner to murder and the body's disposal. She didn't want to talk about that, nor about her relationship with Schul, since even now, when it came into her mind, she was filled with revulsion.

Like an animal . . . She had behaved like a primitive beast . . . and she could never confess to that.

"Frances," her mother said, leaning forward in her chair, head tilted slightly. "You know, of course, that we Devereuxs are a very *psychic* family."

"Don't start, Mother."

"Well, it's true, isn't it? And I'm not just talking about myself. I also think that you might have such powers but simply don't know it."

"That's nonsense, Mother."

"Are *my* powers nonsense?"

"That's different."

"Not really."

Frances's mother was a practicing spiritualist medium who held séances right here at home every week and had been trying for years to contact her dead husband. She had not succeeded in that, but she *had* succeeded in bringing to the house each week a collection of extremely odd characters and in producing during the séances some very odd effects.

At her mother's insistence, but with very great reluctance, Frances had sat in on a few of the séances and been very surprised by what she had witnessed. The round table had rocked and actually risen in the air. Pencils and papers had also floated in the air while her mother spoke an indecipherable alien language. There was clearly no trickery involved—Frances trusted her mother implicitly—and so, if bewildered, she had also been nervous about what had occurred.

"Do you *remember* what happened at those séances?" her mother asked, lighting up a cigarette.

"Yes, Mother, I do."

"They were impressive, were they not?"

"Yes, Mother, they were."

Her mother nodded contentedly and leaned a bit closer. "Well," she said, "I'm going to tell you something that I never told you before. We never obtained such impressive results when you were *absent* from the séances. The things you saw—those very powerful manifestations—were produced by *your* presence."

Mrs. Devereux nodded vigorously, exhaling cigarette smoke, her eyes glittering behind the round spectacles when they focused on Frances.

"I don't get what you're driving at," Frances said, wanting to stand up and leave.

"I think you're highly psychic," her mother said. "And if that's true, it makes you powerful. It would mean that you can see things most mortals cannot see, make visible what is normally invisible, travel outside your own body and contact the spirit world."

"Please, Mother, *stop* this!"

"No, dear, I won't! You just have to face up to the possibilities. And the point, my dear, is that you possess unusual psychic powers that could be the cause of, or a contributing factor to, what happened to you and those with you. There *are*, after all, other worlds—*spirit* worlds, for want of a better term —where time and space have no meaning in any sense that *we* understand. What is death, dear? We simply don't know. And where does human energy go when the soul leaves the body? Again, we don't know, but logic demands that it must go *somewhere*. And it *is* widely believed—and certainly believed by *me* —that that energy must remain in circulation, possibly in a kind of parallel world where it can still serve some purpose."

"I'm sorry, Mother," Frances intervened, "but this conversation is going to give me a headache, and I think we should—"

"Nonsense," her mother replied. "You're just trying to wriggle out of this. What I'm saying is that psychic phenomena, other phenomena such as flying saucers and inexplicable disappearances, and even so-called hallucinations, could simply be manifestations of parallel worlds. Ghosts, my dear, don't have to rattle chains—they might be perfectly normal."

"Why don't you take up knitting or something, Mother? I'm sure it's much healthier."

"Sticks and stones, dear. I am immune to your sarcasm. But I must insist on reiterating that a lot of strange things have been happening recently—indeed, to an unprecedented degree. Glastonbury Tor *did* disappear and has never returned; that American, Schul, *did* insist that he had fallen asleep in Glastonbury before awakening in Iraq; and there *are* an increasing number of stories in the papers about people and objects disappearing. In fact, only yesterday there was an awful story on television about a woman, in Surrey, whose child walked into the middle of their garden, abruptly disappeared, and though apparently invisible, kept calling repeatedly for her mother until after an hour or so the poor child's voice faded away completely—and that child has not been seen since. So, my dear, I'm sure you must get my drift by now. What happened to you is not an isolated incident. The only difference is that you returned to tell me about it."

Agitated, Frances stood up and walked past the piano to the window. The sun was going down, and the fading light, turning the garden gray, also darkened her mind.

I'm going crazy, she thought. *I cannot believe what I am hearing. Perhaps I'm not hearing it at all; maybe I'm simply imagining it.*

Home? Was this it? Had she actually expected to find a cure here? In this house with its music, memories of loss and spiritualist séances? She was angry at herself, then directed it at her mother. But when she turned around to look at the old woman, she felt love's cleansing emotion.

Her mother was squinting up through her spectacles, her face wreathed in cigarette smoke, her lips pursed rather primly.

"I don't want to think about this," Frances said, "so I'm going to bed."

"A jury cannot ignore what it has just heard," her mother replied, "even though it may be stricken from the record." She nodded, smiled with triumph, then sat straight in her chair, tensing like a bird about to snatch up a field mouse. "Sooner or later you'll remember what I've just said . . . and it might start to make sense."

It did not make sense that night when Frances tossed and turned in bed, her thoughts colliding like cars at a junction, bringing chaos and pain. She was back in civilization but did not feel that way, her clothing and demeanor concealing emotions that were close to the primal. She dreaded sleep because of the dreams, seemed to dream when still awake, closed her eyes to the shadows on the walls and instantly saw what she still feared.

It was the bright, sunless sky over the garden of Eden, the great lake and marshes turning into a vast dust bowl, while another light, greater than the sunless day, burned a hole right above her. It was that—a familiar memory—but it was also something else: She had always sensed the presences around her, but now she could see them.

They were there and then gone, materializing and disappearing, faceless, distorted shadows in the burning haze that made eyes and flesh weep. Were they human shapes or not? Had they faces or were they masked? In that light, and given her blinding fear, it was impossible to tell.

Frances cried out in that dream, but heard her own voice in the darkness, forcing her to open her eyes and stare fearfully around her. She was alone in the room, her gaze focused on the window, which framed the gray-smudged darkness of the northern sky between the fine white-lace curtains.

Her gaze roamed, still fearful, taking in the rest of the room, letting familiar items materialize out of the gloom and lend reassurance. She had slept in this same room as a child, and inside was that same child.

Now she viewed the past and present as a single, haunting entity. Her memories, brightly lit and vivid, simply would not release her. She saw herself on her father's knee, felt his breath, heard his voice, then felt a searing pain and fell through darkness to arrive at a graveyard. Her father's grave was a mound of earth (they had obviously buried him years ago), but she wept and threw herself on the dirt and tried to bring him to life again.

She opened her eyes to the sunlight, feeling older but no happier. The bells of the town church were ringing out above the hills of Ravello. *I love you,* the Italian murmured. *My beautiful English rose.* Naked, at seventeen, she lay beneath him and was gradually crushed by him. Frances groaned at the memory of it. First love, then humiliation. "My beautiful English slut," he had whispered in his melodious Italian. She had wept, but accepted it, wanting someone older and wiser, then one form of dependence became another and left her enslaved.

She saw herself on her hands and knees, felt him stretched out on her spine; she strained against the thongs of silk in a helpless anguish that soon turned to ecstasy. "You were born for this," he said. "To submit. To be a slave." And she knew that to be true when she found herself in Eden, submitting to Schul's domination and rapacious demands.

Frances tossed and turned all night, as she had done for so long now, caught in the conflicting web of guilt and lust, trying to reconcile opposites. She fell in and out of sleep, finding exhaustion rather than rest, and once having found it, lay stupefied all morning, letting the hands on her wristwatch turn toward noon, but still unable to rise.

She suffered dark premonitions, sensed disaster in the air. Her mother entered the room and stood beside the bed, peering down through her spectacles, her flushed, birdlike head tilting a little as she coughed into a clenched fist.

"You better get up," she said. "You have a visitor. . . . It's that American, Laurence."

13

FRANCES took Laurence to Jack Straw's Castle for lunch, feeling as she did so that she was walking beside a ghost. The journey to that famous pub was accompanied by a conversation whose long, awkward silences were only broken by words of the utmost banality. During this time they desperately avoided each other's eyes, but once seated in the upstairs restaurant, overlooking the sea of trees on the hills of West Heath, Frances, forced to stare directly at Laurence, was shocked to see just how pale and aged he looked.

He obviously knew what her startled glance signified, for he shrugged, grinned painfully, and said, "Lots of sleepless nights in Virginia. Lots of very bad dreams."

In a moderate way, the acknowledgment that Laurence had shared Frances's traumas, albeit from a great distance, was enough to ease the embarrassment and shame between them. Since Laurence was an American on his first visit to England, Frances relaxed him further by telling him a little about the old hotel, most notably that Jack Straw had nothing to do with it, but that Charles Dickens, Washington Irving, Karl Marx, and Max Beerbohm had frequently visited it—then, still in the spirit of entertaining a foreigner, she ordered roast beef and Yorkshire pudding for both of them. While they were waiting for the food to come, and settling their ragged nerves with a bottle of red wine, Frances, hardly knowing where to begin, said, "Well, it's a shock."

"Touché," Laurence replied. "I can hardly believe I'm here, but I just had to come."

"Why?"

Laurence shrugged. "Lots of sleepless nights," he repeated. "Too many, in fact. Wondering if it had really happened. Going crazy because I couldn't discuss it with anyone—except you, of course. In the end, I think I *was* a little crazy, so I just had to see you."

"To hear me confirm that it actually happened?"

"Yes."

"It happened. Now what?"

Laurence shrugged again. "I don't know," he said. "I have to find a way to forget it. And I think that to do that I'll have to find some kind of rational explanation."

"I can't give you one, Laurence—"

"I know that."

"—and I don't think you came all this way just for that. I know no more about what happened than you, so why have you come here?"

Laurence rubbed his eyelids with his forefinger and thumb; when he looked up, his eyes were slightly bloodshot, doubtless from weariness.

"I just had to talk," he said. "And who else can I talk to? Only someone who shared the experience with me could believe that it happened."

"I'm sorry, Laurence, but *I* don't want to talk about it. In fact, I can't even bear to think about it—for understandable reasons."

Laurence blushed when she said that, then he gazed out of the window, trying to find escape in the heath that rose and fell under low clouds.

"You've nothing to be ashamed of," he said. "You weren't yourself and neither was I. *None* of us was."

The unconscious reference to the dead Schul made them both uncomfortable, but Laurence, no longer an amiable innocent, was able to force his gaze back upon her.

"I've more to be ashamed of than you," he said. "And you know what I'm talking about."

Frances thought of Schul's body sinking into the lake, and was relieved when the waitress arrived with their food. While Laurence was tentatively tackling his typical English pub lunch,

Frances filled up both glasses with more red wine, appreciative of its anesthetizing qualities during discomfiting experiences. The bottle, she noted with alarm, was almost empty already.

"You used not to drink," she said to Laurence.

"I started when I got back from Iraq," he said. "At least it's safer than drugs."

"The sleepless nights?"

"Yes."

"So we're both having trouble sleeping," she said. "In our separate beds, of course."

Laurence blushed again and busied himself with his eating, while Frances, amused even in her general depression, sipped some more wine.

"It wasn't us," Laurence said eventually, putting down his knife and fork. "I don't know who Schul was—man or monster, or just a victim—but I *do* know that it wasn't the normal you or I who took part in those terrible events."

"It was us, Laurence. Let's face it: It was us. We may not have been rational at the time, but certainly it was us."

"No, I'm not sure of that. I think we were *inhabited*—that when time changed and we found ourselves in that other world, we were actually taken over in some way and weren't remotely ourselves."

"If that's so, then you needn't feel guilty."

"Yet I feel it. It haunts me."

He shuddered, then glanced down at his plate, studying the unfinished food in a distracted manner.

"I feel guilty because I was aware of who I was and what was happening—but I *still* feel that I was somehow inhabited—that the three of us were. We were in another time, another place, but we were being . . . *controlled.*"

They were silent after that, unhappily struggling through the meal; then, when the waitress came to remove their plates, Frances ordered another bottle of wine. When it was delivered, she filled up both their glasses, then settled back in her chair, feeling a little bit better.

"I killed a man," Laurence said, "and I'm not sure why I did it. And even now, I wonder who Schul was or how he came to be there."

He was staring intently at her, trying to gauge her reaction, but she simply had a sip of her wine and remained very cool.

"You said that when you got back to the States you were going to check with the authorities to find out what they'd discovered about Schul. Did you ever do that?"

"Yes," Laurence replied. "And that's why I'm even more baffled. 'Schul' was his name all right. Jack Schul. He was a perfectly normal American citizen, born and bred in Atlantic City, and with a long list of petty misdemeanors to his credit. Mainly boardwalk and casino confidence tricks and muggings —nothing too serious—but he'd been in and out of corrective institutions and jails most of his life. Nothing special about his parents, either: his father a garage mechanic, his mother a cleaning lady, both dead in a highway pile-up when Schul was still just a kid. And it was also confirmed that he had an American friend who was married to an Englishwoman and lived with her in Glastonbury. Finally, I discovered that our misleading report of Schul's drowning in Iraq is the only record they have of him since his initial arrival in Great Britain. So, it would seem that when Glastonbury disappeared, Schul did indeed vanish with it."

"When Glastonbury disappeared, so did most of its inhabitants. However, none of those people was ever seen again, whereas Schul turned up in Iraq."

"Right," Laurence said.

His cheeks were flushed, either with alcohol or excitement, and he had another sip of his wine, then nodded abstractedly.

"This was not an isolated incident—" he began.

"My mother said that," Frances intervened.

"Well, your mother was right. Since the disappearance of Glastonbury, there's been a worldwide series of reports of disappearances—mainly of individuals and vehicles—many of which were related to UFO reports. Naturally it was widely assumed that such reports were largely hysterical reactions to the Glastonbury disappearance, but it soon became clear that many of the reports *were* in fact genuine mysteries, most of them remarkably similar. All the reports came from seemingly sane people who claimed to have watched friends or relatives disappearing abruptly before their eyes. And naturally what was most horrible was that most of the victims were reported to have called out repeatedly for help from the very area into which they had disappeared, their voices often crying out for hours before fading away completely."

Through the window, Frances saw the clouds moving over the green hills of the Heath, casting their shadows on the winding, red-rust paths that wound through the densely clustered trees. The clouds were starting to cover the sun and turn the afternoon gray.

"Anyway," Laurence continued, "according to various newspaper reports, examination of some of the more notable sites has shown them to be displaying an unusually high degree of magnetic fluctuation—which, as you may recall, is exactly what we noticed when the dark mass first started dropping around us."

"Magnetism?" Frances said, feeling drunk and a little confused.

"Gravity," Laurence explained. "Gravity or magnetism. When that dark mass dropped over us, we all felt a lot heavier, as if the earth's gravity had increased and was pulling us down; then, during those periods when the dark mass had disappeared, the pull of gravity, or earth's magnetism, returned to normal."

"I still don't get what you're driving at," Frances said, pouring herself another glass of wine.

"Examination of the Glastonbury area," Laurence continued, "has so far revealed that it's undergoing very dramatic magnetic fluctuations. Also, the few witnesses who luckily managed to remain outside the so-called vanishing zone confirmed that what appeared to be an enormous dark mass—just like the one we saw near Al-Qurna—dropped over the area that disappeared. Finally, a great many of the other vanishing zones have shown the same kind of unusual geomagnetic disturbances. So Glastonbury, Al-Qurna, and those other, smaller areas all seem to be part of the same phenomenon."

"*What* phenomenon?" Frances asked.

"I don't know," Laurence replied. "Obviously they represent some kind of spatial-time zone that can suck people and objects into it, and from which no escape is likely."

"*We* escaped," Frances said, wanting to stand up and run away. "*We* finally got out."

"Right," Laurence said. "And that only makes it more baffling. But I think it may be tied to the fluctuating nature of the geomagnetism."

"Laurence, can we please talk about something else?"

"No," he replied, sipping some wine and looking excited. "That dark mass kept dropping over us and then disappearing again, as if affected by the fluctuating magnetic field. However, each time it returned, it stayed for longer than the time before, which suggests that it was gradually gaining strength and durability with each of its visits. So it's possible that at Glastonbury and those smaller areas, the vanishing zones were strong enough to suck in the present, then, when the masses moved elsewhere, to carry the present off with them. While that *may* have happened, it's also possible that in our case the dark mass was only gradually gaining strength—which is why it was still coming and going—so we may have made our escape just before it became permanent and trapped us for good."

"And where did all those *other* poor bastards get transported to?" Frances asked sarcastically.

"I don't know," Laurence replied, ignoring her sarcasm, "but it's possible that in one sense they could be exactly where they were before, but in some kind of invisible, parallel world outside known time and space."

Frances thought of what her mother had said about this same subject, and that made her feel even more uneasy. . . . *Ghosts don't have to rattle chains,* her mother had said. *They might be perfectly normal. . . .* Recalling those words, and also thinking of her own secret condition, Frances could not prevent her hand from shaking when she picked up her glass.

"Are you all right?" Laurence asked.

"Yes," Frances replied, sipping at her drink. "So what about Schul?"

Laurence sighed. "God knows. I've thought about it often enough, but the more I think of it, the more it baffles me. Apparently he fell asleep on a bench on the lower slopes of the Tor, just outside the range of the vanishing zone. Maybe that's why he didn't disappear for good. Maybe he was just trapped in the fringe of the vanishing zone and was transported somehow to Al-Qurna. I'm convinced that the two dark masses were linked together some way—that they were gateways through time and space—and that Schul, being sucked in through one gate, was spat out the other." He shrugged. "It's a mystery."

The afternoon had turned gray and the pastoral heath now seemed ominous; the shadows of the trees stained the paths that coiled into the darkness.

Frances sighed and started nervously tapping a silver spoon against its silver-rimmed sugar bowl.

"So," she said eventually, hardly knowing what she meant. "You've come all the way from the States just to discuss this?"

She felt his thin fingers tightening over her hand, forcing her to stop her nervous tapping and turn back toward him.

"No," he said. "It's not the *only* reason I'm here. I'm also here because I can't forget what happened between us in that awful place."

"Between *us?*" Frances replied. "It was between me and *Schul.* And God knows, given the circumstances, anything that happened between *us* has no meaning now—other than as some kind of nightmare we have to try to forget."

"No, Frances, I don't think we should do that. And I don't want to forget what I did because Schul was abusing you. There's a meaning to all this. I think it may have been preordained. According to all the evidence we were near the original Garden of Eden—and I'm convinced that in some way we were reliving the birth of mankind."

"Oh, dear God," Frances murmured.

"It's *possible,* Frances! I'm certain of it! That thing took us back in time, to when we were still clearly human—to Eden. Then it took us back even farther—to the dawn of mankind."

Frances stared wildly around the restaurant, noting how crowded the tables were, trying to lose herself in that generalized human chatter but dismally failing to do so. Laurence was squeezing her hand more tightly, tugging at it to draw her attention . . . and it was then that she remembered her condition and thought of a way to protect herself.

"Don't you see?" Laurence said. "It might have been preordained. I wanted you, Frances—in that hell I learned to love you—and I killed Schul, the serpent in our Eden, because of that love. I loved you then, Frances, as I love you now . . . and I think it was preordained."

Frances jerked her hand from his, feeling as if she had been stung, then sat up very straight in her chair while she studied his face. His hazel eyes were almost weeping, brimming over with emotion; his lower lip was visibly trembling as he breathed far too loudly. *Religious mania,* she thought. Maybe he had that tendency . . . But she thought of what had happened in Iraq and her fear washed that hope away. Her mother's words rang in her head—*Ghosts don't have to rattle chains*—then she thought of the condition she was in and almost gagged in her panic.

She soon managed to control herself and sat up straight in her chair, after which, stretching her hands out on the table, she spoke in a level tone.

"I think you need a good sleep," she said. "You must be suffering from jet lag."

And forced a smile when she said it.

She was not smiling that evening when, after Laurence had gone to bed, she had a brandy and coffee with her mother in the elegant drawing room. Her mother immediately launched into a discussion about Laurence, eventually arriving at the conclusion that he seemed a decent sort, if rather nervous.

"He might be good for you, dear," she said. "At least he's not gross and bullying. And we should not let the fact that he's an American detract from his main virtue, namely, a distinct sense of decency that should make him worth having."

"I'm not interested in him, Mother."

"Why not? He's besotted with you. And I *do* think that a younger man—and one who worships you—could give you stability."

"I'm stable enough, thanks."

"No, you're not."

"Then I have good reason not to be."

After the wine in the restaurant and a third, even stronger bottle over the evening meal with her mother, Frances was hoping that the large brandy would help her to sleep. Unfortunately, even as she sat there talking to her mother, she realized that she had drunk herself beyond sleep and would probably be in for another restless night.

"Don't torment me, Mother," she said. "I feel bad enough already. And Laurence's turning up here doesn't help—it just makes me feel even more haunted. I keep reliving what happened, over and over again, to the point where I'm losing track of the real world, or maybe going insane."

"Nonsense," her mother said. "Not while *I'm* here. So, what did he say to you over lunch that made it all worse?"

"Parallel worlds," Frances replied. "Almost the same thing

you said. Except that he seems to think it was preordained for some as yet unknown purpose."

Her mother stared oddly at her, as if disturbed by her own thoughts.

"Well, my dear," she said eventually, "he may be correct. Who knows in such matters? As for turning the event over and over in your mind, I need only remind you that many so-called ghosts are noted for endlessly repeating the same action, and that most of we mediums have always insisted that the world is full of bewildered spirits who, unaware that they are dead, wander around helplessly. Accepting, then, that death does not really exist—as I do—we are left with the question of just *where* such creatures are wandering about. Parallel worlds? Thought-matter imprinted upon time and space? A world where past and future do not exist, but only the eternal, ever recurring present? It's worth thinking about."

"Are you saying we were reliving our lives in an eternally recurring present? That we were witnessing the ghosts of *ourselves*? That *Schul* was a ghost?"

"It's possible, dear. *All* things are."

Frances wasn't amused at all. In fact, she felt panic. The walls of the room seemed to be closing in on her, threatening to crush her.

Her mother sniffed, obviously thinking, then glanced across the room, her eyes magnified by her spectacles and clearly still intelligent, taking in the furniture, paintings, and antiques with an expression that suggested she was recalling her whole life.

All human lives were artifacts, constructed from bits and pieces, marked at their passing by possessions and a lifetime of paperwork. This room was time immemorial—past and future in the present—and Frances felt, as her own childhood came alive before her eyes, that what had happened in the Garden of Eden may not have been so miraculous.

She shivered, badly shaken, thinking of Laurence in the room upstairs . . . and, in so doing, was inevitably reminded of her own secret, frightening condition.

Her fear turned to a terror that actually made her hands shake, but she managed to put the glass to her lips and finish the last of her brandy. It burned down inside her, then made her mind glow; she felt wide-awake to the point of incandescence, seeing everything brilliantly.

Yet what she saw with such clarity was an unremitting night-mare, a mystery whose nature, if revealed, could be beyond her poor reasoning. She could not face that alone, nor endure it in noble silence, and as she thought of Laurence sleeping, and of what she must do, she turned to the only person she could trust, then gave voice to her terror.

"Don't tell me that Schul was a ghost," she said. "I'm carry-ing his child."

14

FRANCES tossed and turned in bed, feeling as if her skin was burning, torn between some last vestige of puritanism and her desperation and lust. The room was dark but moonlit, pale light beaming in through the window, and she saw her pale, ghostly reflection in the mirror across the room.

She sighed and cursed softly, gripped the sheets, stroked herself, remembered being an adolescent in this same room, tossing and turning the same way.

She decided to do it, but abruptly changed her mind. She changed her mind again and decided to do it, then muttered a soft oath. She thought of her mother in the adjoining room and of Laurence along the hall, then, torn between shame and need, accepted that need would prevail.

Eventually it did and she slid out of the bed, put on her nightgown, tied the belt loosely around her waist, and stood there for a moment. She let her eyes adjust to the darkness, listened for movement outside, heard nothing, so quietly opened the door and looked into the hall.

All the lights were out. There was no sound from her mother's room. Her mother was asleep and could not easily be wakened, and Frances, knowing that, stepped into the landing and quietly closed the door behind her. She then walked along the carpeted landing on her bare feet and, without knocking, opened the door of the guest room and walked in, then closed the door behind her and stood there with her spine pressed against it, studying Laurence.

He had been lying flat on his back, his gaze on the ceiling, but startled by her unexpected entrance, he pushed himself upright and whispered her name querulously.

"Frances?"

"It's all right," Frances said. "Don't say anything. Just lie back on the bed."

"What—?" he replied, confused.

"You heard me," Frances said, speaking firmly. "Just lie back and be quiet."

Laurence made no move but merely stared disbelievingly at her, so she walked up to the bed and stood there looking down at him. He seemed a lot less naive than he had been when they first met, but his upward gaze still held the light of a mild sexual panic.

Taking a deep breath and slowly untying her nightgown's belt, Frances remembered how her Italian lover had stood over her in a similar manner—smiling at her, first with tender regard, then with arrogant mockery. She did not smile at Laurence but simply held him with her gaze. Then she let the belt fall, opened her nightgown, and watched his eyes widening.

"Frances, we—"

"Don't say a word. Just lie back."

He did as he was bid, sliding down under the sheets, letting the moonlight fall back over his face and naked white shoulders. Frances let her robe drop off, knowing just what she was doing, and felt the cool air on her warm skin, making it tingle. Then she jerked the sheet away and slipped in beside Laurence, turning sideways, her breasts pressing against his arm, stomach touching his hip.

"Your mother—" he began hoarsely.

"She's well asleep," Frances said. "And she couldn't be wakened by a bomb, so there's no need to worry."

He offered no reply, but she heard his heavy breathing, felt the heat of his arm against her breasts, his hard, heavy hip. He was wearing pajama bottoms, which mildly amused her, and when she placed her outspread fingers on his chest, his heart started racing.

"Are you a virgin?" she asked him.

"Frances, *please,* you know I can't—"

"All right," she murmured, breathing into his ear. "You don't have to answer."

She pressed herself closer to him, breasts flattening against his arm, felt a tremor rippling through him, his thigh's heat at her stomach. He closed his eyes—like a virgin—then his body quivered lightly. His shoulder's heat was enough to harden her nipples as she breathed in his ear. He kept his eyes closed while she bit his earlobe. She slid her tongue into his ear, licked and sucked, and he gave a light gasp.

Her fingers were still spread out on his chest above his quickening heartbeat.

"Oh, Frances," he sighed.

She did not kiss him. Instead, she ran her tongue over his cheek and closed lips, slid it down his unshaven chin, opened her lips to suck the side of his sweating neck. He sighed, breathing quicker. She ran her fingers across his chest. She remembered the Italian running his fingers over her belly as she did the same thing to Laurence. The Italian had been an expert, removing her clothing as if by magic; she thought of that as her fingers crept down Laurence and slid through his pubic hair.

"Oh!" he groaned as he hardened, unable to resist his growing flesh; then she removed her clinging lips from his neck, sucked his chest, then a nipple.

"Please, Frances," he whispered.

Yet he made no move toward her but just lay there quivering lightly, momentarily paralyzed by his own innocence, lost in his helpless needs.

She slid her fingers down lower, touched the root of his rising penis, sucked his chest as she turned her hand around to undo his buttons. She felt his fingers around her wrist, trying to tug her hand away, but she merely bit his nipple and felt his fingers slide off her, his hand falling back onto the mattress with the sound of a light slap. His body arched as she unbuttoned him and pulled his clothing apart; she smiled and pressed the palm of her hand into his groin, her thumb and forefinger forming a ring that slipped smoothly over him.

"Take them off!" she commanded. *"Take them off!"*

He did as he was bid, automatically, like a child, instinctively managing to wriggle out of his clothing without slipping out of her grasp or moving away from her body.

She was still lying on her side, breasts and belly pressed against him, but she curled up, knees sliding across him, to press her lips to his stomach. He quivered like a bowstring, breathing in spasms, gasping loudly, while she slid her tongue into his navel and felt his groin heaving.

Her Italian lover had done that to her and she melted at the memory of it: he had turned his wet tongue like a corkscrew inside her until she was sobbing. Now Laurence was actually groaning, rolling his groin against her mouth, and she squeezed the bone-hard muscle searching for her as she lapped up his sweat.

The bells seemed to be ringing over the rooftops of Ravello as she pulled the sheet off Laurence's body and curled over his white skin.

"Oh, Frances! *Oh, God!*"

He had finally nerved himself to touch her, but only to stop her foraging, fingers sliding through her hair to grip her head and try to pull her back up. Frances knew what he wanted—the absolution of a normal kiss—but she also knew that would return him to an inhibiting awareness of his lack of sexual experience.

So she ignored him and simply moved a little lower, forcing him to release her head and instead place his hands on her bent back. His erection was hot and smooth, slipping easily through her fingers; she let the tip of his penis graze her lips as she breathed warmly over him. He gasped and groaned some senseless words. She thought of how her Italian had taught her. He had thrust in and out in languid motions that made every nerve sing. His hands on her hips. Making her undulate and roll. He had waited until he had coaxed her into a state where will and pride had no meaning. Her skin melting divinely. Rivulets of flesh and sweat. He had waited until her lips had lost control and then pressed his thumb over them. She remembered as she breathed on Laurence, her lips opening, tongue extending: the Italian had insistently pressed her lips with his thumb until she had sucked it into her mouth like a child with a nipple. So hungry to have it. Sucking greedily, seeking life. She had hardly noticed the difference between his thumb and the larger probe of his penis. Her lips had parted to let him in, without awareness, drinking thirstily; and after that, again, then again and again, until, with awareness, came greed and yet another addiction.

So it was now with Laurence. His erection had no pride.

Frances opened her lips and sucked him in as his groans sounded distantly.

"Oh, Christ!" he blasphemed.

His groans sounded like distant bells, filling her head in that stifling apartment, people chattering in the street just below where the white walls met Roman stones. It was summertime in Ravello, the afternoon bright and hot, and she watched her sweat dripping off her breasts and falling onto his belly. *"Sì,"* he murmured. "My little whore. You learn so well, so quickly." And touched her with his hardness, divided her thighs and lips, showed her how to lean across him as she now did with Laurence, moving her lips up and down the smooth, pulsing length of him.

Laurence groaned and whispered something. He took hold of her head again. This time he didn't try to pull her away, but instead coaxed her lower. She held him in her hand, lightly pressing on his scrotum. When he quivered she slid her lips off him and slowly sat upright.

He was writhing on his back, his hands clawing at empty air. He opened his eyes to stare blindly upward through oblique lines of moonlight. "What—?" he said, his voice hoarse, hands falling back by his sides, rolling his groin to raise himself higher as she slid one leg over him.

An innocent . . . no more. She would enslave him through his flesh. She raised herself on her knees above his body, her legs spread out across him. She felt her sweat trickling down between her breasts as his eyes fixed upon them. Dazed eyes, almost mad. Eyes drinking in her body. She leaned forward while rolling her hips to locate and then hold him. He touched lightly, divided her, slid smoothly in, entering as she leaned lower, still swinging her hips, to let his hungry mouth suck her breast and release more old memories.

Night. The silvery moonlight. Her Italian lover had taught her well. She thought of her mother sleeping in the next room as Laurence pushed up more frantically. Filling her. Melting her. Making her lose her senses. She moved her other breast to his mouth to let that be sucked as well. He was thrusting up, quivering, and she slid her hands beneath him, taking hold of his constricting buttocks and pulling him higher.

"God!" he sobbed. "Oh, that's wonderful!"

She sat upright again, still rolling her hips, turning left and then right, staring down and taking pleasure from his face, which was a wide-eyed, slack-jawed mask of ecstasy. He was running his hands around her body, exciting himself by watching, then she felt herself rising off him, sinking back and flowing warmly around him.

Her Italian had taught her to lose herself and she was starting to do that now; her head filled with fleeting visions and echoing sounds: of motes of dust at play in striations of sunlight while church bells tolled mournfully from the square above the steep, pirouetting roads. Italy: *Ravello.* A mother and daughter on vacation. She had seen her own virgin blood on the white sheet and blushed like a child. A beginning. No more than that. First love, then humiliation: she had ended on hands and knees on the floor, being told what to do.

How could she have resisted? No more than Laurence could right now. He was crying out, convulsing, spilling himself inside her, as a clock chimed downstairs in the dark hall, announcing the midnight hour.

"Oh, God!" he cried. *"God!"*

Frances sank back upon him, plunging into her own feelings, letting his convulsions subside before rising off him. She twisted onto her back, felt him trembling beside her, again placed her hand on his chest to feel his heart racing wildly.

She kept her hand there for some time, listening patiently to his gasping, aware that she had wanted him desperately as her only protection. She was pregnant with Schul's child and could not face that alone. She didn't know who Schul had been, nor what his child might become, and the possibilities lay upon her thoughts like acid on bare skin. Terror shook her leaf and bough, reminding her of what she was doing here: She had to enslave Laurence through his love and make him stay with her.

She started again for that very purpose, massaging him, making him harden, spreading her legs as he groaned and rolled on top of her, his eyes blind with rapture.

"God, I love you!" he whispered, poised above her, bewildered, his body shaking with the tension of desire, beads of sweat on his skin.

She raised her hips to take him in, curling her legs around him, pulled him down and tasted his tongue for the very first time. He sobbed, his tears glistening. She stroked his spine and sweaty flanks. She heard the bells of Ravello, saw the light outside the window, felt the Italian pressing upon her before burning up into her. He had taught her many things and now she passed them on to Laurence, carrying him up to where love became so strong that it rendered him senseless.

"Oh, God!" he sobbed. *"Please!"*

He moved rapidly in and out, penetrating her deeply, his instincts taking over his inhibitions and giving him confidence. He moved faster, still faster, breathing harshly and groaning loudly, until she felt him coming, the spasms starting deep inside him, rippling up through his straining body before exploding out of him, making him go into a series of convulsions, then quiver and sob.

He writhed helplessly on top of her, twisting this way and that, then raised his body and pressed down with his groin, gripping her so hard she hurt. The spasms whipped repeatedly through him, making him seem like a man in torment, but eventually, with a loud gasp, he fell back down upon her, collapsing within himself, then pressed his left cheek to her breasts, to just lie there, trying to get his breath back.

Frances slid her hands over him, stroked his tangled hair, studying the moonlit ceiling above her and remembering Italy.

Shortly after, Laurence wept, kissed her breasts, sucked her fingers. He dried his eyes, then lay beside her in the darkness, staring up at the moonlight. Neither spoke for a long time. Frances let the silence linger. She knew that sooner or later the silence would force him to speak to her.

Eventually he did, taking a deep breath, sounding nervous. He told her that he loved her, that he would never stop doing so, that he worshiped the very air she breathed and would do anything for her.

When he had told her that she smiled, slightly, enigmatically, then rolled over with the elegance of a cat, onto her stomach. She stretched out her right hand, groping blindly behind her, searching for him and, quickly finding him, guiding him into her.

"Do it this way," she said.

IT was soon clear that Laurence didn't know what he had let himself in for. He didn't so much move formally into the house with Frances as simply, at her request, make no visible attempt to leave. At first he had been reluctant, embarrassed about her mother, but Frances insisted that it was absolutely necessary, and her conviction, plus the fact that Laurence now felt feverish just looking at her, guaranteed his acquiescence in the matter.

"You've got to stay," she said. "I can't bear to face it alone. I think that what you told me is true—that this was all pre-ordained. You and I were meant to meet, we were destined to share what's coming—and whatever it is, good or bad, we have to face it together. So stay here. You *know* you want to stay. You know you want *me.*"

She didn't tell him she was pregnant, least of all by Jack Schul, and admonished her mother not to tell him either, lest he hurry back home. He might still have the will to do that—it was highly unlikely, but possible—and she wanted to be sure that when her pregnancy became obvious, he would then be so addicted to her, he would find it impossible to leave.

"You should tell him you're pregnant," her mother chastised her. "What you're doing is immoral. You're keeping him here under false pretenses, which will only make things worse later, but I'm sure that if you tell him the truth, he will treat the matter most sensibly."

"I *can't* tell him, Mother. He'd just take fright and run. He still can hardly bear the mention of Jack Schul's name, so discovering that I'm carrying Schul's child will, particularly at this point, scare him into doing God knows what."

"Perhaps you're right, dear. In this matter you may know best. And it may indeed have been preordained, so the child must be protected."

The thought of the child terrified Frances and overwhelmed her shame, helping her to justify the deception involved in her whore's game. She sincerely believed that Laurence was part of this, that he was somehow meant to be here, but she also knew that what she was doing with him was more than she had to. She certainly did not love him, but she genuinely felt bound to him, perhaps because of what they had been through together in that place which still haunted her. There was that and her own lust, her desperate need for obliteration; and because since her return she had not been able to approach any other men, Laurence, if not her usual type, was at least someone to cling to.

And cling to him she did, letting her body find expression, drowning her fear in that overriding sensuality which, though always a weakness, had recently become even more pronounced, fanning the flames of lust night and day. So she made love in Laurence's bedroom like a whore in a brothel, and Laurence, though unable to resist her, was appalled and ashamed.

"What does your mother think?" he asked her. "She must know what's going on."

"She thinks we're a young couple in love," Frances lied, "and she's a very modern mother that way."

Laurence was skeptical but tried not to show it, already caught in the web of his desire and puritanical guilt. He wanted Frances—yes, he could hardly wait to touch and be touched— but his lust was like a rose caught in the thorns of disbelief and inhibition. He had often thought of love, wanting the heat of its tender flame, but nothing had prepared him for the shock he had felt that first night at the discovery that Frances, the woman he loved, knew tricks which he had never imagined decent women would practice.

"Do it this way," she said.

"Frances, no!"

"I like it—so do it."

Frances knew what she was doing to him, but extracted pleasure from it, remembering that apartment in Ravello where her childhood had ended. She passed on what she had been taught, letting pleasure lead to addiction, often thinking of Laurence looking on in revulsion as she did the same things with Schul.

She thought constantly of Eden, of that lush garden beyond time, of that even earlier time in which a bitch-beast had rutted in the dust, squealing either in pleasure or in rage. Had the other beast been Schul or some bizarre apparition? She was haunted night and day by that question, and knew that Laurence was too. So, she used that, making him do what Schul had done, letting his ecstasy overrule his moral qualms, turning him into her slave.

"You like it," she said to him.

"Please, Frances! Dear God!"

"If you find it that disgusting, just stop."

"You *know* I can't! God forgive me!"

She used his religious beliefs against him, destroying his faith as she freed his lust, turning him into an addict who lives for his fix. She showed him what she had been taught, blandly ignoring his disgust, then observed his disbelief at what he was doing, even as he surrendered.

He was shocked, humiliated, tormented by his growing needs —and ashamed of himself at night, he would be more so by day when he had to sit in the drawing room with Frances and her mother, sipping tea and making idle chitchat. He could barely look in a mirror, much less at Mrs. Devereux, but the old lady lacked similar inhibitions when she fixed her gaze on him.

"You had a good sleep, Laurence, dear?"

"Yes, Mrs. Devereux, fine."

"Most Americans don't know how to relax, dear, but you're obviously more sensible."

Laurence thought that Mrs. Devereux knew nothing about Eden, and so, given instructions by Frances, he avoided raising the subject. However, Frances talked about it—frequently and fearfully—usually when they were in Laurence's bedroom in a tangle of soaked sheets. She often did it when they were naked, tangled up just like the sheets, their sweat glistening in the fractured, moonlit darkness, their words cleaving the silence. She talked even as Laurence groaned, quivering helplessly at her silken touch, coming into the velvet glove of her fingers while she nibbled his ear.

"I knew what I was doing," she said, "but didn't always know who I was. When we went back in time, right back to the dawn of man, I *felt* things, rather than thinking them, though I did have awareness. Sometimes I remembered names. I was aware that you were watching. Even when we did it on all fours, like animals, I was only dimly aware of my shame, and might not really have felt it—I might just have remembered it."

When she talked about it, she excited him almost to the point of mania, rendering vivid in his mind what he had witnessed in outrage and revulsion. Yet even loathing it, he wanted it; despising himself, he had to have it; and often shivering at the thought of his weakness, he still had to give in to it.

Frances knew by his beating heart, gauged his needs from his widening eyes, made him keep them open and focused on her while she spread her legs and lowered herself patiently on his hard, slick erection. She writhed in abandonment above him, rising and falling with blatant relish, tugging his hands to her breasts, to her buttocks, sliding herself through his sweating palms. She did all that and more—much more—and made him keep his eyes open.

"You have to *look,*" she said. "Seeing is almost as good as touching. You think you love me, but you really lust after me because of what you have seen: Schul and me in that awful place, both naked, on the ground, me either on my knees while I used my mouth on him, or on hands and knees with him behind me, displaying his strength. That excited you—yes, you explored yourself because of that—and doing that, you had to remember what you had seen and relive it in darkness. I saw you. We *both* saw you. Trying to satisfy yourself. And Schul, when watching *you*, would become excited and have to take me again."

Laurence cringed at such stories, but became more aggressive, almost fighting through his puritanical, Christian guilt to dominate her more fully. She wanted that, needed it, could not be satisfied without it, and plunged him into new depths of despair because he could not make her climax.

She writhed wildly in her frustration, gripped the sodden sheets, groaned and cursed, clawed his spine as she pulled him down and rolled upon him to slide her body along him. In that soaked bed in the dark room, in that house in the silent night, Frances took him and made him a part of her until they both became one, molded to the pores of each other's flesh by the heat of their passion.

Yet Laurence, though exhausted and dripping with sweat, could only express his despair.

"This isn't love," he said. "It's lust and self-satisfaction. It's not even healthy sex—it's depravity—and it cheapens us both. Why do you act like this? Why do you make us do these things? I despise myself for doing what we do, yet once I start I can't stop. You like that, don't you? It turns you on more than the sex. Maybe it *was* the real you in that place, performing for Schul. Oh, my God, I feel sick."

"There's more," Frances replied, her voice mellow. "We haven't really begun yet. Now pass me the oil."

Most assuredly, Laurence didn't know what he had let himself in for. And as the days came and went, as his lust swamped his disgust, he began to feel even more bewildered by what had happened in Iraq, was happening right here in London, and would surely come to some kind of conclusion in the frightening future. Frances talked constantly about it, when Laurence was calm or in a fever, and soon, when he wasn't being tormented by that subject, he was being haunted by the conviction that this house itself might be unreal, filled as it was with ghostly knockings and bizarre manifestations.

"That's just Mother," Frances explained.

Laurence had already been compelled to adjust to the stream of elderly people, many of them very strange indeed, who poured twice each week into Mrs. Devereux's drawing room where, before the doors were shut in his face, he would see them partake of tea and biscuits.

When Frances explained to him that the people were gathered there to have a spiritualist séance, Laurence at first put it down to typical English eccentricity. However, during one of those evenings—when he was flat on his back in the darkened bedroom, with Frances's lips sliding diabolically over and along him; when he had just clutched at the bedsheets and opened his eyes to beg "No more!"; when in fact he was on the verge of another delicious, guilt-ridden climax—he was jerked out of his reverie by a distant, steady knocking that seemed to emanate from the floor directly below him and reverberate, as if magically amplified, through his dazed, spinning thoughts.

"Oh, God," he groaned, "what's *that?*"

"That's just Mother," said Frances.

On that and subsequent nights he was forced to continue
making love to Frances (or, more precisely, being made love to)
while the floor resounded with knocking, tables tapped, crock-
ery rattled, or macabre shrieks and groans arose from the elegant drawing room directly under his bedroom.

Already lost in a bewildering, hallucinatory world of flesh,
sweat, moonlit darkness, and burning breath; of tears, entreat-
ies; prayers and whispered obscenities; of mortal shame and
profane desires that often carried him close to delirium—already trapped in that incandescent dream of sexual madness,
Laurence could scarcely take in the reality of this latest en-
chantment.

Indeed, with his every pleasure tainted by the persistent
thought that Mrs. Devereux might overhear his ecstatic cries
and gasps, Laurence was thrown deeper into the vats of his fear
and confusion by the knowledge that a collection of English
lunatics was attempting to speak to the dead in the room below
him, even as he was engaged in a sexual adventure of the most
unspeakable kind.

Unspeakable at least to him, or to the puritan he had been,
since he wanted to love and be loved in return, but instead
found himself with a woman whose appetites outraged his
moral nature even as, in attempting to satisfy her, he was shuddering helplessly.

"What's *that?*" he whispered.

"That's just Mother," Frances said. "She's a medium and
claims the spirits speak through her, which is what you're hearing right now. They groan and shriek a lot. I really don't know
why. I haven't joined in on a séance for years. Now pass me the
oil."

He passed over the oil and let her soaking hands massage
him, felt himself melting into her fingers and becoming part of
her. He often stared in amazement at her, disbelieving her lewd-
ness, hardly able to credit that she was actually Frances Devereux, unable to reconcile that cool, middle-class English doctor
with this aggressively wanton woman who, naked and
unashamed, displayed the most unsavory appetites imaginable,
making demands that he tried to resist even as they aroused
him.

"You drive me wild," he said. "You reduce me to moral tur-
pitude. You get me to do things that I can't believe I'm actually

doing—and yet it isn't enough for you. You never seem to get satisfaction, and you hate me for that."

"Tie me up," she replied.

"Oh, my God! No, I won't!"

"There's no harm in it."

"It's not right! *I won't do it!*"

At such times he could take no more and would break down into tears, these often leading to waves of religious guilt and the need to confess. A good Catholic, a mission worker, he would fall to his knees on the floor and there, stark naked, tears flowing, pray with deep fervor.

Yet even that was no solution, and certainly no protection from Frances, since she would often, even then, in the very middle of his praying, move directly in front of him, her groin close to his face, silk panties small enough to accentuate her mons veneris; then, as he was praying, she would slip her fingers between his lips, immediately stopping his talk, transforming his confession into a greedy devouring and making his shame crumble before his lust. So there in that fraught darkness, signifying a fresh surrender, he would try to take his fill, drinking drunkenly of her essence, his senses flying away as he heard her seductive whispering, felt her fingers in his hair, smelled the oil on her writhing, gleaming skin when his nose lightly grazed it. Then she would drop down past his face, spreading herself out below him, making him bury his face in her, smelling and tasting her, his lust blending with guilt and inevitable remorse.

The latter would make him tremble when, the next morning, he would have to sit in the drawing room, nibbling biscuits and sipping tea, listening to Frances's mother, the very peculiar Mrs. Devereux, offer the hope that her spiritualist activities in the drawing room directly below him had not disturbed the sleep he surely needed.

"No, Mrs. Devereux, not at all."

"I'm *so* glad," Mrs. Devereux said, biting delicately into a biscuit, then tilting her head to peer at him through her spectacles. "Thing is, my dear boy, that the séances *are* important in that they do, if nothing else, bring great comfort to the poor wretches who come here. They have all, you see, at one time or another, lost someone quite close to them."

"I hear groaning and shrieking," Laurence said. "I wonder what they might be."

"The dead speaking," Mrs. Devereux replied. "Alas, communication is imperfect. There seems to be a great lack of comprehension between the dead and the living. Thus, they make the table tap—once for yes, twice for no—and when angry, or possibly just frustrated, they throw things about. The groaning? The shrieks? I must apologize, since that is me. Not *really* me, of course, but one of my spirit guides speaking through me—either in some unknown babble or in the sounds that you heard. Do you have an interest in such matters, Mr. Gilbride? Then perhaps you should join us."

Frances had told Laurence that her mother knew little about their experience in Iraq, but sometimes when Mrs. Devereux spoke to him, Laurence was convinced that she was reading his mind. She was, of course, a spiritualist medium, and had hinted that Frances might be psychic as well, but Laurence only knew that he felt strangely uncomfortable when she gave him her sweet smile.

He meant to ask Frances about it, and tried to keep his mind on it, but when she came to his room that night, and crept seductively into his bed, her oiled body too quickly found his hardness and splintered his every thought. He was blinded by the pale moon, hypnotized by the fluttering curtains; and bent across Frances, seeing the white line of her spine, feeling her small breasts in his hands and her rump against his belly, he was shriven in the heat of his revulsion and swept back through time.

He saw the fig-leafed gates of Eden melting into the dazzling haze, the green trees turning into stone that was bleached by the sunless sky. She was in the middle of the clearing, hands and knees in the dirt; he knew her name but could not quite remember it as she grunted and heaved. He was filled with lust for her, wanting to do what the other did, and when he looked at the other thrusting behind her, he wanted to kill him.

Then it all dissolved before him, the sky brightening and descending, a fierce light spreading out to obliterate the features of those standing around him. God it was who came down, then His angels took command, making everyone feel terror or awe as they went into hiding.

In the rock hole he still saw her, being taken again, grunting.

He whimpered as the other, standing behind her, displayed his great pleasure. Then the cave was flooded with light and silhouetted creatures entered, advancing on those trembling just out of reach. Different creatures, tall and upright, not speaking, but making strange music as oblivion came. . . .

"—love you, Frances! I love you!"

Returning to her arched spine and the rolling of her buttocks, he would hear himself whispering those words with an almost anguished intensity. Yet she never replied but merely drove him to a greater frenzy, moving with the suppleness of a cat, her heat making his blood boil. He worked at her, in despair, vainly performing as she had taught him, but always found himself exploding ecstatically into a great isolation—aware that once more she had not come and would display her frustration.

"Christ!"

"Please, Frances!"

"Jesus Christ! Oh, my God!"

"Please, Frances!"

"Just tie me up and that will do it. *Damn you, I need that!"*

He refused such demands, his body shuddering with revulsion, his mind still unable to grasp that his love had brought him to this. Was it love? He wasn't sure. He didn't want to face the question. He only knew that he was no longer capable of telling the difference between love and this relentless, enslaving lust and the shame it engendered. Her demands disgusted him, but his compliance shocked him more, and when she begged him to tie her to the bed, he made that the limit—since he sensed that his compliance would cause him to be totally damned.

"Why do you want that?" he asked her. *"Why?* It's not natural! It's *sick!"*

She laughed harshly at that, throwing her head back on the pillow, her swollen breasts thrusting up toward him, her thighs trapping his sweaty hand.

"Natural?" she said mockingly. "You don't know what that word means! What's natural is what comes easily to us—as this does to me. Tie me to the bed, damn you! You've had your pleasure, now give me mine. I can only get satisfaction when I'm helpless, so for Christ's sake unbend."

"Don't blaspheme!" he said.

And yet he thought it *all* a blasphemy, a denial of his faith, and continued, even as he was sinning, to pray for forgiveness. And with those prayers, another, an entreaty for revelation, for the truth of what was happening and *had* happened to be revealed to him.

He was still haunted by Eden, by constant visions of that nightmare, and often, even as he made love to Frances, thought of Schul and her doing it. She had said that she did the same, so he tried to hide behind that, convincing himself that her perverse, shocking needs were a form of escape.

She cupped his testicles in her hand, slid him through well-oiled fingers, licked him and very gently bit him until he was whimpering—yet her skill, which was diabolical, had its roots in despair, her exquisite refinement of touch seemed to spring from her torment.

He often begged her to tell him who had taught her such things, thus reducing her to such baseness, but invariably she replied with a soft, mocking laugh, before making him quiver once more in passion's uplifting agony.

"God forgive me!" he gasped.

With his guilt growing daily in direct proportion to his desire, Laurence still had to suffer the memory of what had happened in Eden. Indeed, there were times when, making love to Frances, he would have of that awful place a recollection so vivid that it would take on a hallucinatory quality. He knew that Frances suffered the same and that her lust was mixed with fear, but this knowledge did not help to ease the pain growing inside him.

In fact, as he gained experience with her, learning the manifold ways of sex, wallowing in his lust and viewing his desires as depravity, his guilt and shame grew, sweeping away his romantic notions, eventually leaving him in a mire of hatred for her because of what she had made of him.

"You've destroyed me," he accused her. "Stripped me of love and pride. You've shown me the gutter, rubbed my nose in the mud, and ensured that I'd become addicted to it, no matter how it disgusts me. Even knowing what I was—a practicing Christian—you did all that to me."

"Stop being so hypocritical," she replied. "I gave you what you were yearning for."

"I'm going home," he said. "I'm returning to the States. I can't live with this any longer, so I'm going to leave."

"Leave?" she replied dreamily, on her knees, between his legs, her warm breath pouring over him as she spoke to make him erect. "I don't think so. Not yet . . ."

He closed his eyes—she now let him close his eyes—and concentrated all his senses on his groin, his new soul, to experience sensations of unbearable intensity, his body quivering like a bowstring, his pores rippling like grains of sand, his fingers electrical on her scalp, seeming to sparkle down her spine, his heart racing as he grew and kept expanding to the point of explosion. And there she stopped him, controlled him, using the contracting rings of her fingers, holding him back while she stroked him to a sensual pitch beyond which lay delirium.

Even then he learned to hate her because of the power she had over him, and would view her as some kind of dark witch who could exalt or debase him. Just that: her expert fingers; his mouth filled with her swollen breast; her white skin gleaming under a sheen of oil against which he could rub himself. Moonlit darkness, writhing limbs, oil, sweat and heat, nimble fingers playing delicate refrains, mouths and tongues joining greedily.

All that and more: Mrs. Devereux; the house itself; the twice-weekly séances; the dead communicating in strange tongues or with sounds that made his flesh crawl. He plunged into despair and rage, hating himself as well as Frances—and then grew more paranoid each time he had to descend the stairs to have tea with the eccentric Mrs. Devereux in that elegant drawing room.

"Frances isn't happy," Mrs. Devereux said. "Alas, poor child, she never was. And unfortunately I do not think your presence here has made an improvement. I must confess, I had hoped for more—but please don't misunderstand me. If I say this, it is not to blame you, but simply to point out the facts. She has *always* been unhappy. I blame that on the loss of her father. I also blame it on that unfortunate affair in Italy, about which, the less said the better."

"Italy?" Laurence murmured. "An affair . . . ?"

"No," Mrs. Devereux continued, smoking a cigarette, puffing smoke, "that was her affair and I refuse to resurrect it. I would just like to discuss, my dear Laurence, your relationship with her. You both shared a terrible experience—we need not dwell

on the details—and this has naturally drawn you closer together than you might have been otherwise. It is therefore good
that you should be here—I think the positive aspects are obvious—but I *have* noticed disturbing changes in Frances that cannot be ignored. I think she is having a breakdown, Laurence.
She cannot forget what has happened to her. And for that reason, no matter your own feelings, I think you should stay on."

"Is Frances psychic?" Laurence asked.

"I beg your pardon?"

"Is she psychic?"

"Her psychic powers are greater than mine, but she refuses to
face that fact. She *feels* things, Laurence—things beyond our
normal perceptions—and I think that's her problem. So, will
you stay on?"

"Yes," Laurence said.

So he agreed to stay—because he thought Frances might be
psychic, because he felt that if she *were* indeed psychic, that
might explain what had happened. He understood what was
happening here—it was why he had turned to God—he had
always felt the breath of the spirit world breathing over his
shoulder. Thus it was possible, as Mrs. Devereux seemed to
think, that his adventure with Frances and Schul had been preordained.

"Why?" he asked Frances.

"God," she said, "I don't know. I only know that I want to
forget about it, but I can't seem to do that."

"Are you all right?"

"All right?"

"You don't feel ill or—?"

"Deranged?"

"I just meant—"

"Just tie me to the bed, Laurence. I can't come any other
way."

In that instance she said it mockingly, but he knew that she
also meant it, and he felt his resolve to stay fading away in the
light of what she was asking. He stared at her, frightened, wondering who he was looking at, still bewildered by what he felt
was her depravity and almost too shocked to speak.

She was sitting in front of him, wearing only her nightgown.
Her brown hair was bathed in moonlight, dark eyes glinting
steadily, and she sat on the edge of the bed with her very long

legs crossed, the lower half of the gown falling off her thighs in a provocative manner.

Laurence despised his hapless lust but remained a victim of it, his breath quickening immediately when he gazed at her pale, unlined skin. He was lost to her and knew it, wanting her more than life itself, but as his hand fell on her knee, clearly out of his control, he tried with the last of his willpower to resist what was coming.

"Tell me about Italy," he said. "I want to know all about it."

She didn't actually move, but he sensed a change in her, then saw an almost imperceptible stiffening of her lithe, treacherous body. His hand slid up and over, finding a space between her crossed legs, and he felt himself hardening as he watched her, wondering how he could do this.

She just stared steadily at him, offering an enigmatic smile, then raised one leg a little, letting his fingers slip into her, and slyly pressed her tender inner thigh back down on his knuckles.

"Italy?" she whispered, while his hand burned and he hardened more. "Why do you want to know about Italy? Has my mother been talking?"

Laurence moved his hand up farther, hardly knowing what he was doing, aware only that the radiant heat coming from her was flooding his loins. He squeezed and stroked her automatically, his hand trapped between her thighs, and was captured by the fathomless depths of her ambiguous gaze. His body shuddered against his will—he tried to stop it, but failed—then he found his fingers touching that softness where one thigh joined the other.

"She just mentioned Italy," he murmured throatily. "Some trouble you had there . . . Now I want to know everything."

Frances opened herself to him, making his heart leap dramatically, and he touched that melting warmth with a thrill that threatened to drown him in pleasure. She sensed that, and smiled, stretching her body like a snake, then managed with a slight roll of her hips to take his fingers right into her.

"Pornography," she whispered. "That was Italy. . . . And that's what you want."

He heard his own choked sobbing, a strange, childish sound, as she smiled, sat up straight, placed her hand on her neck, then slowly, theatrically, with a stripper's practiced skill, tugged the dressing gown off her gleaming shoulders and smooth arms, until it was lying behind her on the bed, leaving her top half exposed.

He saw the marble of her bare skin, the rise and fall of her bosom, then his gaze was captivated by her nipples as they visibly stiffened. *Italy,* he thought obliquely. *I want to know what happened there.* He was contemplating that when her legs moved and his fingers slid farther into her. He sucked his breath in simultaneously, heart racing as he stared at her, then sobbed again, scarcely knowing he was doing it, and, with his free hand resting lightly between her breasts, gradually pushed her back onto the bed.

"God, I want you!" he groaned.

"If you tie me to the bed," she replied, murmuring, "I'll tell you all about Italy."

Laurence felt himself breaking, unable to resist his own greed, and he untied the knot at her waist and jerked the gown from her hips. He stared at her, breathing harshly, leaning over her like an ape, aware only of her supine naked body and his aching erection. His consciousness drained down to there, flooding into his loins, responding in a flare of awareness to the touch of her hand. Her fingertips stroked his penis, one nail scraping along it, and he heard his own breathing like a storm blowing through a deep gorge. Her body lay beneath him, oil-slicked limbs curved in surrender, pale skin smooth on shoulders, soft breasts and a sublime mound of belly.

He shook with shame and longing. Her free hand held his erection. Her fingers slid like well-greased rings along him when he tried to resist her. At that moment he was doomed. His tears came when he saw her smile. He thought of her in that awful place, then of Schul penetrating her, and was starting to fall upon her burning body when her other hand stopped him.

"No!" she said. "Not yet!"

She was supporting him with her free hand, pressing him back with surprising strength. Her other hand was sliding along his penis to press it gently against her. His body quivered and he failed to stop his tears. He stared down at her, stricken, comprehending her through his loins, then noticed something dangling from the hand that was holding him off her.

He cried out in despair. Her other hand slid him inside her. He saw the cords of silk in her free hand, but by then it was too late.

"All right!" he gasped, blinded by tears. "All right, damn you, *yes!*"

He tied her to the bed and did her bidding until the dawn broke. After that, they were enemies.

Book
II

The Present

THE woman who sat in front of Michael in his office in the psychiatric wing of the Royal Free Hospital, recounting her extraordinary experiences in southern Iraq and telling him about a murder that may well have taken place only in her imagination, did not give the appearance of someone suffering from any kind of mental disorder. A rather severe, dark beauty with her long hair hanging loose, she *did* look, in some manner which he could not quite define, slightly older than her stated age; but the simple elegance of her clothing and the unconscious dignity of her poise marked her indelibly as an educated, middle-class woman of considerable refinement.

She answered his questions precisely, talking softly but clearly, her hands folded primly in her lap, resting on top of her handbag. Her lovely legs were crossed, her skirt's hemline above the knees, and although it was true that in general she did not fidget, he noticed that her left leg, crossed over the right, frequently made an almost imperceptible swinging motion which suggested erotic arousal.

When most of the details of her strange adventure had been recounted into his tape recorder, Michael gazed down at his extra notes and sighed disconcertedly. Buying time while he thought, he offered Miss Devereux a cigarette; when she accepted, he lit the cigarette for her, then lit his own and inhaled.

"Do you smoke a lot?" he asked her.

"Very rarely," she replied. "I always carry a pack in my handbag, but I don't often smoke them."

"A bad example to your patients, I suppose."

"Maybe that's it," she said.

She smiled at him for the first time, a remote smile, quietly radiant, and he realized how very attractive she was.

"Before we go any further," he said, "can I just confirm this one vital point: What you're telling me is that God is speaking to you and that you may well be carrying His child. Is that correct?"

"Yes."

"Do you have any conception of who, or what, this God is?"

"No. Just that He is."

Michael nodded and inhaled on his cigarette, realizing that he had a special case here and becoming more interested. "Fine," he said conversationally, exhaling the smoke and watching it disappear. "We'll probably return to that later. Right now, however, I would like to ask you a series of questions, many of which may seem unduly personal and of no relevance to your case, but which are, I can assure you, of great importance. Should any of these questions offend you, please don't hesitate to say so, but try to answer as many of them as possible. Okay?"

"Yes, Doctor."

"You're a doctor yourself, I believe."

"Yes, a general practitioner specializing in tropical medicine —but I haven't worked since I returned from Iraq."

"How are you managing to support yourself?"

"I live with my mother, who has her own income."

"Ah, yes, Mrs. Devereux. I've talked to her. She told me she was a spiritualist medium and seemed to take it quite seriously."

"She takes it *very* seriously, Doctor."

"She also said that psychic abilities ran in her family, and that you had inherited them to an exceptional degree. Is that true?"

"I didn't think so before because I wasn't really interested, but now I think my mother may be right. Normally at her séances she would only obtain routine results—communication through tapping furniture, the odd poltergeist effect, spirit guides speaking through her—but each time I attended there was a dramatic improvement, including some extremely vivid images, or materializations."

"Of the dead?"

"Of people." Miss Devereux shrugged, glancing at the framed diplomas that adorned the plain walls of the office.

"Do you think," Michael asked, "that your psychic abilities had anything to do with your experience in Iraq?"

"I don't know. I think constantly about it—constantly—but I simply don't know."

"And your mother?"

"She believes that my psychic abilities are the channels through which I've been contacted."

"And does *she* believe you're carrying God's child?"

"She says anything is possible. Of course, my mother, as you've doubtless gathered, is a little eccentric."

Michael had in fact been charmed by Mrs. Devereux but not fooled by her. It seemed to him that if Mrs. Devereux had, over the years, picked up more than a few eccentric habits and interests, she had nonetheless lost little of her sharp intelligence, intuition, and perception—to the degree, indeed, where she simply could not be ignored.

"I take your mother's eccentricity with a pinch of salt," he said. "But tell me: Do you know *why* your mother sent you to this particular department?"

"Yes. She thinks I'm having a nervous breakdown."

"Are you?"

"It's possible. I think about this thing night and day, and it's certainly affecting me."

"That shows a healthy degree of self-awareness."

"I'm no fool, Dr. Phillips."

Michael smiled at that, but lowered his head first, fixing his gaze on his notebook but not really seeing it. When he looked up again, she was staring steadily at him, her brown eyes very calm, the smoke from her cigarette spiraling in front of her pale face.

"Call me Michael," he said.

"I'm sorry, but that's too familiar."

"I don't mind that kind of familiarity."

"I do, Dr. Phillips."

Michael studied her at length, surprised by her response, but also finding her severe beauty very attractive . . . indeed, oddly disturbing.

"And what about the man?" he asked. "Laurence Gilbride. Is *he* having a breakdown?"

"Yes," she replied. "I think he's heading that way—and for more than one reason. I think—"

"We'll get back to that later. I need to know other things first."

The very mention of Laurence Gilbride's name had made the woman start gently to swing her left leg again; and when Michael's attention had been drawn to that motion, his gaze automatically narrowing down to where the folds of her thin dress met in the cleft of her compressing thighs, she had instantly ceased the movement but smiled at him, as if reading his mind.

Michael, very much to his surprise, felt aroused and embarrassed.

"Your mother," he explained, grateful for the distraction, "didn't send you here *just* because she thought you were having a nervous breakdown. She also sent you because this particular department is engaged in research into psychological disturbances relating to reported experiences with unusual phenomena. In that respect this department is also involved in investigating the psychological responses of those who have in one way or another been involved with the increasingly widespread incidences of human or material disappearances, notably Glastonbury and its inhabitants; encounters with so-called aliens; sightings of UFOs or mysterious masses of the kind that came down over Glastonbury—and, according to you, over that area in southern Iraq. Your mother, then, wanted you to come to me because your experience is not an isolated one, and because I specialize in just this kind of case."

Miss Devereux leaned forward to stub out her cigarette. She stayed like that for some time, as if in a trance, but finally managed to shake herself from her reverie and sit straight again, crossing her legs in that elegantly sensual manner, leaving her knees and calves exposed to his increasingly disconcerted gaze.

"And you believe that such phenomena are now widespread?" she asked, speaking levelly.

"Yes—and increasingly so." He folded his hands on the desk, strangely pleased by her interest. "This department is currently filled with people who have either had nervous breakdowns, gone totally insane because of—or can simply supply firsthand accounts of—bizarre and frightening events of the kind we cannot rationally explain. Now, while many of these cases undoubtedly are rooted in commonplace trauma, our main interest lies in those cases that are allied to a phenomenon that, though almost too incredible to credit, is becoming common worldwide: namely, the inexplicable, usually permanent, disappearance of people and objects after the materialization of a linear dark mass of variable size. . . . As I said: the very same kind of mass that descended over Glastonbury and, according to you, over your so-called Garden of Eden in Iraq."

"It was not *so-called,* Dr. Phillips. It was definitely Eden."

"Perhaps," Michael replied, not ignoring her note of firmness. "We can leave that aside for now. What matters is that you're convinced that you were transported to another space–time continuum, and your description of that experience tallies remarkably with those of most of our other patients."

"Well," Miss Devereux replied tartly, "it's heartening to know that at least I'm not *completely* alone in my lunacy."

"No," Michael replied with a gentle smile. "Not completely."

"May I have a drink?"

"Tea or coffee?"

"I mean alcohol."

"No, I'm afraid not."

She displayed a flash of anger, then glanced restlessly around his office, again studying the diplomas with what appeared to be professional interest, then letting her gaze roam out the window and up to the sky. She studied the sky for some time, then turned back toward him, watching him as he stubbed out his cigarette and leaned back in his chair.

"So," she said, "you've been investigating the dark masses. What have you found out?"

"Naturally my own concern is with the psychological and, in some cases, physiological effects on those patients who have either been actually engaged with, or witnessed, a dark mass."

"What do you mean by 'actually engaged with'?"

"I mean those people who have actually found themselves *inside* a dark mass, but somehow managed to get out—people like you."

She nodded solemnly. "Go on," she said.

"Let me repeat: My own concern is with the physical and

mental health of the people involved—but my department *is* working hand in hand with a team of specialists who have been attempting to ascertain, scientifically and with the aid of first-hand corroborative evidence, the exact nature of the dark masses—which, it now seems, are starting to gobble up whole portions of the earth. Much more of this has been happening than has generally been revealed by the media, but the situation is becoming more dramatic—*very* dramatic, in fact."

"You mean an increasing number of dark masses are appearing?"

"That's right. A *lot* more."

Miss Devereux uncrossed her legs, then crossed them the other way. Michael, to his consternation, found himself watching that movement with an intensity not experienced since his adolescence. When he managed to raise his gaze from the hands placed back in her lap, he saw that to her calm gaze she had added a slight, enigmatic smile.

"So," she asked, *"what* are they?"

Relieved to be thus distracted, Michael clasped his hands under his chin and said: "Do you know anything about earth's magnetism?"

"Hardly my best subject," she replied, "but I'm sure you'll forgive that."

Michael smiled, actually pleased with her gentle sarcasm. "All right," he said. "Let me give you some background. I'll be as brief as I can."

"I'm very glad to hear *that,"* she replied, then sat back to listen.

"Two points about your own report," Michael began. "One: that when the dark mass was taking shape around you, the atmosphere turned very cold—"

"Correct."

"—and, two: that once inside the dark mass, when the whole space–time continuum changed, you all felt a lot heavier, as if the magnetism of the earth had increased."

"Correct again."

"Okay," he said. "The earth's magnetic field is caused by the electric currents set up in its core by the revolution of the planet about its own axis. However, the magnetic field isn't constant. Short-term variations in the magnetic field can be caused by disturbances of the electrical currents in the ionosphere—and those disturbances are in turn caused by the changeable properties of particular rock formations on the surface of the earth itself, notably the rock known as 'lodestone,' which loses its magnetic properties when heated, but gains *more* of those same properties when *cold*."

He stopped for her response, but she simply smiled a little, then said, "I am listening, Dr. Phillips. I am all ears. Please *do* continue."

He coughed into his fist, tried not to look at her long legs; that forced him to look at her face, which made him just as uneasy.

"It's already well established," he continued, trying not to sound too pedantic, "that under the action of an *external* magnetic force, *all* substances become magnetic to a greater or smaller degree. That's what seems to be happening all over the earth wherever one of those dark masses appears. It would seem that part of the composition of the dark mass is a dense core of electrons that are being affected by—or are utilizing—the more extreme fluctuations of the earth's magnetism, such as those found in areas containing large deposits of the highly magnetic mineral magnetite—in other words, *lodestone.*"

Miss Devereux took a deep breath, then let it out, thus causing her breasts to rise and fall again under her thin cotton dress. Remarkably, although she still looked severe, her sexuality seemed radiant.

"And what areas might those be?" she inquired.

"Generally speaking, areas that are noted as convergence points for what in Britain would be called ley lines; in China, *lungmei,* or the paths of the dragon; in Ireland, fairy paths; in Australia and North America, creation paths. What I'm talking about is geomantry: the theory that the earth is crisscrossed with an enormous network of largely invisible straight lines— the most noted visible ones being those of the Nazca plains of Peru and the unnaturally straight so-called antelope tracks of the Himalayas—and that such lines are known to possess unusually powerful currents of terrestrial magnetism of the kind that can cause atmospheric phenomena. For some unknown reason, all but the few visible magnetic paths converge at points noted for their large quartz or metal content—in other words, lodestone—or in areas to which the lodestone has actually been transported and used for construction purposes, such as the

numerous megalithic-stone rings of this country, or the pyramids or other great buildings around the world."

He paused to gauge if Miss Devereux was actually following
what he was saying. Clearly she was, since she merely stared
steadily at him, then said, "Go on."

Michael sighed. "Recent surveys have shown that in the past
few months there has been an unprecedented drop in temperature—and subsequent increase in magnetic strength—in most
of those areas, with some, such as Glastonbury, displaying a
much greater fluctuation than others. Glastonbury, which
quickly became the coldest and most magnetic of all, was the
first to suffer the visitation of the mysterious dark mass; but
some of the other, less publicized areas that vanished displayed
the same atmospheric conditions as Glastonbury. So it's
thought that if things continue as they are, we can anticipate
the same fate for a large portion of the earth, including some of
its most renowned sites, great cathedrals and buildings known
to be built over highly magnetic prehistoric mounds and, of
course, the world's most famous megalithic monuments, including Stonehenge and Silsbury."

Miss Devereux was now studying him more intently, her
handsome brow wrinkled in thought as she leaned forward
slightly.

"And when the dark masses swallow up parts of the earth,
they replace them with—?"

"Marshland," Michael intervened. "Just like your Garden of
Eden."

She straightened up again, giving prominence to her breasts;
and Michael, disconcerted by his own feelings, took another
deep breath.

"And can I take it, Dr. Phillips, that if we project this theory
further, we have the prospect of a disappearing earth—and the
emergence of a new one very much like the areas already ef-
fected. In short: a new world of primal marshlands."

"So it seems," Michael said.

Aware that he was thinking of Miss Devereux as an attractive
woman as well as a patient, he shifted uneasily in his chair,
vainly attempting to put his thoughts in order. He tried to distance himself from her, to think of her as a patient, but felt his
senses slipping away into a sensual mist. She was sitting very
straight, her brown eyes fixed on him, revealing a peculiar, quiet

mockery and sexual challenge. Was she mad? He thought not. Yet her condition was not normal: he sensed that her calm exterior was hiding terror and obsessional introspection.

God's child. She believed she was carrying God's child. That was something to think about.

She leaned toward him again, her elbow resting on one thigh, the movement pulling the dress back over one knee and emphasizing her long legs. Michael, shocked to realize what he was thinking, kept his gaze on her face.

"I got out," she said. "Laurence and I both got out. How did we manage to escape when no one else has?"

"You're wrong," Michael said. "Other people have escaped also. Admittedly, most of those people were caught on the very edge of the dark mass—which probably explains your other American, that fellow Schul—but certainly they've at least been sucked in and managed to get out again."

"How?"

"I've already explained how the magnetism fluctuates and subsequently affects the electrons within the dark mass. So when the mutual magnetic attraction between the dark mass and the earth is very strong, the dark mass—which we now call the 'Gateway' to the other space–time continuum—temporarily materializes. However, it disappears again when the magnetic field weakens. Laurence and you were obviously sucked into the Gateway when the magnetic field was particularly strong; then, when the magnetic field started weakening—which, incidentally, is why your 'visions' started fading away—the parallel world gradually disappeared and let you escape."

"If that's so, why did Glastonbury and those other areas disappear for good?"

"Because the dark mass comes and goes, growing more powerful each time it returns, until eventually it gobbles up what it's covered and takes it away for good, leaving behind a part of the earth as it must have been many millions of years ago. You made your escape while your dark mass was still fluctuating, but sooner or later that area will disappear for good and the primal marshlands will be left in its place. In other words, your Garden of Eden will eventually be permanent."

She shuddered visibly, glanced around the room, briefly massaged her forehead with her fingers, then stared at him again.

"So," she said, "what actually *started* all this?"

Michael shrugged and spread his hands out in front of him, palms turned upward in a sign of defeat.

"We don't know," he said. "However, our researches into the kind of people who have been involved with the manifestations have given us the notion, alas unconfirmed, that certain people —those who, whether or not they know it, possess exceptionally powerful psychic or paranormal abilities—may actually be releasing the magnetic attraction between the earth and the dark mass, possibly because they have a very high degree of mental disturbance of the kind that can actually affect certain elements —in this case, the electrons that cause magnetic fluctuations to react on the dark mass, thus causing its power to wax or wane."

Miss Devereux responded with a disconcerting silence, before managing to shake herself out of her reverie.

"Then Schul, as well as Laurence, might have had psychic abilities?"

"Yes," Michael replied, feeling drawn to the mystery surrounding her, "that would seem very likely."

"I don't think Laurence is aware that he has any such abilities. In fact, I think he's rather skeptical of such abilities in general."

"But he is, according to your report, a deeply religious person."

"He *was,*" she corrected him.

"Are you telling me that his experience in Iraq *destroyed* his faith, rather than strengthened it?"

"Why should it strengthen it?"

"It strengthened yours."

"That's because my interpretation of what happened was very different from Laurence's—and for a very good reason."

"Your pregnancy?"

"Yes."

Michael thought of lighting another cigarette, but decided against it. Miss Devereux was staring at him, her face severe and oddly sensual, its beauty a combination of intelligence and controlled emotion—or possibly hysteria. There was something fierce and desperate about her, but she was keeping it bottled up, refusing to let it blow her apart as it was threatening to do.

Her left leg, crossed over the right, was still swinging slightly, forcing Michael to remove his gaze with the guilt of a school-boy.

"Okay," he said, trying to sound as casual as possible. "Let's talk about this child you're going to have. According to this new report, Schul wasn't actually drowned *before* being sucked into the dark mass, but was killed by Laurence during your experience in the other space–time continuum."

"Yes, that's correct."

"And that explains why Laurence refused to come here with you."

"That's one of the reasons."

"And the other?"

"His present relationship with me."

"Your sexual relationship?"

"Yes. He thinks that's all tied to the Garden of Eden and what happened there."

"The murder?"

"*And* my relationship with Schul. He thought that I was possessed—that Schul was the devil's disciple—and that what subsequently occurred between him and me had turned him into a sinner. He was disgusted *and* frightened by our affair, so has since turned those emotions directly against me."

"You mean that you now personally frighten and disgust him?"

"Yes, Doctor. Precisely."

"Which means that this child, whom you consider to be God's child, is to Laurence the child of the devil."

"He's wrong," she said instantly.

Her leg stopped swinging, her knuckles tightened in her lap, and her eyes, formerly calm, suddenly flared with a disturbing intensity. Michael, who prided himself on his objectivity, felt that tension sweep over him.

"You definitely had no sexual relations with Laurence in the Garden of Eden?"

"No," she replied, relaxing again. "Only with Schul."

"And did Laurence develop the idea that you were possessed during that time?"

"No. Only after our sexual relationship here had termi-nated."

"What finished the sexual relationship? Did it end when you told him about Schul's child?"

"No. It ended before that. It ended because of the nature of my sexual demands, which he thought were both excessive and unnatural."

"How many times did you have sex each week?"

"Each week?" she asked him. "Or each night?"

Michael stared thoughtfully at her, slightly shocked, quietly amused, then said, "I think you've answered my question." She smiled at him, also amused, but with a challenge in her gaze, so he coughed into his fist, studied his notes, and continued: "It would help if you could tell me why he thought your sexual demands were unnatural."

She shrugged at that, opened and shut her clasped hands, swinging her leg again as she recounted, in a clear, perfectly neutral tone of voice, exactly what she had taught the innocent Laurence each night in her guest room.

Michael listened patiently, then with growing surprise, then found himself staring at her swinging leg and finally into her steady gaze. Her brown eyes were gleaming brightly, then they melted and turned to liquid, limpid pools that drew him in through their darkness to that quiet, moonlit bedroom.

No: not Frances Devereux. It could not be the same person. That severe beauty in the middle-class clothes would not be capable of such things. Yet he heard her and saw her, wanton, unashamed, and his disbelief was mixed with growing desire at what she was telling him.

He lit a cigarette, inhaled deeply, coughed the smoke out, rubbed his eyes and squinted through the smoke to see her slight, enigmatic smile. She had finally stopped talking and was now staring at him, aware of his helpless discomfort and obviously amused by it.

Michael, normally at ease with the opposite sex, endured a self-imposed silence that seemed to last forever, then coughed without reason into his right fist before speaking again.

"Why do you need all that?" he asked carefully. "I wouldn't exactly call it unnatural, but it does seem . . . *extreme.*"

Miss Devereux smiled slightly, then shrugged. "I just need it," she said.

"There *must* have been a *reason,*" Michael insisted.

"It's all in the past," Miss Devereux replied. "It's simply what I got used to."

"What you got *used* to?"

"Never mind."

"And it brings you happiness?"

"Yes."

"I don't think so."

"Think what you will." She did not say it angrily, but as a simple statement of fact, then leaned forward, over her crossed legs, to study him thoughtfully. "Tell me, Doctor," she said, "are you married?"

"I'm divorced," he replied, taken by surprise. "It happened eight years ago."

"I'm sorry to hear that."

She nodded and pursed her lips, obviously still deep in thought. "Do you mind telling me your weight?" she asked eventually, surprising him even more.

"A hundred and seventy pounds," he replied, trying to hide his bewilderment.

She nodded again, then sat back in her chair. "You're very solid," she said. "That's good. I like a man of some substance."

Again taken aback but trying not to show it, Michael inhaled on his cigarette and took his time blowing the smoke out. He tried to meet his patient's gaze, but could not do it for long, and soon found himself glancing down to take note that her left leg, still crossed over the right, had started swinging again.

Disconcerted, almost sighing, he returned his attention to her face, and was at least relieved to see that she was no longer smiling enigmatically but was instead offering a mask of blank, middle-class composure. More confident, if drowsily sensual, he decided to press on.

"Has the intensity of your sexual needs increased since your remarkable experience?"

"Yes," she said. "Definitely."

"Does this bother you?"

"Only in that it forces me to find men . . . and I don't like being reduced to picking up strangers."

"But it doesn't bother you otherwise?"

"No. Why should it? Sex is perfectly normal. In fact, its only abnormality is its ability to help us transcend ourselves. Sex is a doorway to another world, which is why it obsesses us."

"Have you *always* seen sex that way? As a means of transcendence?"

"I've always needed sex very badly—*very* badly—but until

my experience in the Garden of Eden, I had only thought of it as a form of release."

"And since Eden?"

"I need it all the time. It takes me out of myself."

"And why do you think this all started in Eden? Had it something to do with the new environment, or was it the manifestations?"

"They were *not* manifestations, Doctor. Those events were very real. God came down upon us—it was God: He could control us—and His angels, or children, encouraged Schul and I to do what was done. It was not like normal sex—it was transcendence through self-abasement—and its purpose was to raise us beyond ourselves and propagate a new species. Yes, Doctor, a new species: the seed of a new dawning. What I learned in that place is that the body is more than mere flesh . . . it's immortality's doorway."

"So you feel no guilt about your relationship with Schul in that other world?"

"I felt shame at the time—particularly because of Laurence —but then I came to accept that it was God's will: that He had wanted this pregnancy."

"Schul, then, was His instrument?"

"Yes. And died by His hand."

"Why God and not the devil?"

"The devil is in the mind, a creation of man's guilt. It was the eye of God I saw—a great white light descending—and then I felt His children all around me and heard the song of their speech. Their language sounds like singing, but it isn't singing —it's speech—and I understood enough to learn from them that I was one of the first."

"Pardon? One of the first of *what?*"

"One of the mothers to mankind as we know it," Frances Devereux said. "And now soon to be mother to this child— God's child—which will be one of the first children of the new world that you've already described."

She took a deep breath, stretching herself, smiling at him, then spoke with an oddly quiet fervor that he thought might be madness.

"Don't you see, Dr. Phillips? When we were trapped in that dark mass—what you term another space–time continuum—we first found ourselves in what might have been the Garden of

Eden, but then were taken back to an *even earlier* age, at the
very dawn of mankind. We were like apes, Dr. Phillips, with the
most primitive consciousness imaginable, but then that light
came down, and those beings surrounded us, and they somehow
imprinted upon us all what we *and* our offspring would become.
I was an *animal*, Doctor—existing at the dawn of time—and
then I gave birth to a child that was very different from myself,
and that child and his offspring evolved into the first of the
human race. Time shifts back and forth. All exists simultaneously. I found myself in a barren landscape, as some primitive
controlled by gods, then I found myself in that Garden of Eden
as at least a *recognizable* human being. I was a mother to the
human race—not alone, but one of many. Now I'm about to
become a mother to the new race in the world that is dawning."

Michael stared steadily at the woman in front of him, trying
to stay calm and keep his thoughts ordered; to relate what he
had just heard to the woman who had spoken, as well as to the
extraordinary events of the past two or three months.

More dark masses were appearing all over the world, materializing, disappearing, returning again, then gobbling up whatever they had covered and depositing marshlands. Time was
stealing back its creations, space was opening out to accept
them, and springing out of the nothing left behind was a clean,
virgin earth.

And now this woman sat in front of him, one of many spread
worldwide, claiming to be pregnant with the first of a new generation.

Not *just* a new generation—according to her, a new species—
and if that were true, what would the world be like when the
last dark mass had come and gone?

Michael leaned forward, stubbed his cigarette out, then
rested his elbows on the desk and his chin in his hands. He
looked at the calm exterior of Frances Devereux and felt her
stirring emotions.

"God's child!" he murmured.

MICHAEL told Frances that he wanted her to meet someone, but first he relented and let her have a drink, escorting her to the staff cafeteria high above the city, where he bought her a large gin and tonic. He had purchased a beer for himself and sipped at it with relief, aware that the woman's chaotic emotions were somehow affecting him.

"Are you enjoying the drink?" he asked her.

"Wildly," she replied.

"You drink a lot?"

"Yes, I drink a lot—at least since I returned from there."

"Drink and sex."

"Precisely."

"What about your faith in God?"

"I believe that I'm carrying His child, but I don't know what He's like."

"The thought of what He might be like frightens you?"

"It terrifies me. I'm scared because I don't know His nature —nor what my child will be."

"What makes you so sure you're pregnant? Have you seen a gynecologist?"

"I *don't want* to see a gynecologist. I'm frightened of that as well."

"Of what he might discover?"

"Yes, I suppose so."

"I understand your concern, but you can't possibly say you're pregnant until—"

"I'm a woman *and* a doctor. I *know* the symptoms of pregnancy. I haven't had my period and can actually *feel* something inside me. Damn it, I *know!*"

She was obviously angry, so Michael spread his hands in a gesture of apology until she smiled her forgiveness.

Relaxing, she sipped her drink, gazing around the crowded cafeteria with interest. "White smocks and stethoscopes," she murmured. "It reminds me of old times." She shook her head from side to side, smiling with weary self-mockery, then turned back toward Michael, studying him frankly. "Michael," she said. "Michael Phillips. Why *not* be familiar?"

"Why not indeed?" He grinned at her and raised his beer as if offering a toast, then drank with a thirst that revealed how tense he was. He started drumming with his fingers on the metal-topped table, but when he saw that this was annoying her, he stopped it immediately.

"Can I get back to your relationship with Laurence?" he asked her.

"You're the doctor," she said.

"Why did you eventually tell him about the child?"

"Anger," she replied. "It was no more than that. When he refused to have more sex with me, when he found the courage to reject me, I simply flared up in a most unpleasant manner and told him the truth."

"And?"

"It just made matters worse. My sexual demands had actually revolted him—convincing him that I was either perverted or possessed—then, when I told him about the child, the news filled him with fear. Like me, he's not sure what kind of pregnancy this is, which is something that doesn't make him any happier."

"And yet he still lives there with you and your mother."

"Yes—because no matter what he thinks of me personally, he's convinced that all of this was preordained and therefore has to be seen through to the end, no matter the outcome."

"And your mother? How does *she* react to all this?"

Frances actually smiled, then shrugged in a laconic manner. "My mother is convinced that Laurence and I are on the way to nervous breakdowns, which is why she encouraged me to come here. She wanted Laurence to do the same, but he refuses to talk to you or anyone else."

"Perhaps I could go to see *him.*"

"I have no objections."

Michael felt Frances's knee grazing his under the table; whether an accident or not, it sent a slight electric tingle through him.

"What age are you, Michael?" she asked him, her gaze steady and candid.

"Forty-six," he replied.

"You look it," she said, "but in the best possible way. Most men of your age are still schoolboys in disguise, but you look rather worldly and mature, which I find most attractive."

"I'm delighted that you like older men."

"I like *experienced* men, Michael."

Aware that she was staring very directly at him, that her knee was still pressing insistently into his, Michael had another sip of his beer and tried to keep his mind clear. He could feel her throttled tension, but she only smiled the formal smile of a well-brought-up woman.

A *formal* smile? Not quite: that smile was also slyly challenging, as if in defiance of her fear she was determined to have autonomy over her fate and, if necessary, steal it.

Perhaps aware of the uneasy silence, she abruptly changed the subject, saying, "Since you've met my mother more than once, are you aware of her ideas about the spirit world?"

"More or less," Michael replied. "She seems to believe that we don't necessarily pass over to the spirit world through death, but may in fact exist simultaneously in that world; that it's a mirror to our own world; and that past and future may *also* exist simultaneously in that parallel world."

"Correct," Frances said. "And she also believes that just as we're trapped in our own time and can't see beyond it, so, too, are the beings in the parallel world—they exist in their own time frame, repeating their lives endlessly, unaware of any other world or period. . . . Though sometimes, just occasionally, they get *lost* in another space–time frame and materialize as what we think are *ghosts.*"

"That might explain why you thought you'd been gone for months when you had in fact been gone for only twenty-four hours of earthly time."

"Yes," she replied, "that could solve *that* particular little riddle."

"And do you believe in ghosts, Frances?"

"I'm not sure. I *almost* did last night. Because last night, perhaps trying to prove her point to me, Mother persuaded me to sit in on a séance, and during it I heard what I'm convinced were the same voices that I first heard in the Garden of Eden—voices speaking in a language that sounded oddly like singing—and also saw shadowy figures passing *through* the other women around the table. As that was happening, I became overwhelmed with the same feelings I had in Eden: primitive emotions and dull thoughts, dominated by inchoate fears. Then, just as those feelings became unbearable, I fainted. When I recovered, Mother told me that she also had heard the singing voices, that she had not recognized or understood them, but that she was convinced I had been in contact, *not* with the dead but with creatures from a parallel world, which could have been in the past *or* the future. . . . So there could be something in what she says."

Michael noticed that her eyes were glittering, no longer calm but fraught, so he reached out and patted her wrist as if comforting a child. When he did so, she placed her hand on his, her fingers pressing his skin.

"You feel nice," she said. *"Warm."*

Michael instantly withdrew his hand, feeling his heart racing suddenly.

"According to that theory," he said, "the people disappearing from this world are going to materialize elsewhere as ghosts."

"That's it. That's her theory."

"And do you think that you, Laurence, and Schul were like spirits in your Garden of Eden?"

"Yes," she replied, "I think so. The experience was extraordinarily vivid, yet completely unreal."

"And your child? How does that fit in?"

"Oh, dear God, my child."

She shuddered and looked away, her gaze scanning the crowded cafeteria. Eventually she returned her attention to him, letting her knee press against his, taking comfort from flesh and bone.

"I feel like running away," she said. "I just want to get out of here."

"Not yet," Michael replied. "I want you to meet someone first."

"Who?"

"An in-patient."

Before she could refuse, he stood up and took hold of her elbow to lead her away. Guiding her out of the noisy cafeteria, he marched her to the psychiatric wing, entered it, and stopped at a solid wooden door, painted lime-green with a sliding panel instead of a window.

While Frances stood there, increasingly agitated but offering no verbal protest, Michael slid the small panel back and stared into the room. Satisfied at what he was seeing, he nodded, opened the door, and walked her inside.

"Frances," he said, "this is Miles Ashcombe."

Sitting quietly on the edge of his steel-framed single bed, Ashcombe was wearing what appeared to be slightly oversize clothing—crumpled gray slacks, open-necked white shirt, blue-gray pullover—but a closer inspection revealed that he had in fact lost a lot of weight and although completely white-haired, was actually only in his mid-thirties.

Frances seemed to be puzzled by him, her brow furrowing in thought; she glanced inquiringly at Michael, received no response, so shook her head and returned her gaze to the silent man. He met her gaze boldly but did not attempt to rise, merely opening and shutting the fingers of the hands in his lap.

"I'm sorry," Frances began hesitantly. "I . . ."

"Miles is one of the victims of the Glastonbury disappearance," Michael explained. "He lived just west of Glastonbury, with a clear view of the Tor, and was professionally immersed in the area as a noted center of magic. He is, in fact, a well-known writer who specializes in the history and myths of that area and is renowned for his unusual psychic gifts. He's suffering extreme trauma, and for a few weeks after the event could only speak a kind of primitive English. Now he talks properly, but will only speak when spoken to—though we *have* learned that during the early hours of that fateful day, he was jerked out of sleep by inexplicable terror and felt compelled, even against his will, to go to the summit of the Tor. He was there when the dark mass materialized, and tried hiding himself in the tower of St. Michael's Church; but when the darkness surrounded it, he ran out again and saw that Glastonbury had vanished. Like you, he found himself in what seemed to be a prehistoric world, filled with animals that have long been extinct. He also saw marshlands and lagoons—and a volcanic mountain."

Obviously shaken, Frances stepped away from Miles Ashcombe. Michael put his hand on hers and felt its febrile burning; he then turned to the man on the bed and spoke quietly to him.

"Tell us what you remember of your past, Miles. Please tell us everything."

The man seemed perplexed, his eyes as empty as the moon, then he offered a shivering, demented smile and raised both his hands.

"Water and fire," he said. "A great light in the darkness. I saw a creature beating wings of skin, but it wasn't a bird. It looked prehistoric—at first I thought it was a pteranodon—but then I saw that it was actually the Archangel, descending from heaven."

He closed his eyes and took a deep breath, held it in for some time, gasped, and eventually stared at Frances, offering his awful smile.

"Wings of skin," he said. "Floating between heaven and earth. And he descended out of the blazing heart of God to weigh the souls of the dead. He touched me and I died. He weighed my soul and set me free. My former self cried out and disappeared as I awakened to glory. . . . St. Michael! The Archangel! The Last Day! *I remember it all!*"

He closed his eyes again, held his breath, put his head back, slid down the wall until he was stretched out on the bed, his hollow-cheeked, deathly-white face turned toward the ceiling. Only then did he let his breath out, but kept his eyes shut, his hands opening and closing repeatedly by his sides, his shivering lips holding their crazy smile as he drifted away.

Frances shivered also, then moved toward the door, letting her hand fall off Michael's arm as she turned away from him. A choked sobbing escaped her as she reached for the door handle, but Michael quickly grabbed her and jerked her back, making her spin in toward him. She fell into his embrace, breasts and belly crushed against him, hands digging frantically into his shoulder blades as she sobbed and shook in his arms. He rocked her very gently, offering comfort as he surrendered, feeling something emanating from her that he had known in other women, but never with such palpable presence or fierce, overwhelming intensity. It was heat. Sexual heat.

THOUGH the wind was beating around her, Frances felt hot and drowsy, her thoughts scattering each time she closed her eyes, letting her fall close to sleep. When that happened, she was disturbed, remembering Ravello and Eden, one merging imperceptibly into the other and making her more confused. *Sex,* she thought. *Flesh.* And felt her clothes sticking to her, thus making her open her eyes again to stare out of the car.

No, it was not Ravello. Nor the lush greenery of Eden. Instead it was the low-rolling hills of Salisbury Plain, the grass rippling in the wind like the waves of a green-colored sea. They had just left Devizes and were driving along the A360, Michael guiding the steering wheel with his fingertips as if playing with it.

"God," Frances said, "I hate the English countryside. Even when the sun shines it's empty, and it makes me feel lonesome."

"I love it," Michael replied. "After the city with all its filth and noise this seems so clean and peaceful."

He glanced at her, grinning, revealing wrinkles under his gray eyes, and she felt the languorous warmth of her blood even in her despair. Laurence was in the rear seat, his troubled gaze downcast, the white-walled village through which they had just passed receding behind him.

"Are you all right?" she asked him.

"Yes," he said, "I'm fine. I can think of better days in my life, but otherwise I'm okay."

He smiled and shrugged, obviously trying to conceal his fear, and she felt a real gratitude for the gesture, knowing how he was feeling. He was suffering guilt over Schul's death, and shame because of his affair with her; and even though their sexual relationship had ended some time ago, she knew that he was still torn between his love for her and his loathing for what she had made him do.

During the past few weeks at home he had lived like a recluse, only leaving his room when necessary and even then hardly speaking, except to trade polite words with her mother, who always managed to charm him. Thank God for Michael, who had insisted on seeing him and, receiving too many refusals, had simply knocked on his bedroom door. Michael must have told Laurence what he had already explained to Frances, because since then, though obviously still not without problems, Laurence had reverted to a semblance of his former pleasant self and gradually conveyed some of that old warmth to her.

Now, returning his smile, Frances felt a little better, less ashamed of how she had used him, but still not without guilt.

Sighing, she turned back to the front, breathing the fresh air. They were crossing West Down, where the British Army held maneuvers, the fields suitably desolate and windblown, as if the end of the world had come.

"God," she said, "have you ever seen anything more dreary? Just send me back to Iraq!"

Michael made no reply but threw her a grin, and Frances, in the warmth of her need, felt herself flowing toward him.

Sex, she thought. *Oblivion.* She would have him sooner or later. So far he had managed to resist her, but she knew what he felt. He wanted her very badly—she knew that as sure as breathing—but the fact that he was her doctor, and his concern at her sexual hunger, were encouraging him to keep a certain distance and remain in control.

Thinking about that, she blushed, ashamed of her speculations. She shivered in her seat, saw the dark clouds drifting slowly, glanced across the rolling, tree-filled fields, and talked to keep herself calm.

"That poor man in the hospital," she said. "Miles Ashcombe. What do you think he was trying to tell us? What did he *really* see?"

"I don't claim any *personal* connection," Michael replied, "but surely you know about the St. Michael churches."

"A little," Frances said. "I know that there are hundreds of them all over the country, and that most of them are on top of hills."

"Exactly," Michael said. "And who was Saint Michael?"

"Some long-dead priest, I would imagine."

"No, Frances, you're wrong. Saint Michael is the Archangel, the captain of the heavenly host, first mentioned in Revelations and Thessalonians. According to the Bible it was Michael and his angels who fought against Satan and his angels and eventually cast them out of heaven. It is also written that he will come down from heaven on the Last Day—"

"Ashcombe mentioned that."

"—in order to weigh the souls of the dead, as also mentioned by Ashcombe. Saint Michael is usually depicted as a feathered, winged, sometimes flaming, always sword-bearing, creature who floats between heaven and earth in his constant vigilance against the devil—and, indeed, on the tower of the St. Michael's Church on Glastonbury Tor there was a carving showing him weighing the souls."

"So why are the churches usually on top of hills?"

"At first it was assumed that it was merely a symbolic gesture: Saint Michael, floating between heaven and earth until the arrival of the Last Day, occasionally settled on mountain summits or hilltops to intervene in the affairs of men—so the hilltop churches pay tribute to his many supposed appearances through the ages. However, it has since become clear that most of those same churches were also built over prehistoric mounds covering the convergence of ley lines, and so must have been built there to act as conduits between the earth's magnetic energy and the ionosphere."

"Oh, Christ," Frances said, "we're back to that again."

"Right," Michael replied. "And it gets us back to your question: What did Miles Ashcombe actually *see?*"

"And the answer?"

"Miles Ashcombe is a religious person, a mystic with psychic gifts, and I think that in his terror at what was happening, he grabbed what he could. *Something* descended over him—as it descended over *you*—and then Miles must have seen some kind of being, or beings, and retreating into madness, seeking protection in trauma, interpreted the loss of his sanity as death, and thus viewed that being—or at least the last one he can recall—

as Saint Michael the Archangel, descended from heaven to inaugurate the Last Day."

"That sounds reasonable," Laurence said. "During *our* particular experience, Frances and I clung to the God we had been told about since childhood: a God quick to anger—and to save. For both of us, though possibly in different ways, he was our hope of salvation."

Michael nodded his agreement, then picked up on his train of thought. "The facts fit," he said. "Ashcombe was standing, after all, on the ruins of St. Michael's Church, and that fact plus his obvious knowledge of the mystical aspects of the Tor itself would have encouraged such a connection in his mind. Glastonbury disappeared, the landscape changed before his eyes, then he saw a winged creature, a prehistoric pteranodon, and finally was surrounded by brilliant, pulsating light, as some being approached him. It must indeed have seemed like the biblical Last Day—and that pteranodon, observed just before his last moment of sanity, would have become mixed up in his mind with whatever being approached him, convincing him that he had seen the Archangel on Judgment Day."

"The millennium," Laurence added in a surprisingly calm tone of voice. "I think that's what the disappearing earth means —we're on the verge of a new age."

Disconcerted, Frances glanced out of the speeding car, expecting to see more green fields and autumnal trees but seeing instead the thatched cottages and red-brick houses of yet another typically empty small town.

"The Last Day," she said to Michael. "That certainly seems to be coming. But who will inhabit it? Will it be this child I'm carrying? And is this child one of the links between the past and the future? *I* saw other beings too. They surrounded me and touched me. I saw them at the dawn of mankind, then saw them in Eden. I existed in both periods—just as much as I do now—and those beings, whatever their nature, filled me with love and fear. Now I burn just to think of it."

And she was indeed burning: feeling scorched by the events she had already been through and the thought of what might yet be coming. She stared defiantly at Michael, anticipating his scorn, but saw only his roughly handsome profile with the bright sky beyond. He looked serious, almost anxious, very far

removed from mockery, and she wanted to reach out to hold
him and take comfort from him.

"You may be wrong," he said. "That possibility remains. I
want a rational explanation—I can't help it: that's what I'm like
—and I'm hoping that if things work out as planned, we might
find one today."

As he was speaking the car moved up over the brow of a
small incline. Frances, expecting the familiar prehistoric stones
to rise out of a desolate landscape, was surprised to see instead
an enormous horseshoe of tall directional antennas and dish-
shaped parabolic radar antennas towering over a mass of aluminum huts, mobile power units, tents, army transport trucks,
and what appeared to be close to a hundred men and women,
some in uniform, others in white, knee-length coats, many gathered around what appeared to be a variety of cameras and
lamps mounted on tripods, all of them wearing heavy, fur-col-
lared jackets over their normal clothing.

Frances could hardly believe what she was seeing, but Michael stopped the car on the brow of the modest hill, and now,
studying the scene thoroughly, she saw that the great stones of
Stonehenge were indeed still there, but that the wire fence normally surrounding them had been removed to make way for
that mass of men and equipment.

"My God!" Frances exclaimed. "What on earth is going on
there?"

"Do you notice something odd about them?" Michael asked
her.

"Yes," Frances said, taking note of the fur-lined jackets. "It's
a warm summer afternoon, yet most of those people are dressed
for the winter."

"Right," Michael said. "Here, just three or four hundred
yards from that road, the temperature's about seventy degrees
Fahrenheit, but just across the road—in the area starting just
before the Neolithic ditch surrounding Stonehenge and ending
about twenty yards beyond the far side of that same ditch;
stretching out, also, about fifteen yards past the Heelstone at
the most northern tip of the monument and a similar distance
beyond its southern perimeter—the temperature has been dropping steadily over the past few days and will, if it continues,
eventually fall below freezing point. So we think something's

going to happen, which is why you see this circus around the monument—and why I've brought you and Laurence."

Along the road, nearly half a mile before Stonehenge, armed soldiers were milling about a barbed-wired wooden barrier.

"The whole area around Stonehenge has been cordoned off," Michael explained, "and will stay that way at least until tomorrow. So you are privileged."

Grinning, he started the car and drove along to the heavily guarded barrier. Stopping again, he showed his identity card and official letter of admission to the sergeant in charge and, when the barrier was raised, drove on to Stonehenge, then turned into the parking lot. After parking and making them all get out, he opened the trunk and took out three fur-lined jackets.

"Here," he said. "I came prepared. And you really *will* need them."

As they were putting on the jackets, Laurence smiled nervously at Frances, rolling his eyes in mock despair; then Michael gave them some thick gloves and said, "Okay. Let's go."

He led them out of the parking lot to the monument's entrance area. The ticket booth and souvenir shop were closed, but the concrete enclosure had been filled with two long trestle tables at which some of the soldiers and scientists were having the lunch that was being served from a mobile canteen. Smelling vegetable soup, grilling sausages, and french fries, Frances instantly felt hungry; but instead of being invited to eat, she was told to follow Michael into the tunnel that ran under the main road and led back up into the grounds of the monument.

Entering the tunnel, Frances still felt quite warm, but halfway along, obviously under the main road, the cold suddenly bit her. She shivered uncontrollably, saw Laurence and Michael doing likewise, then emerged from the gloomy tunnel to the daylight and a more intense coldness.

Once in the grounds of the monument, Frances was almost disorientated by the sheer size and scope of what she found there. With Laurence beside her, she followed Michael across the ditch and stopped beside one of the two-thousand-year-old stones, shivering as she stared past the heads and shoulders of men grouped around a mounted cinecamera at the great sarsen circle crowned with lintels and its inner horseshoe of bluestone trilithons which, even surrounded by the steel and plastic of modern technology, retained their infinitely haunting, mysterious appearance. Nonetheless, the ancient standing stones were, in a sense, dwarfed and aesthetically diminished by the tall steel antennas and gleaming radar bowls that formed a wall around the circular ditch, and by the thick black electric cables that covered the grassy ground between the stones and terminated in the four mobile power-units standing at roughly equal distances apart around the inner bank. Beneath the radar bowls were the arc lamps, also forming a great horseshoe around the monument, while beneath the arc lamps were milling soldiers and scientists, the latter attending to the quite remarkable variety of scientific instruments that had been placed around the monument, including different kinds of telescopes and cameras, most of which were mounted on tripods.

Frances did not recognize any of the other instruments, so Michael, obviously aware of that, explained what was happening.

"We think the dark mass is going to materialize as soon as the temperature drops below, or near, zero. Since some of us also happen to believe that a human element may be involved in the magnetic and electron disturbances required to create the phenomenon, we've brought you and Laurence along for that very purpose. As you can see, most of the people involved have already moved out of the cold zone to that field beyond the ditch"—at this point, Michael indicated the nearby field, filled with aluminum huts, tents, parked army transport vehicles and humans—"and in a few more minutes, when the people around you have made their final adjustments, we'll *all* retreat to there and wait for something to happen. Should the dark mass materialize, we are going to try to ascertain, in scientific terms, just what it is. What you are surrounded with, then, are radiation detectors, ionization measuring devices, ozone-measuring spectrometers, particle telescopes and cameras, infrasonic frequency detectors, geodetic and seismic measuring instruments, and theodolites."

"I thought theodolites were used for tracking UFOs."

"That's right. They are."

More puzzled than ever, Frances was just about to ask Michael what UFOs had to do with the dark mass when a well-fed, rosy-cheeked man wearing civilian clothes, shivering visibly, and blowing into his cold clenched fists, walked up to him and, with a cheery grin, said hello. Michael replied in kind, shook the man's shoulder in a friendly fashion, then introduced him to Frances and Laurence as Lionel Sampson, the London-based projects officer for the Ministry of Defence's Department of Atmospheric and Meteorological Phenomena.

After shaking their hands, Sampson said, "You got here just in time. We think something's happening. The temperature's started dropping more rapidly, and our instruments are showing dramatic fluctuations in the magnetic field. We have five or ten minutes."

"What about us?" Laurence asked.

With the same cheerful, deliberately reassuring grin, Sampson pointed south to the far side of the area inside the encircling ditch.

"All we want you to do," he said, "is sit down on the mound between those two Aubrey Holes, which are marked with white circular chalk patches. Since some evidence suggests that the human element—at least in the case of certain individuals—could be vital to the materialization of the phenomenon, we're hoping that your presence within the field of the dark mass will encourage its eventual appearance."

Frances could hardly believe her eyes and, after glancing at a straight-faced Michael, returned her attention to Mr. Sampson.

"You want us to just *sit* there," she said, feeling the rise of her anger, "while the dark mass emerges? Is *that* what you're saying?"

Sampson nodded, his grin wavering. "Don't worry," he said. "We don't want it to capture you again, and we're not going to let it. All these instruments around you," he continued, waving one hand in the air, "will be recording and measuring every conceivable aspect of the phenomenon—magnetism, radiation, temperature, light intensity, infrasonic frequency, electron and radio-wave density, general particle and ozone content—you name it, we're measuring it. And the minute the phenomenon starts forming, we'll pull you right out of there. We'll be back in the field, near the aluminum huts, but we'll have you wired for sound and as soon as we know it's coming, we'll give you the word to get the hell out of its range and come back to us. Okay?"

"No, thanks," Frances said.

She was stunned by their impertinence, by their willingness

to exploit her, and she let her anger show in her face when she turned to face Michael. She took a step back, moving slightly away from him, filling up with the urge to slap his face and remove the smile from his lips; but he obviously read her thoughts and very neatly took control, reaching out to place his hands on her shoulders and shake her affectionately.

"Please," he said. "Do it. It's important that we try this. I know you think we're exploiting you, but we're not—we've got it under control. Believe me, if it starts materializing we're going to know about it before it gathers strength, so you'll have plenty of time to get out of here and join us back at the huts."

"You bastard," she said.

"No," he replied, "I'm not that. I'm just a man trying to do his job, and I want you to help me—"

"Rubbish!"

"—and, in helping me, perhaps help yourself. It's in your interests, as well as in ours, to find out what that thing is."

"I won't do it," Frances said, speaking as angrily as she could, yet irresistibly attracted to his air of authority.

"You must," he said. *"Please."*

He was still holding her shoulders, shaking her gently, insistently, and Frances felt the heat of his large hands filtering through her cold clothing. Already his touch was making her helpless, destroying her willpower and pride, doing to her what she had formerly done to Laurence in the guest room's dark silence.

"No!" she said firmly.

"I'll do it," Laurence offered, surprising them both. "It's all right. *I'll* do it."

Frances studied him thoughtfully, wondering what had motivated him; she recognized the panic in his eyes as exactly what she was feeling. So, that was it—he would fight his fear by facing its source—and understanding that, as well as knowing what she owed him, she had to give in to Michael.

"All right," she said, not sounding friendly. "I'll stay here with Laurence."

Michael gave a small bow, his grin affectionate and knowing, then let his hands drop from her shoulders as he turned toward Lionel Sampson, who, managing to get back his grin, was already moving away from them, waving his right hand to indicate that they should follow him.

"This way, children," he said.

He led them southward across the grounds of the monument, past the open end of the sarsen circle and the bluestone trilithons, then on to the mound located between two chalk-marked Aubrey Holes at the far side of the ancient, encircling ditch. Once there, he asked Frances and Laurence to sit together on the grassy mound; then, when they had done so, a technician, bulky in his coveralls and heavy jacket, gave them both walkie-talkies, put his thumb up encouragingly, but then too hastily headed off across the field beyond the curved ditch.

"They're set to receive," Sampson told them, "so you'll hear us if we want you to; but if you want to speak to us, press the switch—that's all there is to it. Okay?"

"Okay," Laurence said.

He grinned uneasily at Frances, trying to show his appreciation; then Frances glared at Michael, determined to make her resentment obvious, but was defeated when she saw that his gentle smile was hiding concern.

"All right?" he said.

"Why bother asking?" she replied. "You haven't left me much choice."

He was visibly hurt, but simply nodded and turned away, walking across the ditch, side by side with Mr. Sampson, and continuing across the field beyond it. They both followed the other men who had also left the area inside the ditch and were heading toward the aluminum huts in the middle of the field where, behind a solid wall of heat and impact shields, a great number of soldiers and civilians were nervously gathering.

Frances watched him until he had disappeared into that distant throng, behind the wall of large, rectangular heat shields, then she sighed and turned back to the front.

Deserted, she sat beside Laurence on the grassy mound, staring at the prehistoric standing stones that, with the lintels lying across them, did not look too safe. She glanced sideways at Laurence and saw him gazing skyward, his lips moving as if offering a silent prayer, his eyes sleepless and haunted.

She had liked him in Iraq and now she did so again, understanding that what she had made him do had briefly robbed him of pride. And remembering that, she burned—not with shame, but with helpless lust—then glanced over her shoulder at the wide field behind her, searching for Michael in that ugly collection of aluminum huts, wind-whipped tents, army trucks, and milling men and women. Failing to see him, she felt an even stronger desire for him, beyond shame or conscience.

She distracted herself by looking at Stonehenge, at the Altar Stone by the great trilithon. The stones represented history, imprinting its mysteries upon the present, but the electric cables, dish-bowl antennas, arc lamps, cameras, theodolites, and other scientific instruments had made a travesty of the normally haunting beauty of the ancient site, joining the past to the future in a grotesque and ominous technological union. Frances, no longer trusting in logic or science, was disgusted and fearful.

"I'd like to apologize," Laurence said, speaking quietly, his eyes lowered. "I've behaved very badly toward you, blaming you for my own sins. So I want to apologize."

Taken by surprise again, Frances blushed like a schoolgirl. "*Your* sins?" she managed to say after the silence became too much. "I seduced you. That's all there is to it. Perhaps *I* should apologize."

"This is ridiculous," Laurence said. "How many men receive an apology after being seduced?"

Frances chuckled. "Not many, I suppose. But in this case it's more than a simple case of seduction. I was fully aware of your beliefs, of your religious sincerity and celibacy, and instead of respecting that, I used it for my own selfish purposes."

"Why *me?*"

"I can't answer that," Frances replied, "because I simply don't know. At first, I thought I was doing it because I needed you to protect me—but now I think I did it simply to keep you here until this situation resolved itself. It was an irresistible impulse, Laurence, instilled in me in Eden."

Laurence stared directly at her, as if trying to read her thoughts, then nodded, gave a rueful smile, and looked back at Stonehenge.

"I love you," he said simply. "I want you to know that. I was angry because you made me betray my faith, but throughout it, I loved you. I know you don't love me, but that doesn't matter. I just want you to understand clearly how deeply I feel for you."

Frances was very moved, but she didn't know what to say. In truth, there was nothing she *could* say, and that made her feel worse. Eventually, still unable to put her feelings into words, she took hold of his hand and pressed it to her lips, then let it fall again.

"God," she said, "what a life!"

Laurence smiled at that, and Frances, sighing gratefully, looked back over her shoulder, first taking note of the men and women milling about behind the heat shields, then surveying the giant radar bowls and tall, thin antennas encircling the monument right in front of her.

The temperature was dropping and she quietly cursed the cold. Then Sampson spoke through his walkie-talkie, his voice badly distorted, telling her the atmosphere was disturbed and he thought it was starting.

Shivering again, Frances looked up at the sky, saw nothing but the swiftly moving dark clouds and returned her gaze to the monument. The great circle of stones seemed ominous, isolated from field and sky, the horizon, far beyond it, a green, tree-laden expanse that merged with natural tranquillity into a gray haze. It was a typical English summer's day—the sky cloudy, threatening rain—and even as she studied it, feeling more depressed each second, she turned colder and started feeling distinctly heavier, just as she had done in Eden.

"Look!" Laurence exclaimed.

And even as he was rising to his feet, pointing at the sky, Frances noticed that the crackling of her walkie-talkie had suddenly ceased, signifying that the instrument had gone dead. She pressed the switch and spoke into it, vainly hoping for a response, but knowing that contact had been cut off by some mysterious force.

Nothing. Deathly silence. Even the birds had ceased their singing. She followed Laurence's pointing finger, straining to see through deepening gloom . . . and eventually saw an odd light flashing out around the Heelstone, at the northern tip of the three-thousand-year-old Avenue.

From where Frances stood, the Heelstone looked like a giant fish-head, bowing slightly toward the monument, its top nearly level with the distant horizon over which, in an impossible manner, the sun was now rising.

It was a huge sun, a tropical sun, rising golden and majestic, and its striations were fanning out along the horizon, first yellow, then red and appearing to flicker rapidly, giving the im-

pression that they were flames licking out of the bowing Heelstone as it plunged into jet-black silhouette.

"It's two o'clock in the afternoon," Laurence said. *"The sky
must be changing!"*

Frances jerked her head around and stared obliquely above
her to see the normal sun, pale as the moon, hovering beyond
the dense clouds. She glanced back over her shoulder at the
mass of people across the field, observed that the normal sun
was reflecting only dimly off the huts and army trucks behind
the heat shields. Disoriented, she turned back to the front, saw
that other strange sun rising behind the Heelstone, then, tugging furiously at Laurence's arm, started to run.

"No!" Laurence snapped. "I'm staying here! *I have to know
what it's all about!"*

Frances stopped and gawped at him, not believing what she
had heard, frantically worked on the switch of the walkie-talkie
and received nothing but silence. She felt frozen, too heavy,
divorced from reality, and knew that the dark mass was forming around her to take her away again. She remembered the
child in her womb, was convinced she could feel it kicking, then
sobbed, threw the walkie-talkie aside, and suddenly found herself fleeing.

She ran over the ditch and bank, then raced across the sloping field, heading straight toward the long line of black shields
and the people behind them. She was almost hysterical, conscious only of survival, and her very loud gasping was the only
sound filling the silence. She glanced over her shoulder to see
Laurence beside the mound, his head pulled back as he looked
directly above him, his hands shading his eyes. She saw no more
than that, but looked ahead and just kept running, then mercifully found herself racing between two large heat shields and
falling, almost sobbing with gratitude, into Michael's strong
arms.

"It's all right," he said. "You're all right. It's still just taking
shape."

She felt his heat at her breasts, at her quivering thighs, and
clung to him, pressing herself against him until he turned her
away from him. Leaning against him, letting his hands rest on
her shoulders, she looked across the field to where Laurence
was still standing on the grassy mound, his face turned toward
the sky, the sarsens and trilithons silhouetted behind him in the

golden, almost phosphorescent illumination of that slow-rising, alien sun.

"Christ," Michael murmured, his chin just above her head, his voice floating out of the silence with an eerie tonality. "I can't believe this is happening."

Frances glanced left and right, at the people massed around her, saw that most of them were looking at Stonehenge with fearful, rapt expressions on their faces. Here, also, were telescopes, various cameras, and other instruments, but Frances was only aware of those pale, awestruck faces illuminated in an oddly pulsating light, which was growing brighter each second.

"I shouldn't have run," she said. "I should have remained with Laurence. I should either have persuaded him to come with me or stayed right there beside him."

"No," Michael replied. "You did the right thing. You couldn't have talked Laurence away—and wouldn't have gained a damned thing by staying there with him."

"Jesus Christ!" Lionel Sampson exclaimed softly.

Frances suddenly noticed the small, plump man standing beside her, his mouth open in amazement . . . then she followed his gaze and saw the great darkness forming around Stonehenge.

It was an immense column of darkness, rectangular, its edges wavering, about half a mile wide and reaching up from the earth to the sky, like a pillar supporting the clouds in some mad artist's vision. The alien sun was still rising, beaming its light into the dense mass, and that light diffused to form a brilliance that burned through the darkness. The light exploded, became striations, then turned into countless stars that repeatedly flared up and contracted, giving life to the nothing.

Laurence was still standing there, dwarfed by that spectacular dawning, then a stronger light exploded obliquely down from the clouds to form a great pyramid that, in illuminating Stonehenge, turned Laurence into a silhouette.

"No!" Frances screamed.

She tried to break away from Michael, but he held her close to him, refusing to let her go, while the pyramid of light contracted vertically to become even wider.

Laurence stood there, a silhouette, the brightening light distorting his shape, then the brilliance of the pyramid, whose base was broadening as its apex sank, eventually, in devouring the ancient stones behind him, erased him completely.

The pyramid's vertical kept shrinking until the light turned into a long, thin blade that stretched horizontally from one end of Stonehenge to the other, erasing the whole monument, while the surrounding darkness, half a mile wide, blocked out the real world.

And then, even as Michael's arms tightened around Frances, she *felt* the darkness advancing on her and sweeping around her.

"We're inside it!" she screamed.

Suddenly it was there—directly above them and all around them—a darkness filled with pulsating light and what might have been shooting stars. Frances looked at Stonehenge, searching for Laurence and failing to find him, instead seeing what appeared to be an immense, glowing disc descending over the ancient stones as they gradually dissolved.

The stars were shining *through* the stones, dazzling her with their radiance, but she managed to observe that the enormous disc was surrounded by smaller discs, and that all of them were adding their light to the greater, pulsating brilliance.

"I can't believe this is happening!" Michael murmured. "I don't *want* to believe it!"

And even as she heard his voice, Frances stared more intently into that dazzling haze and saw, in its unreal, shimmering splendor, figures moving to and fro, then spreading out to advance toward her, silhouetted, featureless, but obviously standing on two legs, their arms swinging in a normal fashion as they walked out of what resembled the landscape of a very vivid dream, at once frightening and beautiful.

"It's sucking us in!" someone screamed.

That single terrified cry was the signal for panic, and Frances felt Michael's arm around her waist as he dragged her away. She ran with him, sobbing dryly, trying to hold on to her senses, vaguely aware of the mass of other people racing past her on all sides. They were retreating across the field, trying to get away from Stonehenge, and she saw the gray-hued greenery of the normal world again spread out in front of her.

There was shouting and screaming, then a fierce wind beat around her; she felt herself being sucked into a vacuum, but was pulled back by Michael. It was like the eye of a storm—the wind was rushing and howling around them—then there was buckling metal, collapsing antennas and arc lamps, then the screams of those coming up behind her were sucked back into silence.

"Keep running!" Michael bawled.

She kept running because she had to, being dragged along by him, but eventually they escaped the force that was trying to pull them back, and stopped side by side on the grass at the field's outer limit.

"Christ!" Michael gasped. *"Christ!"*

Together, they turned to look back across the field, noticing that the others were doing the same, most disheveled and windswept.

The pillar of darkness was still there, rising from earth to sky, but now stretching out on either side for a very long way and covering at least half of the field. That area, now unrecognizable, presented an alien spectacle, its darkness streaked with constantly shifting, shimmering light and what appeared to be exploding or shrinking stars.

Obviously it was another world, extraordinary and confusing, dominated by the great disc that hovered over the vanished Stonehenge and was, in its turn, surrounded by many smaller discs. The latter glowed like lanterns where they floated above the vanished monument, their flat bases emitting light that formed luminous pyramids in the stark, seemingly artificial darkness.

And there, most chillingly, stretched across what had been the field, were the silhouetted, distorted, but apparently human-shaped creatures who were moving to and fro, back and forth, very slowly, reaching out as if to touch the human beings mingling with them.

Then, even as Frances stared at them, they started fading away.

Again, it seemed impossible, an insult to intelligence, turning the senses upside down even as it was happening.

The great disc flared up and vanished, shrinking back into darkness; then the smaller discs did the same, one after the other, eventually leaving nothing but that alien sky filled with pulsating stars.

The stars illuminated the ground below, and the creatures moving blindly over it, including the soldiers and scientists who had been sucked into the dark mass and, crying out, their voices echoing ethereally, gave the distinct impression that they were not only lost, but oblivious to the alien creatures wandering among them.

Yes, they were lost, and Frances knew it on the instant, as she heard them crying out and saw them fading away into a whirlpool of receding, shrinking stars and swirling streaks of white light. And then they were gone, and only the pillar of darkness remained, and then it also faded away to leave the normal gray afternoon.

Normal except for one thing.

Stonehenge had vanished.

Standing with her spine pressed into Michael's broad body, feeling his heat filtering through to her as his hands slid around her waist, Frances stared, with all the others massed around her, at the chilling emptiness of the field where Stonehenge had recently been standing.

The ancient stones had disappeared. A fine vapor rose from the green earth. There were no indentations or other marks where the stones had been standing. The great circle was empty. The land beyond was clearly visible. The alien sun had also vanished, and now dense clouds were moving across the sky as if nothing had happened.

Then, her blood turning cold, Frances heard the voices emerging from that empty area . . . disembodied . . . despairing.

"Help! Someone help me! Where am I? What's happening? God, help me!"

The voices cried out for a long time—the desperate pleas of the invisible—while Frances and those scattered around her looked on in numb horror. *"Where am I? Please help me? Oh, God, what's happening to me?"* The voices rose and fell, echoing ethereally in an outer silence, until, after ten or fifteen minutes, they started fading away.

They faded slowly but surely, with heartbreaking inevitability, disappearing into the ether, growing fainter, as if their owners were moving away over a very great distance. Then they faded away completely, first one, then another, until only one remained, and it eventually faded away also, leaving a vast, eerie silence.

That silence lingered a long time and was infinitely haunting; then a single bird sang, and was shortly followed by another; and soon the birds were gliding across the gray, cloudy sky, above the desolate green earth upon which Stonehenge had stood, and from which arose, for reasons as yet unknown, a fine, marshlike mist.

"God help us all," Frances whispered.

§19§

MRS. Devereux examined herself in the mirror and, displeased with what she saw, turned away and went to the French windows overlooking the rear garden. It was late in the evening, the dark garden moonlit, and Mrs. Devereux, concerned that Frances had still not returned from Stonehenge, looked down at her very well-kept lawn and found herself shivering. *Damn,* she thought, *will I never forget it? Will it haunt me even into my grave? And now Frances! Dear God . . .* And yet she continued looking down, seeing the moonlight on the green lawn, remembering what had happened there many years ago and convinced that it was going to happen again, if in some different way.

Disturbed by such contemplations, she poured herself a sherry and sipped it as she stood by the window. Now, with the séance over and everyone gone, the silence of the four-story house seemed oppressive, amplifying every creaking of wood and rustling of curtains.

Mrs. Devereux closed her eyes, remembering the séance in the dark lounge, herself drifting away into that place where time and space had no meaning. Once there, she became a bridge between one world and the other, allowing the disembodied, who could not speak for themselves, to speak their garbled words through her. She had seen them in the starlight, in the glittering void of the nothing, and had watched them moving to and fro silently, obviously lost.

She had seen nothing else—and certainly not her long-lost husband—and when she had opened her eyes again, feeling exhausted and slightly dizzy, she had been faced with a group of perfectly normal women, all holding hands around the circular table. All old. Her own age.

"Silly cows," she now murmured over her glass. "I don't know why I bother."

But she *did* know why she bothered. It was because she had lost her husband and wanted to contact him, desperate as she was to get answers to the questions that had secretly been tormenting her for years. No one knew of her torment (they only saw what she chose to show them) but *she* knew that she would never rest in peace until the truth was discovered.

"That's why I bother," she said. "Those silly old cows aren't silly."

Nor were they. She, Mrs. Devereux, although possessing certain powers, could not get in touch with the other world without aid; so those other old women—frequently grief-stricken but often just intensely curious—had the sort of fierce belief which, when strengthened through their linked hands, could help her, Mrs. Devereux the medium, to break through to the other world.

And what was that world, exactly? Even now, it was hard to tell. Was it actually populated with the dead or with some alien intelligence? Mrs. Devereux did not know and was haunted by her own ignorance, sometimes feeling that the more she found out, the less she actually understood.

She knew the other world existed, but didn't know what it really was; she had never seen more than vague figures moving through star-filled darkness. They were strangely insubstantial, wandering silently to and fro, obviously lost, but not necessarily dead or even human by nature. They existed and spoke through her, their language incomprehensible, but she never saw their faces or heard them speaking, so didn't know who or *what* they were.

"Are you still down there?" she said, staring intently at the moonlit lawn. "Are you going insane, wondering what's happened to you, or have you simply not realized?"

Talking to herself again. Or to the ghost of her lost husband. She put the glass to her lips and took a sip of sherry, still thoughtfully staring down at the tree-filled, shadowy garden and letting her thoughts turn from her missing husband to her very late daughter.

Why wasn't Frances back yet? Had anything happened to her? Mrs. Devereux hadn't wanted them to go—neither Frances nor that poor Laurence—but Dr. Phillips, with his charm and gentle firmness, had dragged them both off, insisting that it was all terribly important and could not be avoided.

Stonehenge. Why that monument? What could they do there? It all seemed rather odd, but she knew Dr. Phillips well, and doubtless he had very good reasons to do what he was doing, no matter how mysterious they seemed at this particular moment.

Mrs. Devereux shivered, still gazing down at the lawn, thinking of her husband and of what had happened to Frances, and wondering how much she was to blame for what was happening now.

I am paying for my secrecy, she thought. *All of this is my penance.*

The front door opened, then closed with a loud bang; Mrs. Devereux immediately relaxed in the knowledge that Frances had finally returned.

She finished her sherry, turned away from the window, sat in a deep, faded armchair and tried to look unconcerned. Frances was obviously taking her time hanging her coat up in the hallway, but eventually she appeared, tall and slim in blue jeans, white blouse, and high-heeled boots, long brown hair windblown and uncombed, her gaze slightly unfocused.

"God!" she exclaimed. "I need a drink!" And walked straight to the cabinet where she poured a large brandy, drinking some while Mrs. Devereux studied her, before returning her thoughtful gaze to the door.

There was no sign of Laurence.

"You look absolutely *ghastly,*" Mrs. Devereux said. "What on earth have you been doing in Wiltshire? Rolling about in the tall grass?"

"That's not too inaccurate," Frances replied, looking quite grim.

"And our American guest? I see no sign of him. Has he gone straight to bed as he usually does, hiding his face in the pillow?"

"Laurence hasn't gone to bed," Frances said, "but he *has* gone for good."

"Gone?" Mrs. Devereux said.

"Yes, damn it," Frances replied. "Laurence has gone, probably for good. He disappeared with the rest of them."

"The *rest* of them?"

"You're really not that stupid, Mother, so please don't act bewildered."

"But I *am* bewildered, dear. Absolutely. What do you mean Laurence has gone for good? And who were the others? I don't know what happened down there, dear, so you'll have to *explain.*"

Frances stared angrily at her, sighed and drank more brandy, let the glass rest on her knee while she explained what had happened. She told her story thoroughly, with great attention to detail, and as she continued talking, her voice low and hypnotizing, Mrs. Devereux saw it vividly in her mind and felt growing fear.

She saw that great pillar of darkness, rising majestically from earth to sky, the alien creatures emerging from that strange, light-filled nothing, materializing, disappearing, becoming visible again . . . as they had also done years ago in this very house . . . and as they still did when she went into her medium's trance and became part of that other world.

She watched her daughter's moving lips, heard her words, dissolved into them, and visualized her husband on that lawn all those long years ago. Yes, a very long time ago, though not long enough to forget; and thinking about it, and of how Frances had been born, Mrs. Devereux knew she would finally have to tell her daughter the truth.

"—then they were gone," Frances was saying. "They just seemed to dissolve. They vanished as the dark mass was disappearing and didn't come back . . . and neither did Stonehenge."

Mrs. Devereux took a deep breath and tried to remain calm; she felt trapped by the silence of the house in which a distant clock ticked. That clock was ticking off her life, remorselessly whittling her time away, and she shuddered to think of what might be coming to those who would follow her.

"All gone?" she said, still stumbling to find an adequate response. "All those soldiers and scientists just . . . *disappeared?*"

"Yes, Mother . . . *and* Laurence. We heard their voices calling out and fading away—then there was nothing."

Mrs. Devereux thought of Frances and Laurence upstairs, conducting their affair nightly on the bed in the guest room, under the illusion that she would not hear a sound. And of course she *had* heard—not much, but enough—and, though shocked a little, had accepted it as a form of catharsis after their terrible experience in Iraq. So she had ignored them, letting them cling to each other but also sensing that their meeting had been preordained and that she should let events take their natural course—which, in view of what had happened at Stonehenge, they appeared to have done. Now Laurence, like her husband, had served his purpose and been spirited away.

Mrs. Devereux studied her daughter and saw lines on her skin, eyes luminous with a terrible beauty, lost in wonder and fear. Trying to ignore that, she leaned a little forward, remembering to keep her voice level.

"And what about those other creatures inside the dark mass?" she asked. "Was our friend Dr. Phillips willing to venture an opinion as to whom, or what, they might be?"

"He wasn't," Frances replied, "but some of his friends were. It's the opinion of the team of scientists with whom Michael's working that the dark masses are entrances to other space–time frames, and that the disappearing people have been transported into some other world, possibly in some other time scale—past, present, or future. Apparently, scientific examination of the areas involved has shown them to have possessed—at least for a short period after the disappearances—certain similarities to the known properties of black holes, and the scientists are therefore convinced that what is being observed inside the dark mass—the strange lights and wandering creatures—are parts of other space–time continuums that are temporarily rendered visible by certain geomagnetic forces and then, due to fluctuations in those forces, fade back into the space and time they originally came from. In other words, what we might be seeing is a race of totally alien beings, who come from a completely different world . . . and possibly another time."

"So the people sucked into that dark mass could still be alive?"

"Yes," Frances replied. "And could in a sense be still right here on earth, in a kind of parallel world, no longer subject to our own laws of time, and perhaps imagining that they're suffering a bad dream from which they'll eventually waken up."

Mrs. Devereux felt the silence closing around her like a shroud, heard the clock ticking in the hall, sounding distant and unreal. She felt profound relief, as if freed from years of pain, but it sprang out of a deep well of fear and might soon fall back into it.

"And you?" she said, leaning closer to Frances. "What do you think?"

"I don't know," Frances murmured.

"You were *in* another world, in another time, and now you seem to be pregnant. So what do you *think?*"

Frances shrugged, her face pained, her gaze wandering around the room, one of her legs crossed over the other, the almost empty glass of brandy resting on top of it. The lamps cast triangles of pale light on the richly carpeted floor, these separated by small pools of shadow and the carpet's striped patterns.

"I thought I was carrying God's child," she said, "and in a sense I still do. I don't know just who or what He is, but I feel that I've been directly touched by him, and that Schul was His instrument. Another world and time. *What* world and *what* time? And if those creatures in the dark mass aren't human, who or *what* are they? I only know that I saw and felt them in Eden, and that everything I did in that place was orchestrated by them. If God truly exists, we're probably *all* His children; and perhaps those creatures, coming out of His light, have been sent here to guide us."

"Perhaps you *are* God's child," Mrs. Devereux said. "You are certainly not *normal.*"

"Not *normal?*" Frances replied, looking bewildered. "Mother, what do you mean?"

Mrs. Devereux went to the windows, glanced down into the dark, moonlit garden, then returned to her chair, shaking her head.

"I lied to you," she said, speaking clearly but reluctantly. "Unfortunately, and to my eternal shame, I've been lying for years."

She folded her hands in her lap, sat up very straight, fixed her gaze steadily on Frances, and spoke as calmly as possible.

"Your father didn't really die when you were a baby," she said. "In fact, he disappeared the night you were born—right here, in this house."

Nervous, and unable to hide behind her usual show of eccentricity, she clenched her left fist, coughed into it, then continued her story.

"A few years after marrying your father, and after trying repeatedly to get pregnant, I underwent a gynecological examination, after which I was told I was suffering from a condition that would prevent me from ever having a child. It was a terrible blow. A really *awful* blow. Your father was a good man, a deeply emotional, gentle man, and having come from a loving family, desperately wanted to have children—or at least *one* child. I was very much in love with him, and naturally wanted to please him, so the knowledge that I would never be able to give him a child destroyed all my happiness."

Mrs. Devereux hesitated, barely able to continue, then looked at the rapt face of her daughter and understood that she had to. There was nothing that could stop what was coming, and the truth might be helpful.

"Oh, he was good about it," she said, "carefully trying to hide his pain, but I knew how disappointed he had to be feeling secretly, and so the more I thought about my condition, the more depressed I became. In fact, as your father tried to bury his disappointment in work, and as we drifted apart because of that work, I, left alone while he spent long days in the film studios, gradually came close to a nervous breakdown."

Mrs. Devereux stopped talking, reliving the pain of those distant years, fully aware that the past, present, and future all shared the same bed. The pain had not died and could be recalled on the instant; and as she stared steadily at Frances, hardly recognizing her child in the mature woman in front of her, she knew that the pain would stay with her even unto the grave.

"I started to dream a lot," she said, "and had very bad nightmares. I dreamed of trees stripped of their leaves, and of flat, barren earth. Then the dreams took over my days, making me feel haunted, convincing me that I was being observed by some unseen force. You understand? It wasn't *people* I felt pursuing me: it was some kind of spiritual or ghostly *force*. And so, from that conviction sprang another, more helpful one: that either I was suffering from very odd hallucinations or was seeing what others could not see—that in fact I was psychic."

She stopped to collect her thoughts, and to control her heavy breathing, feeling a little disconcerted by Frances's large-eyed, unwavering gaze. She sighed, trying to relax, but hearing the silence felt more nervous, her head filled with the ticking of the distant clock and thoughts of mortality.

"I began to see strange things," she said, "both at night and in broad daylight. I saw ghosts in this very house, faces floating in the darkness; heard whisperings and indistinguishable murmurings which seemed oddly ethereal. Yes, faces floating in darkness, then softly glowing forms, most of them at night, always indoors—none recognizable. Then all that changed. I started seeing them in daylight. First I saw Kirlian colors around people in the streets, then I saw their astral bodies emerging from them and dissolving above them. And soon I was seeing lights—the kind that people were calling UFOs—hovering in the sky in broad daylight or, much more frightening, glowing like lanterns and descending over Hampstead Heath, usually at night and always in silence, before dissolving to nothing. . . ."

Dissolving to nothing. Just like her husband. Just like Laurence and the scientists and soldiers and many more worldwide. Mrs. Devereux was sick with fear, cheeks flushed, heart racing, and she felt the malignance of the silence that the clock's ticking challenged.

"Finally," she continued, "I developed *most* of the signs of pregnancy: the loss of my period, morning sickness, and—though even *I* could scarcely believe it—the very *physical* sensation of the child developing inside me . . . though, remarkably, I never gained weight. However, when I went for an examination, my doctor insisted that I was not remotely pregnant—that I was merely suffering from a *hysterical* pregnancy, the product of my desperate wish to have a child. Subsequent visits to other doctors produced the same diagnosis; yet no matter what they said, and throughout the interminable period of the child's gestation—*your* gestation—I retained most of the symptoms of a pregnant woman, and certainly felt you growing inside me. Then, when after eight months another doctor had insisted that I still wasn't pregnant—that my belly hadn't even swollen and there was no sign of a physical fetus—I distinctly felt the nonexistent child kicking . . . and then I went into labor."

Mrs. Devereux straightened up, turning her face toward the

ceiling, closing her eyes and slipping back through the years to
that singular moment. She saw the bedroom upstairs, herself
lying on rumpled sheets, her elegant beauty distorted by sweat
and fresh lines of pain. The room was brightly lit, very warm,
the windows closed, and she felt that and saw the curtains
whipping as the stars disappeared.

The stars disappearing? She must surely be dreaming! She
saw her husband's face filling up with bewilderment; then, with
his voice about to break, he asked her to bear down . . .

Looking into that bright room of long ago, Mrs. Devereux
saw the darkness descending over the whole scene—as it had, in
fact, done so at the time; then, having seen it, she opened her
eyes again, to stare into her daughter's haunted features and
take comfort from them.

"It was in this very house," she said, surprised by her own
voice. "This large house that needed children to fill it with
movement and noise. And here I went into labor, impossibly
pregnant and bearing down, and your father, that gentle man,
that loving husband and composer—knowing what the doctors
had said but taking my word for it that they were wrong—
decided to be there when the baby arrived, if indeed it existed.
Well, it existed—*you* existed, my dear! I labored neither long
nor hard, but soon felt the baby coming; then, as this was happening, as I was bearing down to push you out, an unnatural
darkness slipped down over the house, blotting out the sky,
then filling up with a shimmering light, which pulsated with a
radiant energy that filled the whole room. And then—oh, dear
God, even as I felt you coming!—I saw figures around me,
leaning over to examine me, yet transparent and actually passing *through* your father, where he was standing by the side of
the bed, looking down at me, clearly shocked speechless. Then I
heard their sibilant speech—not talking, something else: an
ethereal, melodious kind of *singing* which, though sounding like
nothing I had ever heard, filled me with unutterable joy and
lifted me out of myself. Then suddenly you cried out—the living child I should *not* have had—and I saw your father holding
you in his arms and rocking you gently."

"But surely, Mother, if there was no *physical* sign of . . . ?"

"There was no blood on the bed. No mess at all . . . Yet
you seemed perfectly normal."

She saw Frances staring at her with eyes as big as spoons,

their brown depths leading into a universe of infinite mystery. In those eyes she saw awe mixed with dread and disbelief; but she also saw the yearning and hope of all the children to come. Mrs. Devereux wanted to look away—to avoid seeing herself twice reflected—but the force of her daughter's gaze mesmerized her and kept her gaze steady.

"And my father? What happened to him? Did he—?"

"Yes, he just vanished."

Mrs. Devereux heard her own sigh like a breeze far away, crooning through imaginary bulrushes, over rippling, dark water.

"I must have slept," she said. "Or perhaps I even fainted. I remember your father placing you in my arms, then telling me that he had to go outside to see what was happening. First he went to the window. That strange darkness was still there. I couldn't see the sky, but I saw the light inside that darkness, pulsating with a magical, beautiful life of its own while that alien, voiceless singing continued and the shadowy, almost silhouetted figures surrounded my bed. Your father looked into the garden, murmured something like 'Good God!' and then, as he turned to leave the room, I must have slipped into sleep."

"And he never returned?" Frances asked, her voice as quiet as the grave, her eyes glittering with a light that illuminated shocked disbelief. "You mean he just . . . *disappeared?*"

Mrs. Devereux sighed, releasing her pain with it, noticing that the darkness between the tall lamps formed an arch behind Frances.

"I awakened soon enough," she said. "Hearing your father's voice calling to me—calling up from the garden below the bedroom and sounding quite desperate. He was begging me for help, wanting to know what was happening to him—and terrified by what I was hearing, not knowing what was happening, I placed you in your cot and forced myself across the room to look through the window. The night had returned to normal. There were stars in the sky. I looked down at the moonlit lawn where your father's voice was coming from, and although I could still hear his voice, the lawn was totally empty. I kept looking, unable to move, horrified and disbelieving, and eventually your father's voice faded away, leaving only the silence."

Mrs. Devereux closed her eyes, opened them again to study

Frances, was lost in the pale beauty of that face, wanting to reach out and touch it.

"After that—I don't know why; some animal instinct, I suppose—I simply picked you out of your cot, held you close to me, lay down with you on the bed and fell asleep quickly. When I awakened, the world was normal—daylight beamed through the window—and you were crying healthily in my arms, though your father was missing. I never found out where he had gone . . . and he never returned."

Mrs. Devereux shuddered, feeling adrift on a cold, dark sea, wondering if life wasn't but a dream populated with dreamers.

"So I lied to you," she said. "I've been doing so for years. I didn't want you to feel unnatural—to be haunted by the past or frightened of your unknown future—but now, given what has occurred, I think you just have to know. . . . Your father didn't die when you were two or three years old—he was abducted by whatever came down and surrounded this house— the same kind of dark mass that you experienced in Iraq, and which today spirited Laurence and those other unfortunates out of this world. Now you know why I practice spiritualism—I'm trying to contact your lost father—and why I think that your experience in Iraq was almost certainly preordained. You were not a *normal* child, Frances—nor will your own child be. *God's* child? I don't know if that's true . . . but you're certainly not mine."

She leaned forward in her chair to watch Frances more closely, noting that her dark, tragic eyes were growing larger each second. The room was lit by pedestal lamps in the corners, and their pale light, falling obliquely from wall to carpet, was shadow-filled and too weak. Frances looked like a ghost, a pale ghost, and her gaze wandered blindly.

"I can't . . ." she began, hardly able to force the words out. "I can't accept that—"

"You *must!*" Mrs. Devereux insisted, reaching out to take Frances's hand and shake it dramatically. "Your own birth was not normal—and the child you're having can't be normal—so you must accept the powers you've been given and learn to live with them."

"*Powers?*" Frances said, sounding dazed. "I don't have any powers! *I don't believe what you're saying!*"

She tried to snatch her hand away, but Mrs. Devereux tightened her grip, staring at her as if wanting to slap her.

"Yes!" she whispered. "You *have* strange powers—and they'll gradually grow stronger—and soon they'll be so remarkable that you'll find yourself wanting to hide them. *Here!*" she snapped, grabbing Frances's other hand. "Concentrate! *Look at me!*"

Frances did as she was told, her eyes large and luminous, while Mrs. Devereux, tightly clutching both her hands, let the power flow between them.

"Look at the glasses on the cabinet!" she hissed. *"Will* them to *move!"*

Frances stared at the liquor cabinet, too dazed to do otherwise, obeying her mother with the docility of a child, her strained face streaked with shadows. Mrs. Devereux held her hands, letting the power flow between them, and eventually Frances started to shake like a leaf in a storm.

Mrs. Devereux felt omniscient, her body consumed by flames, and knew that what had possessed her was now entering her daughter. She gripped Frances's hands even tighter, feeling her fear and tension, saw her lips shivering, heard a gasp as her wet eyes grew larger.

Some of the wineglasses were drifting up into the air, hovering about six inches above the cabinet in that weak yellow lamplight, framed by the panes of the windows and the night sky beyond.

"Yes!" Mrs. Devereux cried. *"Yes!* Now make them all *move!"*

Frances shook even more, as if jolted by electricity, and beads of sweat broke out on her forehead as, striped by yellow light and shadow, she concentrated with unleashed ferocity on the glasses floating in midair. The glasses bobbed up and down, wobbled nervously from left to right, drifted apart, shook violently, and then suddenly exploded, scattering their pieces over the cabinet below and onto the carpet.

Frances stared at the scattered pieces, at the empty air where the glasses had floated, then looked straight at her mother as she sat back, releasing her sweating hands. Mrs. Devereux said nothing, no longer knowing right from wrong, wondering what had impelled her to tell the truth when it could bring no one happiness. Then she saw Frances's face, her dark eyes filled with lamplight, her sensual lips, marked by her own teeth, searching desperately for words.

"I don't believe this," Frances said.

20

"I don't believe it!" Frances snapped into the telephone. "Of *course* I don't believe it. How can I believe what you're saying when I know how I feel. I *am* pregnant, damn you! *I am!* I don't *care* what your doctors say!"

"You're being hysterical," Michael replied. "You've simply got to accept the facts. The examination proved you weren't pregnant, and that's all there is to it."

"Damn you, I am *not* hysterical!"

"Then why did you rush away this morning?"

"I rushed away from your bloody stupid gynecologist and his silly remarks. I can actually *feel* this child inside me—and he says I'm imagining it!"

"You *are* imagining it," Michael said. "You're suffering from clinical hysteria. Now I want you to come back here to discuss what we're going to do about it."

"Damn you!" Frances said, feeling betrayed and humiliated, her cheeks burning in the cool air of the hallway, the light of noon beaming in through the tinted glass of the ornate door and forming a hazy rainbow at her feet. "I will not take sedation or your bloody psychiatric treatment. I won't become part of your rotten experiment. I'm pregnant! That's *that!*"

She slammed the receiver down and stared at it for some time, visualizing Michael in the hospital, doing exactly the same. That alone could excite her—the very thought of his presence—and *his* anger, which she had felt over the line, excited her even more.

"Damn!" she muttered, shaking her head, trying to clear it and think straight. She stared in bewilderment at the front door's leaded windows, at the kaleidoscopic glass that let the sunlight fall on her face to make her skin glow.

She didn't hear her mother behind her, but sensed her arrival, and turned around to find her standing in the living room doorway, small and youthfully slim, wearing a loose dress and flatheeled shoes, her bright eyes magnified by the spectacles, giving her the appearance of an inquisitive bird.

"That was Michael?"

"Yes," Frances replied. "He thinks I'm hysterical."

"Did you tell him about me? About how you were born?"

Frances sighed. "No, I didn't, Mother. I didn't even think about it. Quite frankly, I didn't believe your story myself—and I assumed that when I had an examination, it would prove that my pregnancy was perfectly normal. Then they told me I wasn't pregnant—God, I couldn't believe it!—and then, still not wanting to believe it, I went a bit crazy."

"And stormed out of the hospital."

"Yes. I walked out the minute I heard Michael mention 'hysterical pregnancy.' I shouted at him—I remember doing that—then I stormed out."

Remembering it, she blushed, but also felt desire, her embarrassment merging subtly with lust to make her mind reel.

"I'm going crazy," she said, really talking to herself. "I can't take too much more of this. I can't believe it's really happening to me. It all seems like a bad dream."

"Alas, it's *not* a dream," her mother replied, "and I do believe, my dear, that you should go back and tell Michael about it."

"I can't tell him. *I can't!*"

As she had stormed from the hospital, so she now fled to the living room, scarcely aware of what she was doing, impelled by blind panic. She saw the gilt-framed paintings, the fading, antique furniture, the velvet curtains hanging from the ceiling and framing the windows. The room had been like this for as long as she could remember, and as she surveyed it, taking note of its decaying elegance, she felt like a child again.

She turned her back to the ornate white marble fireplace and faced her mother once more.

"I can't think straight," she said.

She placed her hand on her stomach, wanting in vain to feel it swelling, then remembered that vivid nightmare in Iraq, where she had, on hands and knees, in front of Laurence, behaved like an animal. It had been her, yet not her—it had also been someone else. The real Frances had been lost in Ravello, where the church bells still tolled.

She thought of Ravello now, getting it mixed up with Iraq, both places bathed in the silvery light of a perpetual noon, illuminated in her mind with an intensity born of sexual release. She was dominated by her flesh, held in thrall by her own desires, driven to seduce and submit until her self was destroyed. It wasn't natural and never had been (her skin burned with an ethereal heat), and just as she had been used by Schul and had in turn used Laurence, so did she now yearn to use Michael, then be used by him.

She shuddered, feeling fearful, her fingers outspread on her belly, wondering how she could even think of such things, given what was to come.

"It's understandable," her mother said, "that you can't think too straight right now; what I've told you must be frightening to hear, as well as totally bewildering. That's why I think you should go back to the hospital: to see Michael and talk to him. You have to talk to someone other than me—someone not so involved—and Michael, with his professional interest in this matter, is the best person for that."

"You like him, don't you?"

"He has strength, but lacks brutality. I find that an admirable trait in a man—plus intelligence, of course."

Frances smiled, surprised she could still do so, then looked around the cluttered, Victorian lounge and tried to imagine her father. He would have sat at that same piano, or that Chippendale *secretaire,* composing his music while his pipe lay in its brass bowl, filling the air with its smoke. Her mother had told her he had died, but she had never really believed it, and had kept him alive in her mind as someone to cling to. Yet she had felt his loss greatly—much more than she could admit—and had been angry, as well as deeply pained, at being betrayed by his going.

It was a romantic reaction, rising out of his lost presence, and later, when she was caught in the swirling tides of her adolescence, she had been drawn, irresistibly and forlornly, to older men—father figures. Small wonder, then, that Italy became her personal waterloo; that her Italian lover, in his sunlit and white-walled, sweltering room, while the church bells tolled noon and Ravello's narrow streets filled with noise, had been able to exact complete submission and dependence. He had set her on fire and taught her to love the flames; now, when she thought of his singular, debased artistry and, perhaps more pertinently, failed to separate it from the present, she felt ill and had to turn away from her mother, fixing her gaze on the hallway.

"Yes," she said. "Of course. You're quite right. I'll go back and see Michael."

So saying, she went into the hallway and put her coat back on, then left the house and walked down the street, heading toward East Heath Road. She had to pass the Freemasons Arms, and that temptation was too much for her; she went in and purchased a large gin and tonic, which she then drank too quickly. Instantly feeling illuminated, she left the bar and walked on, turning right at the main road and moving parallel to East Heath, very aware of the lush greenery across the road and the roaring traffic on it. She soon passed the busy shops and arrived at Pond Street, looked up at the towering hospital, then crossed the road, passed through the main gate, and entered the building.

Standing in the elevator carrying her to the top floor, she felt even more removed from her senses, as if enslaved by her burning skin. She thought of what had happened to her, and of what she was undergoing, and only managed to deduce from the abnormality of those experiences that her sensuality, extreme at the least, seemed to come from afar. It was more than herself—it was something outside her—and it was making her behave as she did for reasons still unknown.

The elevator doors opened, letting her make her escape, and she went along to the main door of the psychiatric wing. There was a person on attendance, but he obviously recognized her, and once he had let her in, she went straight to the room of Miles Ashcombe.

She opened the sliding panel (she was a doctor, after all) and looked through the peephole to see Ashcombe sitting on the bed, his eyes glacial and too bright.

Was he mad? It was possible, though she didn't believe so.

More likely he was driven by the mysterious, growing powers that were at this very moment at play in that small room.

Ashcombe was sitting in the sunlight pouring in through the window and, with both hands weaving arabesques in the air, orchestrating the dance of the colored beads he had been given to play with.

The beads were as big as marbles and of many different colors. Having been removed from the strings that had held them together, they were, with the unknotted strings, drifting about in thin air like the planets of some alien cosmos, rising, falling, forming into catherine wheels, coming apart and reforming as kaleidoscopic lines that twisted and turned to his will.

Frances watched, fascinated, remembering her own brand of magic, then glanced at Ashcombe's bright, wandering eyes and turned away in despair. Breathing harshly, she fled from there, took the elevator down one floor, then hurried straight to Michael's office, her heart racing, face flushed.

She opened his door without knocking, walked in and slammed it shut. Michael looked up, surprised, then dropped the pen he had been using. He was wearing a nondescript, open-necked shirt with short sleeves, and she noticed that his muscular arms were tanned, with fine golden hairs.

"I've just visited Miles Ashcombe," she said, "and he seems to be developing very strange powers."

"Yes," Michael replied. "Very strange . . . and growing more powerful, thus potentially more dangerous, every day."

"Dangerous?"

Michael shrugged. "What *else* can they be? The powers you've seen, developing for weeks, have shown no signs of stopping. Ergo, if they continue to develop at the same rate, there's no limit to what Ashcombe might become."

"Godlike."

"Yes, Frances, godlike . . . perhaps a new kind of being."

Michael pushed his chair back and stood up behind his desk. He was wearing fawn-colored tropical slacks, and his belly was flat.

"I'm pregnant," Frances said. "And that's *not* a hysterical statement. I don't know what kind of pregnancy this is, but believe me, it's genuine. Miles Ashcombe is developing some very strange powers, and my pregnancy obviously comes from the same source. Now listen! *Please listen!*"

She told him about her mother, about her own magical birth, and about how her father had disappeared the night she was born. She spoke with controlled urgency, very aware of her racing heart, then noticed the intensity of his gaze as he walked around the desk. He stopped just in front of her, gazing thoughtfully at her, then placed his right hand on her shoulder and leaned closer to her.

"This is true?" he asked.

"Yes," she said. "I think it is. I don't think my mother would lie about such a thing—and I know what I'm feeling."

"What *are* you feeling, Frances?"

"I'm feeling pregnant, Michael. *Very* pregnant . . . And my body is burning."

At that moment she knew she had him. She could see it in his eyes: they widened, then narrowed again as he took a deep breath. Frances smiled and stepped close to him. He moved back against the desk. He couldn't retreat any farther, so she remained where she was.

"What do you mean, Frances?" he asked. "Just what are you driving at?"

"I need it," she replied. "I always need it and want it now. I used to think it was because of the first lover I ever had, but now I know he's only responsible for my predilections—not for my appetite. My body is burning, Michael. It *always* seems to be burning. I'm on fire right this moment. I can't help it. . . . My body rules me completely."

She took hold of his right hand and placed it on her breast, breathing deeply to tighten the cloth against her skin and let him feel her warm softness. He tried to slide his hand away, but she held it there, pressing her hand on his.

"It's not me," she said. "I'm convinced that I'm being used. Whether God or the devil or some alien beings, I'm being used by a force outside myself, and what it wants is my body. I'm burning up, Michael. Feel me! Spread your fingers and *feel* me."

He sucked his breath in, held it briefly, let it out. She felt his fingers spreading over her breast, his palm flattening her nipple.

"For God's sake," he whispered, "I'm your doctor! I can't . . . *I can't do this!*"

But he didn't remove his hand. In fact, his fingers explored her softness. She breathed deeply to make her breast swell out and give its warmth to his fingertips.

"You want me," she murmured.

"Frances, *please* . . ."

"You want me badly—I can feel that. Now I want you to feel me, to know my need, and I want that right now."

"The door's not locked, Frances."

"Never mind the bloody door. Here," she murmured, sliding his hand under her blouse. "Feel the softness of me. Feel my heat. Do it *now,* Michael. *Do it!*"

His hand closed over her breast, fingers squeezing, palm pressing; she was not wearing a bra and she felt the abrasive warmth of his masculine skin. He breathed deeply and closed his eyes, then started opening them again; but she pressed the fingers of her free hand on his eyelids as her body fell into him. He sighed, almost despairingly, then put his head back, letting the fingers on his eyelids slide down and slip into his open mouth. He sucked her fingers and squeezed her breast, losing his senses, giving in, and she artfully rolled her belly against his groin and heard his soft, throttled groan.

"Yes!" she said. *"Yes!"*

She pulled her fingers from his mouth and slid them wetly under his shirt; his groin quivered against her loins as his hands undid the rest of her buttons and pulled the blouse from her shoulders. She felt the air on her naked bosom, then his lips, his lapping tongue, then his fingers were in her hair, jerking her head back to let his mouth cover hers. She writhed against him, losing herself, letting the flames scorch her skin, then felt herself being gripped, turned around, and pressed back down on the desk. There were sounds overlapping—creaking wood, spasmodic gasping, cloth rubbing against cloth—then she felt, as the flames consumed her and she melted, the need to cling to her senses.

She was suffocating, burning, opening her eyes to his sweating forehead, her tongue licking the one deep in her throat as she tried to devour his lips. She jerked her head back, gasping harshly for breath, saw her right leg curved over his spine as he penetrated and filled her.

Her aching throat released a groan as her own knees bent in toward her, then she locked her legs over his straining back and sank her teeth in his shoulder. She tasted sweat, a touch of salt; nipped his skin and tasted blood; heard a grunt and cried out as he pushed deeper and the desk hurt her shoulder blades. She tightened her thighs, drawing him in, gasped for breath, her lungs on fire, locked her arms and legs around him and quivered, then was dragged down.

A wooden chair fell over with a nerve-jarring bang. Michael cursed, gasped, and groaned loudly as her weight forced her down on him. She was writhing, twisting on him, being supported as she sank slowly; was stopped, then lowered onto the floor and felt him on top of her. She opened her eyes to the ceiling, gasped for breath, heard him groaning, glanced over the white skin of his shoulder to see the plain of his heaving back.

Edinu: plain. The plain stretched to a hazed horizon. The light was a whiteness that shimmered with an unearthly glowing. The plain was hot and desolate. Beyond it were the mountains. The peaks of the mountains were distorted in the shimmering heat-haze. She looked away from it, returning her gaze to the immediate vicinity, saw her brothers and sisters huddled fearfully together as the shadowy forms, faceless and silent, moved curiously around them. When she saw them, she cried out. When they touched her, she cried again. That cry was the sound of her terror, but did not last too long. She succumbed to her body's heat, wanting only to please them, then lay down and let herself be opened and entered and filled.

"Yes!" she cried. *"Schul!"*

Frances felt the weight on top of her, the thrusting inside her, opened her eyes as a belly slapped upon her and fleshy hips pounded her. The glistening skin of a sweating shoulder blade was all she could see.

Where was she? In a room. It was white and filled with sunlight. For a moment she thought she was in Ravello with the Italian on top of her. No, not the Italian. And not Schul or Laurence. That warm hardness withdrew, then entered her again, and she heard the slapping sounds of their union as she melted around him.

Michael! Oh, dear God! They were on the floor in his office! She remembered the unlocked door and the terrible chance they were taking; and this thought, while it filled her with horror, also increased her excitement.

"Don't stop!" she gasped. *"Don't stop!"*

It was a useless command, falling on deaf ears, but she felt the electric jolting of his orgasm as he flooded her insides. The flames consumed her and made her melt, letting her flow into the ether, and she gave herself to him, pouring around him, drowning him, and felt herself becoming one with him as his throttled cry pierced her.

He shuddered and groaned, as if being whiplashed, then shook violently and turned to a block of stone when he subsided on top of her.

She had wanted to find transcendence, to be taken out of her mortal self, to feel the glory of her untrammeled spirit before being recaptured. But that eluded her once more—her churning emotions found no release—and when she opened her eyes and legs, and let her hands fall from his spine, as she lay there on the floor, being crushed by his cooling body, she heard his harsh gasping, his anguished groan, and felt the burning begin again.

"Oh, Christ!" she said. *"Damn it!"*

21

MICHAEL groaned again, slowly rolled off her, lay beside her for a moment, staring blindly at the ceiling, then adjusted his clothing as she turned away from him, curling up on the floor like a ball, and slid her hands between her clenched thighs to hold herself where she ached. She just lay there, curled up, trying to regulate her breathing, then heard Michael zipping his trousers, standing upright and locking the office door.

"Madness!" he exclaimed. "Pure madness! I can't believe we did that!"

She remained where she was, holding her aching center, letting her racing heart settle and her breathing return to normal, frustrated even more than before and burning all over. Was she mad? Not yet. But she could not stay sane like this. She thought of what she needed for satisfaction, then shuddered helplessly.

Michael must have seen that, because he suddenly knelt beside her. He ran his hand lightly down her side to her raised hip, then very gently rolled her over, onto her back.

"Are you all right?" he asked her.

The question made her smile. "Why do men always ask that after sex? Are their egos that fragile?"

Michael remained grave, his face showing his concern. "Maybe," he said. "But perhaps I'm just worried about what really went on here. I'm in love with you—"

"It was sex."

"I repeat, I'm in love with you—it's not just sex; it's more than that—and I'm worried about what you actually experience when you need sex that badly."

Frances closed her eyes, trying to look into herself, having to fight back the tears as his words resounded through her, giving life to the love she had sensed in him and washing her clean. She bit her lower lip, choking back her emotions, letting tears fall on her cheeks to cool her warm skin. She loved him—at least she *wanted* to love him—but was frightened of showing it.

"We didn't make *love,*" she said, opening her eyes again. "We simply had sex."

He stared down at her, very gravely, then with slowly rising anger. "Don't speak for me," he said. "Speak for yourself—but not for me. It's not just sex—it's love. I know what I feel, damn it! I'm not a child, Frances; neither am I given to self-deception. I love you and want you."

She remained on the floor, taking deep, even breaths, looking up into his gray, intense eyes and fighting her overbrimming feelings. She had not wanted love—not after Ravello—but she could hardly resist the emotions that were now washing over her, so she nodded to let him know that she had heard him, but made no reply.

"Okay," he said. "I just wanted you to know. Now tell me why you called out Schul's name—and I'm *not* being jealous."

Frances sighed. "All right," she said. "I'll tell you, though I doubt that you'll believe me. For a while there I thought that I was back in Iraq, in Eden, being taken forcibly by Jack Schul while those other creatures stood over us."

"The *other* creatures?"

"Yes," Frances said, "the other creatures. When I went back in time, to what I think was mankind's dawning, I was usually surrounded by other primitives, whom I assumed were just like me—let's say members of the same tribe—but at some point was also surrounded by other creatures like the ones we saw at Stonehenge. I thought of them as God's children because they'd emerged from disc-shaped lights which had, in their turn, emerged from a greater light, which I thought was God. Whether right or wrong about that, I *am* convinced that those creatures, whatever their nature, were controlling our actions, and that even now I'm under their influence and cannot escape it."

Michael nodded, then stood up and stretched himself, looking very tall and broad above her.

"And your sexual appetite?" he asked levelly. "Do they control that as well?"

"If you're talking about my need for the kind of things I did with Laurence—"

"I'm not."

"—then the answer is negative, since all of that—which doubtless disgusts you—I picked up from my first lover at a time when I was emotionally very vulnerable. However, if you don't mean that—"

"I don't."

"—but are talking about my increasingly abnormal need to simply *have* sex, then, yes, there's no doubt that it began during my experience in Iraq and has been growing stronger ever since. And if it continues doing so, it will almost certainly drive me out of my mind."

Michael shook his head, displaying his bewilderment. "It doesn't make any sense," he said. "There's just no logic to it."

Frances sat up, adjusted her clothing, glanced around her. Then, seeing the key in the locked door, she smiled and climbed to her feet.

"Maybe that's your problem," she said. "After all, what *is* logic?"

"You mean, whoever they are, they may not have *our* kind of logic?"

"That's right," Frances said.

Michael went to the window and looked down on Pond Street, then turned away and started to place his hands on her shoulders. Frances, feeling the heat of her own desire, stepped back out of his reach.

"Don't touch me," she said.

Michael sighed, looking hurt, then nodded his understanding; he gave her a slight, knowing smile, but made no move toward her.

"So," he said, "who *are* they?"

Frances shrugged, feeling helpless. "I don't know, Michael. I only know that when I was sucked into the dark mass, I first found myself in a place of lagoons and marshes, then found myself in a completely different time, if possibly the same place. I think it was the same place: it was just thousands of years earlier. I was a primitive creature, living with others at the edge of a great dust bowl, which I believe became filled with water, probably the sea, over subsequent centuries. So, first I was that primitive creature in a parched, primal landscape; next, I was a recognizable human type, living in lush greenery by the edge of a great lagoon—a lagoon I believe was originally no more than that very same dust bowl or, perhaps, meteorite crater. What I'm talking about is reincarnation: the possibility of multiple lives. I now believe that I've lived at least twice before—and that somehow or other that dark mass took me back to my former lives."

"A parallel world," Michael said. "Or alternate universe."

"Pardon?"

"The theory of parallel worlds is difficult to explain, mainly because of the bewildering nature of time. However, the main point is that if alternate universes *do* exist, they would do so in a completely different time scale from our own, which gives rise to the possibility that there could be a virtually identical *you* living in a different time and place, right now and always. It is also possible that what we dream is as real as *we* are, and exists, side by side with our own existence, in an eternal present containing its own past and future."

"I'm bewildered already."

"Once the dream is dreamed, it takes on a separate existence and will therefore create its own world, with past, present, and future—and *that* world, in turn, does the same—and so on to infinity."

"You're driving me crazy," Frances said.

"It's easy to do," Michael replied. "Better minds than ours have gone crazy trying to prove this—but the theory, if hard to grasp, has a high degree of probability, and *has* been used as an explanation for reincarnation, dreams, automatic writing, extrasensory perception, precognition, ghosts, and UFOs, which, according to many including Carl Jung, are psychological projections from the common racial memory of mankind."

"And the dark masses?" Frances asked, sinking into confusion. "Where do they fit into this elaborate theory?"

"Black holes," Michael said. "As I told you before, we've already found out that most areas where the disappearances occurred, possessed—at least for a short while after the disappearances—a great many of the characteristics of black holes.

Now, we *do* know that matter falling into a black hole disappears from our universe, but the million-dollar question remains . . . Where does it *go?*"

"Where indeed?" Frances murmured, hoping to get a smile out of him, but failing to do so.

"Assuming that the matter doesn't simply *disappear,*" he continued, "—which, in theoretical terms, it should not—we're left with the choice of it either reappearing in another part of our universe—maybe emerging from a white hole—or reappearing in an *alternate* universe. Accepting this second hypothesis—that the matter sucked into the black hole could reappear in an alternate universe—we have to bear in mind that there'll be no relationship between the time when the matter was sucked into the black hole and the time of its escape into the alternate universe. The black hole, then, could be a doorway through time and space, linking past, present, and future together in a simultaneous reality."

"Which means that the creatures I saw, as well as the people who disappeared, are now existing simultaneously in the past, present, and future—right here on earth, in a parallel world that we can't see."

"Yes," Michael said, "put crudely, that's just what I mean."

"So I could, in fact, have been that primitive creature at the dawn of mankind, as well as the evolving human being in the Garden of Eden?"

"Correct. Figuratively speaking, an original Eve. And now you're Frances Devereux of Hampstead, England . . . giving birth to the future."

"Oh, no!" Frances groaned.

She covered her lips with her right hand, stopping the scream she felt coming, then let a shudder of dread ripple through her before controlling herself. She thought of those creatures around her, their wavering, faceless forms, then imagined them watching her this very minute . . . silent . . . invisible.

Were they actually in this room? Was Laurence still at Stonehenge? Was her father still on the lawn, lost in another time frame, convinced he was having a bad dream and would soon wake up? It chilled her to think about it, made her feel that she was suffocating, as if the walls were closing in upon her, threatening oblivion.

"I still can't believe this," she said.

"It's only a theory," Michael replied, "if a rather persuasive one. But you're not physically pregnant—though showing most of the symptoms—and your mother is convinced that you have unusual psychic gifts, which could relate to this. Miles Ashcombe possessed psychic powers of a rather modest nature, but since emerging from that dark mass his powers have been developing remarkably. What about you?"

Frances trembled, stirred to fear by his words, remembering what she had done with the wineglasses at her mother's insistence.

"Yes," she confessed, "I'm developing such powers. Already I can do what I just saw Ashcombe do in his room."

"You can make objects float in the air?"

"Yes."

"That's just the beginning," Michael said. "Ashcombe now *amuses* himself with those games, but he can do a lot more. As I said, we're wondering when, and if, it will end—or if he'll turn into some kind of superman. Come on, let's go see him."

He took Frances by the elbow and led her out of the office, then straight to the psychiatric wing. As they approached Ashcombe's room, Frances felt her fear rising, a tide of heat that reached up to her face and made her cheeks burn. She stopped just before the room, reluctant to go any farther, but Michael, smiling encouragingly at her, tugged gently at her elbow and coaxed her right up to the door.

He slid the peephole open, looked in, his brow furrowing, then stepped aside and indicated with startled eyes that Frances also should look in. She did so—and instantly felt confused and terribly frightened, at first not understanding what she was seeing, then not quite believing it.

There were two Miles Ashcombes in the room. One, perfectly normal, was stretched out on his bed, flat on his back, his face turned toward the ceiling, a gentle smile on his lips. However, the other, not so normal—or at least the same, but surrounded by shimmering light—was hovering above the bed, lying flat on his back in thin air, his face also turned toward the ceiling, the same smile on his lips.

Frances gasped and turned away, hiding herself in Michael's embrace, shocked and frightened by what she had seen, hardly able to credit it. Michael held her close to him, patted her reassuringly, then eventually pushed her from him and, holding her lightly by the shoulders, gave her a gentle smile.

"Yes," he said, "now you see what he can do . . . and now we're going in there."

"No!"

"Yes," Michael insisted. "He's started talking and I want you to listen because it could be of use."

Again she started to protest, but was given no chance because he quickly opened the door, pushed her into the room, followed her, and closed the door behind him.

Frances stood there, terrified, trying to reject what she was seeing, but that other Miles Ashcombe, that bizarre doppel-gänger, was still hovering in the air above the original Miles Ashcombe, both wearing the same clothing and smiling the same sly smile, both stretched out in exactly the same manner . . . the only difference being that the one hovering magically in the air was encased in an eggshell of shimmering light.

Frances stared at that apparition, then lowered her gaze. When the man on the bed turned his head to stare at her, the man hovering above him did exactly the same.

Frances felt disorientated, rendered dizzy by faulty vision, but then Ashcombe, noticing her, stopped smiling and sighed—and as he did so the shimmering creature above him drifted down very slowly. It started fading when it touched him, and soon disappeared altogether, becoming no more than an egg-shell-shaped light that shimmered brightly around him, then was sucked into his body until it was all gone.

Ashcombe remained there, lying stretched out on the bed, staring steadily at Frances.

"I know you," he said, his voice hollow. "You were there on the other side."

Hearing those words, Frances felt that she was suffocating, and she stepped back until stopped by Michael's body, by the hands on her shoulders.

"It's all right," he said. "Just stay calm. There's nothing to fear."

His strong hands were a comfort, as was the heat from his body, but Frances still trembled with fear as she gazed down at Ashcombe. Because of his white hair he looked older than his age, and the smile returning to his thin lips seemed slyly triumphant. He examined her face, then her flat stomach, finally nodded judiciously and sat upright, resting his feet on the floor.

"You were there at the beginning," he said. "You were blessed, as I am."

Frances found it hard to speak, but she managed to force the words out. "What do you mean by the 'other side'?" she asked. "And the beginning of *what?*"

"You know what I mean," he said. "You have been there yourself. You were there at the dawn of mankind, and have returned more than once."

"You mean inside the dark mass?"

"Yes," he said. "Naturally. But the dark mass isn't dark—it's filled with light—and that leads to our origins."

"What origins?"

"You were blessed, as I am. You were one of those chosen to link the past to the future, to help plant the seeds of each new age as the old passed away. They came four hundred million years ago, returned ten million years ago, then came two million years ago to bless those who were chosen. First the reptile, the monkey, the upright ape, *Ramapithecus;* then they returned again, one hundred thousand years ago, to ensure that Neanderthal man would evolve into Cro-Magnon man—the true ancestor of modern man. You were there even before that, living in caves, eating your own flesh; then the landscape changed, filling with water and becoming verdant, and you—the different you that was passed down through the centuries—learned to worship them and make carvings of them before the next change was ordained. You were there at the start—at every ending and new beginning—as you are here, right now, to take part in the end of the old world . . . and the start of the new."

Frances trembled in Michael's grip, feeling disordered and unreal, her heart racing and making her skin burn with a new kind of fever. She licked her lips, thinking them parched, then forced out more words.

"Who *are* they?" she asked. "The ones who came . . . and are coming back now?"

"The gods," Ashcombe said, his eyes gleaming with a distant light. "They come from afar, from the double star, slipping through time and space. They are bodiless, but materialize before us that we might recognize them. They are here to inaugurate the new dawn—and a new breed of man."

"A *new* breed of man . . . ?" Frances almost lost her courage, but when Michael reassuringly squeezed her shoulders, she found it again. "What *kind* of new man? Will the new man have powers like your own? Like the . . . ?"

"Yes," Ashcombe answered proudly. "Like those of the gods . . . the powers that you and I have."

He raised his right hand to spread his fingers like a web, and the curtains, hanging motionless over the window, started fluttering gently. He kept his hand there, staring steadily at Frances, then the gently fluttering curtains were whipped up dramatically, flapping and snapping as if attracted to his fingers by an invisible force. Then the window exploded, sending shards of glass flying, and a fierce wind rushed into the room and slapped Frances's face.

Startled, she gasped and covered her mouth with her hands. Michael gripped her tighter and pulled her close to him as the wind, suddenly swirling around them, rushed back out, leaving silence. Then the walls of the room cracked and lumps of plaster fell to the floor. The walls spat white powder while their beams split apart, then the cracks became bigger and suddenly crisscrossed the walls like great webs.

"No!" Frances shouted desperately at Ashcombe. *"Don't tamper with this!"*

Yet even as her voice rang out, the walls were spitting more dust and plaster; then the window frame exploded from its breaking wall in a great many pieces. Frances and Michael both ducked as the pieces shot past their heads, straightened up as the carpet flew off the floor and fell over the bed.

Miles Ashcombe stood up as the floorboards started buckling and rusty nails were shot from the splitting wood like bullets to embed themselves in the ceiling that, now cracking like the walls, was sending down a fine powder.

Ashcombe smiled with sly triumph, eyes gleaming with a distant light, then raised his hands in the air about three feet apart. Sparkling lines of electric current passed from one to the other, erratically illuminating his face and making him look totally mad.

"Stop it!" Frances screamed. "Stop it! *For God's sake, don't play with them!"*

But Ashcombe didn't stop. He just stood there, smiling triumphantly. The sparkling lines of electric current jumped be-

tween his outstretched hands while the floorboards, still buckling noisily around his feet, started breaking up and flying about
the room.

"Let's get out!" Michael bawled.

He started to pull Frances out, moving back toward the door,
but large chunks of the walls exploded violently, showering
them in plaster, and they both dropped to their knees while
more floorboards snapped loose around them.

The noise had reached deafening proportions—a cacophony
of snapping wood, screeching nails, and exploding plaster—
then the fierce wind rushed back in, sweeping around and beating at them. As Michael grabbed hold of Frances and pulled her
tightly to him, she glanced up and saw that Ashcombe, still
standing by the bed, had turned into a human torch, his fingers
blackened and burning from the electricity charging between
them, his whole body from head to toe surrounded by a phosphorescent light that forced her to close her eyes.

"No!" Ashcombe shrieked. *"No!"*

Frances felt the wind departing, though its roaring still filled
the room, and at the sound of Miles Ashcombe's desperate cry,
she looked up again.

The wind was still there, forming a whirlwind around Ashcombe, who, frozen in its vortex and surrounded by the dazzling light, was releasing a high-pitched, macabre wailing that
added dramatically to the general bedlam. The whirlwind
roared and swirled, sucking up plaster and broken floorboards,
and Ashcombe, growing fainter in the brilliance inside the
storm, remained in that pose of stark, frozen terror while his
screaming also started fading away, growing more and more
distant. He rapidly became less real, then seemed to be transparent, then dissolved into the dazzling light and faded out with
his screaming.

The whirlwind was still roaring and swirling at a furious rate,
but now surrounded only the globe of shimmering light—then
that, too, started fading away to let the storm settle down. The
whirling floorboards fell to the floor, as did nails and pieces of
plaster, then the wind gave one last, defiant whisper and died
out completely, leaving nothing but a devastated room, filled
with drifting white powder.

Then Miles Ashcombe called out of nowhere. He was appeal-
ing desperately for help. He kept calling out of thin air, his

voice ethereal and haunting, until after a few minutes it faded away completely, lost at the other side of the universe, leaving a stark, chilling silence.

Frances remained kneeling on the ruined floor, safe in Michael's embrace.

They both stared at the empty room.

"Y ES," Mrs. Devereux said, picking flecks of cotton off her brightly patterned Victorian dress and squinting upward out of the gloom through her spectacles, "but what did he *mean* exactly? What was he trying to convey before he performed his Houdini act?"

"Please, Mother," Frances admonished her, "it's not funny. That remark's out of place."

"*Nothing* is out of place, dear," her mother replied. "Nothing is out of place, anywhere, anytime, and my remark was designed simply to make you feel less gloomy than you look."

"It seems clear," Michael said, ignoring the minor altercation, "that he was talking about the different stages of mankind's development, and about the fact that these creatures have materialized on earth at each of those stages. The first visit mentioned by Ashcombe was four hundred million years ago, which would be in the early Devonian, when the first fish crawled out of the sea and onto the land. The next visit, according to Ashcombe, was ten million years ago, which would be about the time of the first upright man, *Ramapithecus.* The next visit mentioned was during the time of Neanderthal man, who, for reasons not yet fully explained, disappeared to make way for Cro-Magnon man."

"A disappearance that could be explained by our visitors," Mrs. Devereux intervened.

"Correct," Michael said. "He then went on to talk about how the landscape gradually changed, becoming more verdant, and suggesting that the ancestors of Cro-Magnon man evolved into a race that learned to worship the so-called gods and make carvings about them. Since even *we* know that the aliens materialize out of disc-shaped lights, that would explain why Cro-Magnon man was known to have carved stones into disc and spherical shapes, and why many of his cave paintings—the world's first paintings—were basically magical. What Ashcombe was implying, then, is that the so-called gods have visited the earth at each vital stage of humankind's development in order to specifically shape, or guide, its progress; and that Frances, and others like her, have been used—and are still being used—as channels through which each new stage of development is ushered in. If the dark mass is a kind of black hole—at least in the sense of being a space–time warp—it *could* contain every event in history, as well as the future; thus Frances, Laurence, and Schul—and everyone else sucked into the dark mass—could have relived their previous lives, all of which exist simultaneously in the dark mass's space–time continuum."

"This sounds distressingly complex," Mrs. Devereux said. "It makes me wish I were dead."

"It may be complex," Michael said, "but it also seems likely —and Miles Ashcombe *did* say that those creatures can slip through time and space."

"So," Mrs. Devereux said, "accepting that, where do they *come* from?"

"They come from a double star," Frances said, "wherever that is."

"I think it's Sirius," Michael said.

Frances noticed that her mother was leaning forward in her chair, her slim body looking even smaller in the loose Victorian dress. There was only one lamp turned on, beaming its light on two walls, romantically illuminating the paintings on those walls as well as the area in which they were sitting. Frances's mother, staring up at Michael's broad bulk, seemed spectrally beautiful.

"Sirius?" Mrs. Devereux said sweetly. "I don't believe I recall it."

Michael smiled at that. "Sirius is the brightest star in our sky. It is, in fact, a double star whose invisible companion—invisible at least to us—is now known as Sirius B. However, one of the most remarkable things about Sirius is that while its invisible companion, Sirius B, was not discovered until 1862, a so-called primitive African tribe, the Dogon, have always known about it, always described it as the smallest and *heaviest* of all stars, and always knew that it rotates on its own axis, revolves around Sirius A every fifty years, and has an elliptical orbit. Modern astronomical knowledge supports all these facts, but how a primitive tribe like the Dogon could have known them throughout their history is a mystery that has never been solved. However, we *do* know that the Dogon believe all creation originated in Sirius B, that Sirius was the sacred star of the ancient Egyptians, and that an Egyptian dissertation attributed to their legendary founder of magic, Hermes Trismegistos, states that he, Trismegistos, landed on earth to teach men the arts of civilization, then returned to his home, quote, *in the stars.* It's also interesting that the Dogon are in Africa where the upright ape, the *Ramapithecus,* first appeared during one of the periods mentioned by Miles Ashcombe. Finally, it's worth mentioning that Stonehenge—*and* other renowned megalithic circles built over geomagnetic-line convergence points—had originally sixty stones in its outer circle, which relates to the sixty-year cycle of the astronomy of the Dogon, as well as to that of the Hindus and the Chaldeans, the latter being the founders of astronomy.''

Listening to Michael speaking, Frances had gone into a trance; she now found herself staring past her mother's head at what she could see of the gray sky through the tall window. She was thinking of space, of the boundless realms of the cosmos, and of how if space were curved, as theoretically seemed likely, it might be possible to travel from one point to another by dropping *through* space, thus circumventing time, instead of traveling around it.

A black hole, she thought. *Where time and space have no meaning . . .* She tried to imagine that place, to visualize that eternal All, to see herself and her father, Laurence and Schul, and all the others repeating their multiple lives over and over, outside all known dimensions. It was like trying to conceive of God—His nature foiled comprehension—so she sighed, sinking back into defeat, that very mortal emotion.

"And can I take it," her mother asked, undefeated and inexhaustible, "that we're still talking about bodiless, or incorporeal, creatures who materialize before us only that we might recognize them, or at least relate to them?"

"Yes," Michael said, "that appears to be the case."

"Which gets us to *ghosts* or *spirits,*" Mrs. Devereux said. "And thus back to spiritualism."

Michael sat back in his chair and stared steadily at Mrs. Devereux, then unconsciously reached out for Frances's hand and squeezed it affectionately.

"Yes," Mrs. Devereux said, "spiritualism. Contact with ghosts or spirits. For years it has been assumed that if we make contact, it's with the dead; but what has baffled a great many, and turned others into cynics, is that the dead, when they talk —either through the speech of mediums, automatic writing, or table rapping—do not make intelligible conversation or impart worthwhile knowledge. Incoherency, confusion, or ambiguity is the standard fare, and since those communicating—the so-called dead—are supposed to be familiar with the living, it has never been explained why that intercourse is on such a low level."

Mrs. Devereux stared steadily at Michael, eyes enlarged behind the spectacles, her head, perched on top of the billowing dress, looking unnaturally small.

"Do you follow my train of thought? It may *not* be the dead. Or if they *are* dead, they've simply become part of that alternate world, where time and space have no meaning. We may be communicating with *that* world—actually talking across the infinite—and that distance, which may not relate to any dimensions we can comprehend, could well make *all* attempts at communication unintelligible and suspect. No, Michael, we may be talking not of the dead but of your alternate universe; one— perhaps one of many—that keeps invading our world, in some cases by deliberate design, in others by accident."

"I'm sorry," Frances said, feeling the need to hear her own voice, convinced that she would otherwise disappear down the funnel of her own abstract thoughts. "I'm sorry to interrupt, but all the evidence points to the fact that these creatures have been coming here *deliberately* for a definite purpose."

"Of course," her mother replied. "I've not forgotten that at all. I'm merely suggesting that these creatures, who coexist side by side with us, divorced from considerations of known time and space, may sometimes *accidentally* materialize in our world and be viewed by us as so-called ghosts, or spirits. Similarly, unfortunate souls like your father and Laurence may be sucked into their alternate universe—or, much worse, some ghastly purgatorial void in between, and remain there, convinced they're having a bad dream, perhaps for eternity. So we see ghosts—and *they* see ghosts . . . and we haunt one another."

Frances took note of Michael's stupefied expression, then gently jerked the hand she was holding and drew his attention. He smiled and shook his head, obviously weary but fascinated, then squeezed her hand and turned back to her mother.

"Do you understand, dear Michael?"

"I think so, Mrs. Devereux. I'm trying to align your theory with mine. What we're saying is that the dark mass is a sort of time–space warp, a gateway through time and space, and that it enables those on Sirius, who are bodiless anyway, to materialize instantaneously in our world at any point in its history, past, present, *or* future. We're also suggesting that such space–time warps exist all over the earth, that they have always waxed and waned in strength and, in so doing, often sucked unfortunate souls in, making them disappear from our own space–time frame. Finally, we're suggesting that those space–time warps, which formerly waxed and waned according to fluctuations in the earth's geomagnetic field, are now growing progressively stronger, to suck the old earth, piece by piece, into another space–time continuum and, as it were, spit out a new world, which will likely include a new breed of man—by our standards, a superrace. Finally, we're suggesting that this superrace, which will be incorporeal like those on Sirius, is being given life through women like Frances—all over the earth."

Mrs. Devereux nodded, no longer smiling, the lamplight reflecting from her spectacles and distorting her eyes. "Yes," she said, "that sums it up admirably. I think that's what is happening here."

Frances stared at her, stunned, then shook her head despairingly from side to side and glanced desperately at Michael. He did not turn his head, but instead kept his attention on her mother.

"I am psychic," her mother said. "Frances, also, is psychic. I think we should join hands in a séance and try to contact the other world. I believe that with Frances and I doing this together, we should at least obtain some interesting results. It's important to me—I'm convinced my husband is still alive—but it's also of vital importance to Frances, who is involved more deeply than either of us in this singular mystery. Do you agree? Will you do it?"

Michael glanced questioningly at Frances, but with underlying enthusiasm, and she felt the fear descending on her like a dark, heavy blanket. She closed her eyes, trying to think, wanting the courage to refuse but knowing that no matter her own fears, she would have to consent. She would do it mainly for her mother, and possibly for Michael, but also quite selfishly for herself, out of fear's desperation.

Like her mother, she was obsessed—with her father's loss and her need for him—but unlike her mother, who had tried to assuage her obsession in spiritualism, she had tried to do the same by finding a man who might act as replacement. So, she had looked to older men, to mature men, father figures, and in so doing had courted the disaster that had subsequently come to her.

Ravello, she thought. *My waterloo was in Ravello. . . .* And recalled that white-walled room above the narrow street off the square, the church bells that tolled for the godly while she writhed on a sweat-soaked bed. She had not found another father, but had found an older man, one with a predator's instincts and a pimp's idle fancies. He had released her sensual self, and enslaved her through that; then, having enslaved her mind and flesh, had stripped her down to the naked bone. There was no place for shame, then, no possibility of resistance, no hope for redemption or self-assertion while degradation was paramount. She did all that he asked of her, then more, and more again, and when she was leaving, when he laughed in her face, she saw no future before her.

Yes, she thought, *that is it: I sold my soul for a father figure. I gave everything I was, heart and soul, mind and body, because I could not admit to myself that my father was gone.*

Now she shuddered, remembering, and felt Michael squeezing her hand; looked at him, then at her mother, and knew she owed it to both of them.

"I'm agreeable if you are," she said to Michael.

"I'm agreeable," he said.

Mrs. Devereux nodded, straightened her dress, and stood up. "Fine," she said. "Just let me draw the curtains. We can do it right here."

She went to the tall windows that overlooked the rear garden, drew the curtains to plunge the room into a darkness only broken by the triangular light beaming obliquely from a tall lamp. Next, she removed a potted plant from a small, round table and placed three straight-backed walnut chairs around it. After turning out the light—leaving the room completely dark but for a sliver of grayness beaming through the curtains—she indicated that Frances and Michael should join her. They did so, Frances sitting on one side of her mother, Michael on the other, the three of them linking their hands together in an oddly charged silence.

"You don't have to do anything, Michael," Mrs. Devereux said. "Just keep holding our hands, irrespective of what you might see or hear. Frances, I want you to close your eyes, as I will be doing, then simply concentrate. Try to block out your thoughts. That's all: simply empty your mind."

Frances stared across the table, seeing Michael's face in darkness, taking comfort from it before closing her eyes and letting the silence enfold her. At first she felt foolish and even had to resist giggling, then also had to resist the temptation to let go of their hands; then she felt Michael's grip tightening her fingers, and the feeling she derived from that contact made her more passive.

She concentrated on her closed eyelids, studying the void behind them, trying to will herself to drift into her mind as if into the sky. It was quiet and very dark, but streaked with white light, and she tried to imagine it as a universe stretching out to eternity. Michael's hand was warm. An electric charge came from her mother. She felt her body glowing with a heat that made her sleepy, that seemed to dissolve her where she sat and let her drift through the ether.

It stayed silent and dark, still streaked with white light, then the lines of light moved in languid loops, coils, and circles until they resembled a great web that stretched out to the infinite. The web was phosphorescent, illuminating the void, then the spaces between the crisscrossing, glowing lines became filled with stars.

The lines of white light moved apart, racing away in all directions, shrinking to nothing beyond immeasurable distances and leaving only the stars. Everything moved toward her, sweeping around her on all sides, surging above and below in great waves that unfurled majestically. Then there was no up or down, no left or right; only constant movement around her, an unfurling of space and time.

There were Magellanic Clouds, dark and luminous nebulae, glittering whirlpool galaxies, spiraling solar flares, and pulsating star clusters; then a comet streaked across the heavens, leading toward two distant stars that, as space unfurled around her, moved farther apart and spread their fierce light through the void. One star disappeared when the other exploded silently around her—then she saw, in the dazzling brilliance of God's fire, the scorched earth in its timeless core. The light flared up stupendously, temporarily blinding her, then shrank back to a bearable intensity, letting time and space perpetually re-create all—the past, present, and future.

"It's all right," a man's voice said in her mind. "There is nothing to fear."

She saw Laurence's profile floating in a haze before her, then moved back until she saw him on the grassy mound with Stonehenge beyond him. He was staring at the sky, his hand at his forehead, trying to see the eye of God in the great light descending on him.

Laurence did not move. He seemed frozen into that position. Frances willed him to move and he dissolved, as did the circle of ancient stones, and there, where Stonehenge had been, but still surrounded by the green grass, a great pool of water, a lagoon, had magically materialized. Beyond the lagoon was more green earth, the glint of other marshes; then, on the grassy mound before the pool, Laurence appeared again.

This time he looked different, his clothing no more than a loincloth, and he stood gazing over the lake with a woman beside him. The woman was familiar, body slim, long hair dark, and she stood beside Laurence, perfectly silent and motionless, while a mist rising off the darkly glinting water gradually fell over them like a shroud, until they had disappeared.

The mist became more dense, impenetrable, and ominous, then a fierce light, first a pinprick then a great hole, gradually burned the mist away, revealing a scorched, barren landscape hazed in shimmering heat waves. A volcanic mountain spewed in the distance. A desolate dust bowl stretched for miles. There were caves near the dust bowl, with short, apelike creatures in front of them. One of them was fornicating with another; both were faintly familiar.

She watched them, moved closer, became one of them and looked up, saw unrecognizable creatures gathered around her, silhouetted in a shimmering white light that fell down from the sky. Then one of them leaned lower to touch her, and she opened her eyes. . . .

Frances glanced left and right, first at Michael, then at her mother, and saw a creature standing behind her mother, placing his hands on her shoulders.

Frances screamed—hardly aware that she was doing so—conscious only of that creature, a luminous figure in the darkness, an oddly glowing silhouette, human-shaped, without features, now placing its hands on her mother's shoulders and making her luminous also.

Mrs. Devereux jerked her head up, staring wide-eyed past Frances, then Frances glanced at Michael and saw him throwing himself away from his chair, behind which another glowing, spectral figure had been silently standing.

Frances heard her own scream. It slashed her free from her paralysis, making her jump to her feet and twist to the side as a glowing hand brushed down her body. Her chair clattered onto the floor, she heard Michael's frightened cursing, then she saw her mother quivering in a ball of light, while the luminous figure standing right behind her kept its grip on her shoulders.

Her mother shuddered and cried out, then shook like an epileptic, fell sideways when the luminous figure released its grip, just as Frances switched on the nearest lamp.

The light was briefly blinding. Her heart was racing wildly. There was a dull thud as her mother fell to the floor and rolled over to stare up at the ceiling, her face contorting in pain.

"No!" Frances cried out.

She rushed to her fallen mother, dropping onto her knees beside her, only realizing as she did so that the creatures had disappeared and that Michael was hurrying around the table, cursing under his breath. Then she looked down at her mother and saw her deathly-white face, the spectacles askew on her birdlike nose, eyes glassy and lifeless.

A chill slid through Frances, then a fierce, blinding rage; she grabbed her mother and started to shake her and scream into her dead face. She didn't know what she was screaming, hardly knew she was doing so; then someone was holding her shoulders and pulling her back.

She suddenly burst into tears, let herself be turned around,
then buried her face in Michael's broad chest as he gently
rocked her and stroked her spine. She wept a long time, on her
knees, in Michael's arms; then, when she had drained herself of
tears, stared down at her dead mother's body and clenched both
her fists.

"Damn them!" she said. "I've taken this for too long. I'm
going back to Iraq, I'm going to find the Garden of Eden, and
once I get there, no matter what it costs me, I'm going to find
out what's happening."

Michael's lips grazed her tangled hair: a gesture of love and
agreement.

Book
III

The Future

LEAVING the morning fruit and vegetable market of the Cours Saleya, Michael passed the Opera and turned into Quai des Etats-Unis, letting the breeze from the phosphorescent blue bay erase the sweat from his face. As a young, single man he had often visited Nice, never without the feeling that his future was filled with promise; but now, as he walked along the promenade, past the fishermen's *ponchettes* that had become restaurants and art galleries, he was decidedly less romantic about his future prospects, if such existed at all.

Having flown on an impulse from London that very morning, he hardly felt that he had left and could not stop thinking about what he had committed himself to. Frances's mother had been cremated the previous day at Golders Green, and remembering that sad affair, with Frances pale-faced but tearless, Michael knew that he would have to journey with her to the end of the mystery. So his future was in doubt, his horizons limited to Iraq, and it amazed him that even the magnitude of the forthcoming adventure could not dim his very human, paternal concern.

He had come to Nice to have words with his daughter in a two-faced attempt to save her from emotional disaster before embarking upon a journey from which he very likely would not return. Having already deserted her once—eight years ago, when he left his wife—he was now about to do the same thing, and, worse, in a more permanent way. He was therefore not feeling too positive as he walked along the promenade, heading for the restaurants and cafés at the base of Le Château.

Cheryl was already seated under a striped umbrella at a table overlooking the port. Michael's heart lurched when he saw her, but he didn't stop walking, merely took in her expensive denims, low-cut blouse and high-heeled shoes, and noting that her blond hair was much longer, making her look more mature.

Already tired and depressed, what he saw further disconcerted him, but his warm grin was genuine when, after reaching the table, he had leaned down to kiss her on the cheek.

"Bonjour, mademoiselle," he said. *"Comment ça va?"*

"Life's fine," Cheryl replied. "But please speak English, Daddy. I'm *dying* to have a whole conversation in English. If it's pleasant, that is."

Michael ignored the warning and took the chair facing her. She was drinking a glass of Château Simone from the bottle she had ordered, and he noticed that the bottle itself was already half empty.

"Your hair's longer," he said.

"Do you like it?" she asked him.

"Yes," he lied. "It looks very casual—just like your clothes."

"Here, Daddy, let me pour you some wine. You look all hot and bothered."

The defensive edge to Cheryl's voice made Michael realize that this was unlikely to be a pleasant conversation; but he managed to hide that feeling with a smile as she poured him some wine, then held her own glass up in the air.

"Cheers," she said.

The wine was white and chilled, with a light herbal fragrance, and instantly refreshed his dry throat and made him feel marginally better. Putting his glass down, he glanced distractedly over the port, envying those lounging on the many boats, large and small, that sailed colorfully to and fro across the mildly choppy water, under a sky filled with clouds as white and insubstantial as the trembling waves.

"Are you hungry?" Cheryl asked.

"No," he said. "Not very."

"You rarely are at lunchtime, so I've already ordered mussels *and* another bottle of white wine."

"Isn't that a lot to *drink* at lunchtime?"

"I thought today I might need it."

She stared at him with veiled defiance, her blue eyes emphasized by her suntan. Sighing, he drank some more wine.

"All right, Daddy," Cheryl said. "Here you are. So, why *are* you here?"

"You know why."

"I told you, I don't want to talk about it."

"But you told me we could talk on the phone—and then you just disappeared."

"It's my work, Daddy. I'm here because of *work.* We're shooting a *movie* in Nice."

"No," Michael said, "you're not. The crew all returned to London four days ago. The only ones remaining are you and this producer you fancy. Are you staying together?"

"Yes," she replied, surprisingly unperturbed to have been caught out in a blatant lie.

"Does his wife know?"

"No. She thinks he's still here working."

"And this doesn't make you feel bad?"

"That's enough," Cheryl said abruptly. "Just stop right there."

Her visible anger startled Michael, but mercifully, at that moment, the waiter arrived with their large tray of seafood. When he had placed it between them with the second bottle of wine, wishing them *bon appetit* and then departing, Michael filled both their glasses.

"Oh, well," he said. "Cheers again."

They touched glasses and drank, then started on the seafood, which, although delicious, failed to raise Michael's spirits.

"I'm sorry," he said, sampling a mussel, "but we simply can't let this lie fallow. Your affair has caused your mother grave concern; so, if I don't talk you out of it, she might do something drastic."

"Such as?"

"Well, for a start she wants me to talk to this man of yours—to convince him to end the affair and, if necessary, get you out of his life by kicking you out of your job."

"You wouldn't dare."

"I'm afraid I would. I'm a *psychologist,* dear child, and talking to people, no matter how unpleasant the subject, comes naturally to me. I don't want this man playing with my daughter, so believe me, I'll talk to him."

"He won't listen to you. He loves me."

"So, when does he leave his wife for you?"

"He wants to, but can't. He's frightened of wounding her and their children. He says he might do it in a year or two, when the children at least have finished at university and can stand on their own feet."

"A likely story," Michael said.

"It's *true,*" Cheryl replied, chewing a mussel. "We've discussed it at some length," she added, "and I agree with him totally. I love him and I want to live with him—but not with too much damage on my conscience."

"Oh, I see," Michael said. "He also discussed the damage it would do to *you* if you actually broke up his family. Obviously a very thoughtful man—omitting no point of view."

"Don't be sarcastic, Father. Examine yourself before you start casting stones at others."

The transition from "Daddy" to the more formal "Father" was enough to signal that the distance between them was widening; and the pain Michael felt was only increased by the way Cheryl had thrown his past back at him.

"Damn you, Cheryl," he said, "that was mean. That was under the belt."

"You're criticizing the man I love for showing more consideration for *his* family than you showed to yours eight years ago— so don't expect any fairness from *me.*"

"It's true your mother and I divorced," Michael said angrily, "but I've looked after both of you ever since. I'm still your father, I never deserted you, and I didn't desert your mother, either. We just gradually drifted apart, that's all."

"And so you think that David would be a better man if he walked out on his wife and kids?"

"Dammit, Cheryl, I'm just trying to protect you. My situation wasn't the same—I didn't leave your mother for a younger woman. In fact, I didn't leave her for *anyone* in particular—I just needed my freedom. I'm not criticizing your David for not wanting to leave his family; I'm just trying to convince you that this relationship can only bring you suffering; that sooner or later you're going to want him on a more permanent basis; and that in all probability, when that sorry day comes, your David *still* won't leave his wife and children."

"So?" Cheryl asked, still trying to sound defiant, but clearly more nervous.

"You'll then be faced," Michael explained, firmly believing his own logic but ashamed of its brutality, "with the dismal choice of living without him completely or growing old as his increasingly burdensome mistress. Now is that what you want?"

"I want to cross that bridge when I come to it. I don't want to discuss it now."

Michael just stared at her, hurt and angry at her vehemence, wondering why he should be so concerned about her, now knowing what her future might be. He was naturally thinking of the dark masses, of the places that had disappeared, of Miles Ashcombe, Frances, her dead mother, and the mysteries surrounding them.

The world seemed to be disappearing. A new world might be replacing it. He and Frances might be traveling into a future from which there was no return. Did it matter what Cheryl did? Did she have a future at all? Would the earth keep disappearing until there was nothing left but empty marshlands and a desolate, eternal silence?

Asking himself those questions—which he had done ceaselessly for the past four days—Michael suddenly realized exactly why he was going on that singular journey with Frances: If the earth was to disappear, taking those he loved with it, he could not stand by idly and let it happen while there was the slightest chance of finding out the cause and doing something about it. At this point he was willing to risk losing those he most loved because of the faint hope that he might either get them back or find them again in that new world. . . . But he could hardly explain all that to his daughter, least of all in these circumstances.

"I told you before," he said instead, "and I'm going to tell you again: If you don't stop seeing this man, I'm going to have to talk to him—and if *he* refuses to do anything about it, then your mother will step into the picture, and she's less liberal than I am."

"If David says no to you, he'll say the same to Mother."

"If David says no to me, your mother won't even go near him. She's told me—and knowing her, I believe her—that she'll go straight to his wife."

There was a shocked silence from Cheryl as she took in what he had said. She started raising her glass to her lips, but then put it down again, her gaze wandering restlessly around the fashionable, busy port before returning reluctantly to the front.

"She wouldn't!" she finally exclaimed, as if she really could not believe it.

"She would," Michael replied. "And you know it—so don't let it go that far."

Cheryl glanced blindly around her, as if searching for someone who might come and take her away from the real world. She shook her head from side to side, as if denying what she had heard, then sniffed like a little girl, rubbing her face with one hand.

"Oh, Christ!" she whispered.

Suddenly she jumped up and hurried away from the table, pushing the milling people aside as she made her way across the promenade. Michael called the waiter, quickly paid him, and followed Cheryl, also having to push rudely through the crowds of tourists until he reached the sea side of the road. Cheryl was standing with her back to him, looking out at the busy port; and as he approached her and finally stopped by her side, he found himself staring in considerable pain and embarrassment at her suntanned, tear-streaked profile. A light breeze coming in from the bay covered her face with her blond hair.

"Oh, God," she said, "you're right. I know you're right, but I can't stop it. I love him and can't stop thinking about him and that's all there is to it. I think he knows that and uses it, but I can't help that either. He just says he can't possibly leave his wife and I have to accept it. I *know* I'm being used. I keep promising myself that each time will be the last, but then when he tells me that he wants me, I go with him. He insists that he *does* love me—but that he owes his wife and children. He often says that we have to live for the moment—and I accept that as well. What can I do? I've tried to stop it, but can't. Each time I see him, it hurts me even more; but it also makes me *want* him even more, and I just can't control that. God, it's made my life a misery, made me mean and contrary, but I can't bear the thought of being without him, so I live on in hope."

She turned in toward him and let him wrap her in his arms, her body trembling as she silently wept and he patted her shoulders. He was blinded by the light and overrun by emotion, his objectivity melting into the warmth of the love he could not disown.

"You've got to let me work it out myself," she said, sniffing and stepping back a little to wipe the tears from her eyes. "Promise me that, Daddy—that at least you'll give me some time. Don't let Mother go and see his poor wife until I come back to England."

"When will that be? She'll want to know."

Cheryl shrugged. "I can't say. But I promise you, it won't be long—perhaps a week at most."

"You've got to talk to him," Michael insisted. "You've got to make him choose—either you or his family—and this time don't settle for any vague generalities: insist on a straight reply, one way or the other, then make your decision."

"I'm not sure that I can do that, but I'll try. God, it's all such a mess!"

Michael was shocked at how easily he had lost his daughter —but even more shocked when he suddenly found himself thinking about Frances and the extraordinary journey they would soon be making together. He was not a religious man and had formerly prided himself on his pragmatism, but now he found himself floundering in a sea of doubts and self-recriminations, none of which were made any easier by this encounter with Cheryl.

The miraculous events he had witnessed during the past few weeks had undermined the foundations of his former beliefs, convincing him that his life would be meaningless if he did not pursue the mystery to its source, no matter what that might be. Were this not enough, he also had to face the fact that his affair with Frances (even though based on love) contravened his professional oaths and, even more base, branded him as someone who was placing his own needs above those of his daughter and former wife.

He was, after all, about to leave on a journey from which he might not return, was doing it with a patient with whom he had had sexual relations, and now, even trying to protect his daughter from her own blindness, was going to have to tell her about a decision that might strike her as being considerably more senseless than her own affair.

Michael gazed out over the bay, distracting himself with the sailing boats, seeing girls in bikinis stretched out on the decks

while men drank and played around folding tables in the light
of a blinding sun. Feeling totally disassociated from that, he
sighed and turned back to Cheryl, realizing that he was going to
have to tell her just what he was planning.

"All right," he said, "it's time I made my confession. I have
another, more vital reason for being concerned about your future and how that man might affect it. . . . I'm going away, I
don't know how long for, and in fact, I don't know if I'll be
coming back. Please," he added, when he saw her eyes widening, "just let me explain."

He told her about his involvement in the Glastonbury event,
about what had happened at Stonehenge, about the dark masses
that seemed to be eating the earth piecemeal, about Miles Ashcombe and Laurence, about the voices he had heard crying
despairingly from thin air and the figures that had materialized
magically at the séance, about the death of Mrs. Devereux—
and finally, reluctantly, but with no other option, he told her
about Frances, and about why he had to go with her to Iraq to
find the Garden of Eden.

When he had finished talking—and saw the shock in Cheryl's
face—he knew he had made a mistake.

"What *is* this?" she asked, eyes growing large. "I can't actually believe what I've just heard. Just what is this . . . *nonsense?*"

"Cheryl, you *know* what happened at Glastonbury. You've
read all about it. *And* about all the other places. So please believe me, it's true!"

"I don't give a damn," she said, her voice rising to incredu-
lity, "I'm not interested in Glastonbury, nor in your other ho-
cus-pocus; I just can't get over the fact that you came here to
chastise *me,* just before running off on some patently crazy basis
with a woman who's also one of your patients—"

"*Please,* Cheryl!"

"—a woman obviously sent to you because of her mental
problems and who, instead of being cured by you, was actually
seduced by you. God, the hypocrisy!"

"I did *not* seduce her," Michael insisted. "It wasn't like that
at all! As I've already explained, Frances was driven by extremely strong needs that were exacerbated by her experience
in—"

"Right," Cheryl interjected, her rage turning to contempt. "And even knowing that, you—"

"Please, Cheryl! I couldn't help myself! It just happened that way!"

He realized what he had said the second the words left his mouth, and watched in despair as Cheryl took a step backward, nodding and glancing histrionically around her to express disbelief and outrage. When eventually she turned back to him, her gaze was unforgiving, and her lips, normally ripe with good humor, had formed a thin line.

"Go on your damned journey," she said, "and take your demented woman with you. You must be demented yourself to even *contemplate* such a thing! As for me, don't you *dare* talk to me about my future. If you had any concern for that, you wouldn't be running off with that woman for reasons which can only be described as crazy. You left me once and now you're doing it again. I doubt that anything my lover will do to me could be worse than you've done. Damn you, Father, *go home!"*

She turned away and rushed off, the wind whipping up her blond hair, very quickly becoming lost in the dense, lunchtime crowds along the promenade. Feeling naked and torn, Michael wanted to pursue her, but he held the impulse in check, knowing perfectly well that it was useless, and instead just continued standing there staring despairingly about him.

The sailboats filled the bay, their bright-colored sails flapping, and beyond them the sea was a rippling blue that stretched out to where it merged with the azure sky in a silvery haze.

Michael stood there for a very long time, longing to lose himself in the future and never return.

24

FRANCES said little while the moving men did their work. She merely wandered to and fro, from one room to the other, silently observing as her mother's house was stripped bare—furniture, paintings, antiques, and musical instruments—each item, as it was carried out, taking another memory with it, as if her history was being eaten away piece by piece, just like the whole world.

The men, wearing overalls, were fast and efficient, talking constantly as they worked, mostly a stream of ribald banter, oblivious to the fact that their world was disappearing just as surely as the contents of the house.

Watching, Frances wondered why it was happening and what it signified. On the simplest level there was no mystery to it: she was going on a journey from which she would probably not return, so the house had been sold and its contents would later be auctioned off. However, on a more emotional level what was happening was very different: she was getting rid of her past, rendering her personal history obsolete, in order to embrace the future more readily and find her own destiny.

So, as the men stripped the house of its contents, she thought of Iraq, of the Arabs in the marshlands, and, most of all, of that place she now knew was Eden. She had to return there—for her lost father and dead mother; for the magical child she was carrying. And as the pieces of her life were carried out to be auctioned off, she felt a curious mixture of dread and quiet exultation.

It was late in the afternoon when the men completed the removal, by which time Frances had almost finished drinking a bottle of Riesling. She could not recall opening it, but that fact seemed unimportant, and when the van had moved off, taking her mother's possessions to a warehouse, she emptied the last of the wine into her glass and stared out the front window.

The light was gradually fading, making the street gray and forbidding, so she turned away and examined the empty room in which she had grown up.

The people buying the house, wanting to renovate it, had insisted that everything be removed, including carpets and curtains. Now, with the floor as bare as the walls, the very silence seemed to be amplified, and the floorboards creaked each time she moved, giving the room, which once had resounded with music and laughter, a hollow, eerie quality.

Frances sipped some wine and then started wandering about, trying to reconcile what she was seeing with the home she had known and loved. Stripped bare, it was unrecognizable, impersonal, devoid of character; its blank walls, high ceilings, and uncovered floorboards made it seem much larger than it actually was.

She stopped in the music room, imagining her mother at the piano, and immediately felt a wave of pain at her loss. She closed her eyes and breathed deeply, and thought of that final séance. She felt the power flowing through her, saw the oddly glowing figures in the darkness that surrounded her mother. Those same specters had been at Stonehenge, emerging out of space and time, as they had done so many years before on the night of her own miraculous birth.

Now, remembering what her mother had told her about that birth, Frances shook her head in disbelief and walked from the room.

She stopped in the hallway, too aware of the silence, feeling it pressing upon her and forcing her into herself. Buried deeply within her was that other, less-known Frances, and she became increasingly aware of her presence as she walked up the creaking stairs.

Michael was in France, having words with his daughter, but she felt his presence permeating the air, as if conjured up by her. He had held her hand during the séance, and she felt that energy now, rising up from her depths like a light burning through veils of mist. Her need for him made her tremble, seeding the wasteland of her grief, and when she thought of her mother's coffin sliding into the flames, she took solace from the knowledge that Michael's love had been gained from that singular loss.

On the landing she stopped again, gazing at each of the bedroom doors. She had intended checking them all, to ensure that nothing had been left behind, but instead, moved by an irresistible impulse, she opened the door of her mother's bedroom, then stepped inside.

Leaning her back against the door, she drank the last of her wine, then stared at the empty space where her mother's antique bed had stood. She kept staring, concentrating, willing the past to return, and eventually saw the room as it had been, with the bed right in front of her. She kept focusing on the bed, sensing the power flowing through her, visualizing what had happened at her birth, thirty-five years ago. . . .

The light around her darkened, bringing the bed into relief, and she saw her mother lying there in labor, with an abstracted, kindly man, whom Frances knew was her father, leaning down anxiously. Then the darkness was streaked with silver, a shimmering light filled the room, and in that brilliant haze tall, translucent figures materialized and surrounded the bed.

Frances saw herself being born—as her own child would soon be born—and she gasped, almost weeping at this revelation, then let the present return.

She was shocked and shaken, unable to accept what she had witnessed, but when she studied the room, she saw only the normal bare walls.

Her heart was racing uncomfortably, but she took a deep breath, then walked in a determined manner across the room and set her glass on the windowsill. She gazed at the lawn below, closed her eyes, stared through her eyelids, willed the present to roll back to the past with its numerous mysteries.

The afternoon turned to evening, bathing the trees in moonlight. Another darkness descended and swallowed the moonlight, then filled up with tiny, pulsating lights and an ethereal singing. Her father stepped into that garden and looked up at the sky, then shaded his eyes and started squinting as another light blinded him. He dissolved into that light, his body spreading out like liquid. The light faded away, taking the strands of his body with it—then the moonlight returned and her father's voice came out of thin air, calling desperately for help. He called out repeatedly, with a naked, haunting fear, but his voice gradually grew weaker, more shaky and distant, then eventually tapered off in some faraway place, leaving nothing but the occasional rustle of autumnal leaves in the night's clinging silence.

Frances took a deep breath, opened her eyes, and looked out again, seeing nothing but a normal, overgrown lawn in fading afternoon light. She glanced at her wineglass, saw a vaporous moon reflected, shivered, turned away from the window, and walked from the room.

The house was nearly in darkness when she walked back downstairs, but she found that a comfort and did not turn on the lights. She wanted to find herself—that other Frances deep inside—and having just seen herself being born, she understood her own nature. She was frightened and awed by that, scarcely able to grasp its meaning, but she now knew that her destiny lay in the marshlands of Iraq.

She walked back into the almost dark, deserted front room and sat cross-legged on the floor, facing the window. She felt the power flowing through her—the power her mother had said would grow—and closed her eyes to concentrate on the future instead of the past.

She needed something to focus on, so thought of this very house, watching it taking shape in her mind just a year or two hence. It was completely renovated and looked modern, if charmless, but the people moving through it were at their ease, clearly not feeling threatened.

Frances was puzzled. The world should have disappeared. How could this house and its new tenants still exist in that future?

She leaned back against the wall, rubbed against it like a cat, stared through the window directly opposite at the lights of the facing house. Above the house the sky was cloudy, its grayness being erased by darkness, and she thought of her first meeting with Michael in the hospital nearby.

Thinking about him, she yearned for him, but managed to cast her mind into the future . . . and *still* saw the hospital. Outside, it seemed normal, the street in front of it filled with traffic; inside, it was business as usual, with no sign of disturbance.

Again, she was puzzled by what she was seeing, having expected to find marshland where the hospital had been and instead seeing an unchanged, normal world.

She kept leaping farther ahead, another five years, another ten, and eventually, in some distant future, saw the building changing—not because of a dark mass or any other unnatural cause, but because of the normal ravages of time and man's redevelopment.

The world, then, had not disappeared: it had simply followed its natural course.

Stunned and bewildered, Frances gazed around the dark room, trying to will herself to get up and leave the house for the last time. In the pocket of her denims was a key to Michael's apartment, and touching it accidentally with her fingers, she was filled with his presence. He would be returning from France this evening and they would meet at his place; in a few days they would leave for Iraq and a problematical future.

What future might that be? And what did her visions signify? Why did her precognition contradict what was happening right now?

Frances sighed and leaned forward, covering her face with her hands. She concentrated on the darkness behind her closed eyelids, trying to gauge the resonance of the silence and lose herself in the nothing.

The nothing was seductive, almost lulling her into sleep . . . but suddenly she heard the front door being opened, then clicking shut again.

Her heart gave a leap and made her open her eyes. She looked up to see a tall, deep-shadowed, faceless figure standing still in the doorway of the moonlit room.

"What are you doing still sitting here?" Michael asked. "I've already been back to my apartment, expecting to find you there. Is everything all right?"

Frances sighed with relief and let her racing heart settle, then raised her right hand in the air and waved him toward her.

"Come here," she said. "Sit here beside me. I want you to hold me."

He did as he was told, sitting beside her on the floor, kissing her on the forehead, the neck, the lips, then sliding one arm around her and pulling her to him.

"Savoring your last moments here?" he asked her.

"Yes," she replied. "Something like that. So, how did it go with your daughter? Did you manage to tell her?"

Michael sighed forlornly. "Yes," he said. "Just about. Alas, she didn't take it very well, so I'm not feeling too proud of myself."

"And did you tell her about me?"

"Yes, but it only made things worse. Now I'm not only deserting her again—I'm also having an affair with one of my patients. In truth, then, our meeting was bloody awful. So, what about you?"

Frances pressed herself into him, trying to lose herself in his warmth, feeling guilt over what she had done to him. That she had seduced him was something that bothered her little; what disturbed her was that he was going to leave with her, probably forever. She had never met his daughter, but knew how much he loved her; and the sight of the pain in his face was almost too much to bear.

"You know, you don't have to come to Iraq," she said. "You're not personally involved like me. Also, I can go because I have no one left here, whereas you have your daughter and former wife to look after. I really don't know why you're coming—and I don't think you should."

He pressed his lips to the top of her head, let them linger there awhile, then tilted her face up toward him. "You and I were destined to go," he said, "and that's all there is to it. Besides, the more I know about this mystery, the more intrigued I become. What I learned from the Ministry of Defence today simply heightened my interest."

Night had since fallen completely, giving the room over to darkness, but the light of the streetlamps outside cast a glow on his face. He was smiling, very gently, almost in wonder, then his fingertips brushed lightly across her lips and fell onto her wrist.

"Sampson phoned me just after I got back from France," he said, his voice sounding oddly ethereal in the dark, empty room. "The first thing he told me is that monitoring operations conducted by the countries involved have indicated that the time between the appearance of the dark masses has steadily been growing longer, and that there's been *no* new materializations at all over the past month. Even better is that all seismic and atmospheric surveys conducted over the past month have indicated that the phenomenon has probably ceased for good except in a few specific areas where the geomagnetic effects, having produced that marshland, seem to have become permanent fixtures. Those areas include Glastonbury . . . and southern Iraq."

Frances felt as if a great weight was lifting off her shoulders, letting her think and breathe easier. She recalled the visions she had had before Michael's arrival—visions of a world that had not changed as she had expected. Then, filled with excitement and hope, she pressed herself tighter to him.

"So the world is out of danger," she said. "Oh, God, I was right."

"You *knew* the phenomenon was ending?"

"Let's say I sensed it," she replied. "Now what about me?"

Michael sighed again. "Sampson's surveys have revealed that you're not alone," he said. "Other women—all of whom have been involved with the dark masses—have likewise reported their conviction that they're pregnant . . . and every one of those women had formerly been told by their physicians that they would never be able to have a child. Also, in every case it's been confirmed that although those women were displaying *some* signs of pregnancy, none of them is in fact pregnant—at least not in any normal, human way. And, finally, it *has* been noted that a lot of those women have recently disappeared without explanation."

"You mean they might have gone away on their own accord —exactly as *I'm* going to do."

"Yes," Michael replied. "That's what Sampson suspects: that those women—both here and in the other countries surveyed— have returned to where they first encountered their particular dark mass. They've gone for the same reason you're going—to *complete* this affair."

Frances closed her eyes and willed the power to her, letting it rise up like a light from her center to illuminate the geography of the human soul in its flight to perfection. She saw how she had been born, and how her child would be born, then she saw the other women, all of whom were conscious of her, making their secret, solitary journeys back to where the spirit had entered them.

Their old lives had ended and a new life would begin, but the world as they knew it would for the most part remain, coexisting side by side with that equally real world beyond human perceptions. It was the otherworld of the spirit, where time and space were one, a world in which consciousness could leap between Sirius and Earth, between the one cosmos and another, illuminating the eternal present with its light and transcending mere matter.

Clearly, she was God's child—and so were all the others—and God was simply the essence of that great, eternal spirit that multiplied throughout time and shrank back simultaneously to the embryonic purity of the universal Oneness. Her child would be God's child—at once embracing the others and being part of them—and the future, which was merely the other side of the past, would be the natural inheritance of the material and spiritual worlds of a thriving Earth.

Frances pressed herself into Michael, taking life from his warmth. Eventually she started laughing, first softly, then hysterically—exactly as she had done when the helicopter descended like God's eye over the river in Iraq—and then her laughter turned into the weeping of someone released.

She was being set free from bondage, from the doubts of her humanity. She took the warmth from Michael and just as quickly gave it back, pressing herself tighter to him, forcing him down onto the floor, stretching along the trembling heat of his body until he could not resist her. Removing their clothes, they joined together, becoming one in the moonlit darkness, trading souls, then rising as pure energy to the peace of transcendence. And at that moment their flesh turned briefly into spirit, showing them the prismatic glory of their eternal, true selves.

Shortly after, they slept like a pair of newborn babies, then awakened feeling sleepy and refreshed but otherwise normal.

After dressing, they left the house, closed and locked the front door, then walked away without looking back, their eyes drawn to the starry sky.

25

SITTING opposite his former wife in what was once his own home, Michael felt a distinctly materialistic yearning for what he had lost. The house was spacious, elegant, and furnished with great taste, and on the sofa in front of him, a cup of tea in one hand and her long legs crossed enticingly, Janet looked, in her quietly distinguished way, very much a part of it.

Glancing around him, Michael sighed, hardly knowing what to say. He had dropped in to say good-bye on his way to the airport, but now that he was actually in his old home, he was a bit short on words.

"So you're actually going," Janet said, saving him any further embarrassment. "You're embarking upon an obviously mad adventure with an equally mad patient. I couldn't believe my ears when Cheryl told me about it—and can scarcely credit it right now."

"It's not a mad adventure and my patient is perfectly sane. I simply can't explain the matter in detail, which is probably why it sounds a bit strange."

Janet raised her fine eyebrows in mock surprise. "Strange?" she said. "Of *course* not, my dear. Perfectly normal for *you*. You always needed a little adventure in your life, and this journey, which is odd to say the least, certainly fits that old, familiar pattern."

"It fits no pattern, Janet, and has nothing to do with my personal habits. I simply can't tell you why I'm going, but I *do* have to go."

Janet sniffed and sipped her tea, then put the cup back on its saucer, while Michael, trying to keep his expression neutral, wondered why he *was* going.

He was in love with Frances Devereux—that much he certainly knew. He wanted her with a passion he had not experienced before—a passion so strong that it would take him to the ends of the earth for her. That was one reason, and he could not forget it. But what he also could not forget were the words of Miles Ashcombe who, in a rare moment of sanity, had said to him: *I know you. You have been there as well. Soon, in the near future, you will go back to where you have come from. . . .* Those words had haunted Michael for a considerable time, but only after an accumulation of knowledge about the dark masses did he understand what Ashcombe had meant.

Ashcombe's "there" was that other world beyond space and time—the world inside the dark masses—and Ashcombe thought that he had seen Michael in it and would do so again. At first Michael had thought it nonsense—the mere fancies of a deranged mind—but when Ashcombe disappeared just like those at Stonehenge, Michael had started believing in earnest. And now, since the séance with Frances and her dead mother, he believed implicitly in that other world and simply had to experience it.

Thus he was going to Iraq for two very distinct reasons: the first was an unquenchable thirst for knowledge; the second, his overwhelming love for Frances. Whether or not such reasons compensated for his own betrayals, it was too late to stop.

"I think that *some* sort of reason should be offered," Janet said, "when you're telling your only daughter that you might not ever see her again."

"Did I say that?"

"Yes."

"I didn't mean to."

"But is it true?"

"Yes. It's *possible* that I won't be coming back, so at the time I probably thought she should know."

"Well, damn you, Michael, I want an explanation. When Cheryl phoned me from Nice she was frightened *and* guilty— the former because of what you said about possibly not coming back, the latter because, being so angry about your affair with a patient, she scarcely took in what you were telling her. So, are you coming back or not? And what on earth's going *on?* Being so secretive about it merely makes you seem melodramatic and cruel, which *I* certainly think you are."

"I'm not being melodramatic and I'd certainly rather not be cruel, but the truth of the matter is that I may not be coming back—and I simply can't explain it any further."

"But it's to do with that Glastonbury business?"

"Yes."

"According to the news, the disappearances have ended—hopefully for good."

"Yes, that's correct—but my personal involvement hasn't ended, and I can't change my plans."

"And what about Cheryl?"

"I've done all I can. You know exactly what happened between us in Nice, and there the matter still rests. Like you, she disapproves of what I'm doing, so now she won't speak to me. As for this business with the married man, well, there's nothing I can do. I *did* tell her that if necessary you would talk to his wife, but frankly, I don't think you should do so."

"I won't have to," Janet replied. "Cheryl phoned me yesterday to say the affair is over and that she intends coming home as soon as possible. Obviously, once she got over her anger at *you,* she had a good think about it."

It was a victory, if a small one, and Michael felt good about it, even better because he would not be leaving behind an unresolved situation. His love for Cheryl welled up in him, washing away his lingering fears, and he knew that he could now face what was coming with optimism and courage. Nonetheless, even stepping into the unknown, he had to express very human doubts.

"Are you sure she meant it?" he asked. "Or might she simply be speaking off-the-cuff and mean nothing by it?"

"I'm *reasonably* sure," Janet replied in her careful manner. "She said she'd had a long talk with him, that she'd asked him to choose between her and his wife, and that he had—as you had said he probably would—told her that he couldn't sacrifice his family for her. So she told him it was over—*and* that she was leaving her job. In fact, *I* weakened at that point, asking her if that's what she really wanted—God, I'm a hypocrite!—and she seemed fairly adamant that it was. I think his response really hurt her, which is why I think she meant what she said about coming back home."

"Well," Michael said, *"that's* a relief."

"Yes, it certainly is. And I have to admit that I think your visit had a lot to do with it."

"Not *always* a bad father, then."

"You were *never* a bad father," Janet conceded, "when you were actually *here.* It was just that for you the responsibilities of work were always preferable to those relating to more personal matters. You were a good father in absentia; you simply weren't a good family man."

Enormously relieved because Cheryl was returning home, Michael let Janet's reprimand pass without comment, even though he could not avoid the discomfort it gave him by raising a truth he would have preferred to avoid.

He had indeed been a good father, but from a safe distance— and now, when his daughter seemed to need him most—he was once more walking out of her life, this time possibly forever. Surprisingly, then, overriding such considerations, was the unwavering belief that what he was doing was inevitable and possibly preordained.

"Anyway," Janet continued, "that's in the past now. If you're going, you're going, and that's all there is to it. I just think that you should at least try to give us *some* idea of what's going on."

"I can't," Michael said, feeling more remote each minute, his thoughts spiraling off into the ether of that other world beyond comprehension. "Believe me, I really would if I could, but I simply can't do it."

Janet sighed, then glanced around the room, as if measuring what she was losing by counting what she had gained. Satisfied, though not exactly happy, she returned her gaze to him.

"Is it dangerous? Can you at least tell me that?"

"No," Michael said, "it's not dangerous. If I don't come back, I'll still be okay—you can tell Cheryl that much."

"Good," Janet said. "At least it's something. Although . . ." Her voice trailed off unsurely, then she sighed and shook her head. "It just seems slightly mad," she said. "Even this farewell is crazy. You say you're going away and *might* not be coming back, and we won't have a clue where you are or what's happening to you."

"Do you care?"

"I'm not talking about myself. It's Cheryl I'm—"

"But do *you* care?" Michael insisted, wondering, even as he uttered the words, why he needed such reassurance.

Janet looked at him, frankly amazed, her brow wrinkled in thought. "Well, *of course* I care," she said. "What would make you even *think* otherwise? We were married for a long time, we have a lovely daughter, you're the father of that daughter and she loves *you*—and for all that I'm grateful. *Of course* I care what happens to you, Michael. You represent the major part of my life, and all I value most dearly. So quite naturally I *care*."

Her patent sincerity made Michael feel cheap. Ashamed of himself, he realized that he was not the objective thinker he had imagined: that his more emotional, subjective side prevailed over his need for distance. Realizing that, and surprised by the warmth it gave him, he found it much easier to accept the unknown's possibilities. In that sense, what he was getting from his former wife, was the courage he needed.

"I didn't know you still cared that much," he said, actually feeling quite childish. "I thought that the divorce had killed off completely what we once shared together."

She smiled, obviously amused that he could think that, then shook her head.

"No," she said. "It didn't. You never mistreated me, after all. And you didn't even leave me for another woman, which was a lot in your favor. No, Michael, our separation didn't embitter me; it just made me more careful."

"And now that I'm leaving?"

"Right now I'm *glad* we've been separated so long; I don't think I could stand this situation otherwise. However, what if you *don't* come back? And when do we actually decide that you're *not* returning?"

"If I'm not back in four weeks, I won't be returning. But whether I do or don't, I've already transferred all my assets to you and Cheryl."

"That was thoughtful of you, Michael."

"It was the least I could do. After all, the fact that we're divorced has no bearing on what I feel for you and certainly owe you, both emotionally and otherwise."

Janet smiled again, aware what he was doing.

"Touché," she said. "Anyway, I really *am* grateful—and it

takes a real weight off my mind, particularly regarding Cheryl and her as yet—thank God—undecided future."

"Good," Michael said. "That makes it worthwhile. Now I don't feel so bad." He shrugged, then sighed. "And that just about wraps it up, I suppose. I have to be going now."

They both stood at once, both smiling uneasily, then moved closer and embraced each other. Michael kissed her on the cheek, too embarrassed to do otherwise, then hurriedly turned away and walked to the front door, pulling it open, perhaps too enthusiastically, and stepping outside.

The morning light was crystal clear, falling out of a cloudless sky, lending luster to the lush greenery of this countrified pocket of Esher. Michael took a few deep breaths, savoring the unpolluted air, then turned back and looked again at Janet, appreciating her middle-aged serenity and more mature beauty. She leaned forward and kissed him on the cheek, then gently pushed him away.

"I hate good-byes," she said, "and so do you—so let's make it short and sweet. Good-bye, Michael. And good luck."

She wasn't crying, but he sensed that the tears were coming, so he smiled, quickly got into his car, and drove out of the graveled drive.

He turned right into a lane lined with trees and headed directly for Heathrow.

Frances was already waiting for him at the Iraqi Airlines check-in desk in Heathrow's Terminal 2. As soon as he walked through the sliding doors and placed his suitcases on the floor, she rushed forward to kiss him. They clung together for some time, taking comfort from each other, two voyagers on the brink of the unknown. Then, as if caught without clothes on, they self-consciously broke apart.

"Oh, God," Frances said, "I'm so glad to see you. I was beginning to think you'd changed your mind."

"No," Michael replied. "Never."

"And how did the visit to your wife go?"

"My *former* wife," Michael corrected. "And it was fine. Farewells, like deaths, make us forget the bad times and remember only the good. Also, I learned that Cheryl's coming home, which made me feel even better. So, all in all, it was worth it."

Frances hugged him again and he felt her uncommon

warmth, the vibration of a magical sensuality that could not be
resisted. He wanted to take her there and then, on the floor of
this crowded lobby, but instead just stepped back and thoughtfully studied her. She looked drawn, almost haggard, her brown
eyes dark-shadowed. But her beauty had an otherworldly radiance that could not be ignored.

"Well," he said, trying to keep his feet on the ground, "I'd
better check in."

"Yes," Frances said. "I did that when I arrived half an hour
ago. Now that Mother's gone, I can't wait to get away—and
every minute seems endless. So let's get moving."

Michael picked up his suitcases and let her lead him to the
check-in desk. There were very few in the line and the formali-
ties were soon over; then, since Frances wanted to feel that she
was actually on the move, they went upstairs and walked
through the crowded terminal toward the departure lounge.

"How do you feel?" Frances asked him.

"Fine," he replied. "A bit disoriented, still slightly disbelieving, some pain at the thought that I might not be coming back
—most notably regarding Cheryl—but otherwise, I have to
confess to a definite excitement."

Frances pulled him closer to her as they walked. "Well, that's
good," she said. "At least you're still clinging to your sanity—
and I know that in these particular circumstances that can't be
too easy."

"I'm a psychologist. I'm *supposed* to cling to sanity. It's the
least I can do."

"You're not a psychologist anymore. You're one of God's
chosen few."

The remark made Michael uncomfortable and he glanced
sideways at her, noting her almost beatific smile and the joy in
her eyes. She was like a woman transported, vaulting out of her
mortal body; and even as he felt the sweeping force of his love
for her, he trembled at the thought of what she might be leading
him into.

He glanced around the crowded airport, taking in the milling
people, trying to accept that he might be seeing it all for the last
time. He failed to do so, being trapped in the familiar; but then,
as they approached the gates that led into the departure lounge,
he saw someone who immediately made real what he was leaving behind.

It was Cheryl.

Michael stopped walking, forcing Frances to do the same, and simply stared, in love and disbelief, at his beautiful daughter.

She was standing near the gate where the boarding passes were checked, wearing a rumpled sweater, denim jacket, and blue jeans, her blond hair, though still long, now piled up on her head, to once more emphasize her pert features and unblemished youthfulness. She seemed sleepy, but was offering a tentative smile that instantly warmed him.

"Stop staring," she said. "It's really me. I came in on a plane this morning and thought I'd wait here for you. I mean, I couldn't let you go without saying good-bye—so, here I am. It's really me and you're not having a bad dream."

Michael felt Frances's hand falling away from his arm, then he stepped forward, took hold of Cheryl's shoulders, and leaned down to kiss her on the cheek.

"You're not a *bad* dream," he said. "More like a dream come true."

He stared at her for some time, feeling a warm glow of pleasure, temporarily forgetting Frances until Cheryl's blue gaze moved from his face to look past him in an inquiring manner. At that, he glanced back over his shoulder at Frances, but she waved her right hand in a negative manner, indicating that he should, at least initially, speak to Cheryl alone.

Nodding, he turned back to his daughter, looking down at her upturned eyes.

"I'm delighted," he said. "I can't tell you how much. My heart was breaking at the thought of leaving without seeing you. I thought you'd never forgive me."

Cheryl glanced at Frances, then back at him. "I came to say good-bye," she said softly. "Not to forgive you."

"I'll settle for that," Michael replied. "And your mother said you'd left that man for good. Dare I ask if that's true?"

"You may. And it is."

She wasn't smiling now, but simply staring steadily at him, her striking eyes enlarged because she was having to look upward, her body jolted by the passengers who were pushing past her to show their boarding passes before moving on to Passport Control.

"Well," Michael said, unable to believe that he was actually

leaving her, "that at least will send me off with a lighter heart.
What made you change your mind?"

"I changed my mind because you planted the seed of doubt in
me, and when you left, even though I was angry with you, I
kept thinking about it. In the end, I knew you were right—that
I had to gauge my importance to him—so eventually I decided
to do what I'd been avoiding for so long, namely, to put the
choice to him: either stay with his wife or definitely give her up
and marry me. Try not to look self-satisfied when I say that you
were right: when he saw that I was serious, he had no hesitation
in dumping me. 'But *ma chérie,*' he said, 'you cannot *possibly*
expect me to sacrifice my family for a mere *poulette!*' And that,
as they say, was that—I walked out and he let me do so, not
even coming to the airport to wave good-bye. So, no need to
smirk, but you were right—and I've come home for good."

She was leaning against the railing, still being brushed by the
people passing, and at that moment she seemed very frail,
rather than just slim. It was a father's view of her—he understood that immediately—but he still felt a lump in his throat
when he studied her pained face.

"You'll recover," he said. "Believe me, it's all for the best."

"Oh, right," she replied laconically. "That really helps me a
lot."

"Don't be facetious, Cheryl. Most of the most valuable things
we learn come at a price—and in this case, you've paid it."

"I know," she said. "Truly." She smiled and reached down to
hold his hand and bring it up to her cheek, letting it rest there
for a moment, then gently dropping it. "So," she said, "you're
really going off on this magical mystery tour?"

"Yes, I'm afraid so."

"And you can't tell me a thing about it?"

"Only what I told you in France: that it's related to Glastonbury."

"I hope you know I want you to return."

"That's a nice thing to hear."

She grinned, then glanced over his shoulder. He knew she
was looking at Frances, but he didn't say anything.

"That's her?" Cheryl asked. "Your mad patient? The one
you're running away with?"

"Yes," Michael said, "that's her. But she's not mad and I'm
not running away with her."

"She's involved in this Glastonbury business too?"

"That's why she's going."

Cheryl stared over his shoulder again, standing on tiptoes to do so, then returned to normal and looked at him, a slight smile on her face.

"She's very attractive in a straight-laced way," she said. "Are you sure she's worth having?"

"Pretty sure," Michael said.

"Are you proper lovers yet?"

"Can't you tell?"

"Yes. It's written all over you." Cheryl's slight smile turned into a wicked grin. "Well," she said, "I suppose you'd better introduce us. After that, you can go."

Michael felt the healing joy of a man who has regained his daughter, but he still suffered a slight trepidation as he turned away from her and beckoned to the woman who had come between them. Frances stepped forward immediately, her face grave and self-contained. The women studied each other for a considerable time, then Cheryl very formally stretched out her hand to have it shaken by Frances.

"I'm Cheryl."

"I'm Frances."

Michael sought for some words with which to fill the brittle silence, but anticipating him, Frances stepped closer to Cheryl, whispered, "Damn it, this is ridiculous!," then hugged her, kissed her on the forehead, and stepped back again.

"So," she said, "you're the beauty I've been told about so often. Well, your father obviously wasn't exaggerating. I can see why he's proud of you."

Cheryl didn't bite, but instead moved in for the kill.

"So you're the crazy patient," she said, "who's stealing my father away."

Frances blushed instantly as if slapped on the face, but quickly rallied herself and offered a smile that had a hard, cutting edge.

"I'm the woman all right," she said. "The one your father's told you about. And I know him enough to be convinced that he hasn't described me as mad. Furthermore, I'm not stealing him away—he's coming with me because he has to—and although you're his only daughter, you're now a woman, not a child, so it's pointless to pretend you're outraged by what's happened between us."

"All I know is that my father is personally involved with one of his patients—and that morally and ethically it's wrong and should not be encouraged."

"Oh, my God!" Frances said. "How pure you are—for a *twenty*-year-old! Though, come to think of it, from what I've heard about your *own* life, you're in no position to cast stones at me or anyone else."

"My lover wasn't a psychologist, and I wasn't his patient."

"No," Frances said, stepping closer, her eyes widening, "but you *were* having an affair with a man who had a wife and two children. Morality? Don't you *mention* the subject in such self-righteous tones!"

"Damn you, I loved him!"

"And what does *that* prove? Only that you're just like me—a woman who was ruled by her feelings and blinded to all else. Sorry, Cheryl, but you've no right to chastise me. You and I are the same."

Michael felt as though the bottom was falling out of his world, as if everything gained was being lost in this brief, bitter intercourse. He just stood there, helpless, destroyed by feminine reasoning, wanting the world to swallow him up and absolve him from choice. He loved both of these women, each in a different way, but that in itself was not enough to help him solve this dilemma.

Then innocence did that for him: Cheryl blushed and took a deep breath. She glanced nervously left and right, at him, then at Frances, let her breath out in a wistful sigh, and spoke softly but clearly.

"Fair enough," she said. "You're right. I know just what you mean. I was angry at anyone who dared to suggest that I was wrong. So, I was angry with him"—here she pointed at Michael —"and then I tried to pin the blame on you, which was easy to do. But it was neither him nor you—it was me and what I wanted. Yes," she continued, "you and I are the same. We both loved a man so much, we didn't care about anything else—the only difference being that I was fooling myself, whereas you knew the truth when you saw it and refused to let go of it. So, I'm sorry . . . and you really seem very nice . . . and I think my father's a lucky man."

On an emotional impulse, she again stood on tiptoes, this time to kiss Frances on the cheek and give her a hug. She then turned toward Michael, her eyes wet with tears, gripped him very tightly and kissed him, sniffing back her quiet sobbing.

Michael felt her trembling limbs, her warm, cushioning flesh, and his heart seemed to break down the middle to let love and grief rush in. He was leaving her—yes, and now that knowledge seared his soul—and he knew that whatever was to come, he would never forget her. Some things lasted after all—a parent's love, a child's faith—and in understanding that he was released from the doubts that had burdened him.

Unashamed, Michael wept. Watching his daughter, also weeping. Then he saw her rush away, one hand waving, a pale flower, and he turned into the arms of the woman he would love through eternity.

"Oh, my Frances!" he whispered.

THE office of Professor Saddam Khairallah, assistant curator of the Museum of Arab Antiquities in Baghdad, looked more like one of the museum's storage rooms, or perhaps a shop in the Suq al-Shurjah bazaar, with its numerous, often priceless antiques carefully stacked on the wooden shelves or, if they were too large, left leaning against the walls covered with Islamic art.

Saddam himself was a gray-bearded Sunnite Muslim with an amiable, sun-scorched face, but he looked, in his short-sleeved white shirt and gray slacks, like a European just returned from a long vacation. An old friend of Frances's father, he had obviously been delighted to see her, and having taken her and Michael for lunch in the museum's canteen, was giving them each a glass of *arrack*.

"It is made from dates and grapes," he explained to Michael, "and is really quite wonderful. Alas, I cannot drink it myself, but I'm sure you'll appreciate it."

Frances sipped from her tiny glass and watched Michael doing the same. He let his first sip linger in his mouth, eventually swallowed appreciatively, licked his lips, and nodded his approval at the benign Islamic professor.

"You're right," he said. "It's delicious."

Professor Khairallah smiled happily, then sat in the chair behind his desk, fixing his attention on Frances.

"So, my dear child," he said, "I confess your story intrigues me, particularly your conviction that the Garden of Eden of

Christian mythology actually exists and is possibly connected to the bizarre visitations of the past five or six months."

"We've given you the facts, Saddam," Frances replied, "and they seem fairly persuasive."

Professor Khairallah nodded, sunlight pouring in through the window behind him to lend a silvery tint to his steel-gray hair.

"Fascinating," he said. "Particularly in view of what is happening all over the world, with these extraordinary materializations and disappearances."

"Which seem to have ceased," Frances said.

"Indeed," the professor replied. "However, the very fact that the phenomena occurred in the first place—and that certain areas have apparently been permanently changed by them—has encouraged many to think that what we are living through is the beginning of the end—and they don't know what *you* know. And just as there have been an increasing number of religious conversions, riots, assassinations, suicides, and other extreme emotional reactions in every corner of the globe, so we, too, are having similar problems. Some of our great historical sites have disappeared, so the Shi'ites and Sunnites, just to take one example, are already at one another's throats. Therefore, though the disappearances seem to have ceased, we are now suffering the lamentable results of their initial appearance and the fact that some dark masses still remain."

"That kind of hysteria should die away," Frances said.

"Perhaps so," the professor replied.

Frances glanced tentatively at Michael, who was sitting in the chair beside her, and noted that he was giving all his attention to the Arab professor. His expression was thoughtful, but she knew he was tired and fraught, naturally wearied by the sleepless flight from London to Baghdad, then exhausted by the demands she had made in the hotel's luxurious wide bed.

Thinking about it, she burned, felt the melting of her loins, crossed her legs and tried to keep her expression composed while memories of the last fortnight filled her head.

Since that first time in the hospital they had made love every night, passionately and fiercely; but last night and this morning, in their expensive hotel room overlooking the walls and tower of an ancient, golden-domed mosque, and, more blasphemously, with an *imam's* wailing in their ears, they had ventured into the edge of those waters that had frozen Laurence's tender heart. And Michael had complied, surprising her and perhaps himself.

Nevertheless, she had been frustrated, unable to find satisfaction, and her frustration, which was great, had only been increased by the knowledge that she simply dare not ask him to do what she needed. He had achieved orgasm, groaning softly, until she pushed him off, cursing softly as she rolled onto her side and anticipated his anger. But the anger had not come—he had simply fallen asleep contentedly—and the next morning (this morning) he had awakened with no more than an ambiguous smile.

They had not discussed their night in bed, neither able to summon the nerve, and Frances had found herself floundering like a hooked fish dropped on a hot rock. Now she thought of the night with shame (she had not felt that before) and wanted to reach out and stroke his neck, though she didn't dare do so.

Instead she returned her gaze to her father's old friend, who was once more folding his hands beneath his chin and nodding judiciously.

"So," Professor Khairallah said, "you wish to know if our knowledge of Mesopotamian antiquity will support your belief that another world, perhaps one parallel to our own, has had a hand in human evolution."

"That's it," Frances said.

"Well, certainly Mesopotamia has not been called the 'cradle of civilization' for nothing," the professor said. "For a start, the discovery of seven Neanderthal skeletons in the Shanidar Cave in the Zagros Mountains confirmed that a good sixty thousand years ago, when many areas of Europe were still covered by great glaciers, prehistoric man was already well entrenched in Iraq, Turkey, and Syria. Then, some time in the fifth millennium B.C., the farmers of northern Mesopotamia emigrated southward to the Tigris–Euphrates plain that stretches from Baghdad to the Gulf—and therefore includes your supposed Garden of Eden—where, shortly after, they were brought into contact with the invading Semitic nomads of the Syrian and Arabian deserts; and the subsequent mingling of those two cultures laid the cornerstone for the world's first true civilization."

"Which could account for the Garden of Eden myth," Fran-

ces said. "The myth of the first truly human man and woman—
and of the dawning of moral consciousness."

"Quite," the professor said. "The time and the place are
right. If we treat Adam and Eve as figurative creatures, the
myth carries validity. However, if they actually existed as two
of the first of an ancient race, they must have done so at the
very beginning of a long, tangled saga. Certainly, shortly after
the mingling of the Semitic and Arab cultures, in approximately
3500 B.C., the Sumerians arrived on the stage to become the
actual builders of that first real civilization."

"That isn't exactly a secret," Frances said.

"Of course not," the professor replied, smiling slightly at her
impatience. "But if we know what the Sumerians *did,* that's *all*
we know about them. We still don't know *who* they were."

So saying, he climbed out of his chair, went to the corner of
the room, picked up an object and returned with it, resting its
base on the desk, balancing the top with his right hand.

"This," he said, pointing to what appeared to be a roughly
rectangular-shaped stone on which numerous hieroglyphics had
been cut, "is a pictograph, an example of Sumerian cuneiform.
Perhaps more than any other human invention, *writing* made
civilization possible—and over five thousand years ago the
Sumerians invented writing in the shape of crude symbols
etched in with a stylus on clay tablets like this one. And soon—
at least by early in the third millennium B.C.—the Sumerian
scribes had improved the cuneiform by using symbols *phoneti-
cally* and making it possible to spell out any word in the language. At that point, my dear friends, civilization was truly
born—and over the next fifteen hundred years the Sumerians
added to that glory by commercializing agriculture, establishing
the first trade routes between Mesopotamia, Asia Minor, and
Iran, and creating the first politico-religious city-states. As I
said, the very cornerstones of civilization—for good *and* for
evil."

He laid the ancient tablet gently on the desk, then sat down
again.

"The Sumerians," he continued, not without a touch of his-
trionics, "dominated Mesopotamia for fifteen thousand years,
created the first civilization, then faded away with the ascen-
dancy of the Babylonians—but to this day, my friends, we do

not know the origin of the Sumerians. They remain a complete and tantalizing mystery."

Frances thought of the primitive farmers, the Ubaidians, living in their mud-brick huts and naming their crude settlements Ur, Eridu, and Kish. She also thought of the invaders, the Semitic nomads from the deserts, arriving to take over those dusty villages and crude towns, then mingling with the equally simple Ubaidians. No richly creative fruit there. Just the joining of two primitive cultures. And then, out of an unknown past and source, came the mysterious Sumerians to create, from the crude mingling of Ubaidian farmer and Semitic nomad, the most important event in human history: the first civilization.

It hardly seemed possible.

"The Sumerians disappeared," the professor said, "but Mesopotamian civilization continued, refined and passed down by the Babylonians, surviving the invasions of the Hittites, Kassites, Elamites, and Assyrians, rising up to even greater glory through Nebuchadnezzar's dazzling renaissance, then surviving the Persians and Alexander the Great, then the Selucids and the Parthians, until eventually, in A.D. 227, came the equally mysterious Sassanids, better known as the Sassanians."

The professor distractedly reached across his desk to pick up a gray stone statuette of what appeared to be a bald-headed priest wearing a skirt and with his hands folded over his bare chest. He stared at it as if not really seeing it, placed it back on the desk, glanced first at Michael, then at Frances, and nodded unconsciously.

"We know that the Sassanians were an Iranian dynasty," he said, "founded by Ardashir I in A.D. 224 and destroyed by the Arabs during the years 637–651. We also know that they ruled Mesopotamia between A.D. 227 and 636—in short, until the beginning of their systematic destruction by the Arabs. However, apart from those facts, we know remarkably little about life under their rule. What *is* known is that during the course of their reign, over a period of approximately four hundred years, many of the ancient cities of Mesopotamia were buried beneath the sands of the desert, and with them perished one of the oldest and most remarkable civilizations of the ancient world."

Frances had a sip of her *arrack* while the professor, staring keenly at her, scratched his large nose.

"I only tell you this," he said, "to give you some examples of the numerous mysteries which abound in Mesopotamian history. The cradle of civilization appears to have emerged from a series of great waves of intense creativity, interspersed with periods so shrouded in mystery that there appears to be no logical connection between them—as if, indeed, that inchoate civilization was being guided by a god, or gods, who came and went intermittently, perhaps only as they felt was necessary."

"Necessary for *what?*" Frances asked him.

Professor Khairallah shrugged, looking bemused. "Evolution," he said. "I merely append to what you have already suggested, but the possibility is there."

Disturbed again, Frances stared through the window beyond the professor's silvery head and saw the black clock on the white wall beneath the domed tower of an ancient mosque. That same mosque had once stood proudly above the mud-brick huts of its Islamic subjects, but now it was almost lost in the surrounding steel and glass of modern high-rise hotels, offices, and apartment houses. The wailing of the *imam* no longer fought the braying of camels; instead it had to fight the roaring of buses, taxis, and trucks. Down there, on the ground, some bazaars and *suqs* remained, the stalls piled with copper pots, silver bowls, rugs, and quilts; but they were rapidly disappearing, giving way to supermarkets, just as the minarets and mosques were giving way to skyscrapers.

"—and so it was," the professor was saying, as if speaking at one of his lectures, "that after the reign of the Sassanids, or Sassanians, when much of the ancient world disappeared under silt and sand, there mysteriously arose out of that desolation and human conflict one of the most magnificent ages in human history—by which I mean, of course, the Abbasid golden age, which produced an intellectual awakening that extended in its impact far beyond the borders of the Tigris and Euphrates. This was the age of the founding of the original, legendary Baghdad; of the great storyteller Scheherazade; and of Caliph Hārūn ar-Rashīd, considered to be the greatest monarch of his time. Also during this age Arabic numbers and the decimal system were introduced, as was algebra; the great doctor Avicenna produced what was to be the standard medical text through Europe and the Orient, as well as the Arab world; and Maimonides, philosopher and court physician to the mighty Saladin, dealt with

religious and metaphysical questions that were to influence profoundly the major Jewish and Christian religious thinkers. So,
out of that inexplicable desolation, sprang that even more inexplicable, supremely great age . . . then, alas, it was destroyed
by the rapacious Mongols and thereafter endured centuries of a
neglect that has yet to be fully rectified. Indeed, a neglect so
profoundly irrational that it does lead one to think it must have
been ordained by the gods for their own unknown purposes."

The glass of *arrack* had made Frances feel pleasantly drowsy
and sensual, and she turned her head to glance at Michael's
profile, secretly wishing that he would look at her and smile,
aware of why he was avoiding doing that. She thought of her
seduction of him and the many times they had made love since,
then remembered the ambiguous smile he had offered when her
unfulfilled desire turned into frustrated rage.

He had not been able to satisfy her because there was only
one way to do that, and so far, for reasons she had not cared to
examine, she had been reluctant to ask of him what she had so
bluntly demanded of Laurence. Yet now, when she thought of
what that request had done to Laurence, she was forced to
admit that she was frightened of turning Michael against her.
So she glanced at him, yearning to kiss him, then returned her
attention to Professor Khairallah, whose gentle smile gave her
comfort.

"What about my Garden of Eden?" she asked him. "I *know*
that when we were sucked into that dark mass, we were somewhere very close to Al-Qurna. So do you believe there *is* a
connection between that area and my personal experience inside
the dark mass?"

"All myths are based on obscured facts," the professor said,
"and certainly there are reasons for that area being claimed as
Eden—and, of course, as the place where Abraham once
prayed."

He clapped his hands lightly and gave her a broader smile,
obviously delighted to have slyly returned Eden to its Islamic
origins.

"I note that when you were sucked into the dark mass, you
found yourself in a land of marshes and lagoons, then, in an
earlier period, beside the great dust bowl that you thought
might have later become Eden's lake."

"Yes, that's correct."

"It is interesting, then, that most of the early Mesopotamian creation myths speak of watery origins—of water from under the earth joining water from the sea—and floods. This almost certainly refers to the marshlands between the lower Euphrates and Tigris rivers—a view supported by the fact that both rivers regularly flood their banks. As to the importance of that area to the history of man's evolution, the confluence of the two great rivers—where your so-called Eden is located—marks the place where the first civilization *and* recorded history began. Indeed, it was from Basra and its Euphrates neighbor Kufah—both of which began as no more than military camps—that there emerged all the literary, philological, and historical materials that were to form the basis of Arab-Islamic culture; and from there, also, that those prime foundations of civilization, grammar and lexicography, came into being. In short, the whole history of Islam—and therefore the basis of Judaism and Christianity—was greatly conditioned by events that occurred in the land around Al-Qurna—your so-called Garden of Eden."

The professor smiled at Frances, obviously enjoying her growing surprise, unaware that the very mention of Eden had churned up her emotions. She saw it all immediately, vividly real in her mind, and felt a wave of fear and desire sweeping hotly across her.

She reached into her handbag, withdrew a cigarette, lit it, inhaled, and blew the smoke out to ease her heart's fearful beating. When she glanced at Michael and saw his thoughtful gaze, she looked away very quickly.

"I'm still not sure that this relates to the dark masses," she said.

"Well," the professor replied, "there *are,* in those Mesopotamian myths that deal with the time before recorded history, other parallels to your experience."

"Such as?"

The professor shrugged as if the facts were self-evident. "Although much of that history is shrouded in mystery, there can be no doubt that during the earliest stages of the evolution of the various Mesopotamian religions, particularly during the third millennium B.C., the gods were firmly characterized as *human* in shape and, just as surprisingly, as having organized themselves into a primitive, prototypal, democratic structure that strongly influenced civilization thereafter."

"So these gods," Michael said, "laid the guidelines for future social order. They were, in a sense, *teachers.*"

"Quite so," the professor replied. "And while the Sumerian myths—our earliest known records of at least the *consciousness* of the time—say little about the Sumerian view of the creation, the epic of Gilgamesh *does* mention an earlier time—I quote: *after heaven had been moved away from earth, after earth had been separated from heaven.* The same belief—that earth and heaven had once been close together and were later *separated*— occurs also in a Sumero-Akkadian creation text from Ashur."

"I'm not sure I've gotten your drift," Michael said.

"I refer to what happens within the dark mass," the professor said. "Given, as it would seem, that the dark mass is a gateway leading from earth to the other world—a world where time and space are meaningless, and where the living are incorporeal beings who exist simultaneously in past, present, and future— given that, there *could* have been a period when the earth and heaven were one—or, at least, when the people of ancient Mesopotamia *thought* they were one, possibly because the incorporeal but human-shaped gods actually materialized before them, having emerged from the other world beyond time and space which, for our hypothesis, we may call *heaven.* Then, when the gods had departed, leaving man to his own devices, but with certain directions mapped out for him and possibly instilled in his subconscious, earth and heaven—or this world and the other—were indeed separated . . . separated by time and space."

"And now," Michael said, "where parts of the earth have disappeared, heaven and earth may be coming back together again as one."

"Yes," the professor said.

He leaned back in his chair, sighing, then moved his gaze from Michael to Frances, a sad smile on his lips.

Frances stared back, thoughtfully studying his old man's eyes, trying to imagine him as a much younger man and friend to her father. She was foiled in that attempt, but still took comfort from him, feeling as if her father was in this room, letting his spirit console her.

She turned toward Michael, letting him see her fear and hope, and he reached out to take hold of her hand and squeeze it gently, encouragingly. He held her hand for some time, star-

ing at her, smiling slightly; then, when the professor coughed
for attention, placed her hand back on her thigh and turned his
head to the front.

Frances took a deep breath, feeling light-headed and weak, as
Professor Khairallah leaned across his desk, eyes bright, his lips
straight.

"Finally," he said, "and with particular regard to your
strange pregnancy, please let me remind you that according to
Mesopotamian mythology, however man may have come into
being, he existed solely in order to *serve* the gods. In the scheme
of existence, then, man was never an end . . . he was merely a
means."

The full import of those words sank into Frances like a
heated blade penetrating her flesh. At first she felt a quick, keen
pain, which promptly gave way to terror, then she felt she was
losing her senses and sinking into chaos. She stopped sinking
soon enough, coming to rest in a sea of grief, then remembered
her mother lying dead on the floor at home, her father walking
onto the back lawn and never returning. The grief brought tears
to her eyes, but then she was raised on high, transported on the
wings of a mystery filled with fierce expectation. She thought of
the near future, wondering what it might bring, then shook like
a leaf in a storm and reached out for Michael.

She heard the cry of an *imam* in the distance, calling the
faithful to prayer.

27

THE jeep bounced and rattled painfully along what was, to Frances, a very familiar desert road. Her eyes were protected by sunglasses, but the wind was burning her face, and she brushed her flapping hair off her forehead to glance sideways at Michael. He was obviously fascinated by the desolate flatlands, studying them keenly as he drove. His gaze swept across the distant horizon which was, at this moment, obscured in the clouds of sand that spiraled under a leaden sky.

"You can look as long as you want," Frances said, "but you won't really see much. What you're seeing now is *all* you're going to see until we get to the marshes."

"I love it," Michael said.

"There's nothing to love," Frances replied. "It's flat, barren, and depressing—though it *can* come to haunt one."

"If you find it *that* depressing, why did you return so often? You were, after all, a *voluntary* worker and came of your own accord."

"At first I came simply because I wanted somewhere foreign, somewhere completely different, and I couldn't imagine anywhere much different than this. I wanted to get away from the familiar—and certainly from my own past. Then, of course, when I got to know the Arabs, the depressing aspects of the desert, which, believe me, are very pervasive, couldn't stop it from haunting my dreams and turning me into an addict. In fact, addiction to the desert is a trait very peculiar to Englishmen."

"And, of course, English*women.*"

Frances smiled. "Touché, Michael."

She looked straight ahead, following the line of the crude road, and saw that they were now crossing dry, seasonal marsh and racing toward some dust-obscured palm trees that marked the outer edge of the marshes. Observing them, she shivered, remembering her first meeting with Schul, then felt a wave of trepidation sweeping through her to spoil her good humor. The jeep passed the palm grove, then bounced over a pothole, making the two suitcases, standing together on the rear seats, bounce against each other.

"Are we getting close?" Michael asked.

"Yes," she replied. "We'll soon be there."

"How do you feel?"

"Not too good. The closer we get to Eden, the more nervous I feel. Already, all that happened here is coming back to me with an immediacy that makes me feel I'm reliving it. I'm not only *thinking* of Schul—I can almost *feel* his bloody presence— and I keep waiting to see that dark mass materializing in front of me."

"We can always turn back."

"No, I won't do that. I have to see this through. I'm still certain that I'm pregnant and that it happened in Eden; but I'm also convinced that the baby's coming won't be normal, and that whatever is going to occur will do so quite soon. I want it to happen in Eden. I feel *compelled* to go back there. It's almost as if there's a voice in my head, relentlessly nagging me. This was all preordained—I'm sure of it—so what I'm doing, I have to do."

Even as she was speaking she saw the glint of distant water, swaying bulrushes and fig palms, then more water and reed houses growing larger as the jeep headed straight for them; then suddenly, there, where the desert should have been, was a broad swath of marshlands, water gleaming between green banks, the tall bulrushes moving against a cloudy, sludge-gray sky that made the reed houses of the marsh Arabs look impoverished and colorless.

Frances told Michael where to go, and after slowing down he drove past the reed houses nestling under dusty fig palms, then braked to a halt where the first of the bridges led across the shallow ditches to the center of the small, oddly deserted village.

No children came out to greet them, as they had when Frances was last here, and when she climbed down from the jeep, with Michael following her example, she found herself glancing uneasily around her, as if at a ghost town.

"This is it?" Michael asked.

"Yes," Frances answered slowly. "But it seems *different*, somehow. . . . Where *is* everyone?"

She glanced around her again, looking and listening for some activity, then shrugged and led Michael onto the palm-log bridge that crossed the water-filled ditch and led into the heart of the village. Once across, they did in fact see some villagers, most of them old, wearing the traditional *keffiyeh* and *dish-disha*, their eyes peering lethargically from beneath their head-cloths as they squatted, in unusually somnolent poses, at the doors of their reed huts.

"A singularly lifeless bunch," Michael said.

"Yes," Frances said. "Odd."

Feeling more disconcerted, she led Michael across to the sheikh's large *mudhif*, which, soaring high above the more modest reed huts, looked even grander than it was. As usual there was a servant standing outside the door of the flat end—the end facing Mecca—and once they had kicked off their shoes, he solemnly led them through the arched entrance, into the *mudhif's* dimly lit interior.

Michael was obviously taken aback by the sheer size of the *mudhif*. Frances noticed his eyes scanning along the thirteen high arches before returning to fall on Sheikh Hamaid, who was, as usual, sitting cross-legged on the reed matting on the floor beside the coffee hearth with its exotic row of brass and copper pots, where another silent servant was kneeling.

Frances greeted the sheikh in the customary manner and let Michael do the same as he had been instructed. Then, at the sheikh's invitation, they both sat opposite him on the reed matting.

Sheikh Hamaid smiled at Frances, but the humor hardly reached his eyes; the reed fire crackling beyond him filled the air with spiraling smoke, casting flickering shadows and light over his thin, ascetic, and now very weary face.

"It is pleasant to see you again, Miss Devereux," he said,

"even though these times are unhappy. May I offer you food and drink?"

"The food and drink would be appreciated, Sheikh Hamaid —but I'm sorry to hear of this unhappiness. Do you refer to the village?"

"We are not what we were," the sheikh replied. "Which I'm sure you have noticed."

"Yes, I noticed a certain emptiness. There are only old men and women in the village, none of them smiling."

The sheikh nodded in agreement, then turned his head toward his servant and lightly clapped his hands, signifying that the food should be brought in. The servant immediately jumped up and hurried out of the *mudhif* while Frances glanced along its high-arched, cathedral-like interior to that dimly lit far end, her gaze drawn against her will to where Schul had been lying when she first saw him.

She studied that dark spot for some time, thinking of Schul and feeling threatened, but was eventually drawn back to the present by Sheikh Hamaid's soft voice.

"There are very strange things happening here," he said, "as I'm sure you have heard."

"Yes," Frances said. "I have heard certain rumors. And most of them relate to what happened to me when your oarsmen were drowned."

The sheikh nodded again, his face solemn and much older, his eyes no longer studying Frances's body with sensual suggestiveness.

"We have lived here for centuries, but our time has now run out. There are miraculous things happening—miraculous and terrible—and my people, when they are not being devoured with the land itself, are fleeing from this place with their children, leaving only the old behind. I cannot stop them. I have threatened punishment to no avail. They think only of the darkness that comes down to steal the earth and its living."

Frances heard Michael's sigh, but resisted looking at him; instead she kept her gaze on the sheikh and silently fought her own rising fear.

"Is this darkness like the one I told you about?" she asked.

"Yes," the sheikh said. "The same. But not one—more than one—sometimes two or three at once; stretching from the desert floor to the sky and devouring all that they cover. They take

the land that we know and replace it with other land, changing
the shape of the world we live in—therefore, our very lives.
Whole lakes have disappeared to be replaced with swamp or
marsh; many rivers, which have been here since the beginning
of time, have either vanished or taken on a new course far away
from our villages. Thus many fishermen are starving and their
villages slowly dying—dying when they are not being swallowed completely by the pillars of darkness. There is much fear
and despair among the Ma'dan and other tribes, since most of
them, when not grieving over lost loved ones, are convinced
that the end has come."

"The end of the world?"

"Yes."

"That is understandable, Sheikh Hamaid. What is happening
here has been happening all over the world, and *many* people
think that Judgment Day has come. Religious riots and even
wars have broken out in many countries, with church and state
unable to stop it. However, in most parts of the world the disappearances have ceased, so it seems that the world is returning to
normal."

"*Your* world," the sheikh said. "Not mine. For us it is too
late."

There was a scuffling of feet behind Frances. She glanced over
her shoulder to see the servant holding back the door's woven-
reed curtains, while some of the old women, silent and bowing
low, entered the gloomy hut, carrying trays of food.

Frances turned back to the front as the servant near the coffee
hearth passed around the finger bowl, and even while she, Michael, and the sheikh were rinsing their fingers, the old women
were setting bowls of the customary mutton, chicken, gravy,
and rice on the reed matting between the sheikh and his guests.
Frances noticed immediately that the portions were more modest than usual, and that the musician who normally played on
his *al-qanoun* was no longer present. Both observations filled
her with sadness and a great deal of sympathy.

"I'm afraid I cannot offer you more," the sheikh apologized.
"But there are not enough people left to prepare proper food,
and the dancers and the musicians have fled with all the other
young people. As I said, things are not what they were—and,
alas, never will be again."

"It doesn't matter," Frances said.

"You are kind," the sheikh replied. "Nonetheless, though perhaps it does not matter, it offends my poor heart."

The old women shuffled back out of the hut and the eating commenced. Frances noticed with some amusement that Michael was having as much trouble scooping the gravy-soaked rice into his mouth as Laurence had during his visit to this same hut; however, that small entertainment was all she had throughout the meal, since the food was eaten in a silence devoid of its usual pleasant nuances, and the sheikh, eating halfheartedly and obviously just to be polite, gave the impression of a life devoid of hope and spirit.

Seeing the sheikh's unhappiness, Frances lost her appetite. But she grimly plodded on at her task, letting her thoughts spiral up into the cavernous gloom of the great arched roof and take her back to when she had first met Schul.

Just to think of him made her burn with a mixture of lust and shame, and then she found herself glancing surreptitiously at Sheikh Hamaid, who had once had designs on her. She remembered bringing Laurence here, his discomfort during the erotic dancing of the Arab boys, and the pleasure she had taken not only from that embarrassment but from her own sly sexual parrying with the then sensual, confident sheikh. The man now sitting before her was not the one she had known but merely the ghost of his former self, watching his own disappearance. Her heart went out to him, but there was little she could do to help.

Relieved when at last the meal was over, Frances had just taken her first sip of coffee when the sheikh leaned toward her, his aged, dramatically lined face showing grave concern, the fire from the coffee hearth casting flickering shadows over his weakening brown eyes.

"Be careful," he said. "Where you are going is the worst of all. It is said that that place has become the world's navel, and that those who go there enter the netherworld and never return. That place is the source of all things. The pillars of darkness are gathering there. A few Arabs have seen those pillars gathering from a very great distance. Go home, Frances. Do not go near Al-Qurna. If you do, you will not return."

Frances stared at the sheikh, trying to fully grasp his words, her fear starting to be colored with an excitement that defied rational thought. *The world's navel,* she thought wonderingly. *The source of all things. I am venturing into the navel of the*

world and might emerge to the netherworld. . . . She glanced
automatically at Michael, caught him staring thoughtfully at
her; then he shrugged, letting her know the decision was hers,
and looked down at the floor.

"It is our belief," she said to Sheikh Hamaid, "that Al-
Qurna, which you consider to be the world's navel, is in fact
one of many gateways through time and space, and that just as
it can transport human beings to another world, your 'netherworld,' so it has also been used by a race of incorporeal beings
who, originating near a double star known as Sirius, have visited earth throughout the ages by means of dark masses like
those at Al-Qurna, for the purpose of guiding human evolution.
It is also our belief that they first materialized near Al-Qurna at
the dawn of mankind, and that the time has arrived for our
world to become part of theirs."

The sheikh stared at her as if she had gone mad, then a small,
skeptical smile curved his lips.

"Oh?" he said. "And how will this miracle happen?"

"We're not sure," Frances said.

"And this is why you are returning to Eden? To witness this
miracle?"

"Yes," Frances replied.

The sheikh stopped smiling, but kept his gaze on her face;
after a very long silence he shrugged his shoulders and spread
his hands as if praying.

"Who knows?" he said. "Perhaps you are right. Under normal circumstances your story would sound ridiculous, but given
what we know about the pillars of darkness at Al-Qurna, it is
possible that your extraordinary theory is correct. However, I
beg you, Frances, do not go back there. I repeat: If you insist on
going there, you will almost certainly not return."

"I thank you for your concern, Sheikh Hamaid," Frances
said, "but I haven't come this far to turn back. I simply *must* go
there."

The sheikh's face was filled with sorrow and his breathing
seemed too loud, but eventually, when the silence became unen-
durable, he nodded acceptance.

"As you wish," he said. "It is not my place to stop you.
Clearly you will do as you must. Perhaps it was written."

"Is your canoe still at my disposal, even knowing that it may
not return?"

The sheikh shrugged and smiled forlornly. "*Tarada*s are dispensable," he said. "Good friends are not."

The remark touched Frances and made her look away, taking in the darkly shadowed high arches that ran all the way to the back of the *mudhif.* She lowered her gaze, seeing that dark corner where Schul had lain, then shivered, remembering her first sight of him and her intimations of dread. Those intimations had come true, turning her life upside down; yet now, as she returned her attention to Sheikh Hamaid, she felt a hint of excitement rising out of her fear.

"When do you want to leave?" the sheikh asked her.

"Right now," she replied.

The sheikh nodded in sad agreement, then wearily climbed to his feet. Frances and Michael did the same, their bodies brushing as they did so, and stepped aside to let the sheikh lead them back out of the *mudhif.*

Once outside, in the afternoon's unusually dim light, they stood together uneasily for a moment, glancing around the quiet village. Poised precariously between narrow river and wide lagoon, its reed houses on stilts appearing to lean dangerously toward the water, it seemed somehow artificial and temporary, like a film set rather than the genuine article. This feeling of artificiality was, if anything, only increased by the lack of younger people and general activity; and Frances, glancing around her, feeling as if her heart were breaking, thought that even the chickens and wild dogs seemed remarkably lethargic.

She shivered and glanced at the sheikh, who simply shrugged forlornly, then she and Michael fell in at either side of him and were led through the village to the river, where his large, ornamented canoe was tethered.

Once beside the boat, Sheikh Hamaid turned toward them, raising his hands in apology.

"Unfortunately," he explained, "I cannot give you any oarsmen. I cannot, in all conscience, force anyone to go with you when we know that they may not come back."

"I would not expect it," said Frances.

The sheikh looked at Michael, as if assessing his strength. "Where you are going is not far from here," he said, "so you should be able to manage the boat alone. You just use the pole as you would on a punt at Oxford, while Frances here"—and he smiled sadly in her direction—"handles the rudder. Do you think you can do that?"

"I *have* punted at Oxford," Michael replied, "so I think I can manage."

The sheikh nodded again, smiling a little. "One of the benefits of English education," he said. "So, it's good-bye."

He took a step back, turned sideways, and waved them on. Michael walked onto the plank that led down into the low-slung boat, but Frances hesitated, stared intently at Sheikh Hamaid, then, on an emotional impulse, leaned forward and kissed him lightly on both cheeks. She straightened up again while the sheikh shyly touched his cheek, then she smiled, nodded, sniffed a little, and boarded the boat.

A few minutes later the boat was moving along the river, Michael pushing the pole while Frances handled the rudder, looking back over her shoulder as Sheikh Hamaid waved good-bye, his black robes billowing out behind him in the breeze, the reed houses and glittering lagoon receding in a dreamlike manner until, as if it had never been, the whole village disappeared, leaving only the streaming water, the starlit sky, and the river-bank's whispering.

28

THE canoe drifted along the river between bulrushes and fig palms, taking them past the smoke of burning reed-beds, more isolated villages huddled untidily on the water, the dripping, humpbacked buffaloes silhouetted in crimson as the sun began sinking behind the horizon and cast its light on the marshes.

The surroundings were superficially the same, yet subtly, more gloomily altered, and Frances realized as she studied the reed houses perched on stilts, that what was missing was the normally intense activity that had formerly enlivened the river-banks. Now when the boat passed a village, an eerie silence prevailed, and the Arabs, mostly old, but with the odd lone-some child, stared at the boat with a marked lack of expression, as if not really seeing it. Even the animals and birds seemed lifeless, and no one was singing.

Eventually, when the sun had disappeared and been replaced by an enormous moon and brilliant stars, they did hear some comforting sounds: crying geese, croaking frogs, the snorting and splashing of drinking buffaloes; then the yellow flames of campfires started flickering between the trees, illuminating the moonlit, haunting darkness with a weak, spectral glowing.

Frances was sitting at the stern of the boat, her right hand on the rudder, and when she stared straight ahead she saw Michael near the prow, looking immense and silhouetted against the starry sky as his body rose and fell over the long pole propelling the boat along.

He had hardly said a word since leaving Sheikh Hamaid's

village, but she sensed that his silence was no more than preoccupation with what might be ahead for both of them. He had come here with his eyes open, aware that he might never return, and that he had insisted on coming was a measure of the love he had for her.

Thinking about it moved Frances, made her want to return his love, but there was no way in which she could show him what she felt, since even her desires, broad and seemingly insatiable, overruled sentimental emotions and were apparently divorced from love. He understood that and accepted it, but she knew it hurt him; so as she watched him straining over the long pole, his heaving body outlined by the rich, starlit sky, she longed for a release from that unnatural sensuality which, even now, seemed to be quickening her heartbeat and setting fire to her bloodstream.

"Do you know where we are?" he asked her, glancing over his shoulder.

"Judging by how long we've been traveling, we should soon be reaching the lake, but I can't really tell you where we are. I don't recognize anything."

"Nothing?"

"No. It's like being on a different river. I used to know every bend and village along this river, but now I'm hopelessly lost. Let's face it: We haven't seen a village for some time, which is really quite odd. This landscape has changed—dramatically changed—and all the people are gone."

"The dark masses."

"Yes," Frances said. "And I feel strange already. . . ."

Michael made no reply but simply went back to his punting, making the canoe glide more urgently through the water, as if he had decided to get the forthcoming encounter over and done with. Frances shivered nervously. She was cold since the temperature had started dropping as the river grew wider, its dark, foliage-laden banks moving farther away from the boat, eventually forming the mouth of a broad lagoon.

As the canoe glided out into the lagoon, Frances turned on the portable radio she had brought with her. The sound of static filled the silence while she pressed buttons to find a station. Eventually, after managing to pick up an English-language broadcast from Basra, she heard someone announcing that the world's leading scientists were in agreement regarding the re-

cently reported dark masses, and were convinced—a few excep-
tions notwithstanding—that the phenomena had ended. In
other words, said the newsreader in exultant tones, the threat of
a disappearing world had ended.

Frances kept staring at the radio, mesmerized by what she
was hearing, wanting desperately to believe it but finding the
news too good to be true. She kept punching the buttons, hearing the same news from everywhere. Suddenly, as the canoe
drifted out into the center of the lagoon—and as the cold deepened considerably and made her and Michael shiver—the radio
went completely dead and would not come back on.

Frances tried station after station, muttering curses to herself,
then set the radio back down and smiled tearfully at Michael.

"Well," she said, "at least there's something to go back to—if
we ever get back."

"Yes," Michael said. "Oh, God, yes! It's all waiting there for
us."

He was looking steadily at her as the tears sprang to her eyes.
She smiled and wiped them away with her free hand, then
leaned on the rudder.

"So," she said, "let's keep going."

She held the rudder straight, letting the boat stay on its
course, then pressed her free hand to her stomach and plunged
into despair. She stifled the urge to scream and sunder the silence with her presence, but could not stop sweat forming on
her forehead even as she grew colder. Looking up at the sky,
she saw the known constellations, but the vastness of the cosmos pressed on her and threatened to crush her. She stared
longingly at the receding riverbanks, wishing her feet were on
solid earth, then looked straight ahead as the canoe, swaying
gently and making silver-threaded waves, glided out into the
vitreous, reflecting bowl of the star-covered lagoon.

Michael used the pole more forcefully, hurrying the boat
through the water, then glanced back over his shoulder, his
features hidden in darkness. Frances smiled at him, feeling a
light breeze on her face, but was actually less happy than she
pretended, feeling her unease increasing.

She glanced up at the sky, rubbed her eyes, then looked up
again.

"Oh, my God," she murmured.

Michael had heard her and pulled the pole out of the water,

laid it against the hull, then let the canoe drift forward into the lagoon while he, too, looked up at the sky.

The stars were in motion, some fading in and out repeatedly, many winking out completely and being replaced by others, still more drifting up and down, or gliding to and fro, weaving a new tapestry in the sky, gradually making it brighter and much more beautiful. The cosmos was being turned inside out, revealing its far side: a swimming palette of light and color beyond the known spectrum, of darkness that blossomed dramatically just to shrink back to nothing, of great suns and moons that took turns at dominating the spectacle while time and space intermingled as if in a dream.

"Good God!" Michael whispered. "You told me about it, but I just can't believe it! I've *got* to be dreaming!"

"No," Frances said, "you're not. It's getting cold—*really* cold. Remember how cold it was at Stonehenge? We've arrived. This is it."

Michael shook his head, looked up again, then sat down like a man in a trance and kept his gaze on the sky. Frances also looked up, saw the birth and death of galaxies, looked down and saw that genesis reflected in the glittering bowl of the rippling lake. Her eyes went up and down, drawn to lake and sky in turn, and soon she started feeling disoriented, her senses flying away and dissolving into the dreamscape.

"Head for the shore," she managed to say, "before it's too late. We can't tell what might happen."

Her words appeared to fall on deaf ears, for Michael made no move; he just sat there, staring up at the changing sky, his face bathed in the moonlight. Then the moonlight shifted, moving across his face and off it, forming a great pool of light in the black water beside the boat; then it gradually faded away completely and left only the starlight.

Frances saw that the moon had vanished, the stars had stopped moving, and the sky was no longer familiar: its new stars were too large, its brilliance too remarkable, its crystalline, moonless beauty too sublime to be real.

At once enchanted and frightened, she lowered her gaze. Michael was still sitting near the prow of the boat, perfectly still, his hands on his thighs, his face turned toward that strange sky.

"Michael!" she snapped. "Get moving! Let's get off the lake!" This time she got through to him, her words jolting him awake. He stared at her over his shoulder, his normally calm eyes surprised, then took hold of the long pole, stood up, making the canoe rock, plunged the pole into the shallow water and leaned heavily on it.

The canoe glided forward, cutting through the silky water, causing silver-capped, black rivulets to ripple out obliquely and disappear, whispering, in their wake.

Frances stared down at the water, into those star-reflecting depths, remembering Schul's body sinking into white-foamed turbulence while Laurence sobbed in anguish on the raft and she looked on in horror. First shivering with cold, then suddenly burning as if with fever, she forced her eyes from the rippling depths and looking skyward, was again stunned by what was transpiring.

"Oh, my God!" Michael whispered.

He stopped punting on the instant, letting the canoe drift toward the shore, and just stood there staring at the changing sky as if hypnotized.

The sky was an inverted bowl, filled with large, glittering stars, but those stars were disappearing, one cluster after the other, as if being snatched away in large numbers by an invisible hand. They kept vanishing by the score, leaving patches of darkness where they had been. Then the swaths of darkness merged, becoming one great wall, which in its turn widened dramatically, stretching across the wide lagoon until there was only an immense pillar of darkness reaching from lake to sky, its ragged edges defined by the stars still glittering around it.

"Christ!" Michael said. *"Christ!"*

He pushed harder on the pole, making the canoe leap through the water, while Frances held onto the rudder, balancing herself on the swaying seat, and looked up to see that enormous pillar of darkness moving inexorably toward her.

It grew wider as it approached, spreading out to cover the lake. The canoe suddenly slowed down and was held back by a fierce wind that, sucked up from the shore and into the dark mass, eventually threw the boat into a violent spin.

Michael fell back onto his seat, losing his grip on the punting pole; it struck the water with a light, splashing sound, bobbed back up, and then drifted off.

"Hold on!" Frances screamed.

The darkness swept around them, filling up with streaming

light, then a freezing cold gripped them as the canoe, vibrating violently and screeching in protest, spun around in a whirlpool.

Frances held on as the air was sucked from her lungs; she braced herself in the anticipation of being flung into the rushing water, and heard Michael shouting an obscenity into the roaring wind.

She was not flung from the boat. Instead, the wind died abruptly, rushing away as if by magic. There was silence and the water calmed down and let the boat drift toward shore.

The streaming light changed, became a widespread, dazzling white haze. This in turn faded away, was broken up by patches of night . . . and from that jigsaw of light and darkness emerged hundreds, then thousands, of tiny, pulsating lights that moved back and forth rapidly, like sparklers in the hands of invisible children.

The boat drifted toward the shore, illuminated by the sparkling lights. Michael stared at them with wonder, then raised his right hand, spreading his fingers to catch one of the lights and check what it was. The lights passed through his hand, his arms, his whole body, as he studied the glowing darkness, his mouth slightly open but speechless, hand still in the air.

The boat bumped against the shore, rocked a little, and then was still. Frances looked left and right, over bulrushes and grassy earth—and there in the unnatural darkness, slightly obscured by the drifting lights, was a lush forest-clearing with a natural arch of fig palms at its far end.

"This is Eden!" she whispered.

29

Dazzled by the drifting, sparkling lights and foiled by the outer darkness, they spent that first night in the long canoe, wrapped in each other's arms and looking out over the lake at the constantly changing view.

They were inside the pillar of darkness, surrounded by lights. But when they surveyed the lake, trying to see the sky beyond, they saw smaller rectangles forming within the gloom and, within those inky-black shapes, even more distant stars. The rectangles came and went, like windows opening out to the cosmos, and shifted constantly, left and right, up and down, through one another, as if time itself was moving in both directions along curving space.

Frances and Michael watched, fascinated, hardly speaking, losing themselves in the epic grandeur of what was unfolding. They sat thus for a long time, their arms about each other, and when occasionally they glanced at their watches, the hands were either racing forward or backward, or had stopped completely.

It was uncommonly cold and their weight had increased, but they sat in the boat, which swayed gently and silently, watching those great rectangles filled with stars fading in and out magically. Then sometime during that night they fell asleep, both drugged by the splendor.

Frances woke first, opening her eyes to a dazzling white haze, her skin burning from the fierceness of the heat that was beating down from a sunless sky. She rubbed her eyes and licked her parched lips, squinted straight ahead, saw nothing but the convex bowl of the horizon where the lagoon merged with blinding sky.

Wincing, she shook her head, twisted around away from Michael, saw him opening his eyes sleepily as she looked across the clearing—that very familiar garden of orange and lemon trees, fig palms, and tall, untended grass. She saw the natural arch of fig palms at the eastern end of the garden and just in front of it, flapping noisily . . . Jack Schul's tattered tent.

She studied that tent for what seemed like an eternity, her fear mingled bizarrely with a steadily rising, glowing sensuality. She felt helpless, enslaved, victimized by her burning body, but knew that it was no more than the life-force dramatically strengthened.

Michael groaned and sat up beside her, his shoulder rubbing against hers, and that slight touch charged through her like electricity, making her tingle. She placed her hand on her stomach, wanting to feel the child inside it, failed, then stared at Schul's tent and suffered shamed recollection.

She visualized herself naked, legs spread, Schul on top of her, taking her while Laurence wept by the lake, his cries floating in to her. Studying the tent, she remembered vividly, blushing with shame and lust at once; then, placing her hand on her fevered brow, closed her eyes and recalled that earlier time.

Instead of the lake, a great dust bowl, herself a primitive, grunting creature on hands and knees, face turned toward the parched earth, someone heaving behind her. There was that *and* God's eye, the great humming light descending, spreading out until it dazzled her vision and silhouetted the others. Either alone or in the presence of the alien creatures, she had writhed in surrender, beyond self-control, devoid of normal pride but moved by feelings outside herself.

Now, opening her eyes, staring at Michael and the lake beyond him, she again felt removed from herself and controlled from afar. Her very imperfect body, with its pleasures and pains, was no more than a vessel of evolution, a bridge between the past and the future, a mere link in time's endless chain.

"It's the life-force," she said.

"What?" Michael replied sleepily.

"This problem," she said. "This sexual fever that enslaves

me. It's the life-force—the need to give life—dramatically heightened. The visitants, whoever they are, deliberately made me this way. They made me want to have and give life more than anything else. They ensured my continuance."

She hardly knew what she meant herself, but felt compelled to spit it out. Michael stared intensely at her, as if thinking she might be mad, then glanced out over the haze-obscured lake and rubbed his inflamed eyes.

"Christ!" he said. "Everything's so *bright!* What time is it? What's *happening* here?"

He was talking to himself, as if already in a trance, then turned back toward her, his brow furrowing in confusion, sighed, and climbed out of the boat to give her his hand.

"We're here for a purpose," he said, sounding oddly aggressive, "so we might as well get out of this damned boat and wait for something to happen."

Frances accepted his hand and let him help her from the boat. Once on the grass, they both glanced uneasily about them . . . then Michael's gaze came to rest on the tent near the arch of fig palms.

"Schul's tent?"

"Yes."

"You mean it's managed to stand there all this time?"

"It seems so," Frances said.

Michael stared strangely at her, then returned his gaze to the tent. He quivered as if with rage, waved her forward with one hand, then led her across the attractive clearing and right up to the tent. He pulled the flap back, looked carefully inside, dropped the flap and stared at her again, an unpleasant smile on his face.

"So this is where it all happened?"

"Yes, Michael," Frances replied.

"And did you get satisfaction?" he asked her. "Did he do what I can't?"

"Stop it, Michael. You sound like a child. It's all beyond you and me."

His jaw tightened with anger, fists opening and closing; he stared fiercely at her, then eventually, as if realizing what was already happening to him, closed his eyes and shook his head from side to side.

"I'm sorry," he said. "I don't know what came over me. I

just felt this sudden, unreasonable *jealousy.* I've never felt that before."

"It's all right," Frances replied. "It's this place. It brings out very primitive, basic emotions. You'll just have to watch yourself."

Already on the verge of losing control, Michael stared down at the tent again, quivered visibly with rage, then started walking restlessly around the clearing, as if examining the trees. Frances walked with him, not wanting to leave him alone, noticing as they followed the semicircular-shaped line of trees that she could still hear the normal chorus of frogs, geese, singing birds, and buzzing mosquitoes, and that apart from the shimmering white haze over the lake, the dark line of marshes beyond it looked unaltered.

In fact, everything was the same except for the sunless sky; only the lack of a normal sun and the presence of the mysterious haze showed that changes had already occurred—and that she and Michael were still inside the gateway to that other strange world.

"Eerie," Michael said. "This place is weird. I wish something would happen."

He glanced back across the clearing, at the tent near the arch of fig palms, shook his head as if to clear it of unpleasant images, then started walking again. Frances watched him, feeling nervous, sensing his tension and growing confusion; she could see by the very way he walked that he was fighting himself.

"Let's rest," she said. "There's not much else to do. Let's just sit and talk."

"About *what?*" Michael asked abrasively. "About you and Schul and Laurence in this place? I've heard all that before!" He broke a small branch off a tree, waved it like a whip, snapped it into three or four pieces and threw the pieces away. "You're never satisfied," he said. "You remain frustrated. You just can't get enough."

The remark shocked Frances, but she made no reply, realizing that changes were occurring and could not be prevented. She thought of their arrival here, of the gold-streaked, crimson twilight, of the great pillar of darkness materializing and reaching from lake to sky. They had been greeted and then devoured, swallowed into another world, and once inside it, from their vantage point in the canoe, had watched the unfolding of time and space.

She remembered the other dark masses, the smaller black rectangles, coming and going, materializing and disappearing, bringing with them and taking away again whole glittering, constantly shifting, constellations. Yes, she knew where she was now (or at least where she was *not)* and understood that her normal world—the world she had left behind—was simultaneously very far away and right here, all around her.

Accepting that, she shivered, collapsing into her secret self, touching the burning flame at her core and laying waste to her senses.

She reached out to Michael, placing her hand on his shoulder, but he violently jerked away and then hurried down to the lake's edge. Frances watched him more nervously, wondering what he might do, then joined him where the water met the shore, lapping around the bulrushes. A silvery light covered the lake, making sky and water merge, and she felt a great lassitude falling upon her as the heat started draining her. In that lassitude, which also affected her mind, she felt the rise of desire.

She placed her hand on Michael's shoulder, but he slapped it off and walked away. She followed him until he stopped near the tent, between two groups of fig palms. He just stood there glaring at the ground, his fists opening and closing.

"If you want me, you can have me," Frances said.

"I *don't* want you," Michael replied. "I want to hear about Italy."

"Italy? What *about* Italy?"

"You know damned well," he said.

There could be no mistaking the harsh imperative in his tone, and Frances distracted herself by studying the glittering lake, squinting into that dazzling brightness with restless expectation, yearning for God's servants to return and rescue her from this. *Italy,* she thought. *He wants to hear about Italy. We are waiting to be taken into another world, yet he still wants to possess me. . . .* And she understood then that the madness was infecting both of them, that Michael was losing himself just as she had done, and that whatever might now occur between them, it would not belong to them.

"No," she said. "I won't tell you about Italy. It's not your concern."

She walked away from him, feeling drained and unreal, breathing too heavily. She did not walk very far, but stopped beneath the nearest tree, glancing up as a white pollen fell down and covered the green grass like snow. Then Michael approached her, face grim, eyes wild, and grabbed her by the shoulder and shook her with unusual violence.

"I can *have* you?" he sneered. "And what good would that do me? I can come and then watch you roll away and clench your teeth with frustration? No, I don't want that! I want to know about Italy! Your sexual hunger may be tied to what happened in this place, but your tastes relate solely to your past, and I want to know about that. Yes, Frances! I want to know about Italy! I want to know what you learned there. Now tell me!"

"No!"

"Tell me!"

His sudden slap closed her eyes and made her head spin; she fell back and covered her stinging cheek with her hand, then opened her eyes again. She saw him through her tears, a distorted figure in the strange light, then the anger gave back her lost will and lent strength to her voice.

"All right, damn you!" she whispered. "You want to hear about Italy? You want to know how I learned my whore's talents. Well, all *right,* then, I'll *tell* you!"

And in doing so lost herself, returning to that distant time, reliving every moment with a clarity so lacerating that it flayed her to the bone, leaving her exposed to naked pain and letting her rage take command. It had happened a long time ago, but it seemed like yesterday, and her words, spilling out like pebbles dropped on a pane of glass, broke the silence that covered the clearing, bringing the past to the present. . . .

She had been seventeen at the time, far too beautiful to be heartbroken, and the vacation was not soothing her melancholy as her mother had hoped. She had been melancholic for years, ever since she was a child, convinced that her father, who was supposed to have died years ago, was in fact still alive and spoke to her in the night's lonely darkness. Whether dream or hallucination, she had refused to deny his visitations, and neither doctor nor psychiatrist had budged her from the belief that her father, if dead, was still in touch with her, materializing magically in the night and imprinting his presence upon her. They had thought her mentally ill, deranged by her loss; and her mother, an eccentric (or masquerading as such) had eventually, when Frances was seventeen and no better, taken her to Ravello in southern Italy for fresh air and a long rest.

"It was beautiful," Frances said, "but more isolating than home. I painted, read books, and gazed out over the sea, obediently followed my mother through the mandatory sights of the area—the Duomo di San Pantaleone, the Grotta di Smeraldo, the glorious cathedral of Amalfi, the many gardens and ancient palazzos that adorned the cliffs high above the Gulf of Salerno —but in truth I saw little and rarely heard what was said, since I was hiding in my own silence, waiting for someone to release me—a man like I imagined my father had been: witty and wise and certainly older than myself; a *mature* man who would take command of me and set free my fearful soul. And eventually, one afternoon, in the silence of the town square when I was sitting alone having a glass of marsala, I met my Machiavellian Italian and was swept off my feet."

The Italian was in his late thirties, exceptionally handsome and urbane, charming her with his wit and sophistication, the latter in particular being a rarity in that small mountain town. He had bought her another drink, then ordered another while paying her bill, and she, slightly drunk when they parted, agreed to meet him that evening. After that she managed to meet him every day for a week, usually in the afternoon when her mother was sleeping, but almost as often in the balmy, star-bright evenings when, while her mother drank with the other guests in their small hotel, she would pretend to be bored with their adult conversation and say she wanted to watch the nightly promenade in the colorful town square. It was easy, very easy, and soon turned into a game; until, after five days, proving that patience was worth cultivating, the Italian talked her into his hotel room, thus into his bed.

"He seduced me," Frances said, "because I wanted to be seduced, because I wanted someone older and wiser to turn me into an adult. I thought he could do that—that the experience itself would do that—but although I discovered the exquisite pleasures of sex, I also learned that they didn't bring a sense of security, or even herald maturity. Quite the opposite, in fact. I simply awakened to my sensual nature, and the Italian, who was diabolically gifted in that field, soon had me confusing sex with love and behaving accordingly. I swore that I loved him and would do anything for him, and once he heard that, he knew that he owned me and could make me his slave—which he did by simply threatening to leave me when I tried to resist him."

At first she had been in heaven, transcending herself through sexual release, her sweat running in rivulets as her pores opened keenly to receive him; but then he became less loving, more brutal and demanding, eventually making suggestions that simultaneously shocked and intrigued her. When she tried refusing, he threatened to stop seeing her; and in so doing, gained her often tearful acquiescence. First minor improvisations, then more, and much worse, causing her deep shame and pain even as she obliged him. She vowed more than once to leave him, often storming out of his room, but at such times she always returned, humiliated, more malleable.

"My sweet angel!" he often crooned, his tongue licking at her ear. "My little bitch!" he soon started murmuring as she fought back her tears. "Let's do it this way," he would say. "Turn around. Raise yourself. Use the pillow and remember what I told you. Oh, my sweet, my sublime whore!" And she tried to resist but was defeated by her own flesh; and eventually, when he slapped her face to silence her protests, she accepted even that as her due and soon came to expect it.

"He taught me the hell and glory of complete submission," Frances said, "and that there was little that a woman, if in despair, could not turn to her pleasure."

It all happened within five weeks—the last five out of six. The Italian spent one week charming her, cajoling her into his arms, then another four weeks teaching her the arts of sex and enslaving her by them. Once enslaved, she needed him desperately, unable to imagine life without him—and any hope that she could resist his worst demands was very soon shattered. He promised repeatedly to keep her with him in Italy; kept promising, too, that he would speak to her mother about them . . . but as the days ran out and her departure grew more imminent, he refused to make good the latter promise unless she did even more for him. And naturally she obliged, losing her pride in love's grief—letting him turn her onto her belly, or bend her over the table, or cover her with oil to make her slip through his fingers, or take her on hands and knees as he groaned his obscenities, or make her kneel at his feet to pay him homage with her lips while he turned his hands into a vise that threatened to crush her skull—and although she learned to like it, and certainly became dependent on it, even she was not prepared for the shock he gave her when he dangled his cords of silk.

"He tied me to the bed," she said. "It was the ultimate humiliation. I was tied by my wrists and ankles, spread-eagled and open to him, and for hours he did what he wanted to me while I begged him to stop. And why did I beg his mercy? Not because of my *shame*. Oh, yes, there was certainly shame at first, but that passed soon enough. No, Michael, not that. And not because it was unpleasant. On the contrary, I begged him to stop because I thought I was dying. Yes, you heard me correctly—I was dying . . . of ecstasy. I was that way because he aroused me to a pitch beyond control, and yet, in that condition, I could neither hold him nor give myself fully to him. You understand, Michael? Are you willing to accept this truth? I was writhing in an ecstasy that could be neither shared nor eased—I couldn't stop it or control it or share it with him by touching him—and so, as I lay there tossing and straining against my bonds, I came, then came again, and again and again, and thought, because my heart was racing so fast, that I would surely expire. And after that—oh, dear God, after that there was nothing else for me: I had to be tied up, to be rendered helpless, in order to get satisfaction. . . . So, Michael, you wanted the sordid truth. Well, now you have it!"

For a while he just stared at her, as if not recognizing her, but eventually, as what he had heard sank properly into his consciousness, his blank expression was replaced with tight-jawed rage.

"All right!" he said. *"Right!"*

Quivering, he stepped forward and grabbed the flap of the tent's entrance, ripped it back but could not make it move farther, so cursed and pulled harder. The canvas would not come off, so he cursed again and kicked one foot out, knocking the nearest upright away and making the front of the tent collapse. He stared at it, breathing harshly in a veritable trance of rage, then walked to the other end of the tent and did exactly the same: kicking the remaining support away with the ferocity of a demented man. The rest of the tent collapsed, a part of the canvas covering his feet, and he viciously kicked the canvas away, muttering under his breath. He bent down and jerked the thin ropes out of the rings on the crumpled canvas, straightened up again, glared at Frances, then abruptly walked up to her.

"You like to be helpless?" he asked. "All *right,* then, let's *do* it!"

She thought of running away, but there was no place to hide; and before she could think of some other response, he grabbed the collars of her shirt and ripped them apart, until the garment was dangling around her waist, leaving her bare breasts exposed.

"Now take off the rest of your clothes," he snapped. *"All* of them! *Now!"*

At once frightened and excited, Frances did as she was told; then, when she had finished, when she was standing naked before him, Michael grabbed hold of her wrist, twisted it up behind her, and brutally forced her down onto her knees, with her back turned toward him.

"Is this what you want?" he almost snarled. "Let's *see* if it is!"

He twisted her arm again, making her turn around to face him, then threw her onto her back and aggressively leaned over her. She offered no resistance, but simply lay there, letting his rage burn as he spread her arms and legs on the crumpled canvas and, with the thin ropes, tied her wrists and ankles to the wooden pegs that had kept the tent rigid.

When she was lying there, spread-eagled beneath him, he stood over her, panting.

"You look nice," he sneered. *"Very* nice!"

Then he took off his own clothes, very slowly and deliberately, looking at her with contempt, and eventually knelt between her outstretched legs to place his hands on her ankles.

"You're mine," he said. "All of you. Mine . . . And you can't do a damned thing!"

He pushed her ankles back as far as the ropes would allow, causing her knees to rise slightly and spread farther apart. She watched him bending over, as if about to kiss the earth, then felt his lips down there, between her thighs, on her pubic hair, then pressing over the tender labia and forcing her to shut her eyes.

She gasped and bit her lower lip, feeling the arching of her spine, the automatic, helpless movement of her thighs as they cushioned his head. He was sucking and licking, greedily drinking her as she melted, then she felt his hands sliding up her legs and under her hips. He spread his fingers to hold her firmly, nails digging into her soft skin, and lifted her higher, giving himself more access, as his tongue coiled inside her.

She heard something—her own groaning—and desperately bit her lower lip, only dimly aware of what she was doing as her body quivered involuntarily, straining vainly against its bonds, forming a bridge over a chasm of infinite space and time.

Yes, she was a bridge, a thread of life joining two worlds, her physical self in thrall to the demands of sensual pleasure, her spirit rising out of that mortal shell to spiral into the ether. She soared like an eagle, returned to earth, soared again, looked down upon herself from afar, but fiercely clung to her feelings. Michael's tongue was like a feather, first stroking, then retreating; it returned to press wetly and lick, preparing the way for his hungry lips. She melted and was sucked up, pouring into his greedy mouth, then felt the air rushing onto thigh and labia, as his lips, which had been draining her of sense, slid wetly over her belly.

At that moment, in a sea of drunken flesh, she simultaneously touched earth and sky.

Her navel expanded to accept his tongue, opening out like a great lake, and she pushed up, straining desperately against the ropes, trying to reach for the sky. He plumbed her depths, scoured her banks, made her belly's fine flesh ripple, let the ripples run up over her rib cage and spread out through her breasts. Her flesh became a desert, grains of sand in constant motion, a terrain of curves and hollows and languid dunes given life by a burning wind.

She was that, but remained herself, drawing her energy from sensual greed. She felt his warm breath—in her ear, on her throat, then caressing her bosom to further excite her yearning nipples—then the lips again, that mouth drinking her flowing flesh; that tongue, its saliva like warm oil, pouring into her opening pores. First one breast, then the other; one nipple, then its partner; and she twisted and writhed, straining vainly against her bonds, feeling all of her, every nerve and sinew, aching just to take hold of him.

His hand clamped around her chin, shaking her head, making her open her eyes.

He was kneeling between her legs but had straightened up a little, his erect penis thrusting out above her, hard and smooth and blue-veined. He stared down at her, not smiling, eyes gleaming with a kind of blindness. He slid his hands under her, fingers stroking the perineum, then took hold of her buttocks and raised them to thrust his hips forward. His penis lightly touched her, making her groan aloud; she tried to arch her body higher, to spread herself and take him in, but the ropes, not allowing further movement, made all her nerves sing.

She writhed and cried out, trying to will herself around him, her body quivering in its exquisite torment and threatening to turn her insides out. Then she felt his penetration, herself folding around him, and he was quickly inside her, hard and hot, beating rhythmically, swelling more as she tightened, sending waves of heat rippling through her in every direction, soon making her feel that she was glowing with a magical radiance.

"No more!" she cried. *"Stop it!"*

She was about to explode, to burst forth from herself, to become the moon and stars, earth and air, fire and water, and felt that if she failed to find release her racing heart would give out. Fearing that, she also wanted it, her spirit crying for its lost freedom, then understood in a flash of revelation that the gates would soon open. And indeed they did so, letting her spirit have dominion, and she dissolved and flowed away, pouring down to her own center, became no more than the quivering, pulsating heat of her own nether regions.

Her body strained against its bonds, sending pains through her arms and legs, and she cried out again, her voice reverberating in her head, and realized that the self-abasement which for so long had enslaved her was no more than the wall behind which she had hoped to protect her wounded soul. Then Michael's hands were upon her, traveling down her arms and legs. She felt the ropes being untied and falling off her wrists and ankles; then knew, as the opening gates admitted light and air, that her limbs would soon become freedom's wings, letting her fly away.

"We don't need that!" Michael said. "It's an illusion. We just need each other."

And she smiled with joy, agreeing, rising out of her imprisoned spirit, and so wrapped herself around him, arms and legs, heart and soul, and devoured him, absorbed him, made him part and parcel of her, let herself find the release which in turn released him, and heard their two voices as one, rising above the earth's bedlam.

"Yes!" they gasped. *"Yes!"*

Then the earth actually moved.

30

Like the beginning of an earthquake, the ground shook beneath them, then they heard an ethereal bass humming that filled the space all around them. Michael had rolled off Frances and now they both jerked upright, automatically looking over the lake in search of the dark mass.

The ground shook again, growling far down in its depths, then returned to stillness and silence, leaving only the bass humming that, though it seemed to be all around them, was clearly emanating from the direction of the lake. The dark mass had not appeared there, but the white haze had changed: the general brilliance had decreased and now the air was splotched with dark patches that were changing shape constantly.

Michael climbed to his feet, took Frances's hand and pulled her up. They both stood there naked, still dazed by the act of love, and stared silently at what was happening above the lagoon.

The dark patches were growing larger and more numerous, boiling out of the white haze like irregular holes in a cloud—or like black ink splashed on blotting paper—then filling up with distant stars in a more complete blackness.

No longer frightened but charged with excitement, Frances squeezed Michael's hand and saw his heartening smile. She wanted to embrace him, but he had already turned away from her, to stare out once more at that great spectacle above the vitreous water.

Frances followed his gaze and saw the multiplying holes,

originally in their dozens, now in their hundreds, filling the sky
as far back as the horizon where the marshes had formed a dark
line on the convex rim of the lagoon.

The holes kept multiplying, changing shape, growing larger,
until they looked like dense clouds in a misty luminescence that
rapidly diminished in intensity until it seemed like a normal
sky.

The bass humming grew deeper, then became an infrasound,
so low that it formed a vibration that made the ground shake.
That phenomenon shook Frances, sent ripples through flesh
and bone, making her very aware of her body and the child she
was carrying. She touched her stomach with her free hand, no
longer fearful, simply curious, then saw that the holes in the sky
had stopped multiplying.

"They're getting bigger," she said.

That was true. The holes had stopped multiplying, though
there were a few hundred, and now they were growing dramatically and changing their shape, turning from ragged holes into
wavering, perpendicular columns, then widening until their uneven edges became almost straight. They were shaped like rectangles, some close, others far away, and all of them contained
glittering stars that grew bigger and brighter.

The rectangles were windows, looking out on time and space,
and as they became more distinct and spread out above the lake
the white haze diminished more rapidly, eventually turning into
a mundane, pearly-gray light.

Then the star-filled rectangles began drifting up and down,
north and south, east and west, and were soon settling gently on
the marshes and the lake's glittering surface. Once settled, they
started glowing, were surrounded by a shimmering aura; and
that light, growing brighter, slightly erased the stars within as
well as obliterating the land upon which it was bleeding.

The rectangles were great funnels, descending over earth and
water; and as they pulsated and radiated their shimmering light,
that earth and water began disappearing in a magical manner.

The earth seemed to melt, dissolving within the star-filled
windows, making way for other, very different dark masses,
which were forming mysteriously out of that space–time frame.
And as that was happening the lagoon itself was vanishing, but
in an equally different, more dramatic manner: The water was
sucked up in immense, spiraling arcs that appeared to be pour-

ing backward into the star-windows—like waterfalls flowing miraculously in reverse. And as they did so the remaining water in the lake was sinking, the muddy banks climbing higher, thus exposing the circular rim of a giant crater.

It was an extraordinary sight, terrifying and awe-inspiring. Frances glanced at Michael, wondering how he was reacting, saw that he was calm, if slightly stunned, then returned her own gaze to the front and was again mesmerized.

Where the earth had melted away, the different masses were taking shape, becoming sandy dunes, bleached rocks, and jagged cliffs, each viewed like a piece of a jigsaw in the star-filled, drifting windows. And now the stars were fading, receding back into time and space, and the separate pieces of the new landscape, framed within the great rectangles, materialized in ochers and browns, under a new, stronger sun.

So the landscape was changing beyond the sinking lake, while the lake itself, in a spectacle to stun the senses, was sucked up into waterfalls that roared, flowed in reverse, arched back into the hovering rectangles, then disappeared into thin air. The water in the lake kept sinking, turning the banks into high hills, the wet mud littered with tangled weeds, alluvial stones, gasping fish, and polished bones over which, with the rising of a hot wind, a fine dust was swirling.

Frances and Michael just stood there, too stunned to say anything, the small hand of the former held tightly by the latter, the ground continuing to vibrate through them as the surrounding world changed.

The waterfalls poured backward, vanishing into the landscaped windows, while the water in the lake kept sinking and shrinking in width, causing the crater to grow dramatically and gradually turn into a barren valley. A fierce heat had filled the air and a hot wind was blowing; and as the last of the water was sucked up, disappearing magically into the hovering windows, the muddy slopes of the valley, already drying, were being covered in fine dust.

That dust soon settled over everything in the valley, including weeds and plants, alluvial stones and dead fish, and the polished bones of creatures, human and otherwise, who had once walked the earth.

The transformation took many hours, mentally and physically draining Frances; but eventually she found herself, in what

she assumed must be the late afternoon, sitting near the edge of
the enormous circular dust bowl—a barren valley, in fact—
leaning shoulder to shoulder with Michael, staring out, exactly
as he was doing, over that vast, chilling emptiness.

The rectangular windows still filled the sky and went as far as
the horizon, and there, where the marshes had been, was a
completely new landscape of parched rocks, jagged cliffs, and,
in one instance, a soaring, volcanic peak that, illuminated in a
fierce sun, had the color of burnished gold.

The windows, or gateways, had served their purpose and
were fading away, their black edges becoming vaporous then
turning into reams of smoke that, sucked back in upon themselves, shrank rapidly and vanished.

Frances glanced to either side. The same thing had happened
around her. The gateways, or windows, had fallen over the verdant land, swallowing the orange and lemon trees, the fig palms
and bulrushes, and gradually turning the Garden of Eden into
parched rocks and dry dust, the latter blown constantly by a
gentle though very hot breeze.

Here, too, the great rectangles were gradually fading away
until, even as Frances was studying them, they all disappeared,
leaving only a sultry sky.

The infrasound faded out and the earth stopped its shaking.
Then there was another sound—a jagged, high-pitched squawk-
ing—and they both looked up and saw a pteranodon flying
above them, its large beak pointing down in their direction, its
wings of skin beating awkwardly.

The bizarre creature passed overhead, then they lowered
their eyes again.

The dust bowl was immense, stretching away to the horizon,
a great wilderness valley filled with dried plants and bleached
stones and now, to their surprise, containing a few animals,
most of which were obviously prehistoric and, mercifully, a
considerable distance away.

Frances accepted it, feeling at one with it, realizing in some
dim manner that she had obviously changed herself, but not
really examining that fact closely, putting it out of her mind.
She felt heavy, lethargic, devoid of memory and imagination,
and let her hand slip from Michael's grasp as she wearily
climbed to her feet.

There was a large sun in the sky, a bright golden orb, but it was starting to sink behind the distant mountains, its light turning to striations of deep crimson and yellow fire, which were spreading along the horizon like lava poured from a tilting bowl. The cliffs and mountains were changing color, blackening into silhouette, and the shadow of the soaring volcanic peak stretched across the sloping floor of the cratered dust bowl like a giant's crooking finger.

"Nightfall," Michael said. "Coming fast. Soon darkness will be."

He pointed across the clearing, his finger jabbing at a group of rocks. Frances dimly remembered the tent, but now, when she stared across the clearing, she saw the cave she called home. Michael's finger jabbed the air, then he walked toward the cave. Frances glanced around and saw the sinking sun and the forward crawl of the darkness. Shivering, wondering what the night might bring, she hurried after her man.

"Fire," he said. "Keep the darkness back. . . . And no cold to bite us."

She gathered up the sticks and arranged them into a pile; he made the rubbed stones spit many lights and turn the wood into flame. Then he went into the cave, banging something, saying bad words, emerged with a bloody long-tailed creature hanging lifeless from one hand. The other hand held a flat stone honed down to a sharp edge, and he sat by the fire and used the stone to strip the flesh from the animal. He tore the insides out and threw some of them away; the rest he divided between them, and they both ate with relish. The food was bloody, but it filled up their hunger and left quiet contentment.

"Dark," he said. "Demon-night."

An animal snarled from behind the rocks. There was the padding of swift feet. The animal snarled again, something thumped softly against a rock, another animal squealed, then there was silence and a small, settling cloud of dust.

Daybright dying fast. Night creeping over the plain. The demon-darkness edged toward the cave, but was stopped by the fire. He reached out and pulled her to him. She fell against him, feeling better. The dancing flames were dying like the day and letting the cold take its first bites.

"Inside," he said. "Warm-safe."

Dark but warm-safe in the cave where they huddled together.

She looked out through the rock hole, watching as darkness lapped at the flames before covering them up.

Demon-darkness and silence . . . Which brought other sounds to life: distant growlings and howlings, an occasional squawk from overhead, the sudden rush of padded feet, beating tails, snapping twigs, whispering windtalk.

She shivered, cold and fearful, knowing not what she was feeling, pressed herself to his warmth and closed her eyes when they felt very heavy.

Frances found herself in dreaming, her thoughts floating away from the past, returning her to the self with a mind that roamed between past and future. She felt Michael's arms around her and took comfort from his presence, perhaps awakening for a very brief moment before falling asleep again.

In that sleep she returned home, saw her mother dead on the carpet, wept and then went farther back to find her mother alive. She was sitting in the darkness, holding hands with other old ladies; then all of them placed their hands on the table and it started to rock, tapping its legs on the floor. One tap for yes, two taps for no. It was a simple, primitive language between the dead and the living, between one world and another; possibly between the past, to which the dead had returned, and the present, from which the living had departed.

Frances watched the rocking table, heard it tapping against the floor. It stopped moving and the silence rushed in . . . then her mother was talking.

"I kill him," her mother said, her voice ghostly but very masculine. "Silent, I make him. And still. And then God can return . . ." The voice was harsh and guttural, the words as hesitant as an imbecile's, and Frances saw her mother slumping back, her face turned toward the ceiling. "Me weak," her mother said. "He strong. Me need strength in hand . . ."

The old ladies joined hands again, two linking up with her mother. Frances watched her mother choking in the darkness, then getting her voice back. It was not her mother's voice: it was a man's voice, sounding sluggish and primitive.

"Kill," her mother said. "Need stronger hand. Disappear him forever. . . ." The voice trailed off into silence, or the hush of heavy breathing, then eventually emanated again from its dim, distant past. "You, me," the voice gasped. "Soon to be. When his silence is always. Kill him with stronger hand . . ."

The voice faded away again, as did the image of her unconscious mother; then Frances traveled back, farther back, to emerge in another time. She saw Laurence rising up, his body fine-haired and muscular, his hand holding a thick branch over his head and swinging it down upon Schul.

She witnessed Schul's dying moment.

In that instant she saw herself, linking past, present, and future, forming a bridge with her flesh between what had been, what was, and was yet to be. She had lived then, as now, as she would in the future, and she saw it and returned to her beginnings in the dark of her primitive cave.

"Fear is me! I am fear!"

The words dropped from her shivering lips, reverberating in the darkness, perhaps not even spoken but *felt* and then actualized. She rubbed her eyes, still drugged by sleep, felt her mate, looked out the rock hole, saw a circle of stars, a hint of moonlight, distant rocks silhouetted.

"The fear comes from the demon-night."

She spoke the language of her man, which made him waken, growling something. She grabbed his hand and placed it on the ground to let him hear the earth grumbling.

"Coming back. *Come for me!*"

Then he felt it and yelped, jerking his hand off the ground. He held the hand up and studied it closely, turning it to and fro, opening and closing his fingers, glancing at the floor of the cave, and finally, spreading his fingers in the air, pressing his hand down again.

She did the same, trying to help; at least wanting to give him comfort. Like him, she felt the bowels of the earth in the convulsion of rage. The ground shook and made much noise, giving life to clouds of dust, then the noise, which they had thought came from the earth, seemed to come from outside the cave.

"We be good and obey them!"

Had he spoken with his tongue or put himself inside her head? She only knew that she understood what he wished to convey, and that whatever it was she would listen and do as he told her.

"Me good, too! *Me obey!*"

They clung to each other, sharing fear and warmth at once, both looking out through the rock hole at the demon-night stirring. They saw stars, a hint of moonlight, distant rocks silhouetted. Then another light, stronger than the moonlight, made the rocks stand out from darkness, illuminating their rounded, sun-scorched edges and lengthening their shadows.

Even as that light grew brighter and widened, there was a noise in the sky, first faint, then growing louder, and soon it was a terrible, deep roaring—the breath of a giant that whipped up the dust, and then, not satisfied with this show of anger, reverberated awfully through the cave and made their ears ring.

"Mercy, Masters!"

"We worship you!"

Their voices rang out as one, rising above the earth's bedlam, then they fell on hands and knees and bowed low to rub their noses in dirt.

"Edinu!"

"Plain!"

One word meant the other and both filled their thoughts as they felt the earth shaking beneath them and worshiped the gods of the great plain. The great plain was the dust bowl, the vast, desolate crater—*Edinu,* the world's navel, winding down to the netherworld—*Edinu: plain*—the land of Eden, where all started and ended.

They bowed low, eating dust, feeling the ground vibrating through them, hearing the terrible roaring, the gods' breath, reverberating around them.

Suddenly, there was silence. They looked up and saw bright light. It was neither the moonlight nor the stars nor the campfire, but a fierce and very alien light that pulsated and blinded them. They both groaned and lowered their heads, stifled their groans, *felt* the silence; eventually heard other sounds, short and sharp, penetrating, then a much softer, oddly soothing sibilance that merged into . . . singing.

Singing? What is *singing?* Who shared this word with them? They only knew of noise that rose and fell to make other sound-patterns. It was speaking, yet not so. It was not one: it was many. It was vibration, feeling, a *sensation* that gave life to the silence.

It was something outside the cave.

They raised their faces from the dirt, stared through the rock hole, saw the distant rocks—now appearing to be much closer —illuminated in brilliant light.

Not the moon. Nor the stars. Not the campfire that had died.

What they saw was a dazzling, unknown light, which appeared to be filled with smaller lights that were drifting and bobbing. And those lights, long and thin, like cutting stones turned on edge, were bobbing up and down, almost dancing, to what they now felt was *singing.*

Singing-talk. *Talk that sings!*

Feeling soothed, they stood upright, holding hands, fingers touching, then shuffled toward the rock hole that soon became the mouth of their cave. They stopped just before it, weighing fear against curiosity, wishing to go outside and pay homage, but fearful of doing so.

Too late to decide. A blinding light exploded over them. They squealed, staggered back into the cave, and covered their eyes with their fingers. The dazzling light multiplied, quickly becoming more than one, then the many lights moved forward into the cave, illuminating the darkness.

Thin lines of light converging. Moving up and down. Beaming sideways and then along the floor to form a dazzling web.

At that moment they both screamed, two voices as one, rising above the bedlam of the cave with its stabbing noises and singing.

They stopped screaming soon enough, then both looked up in terror. There were silhouetted figures shoulder to shoulder before them, all very tall and thin, but not unlike themselves, all with lights beaming from their bellies or upraised hands, all communicating with singing-talk . . . or with talk that sang alien words.

She dived into her terror then, plunging down to hide herself, refusing to raise her head or return to thought until the gods had departed. Then she heard it—dying singing, fading words, inrushing silence—and the light outside changed, the smaller lights winking out, and then the humming began, became a roaring that did not hurt, and the greater light grew weak and shrank as it rose on high, until the rocks shifted back into silhouette and let the stars shine in glory, radiating through silence.

Exhausted by fear, they both slept, sharing the same dream.

31

AWAKENING the next morning, Frances felt almost normal, though her eyes were smarting and out of focus, her head light and disordered. Nonetheless, she knew who she was and what had happened the day before, and so, as she glanced around her, letting her gaze linger on Michael, she was able to give him a smile of recognition and love.

He was kneeling on the ground, one knee raised, one on the earth, and she noticed that he had torn his pants off above the thighs, so that now, wearing those rough shorts and nothing else at all, with his chin in need of a shave and beads of sweat on his skin, he did indeed look like he might actually belong in this primitive cave.

It amused her, but only briefly, for then the strangeness crept back over her, making her sit upright and look down at her own dirt-smeared nakedness. She felt embarrassed to see herself, so swallowed dryly and shuddered, then observed that someone, obviously Michael, had placed her begrimed clothing on the earth where her head had been resting.

"I brought them in earlier this morning," Michael said, his voice reverberating ethereally around the cave. "I thought you might want them."

"I do," Frances replied. "Thanks."

She dressed herself without hesitation, though she felt slightly ridiculous, then managed to meet Michael's gaze, which seemed no more than curious.

"Are you all right?" she asked him.

"Yes," he said, "I suppose so. I'm back to normal, if that's what you mean, but I feel a bit unreal."

"You remember what happened yesterday?"

"Yes."

"We were different people then."

"I keep thinking I was dreaming," Michael said, "but obviously I wasn't."

"You've been out there. What's out there now?"

"Just that dust bowl," he said.

Frances felt the child inside her, but her stomach was flat. She had been here only three earth-months before, but knew the child would come soon, since, in the matter of its gestation, time was irrelevant. She should have felt frightened, but instead was uplifted, raised on high by the radiant unreality of her wondrous experience.

"Were we visited last night?" Michael asked her, "or did I simply imagine it?"

"They came in here," Frances replied, as if talking about old friends. "We saw the lights of their descent, heard them talking —if that's what it is—then they entered the cave, carrying some kind of torchlights. They examined us, but then, when we panicked, very quickly departed."

"If you knew it was them," Michael asked her, "why did *you* panic?"

"Because I wasn't myself. At least I wasn't the person I am now. I was my original self, that primitive creature, and thought they were gods."

"Maybe they are," Michael said. "Either gods . . . or God's children."

Frances glanced at him, wondering if he was mocking her, but he was staring thoughtfully out of the cave, his face weary and grave.

"Yes," she said, after a considerable hesitation. "Gods—or simply God's children. Like you and me . . . and my child."

Michael's expression was still somber, but he sighed and stood up, reaching out with one hand to pull her to him and warmly embrace her.

"If I seem strange," he said, "it's just the weather. Put it down to the weather."

Frances chuckled at that, then sank her teeth into his shoulder, wanting to draw blood, to suck him into her and make him a part of her.

"Come on," he said. "Let's go outside and face the new day."

Holding hands like two children, they stepped out of the cave —to be instantly dazzled by the light and burned by fierce heat. They shielded their eyes, letting them adjust to the uncommon brightness, then looked around the clearing, at the parched plants, scorched rocks, and slowly drifting dust, then across the immense, cratered plain at the irregular sand dunes and cliffs.

The volcanic peak was still there, soaring high and wavering in heat waves, its long shadow like the black, crooking finger of a giant, stretching down the sloping side of the crater. There were prehistoric animals where the base of the crater leveled out and formed, to all intents and purposes, a vast wilderness valley. The animals, far away, were distorted in the heat waves that shimmered up from the barren, sun-scorched earth.

The heat was ferocious, clamping around them like a fist, making them both sweat profusely and feel drained of strength. Frances hurried toward some rocks, dragging Michael by the hand, the soles of her feet burning until she reached a shadowed area, where she gratefully breathed cooler air. She rubbed her stinging eyes, glancing around her, having to squint, saw nothing but streams of fine dust winding across empty wilderness. Occasionally an animal roared in the distance, or a strange bird squawked in flight, but otherwise time seemed to be standing still in a great bowl of silence.

"So," Michael said. "Here we are. *Now* what do we do?"

"There's nothing we *can* do," Frances replied, "except sit here and wait."

"And what if they don't come back, Frances? What if they never come?"

"Then we'll die," Frances said.

She hardly knew what she meant, but sensed his intensity, so squeezed his hand and made him sit beside her. They sat on a low, smooth stone, sheltering under the taller rocks, and from that vantage point were able to look out of the shadows, at the panorama of burning desolation that stretched away on all sides. The prehistoric animals still roamed aimlessly in the valley, the volcanic peak beyond wavered in the shimmering heat waves, and, above all, the sky was a silvery-white sheet in which the only visible object was a huge sun that blazed gold and orange.

Frances let her eyes roam from that glorious sun to her own feet which, having been bare for so long, were filthy and torn. Then, with a sigh, she straightened up and looked sideways at Michael.

"I'm going to have this child," she said. "I know it. I feel it."

Michael stared somberly at her, then gazed all around him. Seeing nothing, he coughed into his fist and said, "Maybe. Who knows?"

"You don't believe it?" Frances asked.

"What I believe is irrelevant. I only know that since meeting you, the impossible has become commonplace; and that right now, as I sit on this very rock, I can't believe that I'm here. And where, for that matter, is *here?* We're both living a miracle."

"Are you frightened?"

"No. Strangely enough, I'm not. I feel disoriented, a bit removed from myself, but I also feel tremendous anticipation and constant excitement. . . . And you? What do *you* feel?"

"The same," Frances replied, without hesitation. "Like you, I feel disoriented, or at least a bit strange, but otherwise very emotional. I'm moved by a deep sense of joy and gratification, as if I'm in a cathedral and the organ is playing."

"You were frightened last night."

"That was the *other* me. The dawn-child: that primitive creature. I'm not her today."

"Perhaps you will be, before the day is out."

"I've no doubts about that."

And indeed, even as she finished talking, there was a distant rumbling sound, a fierce subterranean explosion, and the volcanic peak shook visibly, then spewed molten lava. The lava poured down the mountain in streams of gold and crimson, which soon broke apart and spread over the slopes like burning fingers. And observing that spectacle, the earth shaking beneath her feet, Frances was able to accept that this was indeed a long-lost dawning: that time and space had been rearranged to take her back, not only to her own origins but to the beginnings of the whole human race.

The earth grumbled again, its bowels erupting in flame and smoke. The streams of lava soon formed a glittering necklace around the mountain peak, and Frances understood as she lowered her eyes that she, too, was changing again.

"I love you," she said to Michael. "I want you to understand that. Before the day's over, we might be separated—either physically or spiritually—and whatever happens, no matter what becomes of us, I want you to know that I love you. I've never felt this way before—I've wanted to, but never have—yet I now know that what I feel for you is more than just sex. I wasted my life searching for the father I could never have, but when I found you, I also found release from the vanity of that pursuit. Now I don't need other men—nor the self-abasement learned in Italy. I only need your commitment and my own faith to help me face what is coming. So, I love you. *Remember* that."

Michael gave his reply without saying a word. He simply nodded and reached out to seal her lips with his outspread fingers, held them there for some time, then removed them and smiled gently at her.

"We're all right," he said finally, lowering his hand and patting her knee. "You and I, we'll survive. Meant to be, we *will* be. It hasn't ended for either of us yet—and I don't think it will. Relax, Frances Devereux, I'm still here . . . and the day is still young."

His last words were almost drowned out by the fresh rumbling of the volcano. Frances looked across the sunken plain, beyond the animals in shimmering heat waves, saw more lava spewing out of the mountain peak to add its gold to the crimson flow.

"I feel strange," she heard Michael murmuring. "I feel very tired . . ."

She wanted to smile and offer words of encouragement, but was distracted by movement and sound where there should not have been any.

Turning her head, she saw a strange group near the cave, gathered around a smoldering campfire in front of the rock face. At first she thought they were normal people, but then realized they were not. They were hairy, apelike creatures, very small, their shoulders stooped, though those not squatting were standing on two legs, even if awkwardly.

Frances glanced at Michael. She recognized him, but he seemed different. He kept fading in and out, like an optical illusion, and each time he came back into focus he seemed that little bit different. He caught her glance and returned it, brow furrowing in confusion, then scratched the back of one ear and turned away from her, leaning forward as if he could not hold his back straight, his head lolling weakly.

Frances studied the cavemen, wondering where they had come from. They were chattering among themselves, using a guttural, alien language, and a few of them were poking at the smoldering fire with branches stripped of their leaves. They did not appear to notice her; nor did they seem too real. Like Michael, they were magically fading in and out, as if merely images being projected by a faulty machine.

Then she heard beating wings. Her dazed eyes turned toward the sky. A prehistoric pteranodon flew overhead, its large beak pointing down in her direction, its wings of skin beating awkwardly.

Filled with fear, she cried out. She sensed that someone was coming toward her. She clung to the hope that that someone would disappear with the rest of it.

At that moment Michael grunted, grabbed her shoulder, and led her toward the squatting cavemen. As he dragged her through the dust she felt more natural, but kept looking around her. There was no one coming toward her, but strange clouds were gathering, boiling impossibly out of a clear sky and growing bigger each second.

Her man dragged her to the campfire, where they crouched low with the others, all of whom were staring at the sky where the clouds were still gathering. The golden sun darkened, a curtain of clouds falling across it, then long shadows crept into the crater and moved across the flat plain. The sky growled and barked, but surprisingly did not weep; then, though the heat was still fierce, a rising wind whipped the dust up.

"Angry wind come," Michael said.

"Sky no cry," Frances added.

Michael? *Frances?* What words were these she heard? She scratched herself in rising agitation and glanced nervously around her. The ground was littered with bones and the debris of dead fires, but otherwise there was nothing to be seen that she had not seen before. She felt a little better, less fearful of the unknown; but the sky roared again, like an animal in a trap, and she then saw a mass of black clouds where pure light had just been.

"Sky wearing cover."

"Warmed by clouds."

"Making cold where we are."

She felt the slight chill when the wind blew across her, letting the dust settle on her arms and legs, making whispering noises. She glanced up and saw that he was staring possessively at her, turned away and saw the other one, Schul, reaching out to take hold of her.

Schul? What sound was this? Was it the sound that made him known? She scratched herself again, feeling very confused; and then, looking across the great plain of the gods, saw that the shadows were creeping forward to swallow the animals.

"Dark cold is nearing."

"Wind talks louder."

"Sky no the same."

They huddled closer together, all looking up at the sky. There was an immense circle of dark clouds right over the circular plain, blotting out the light from the plain and making it look bleak and frightening. She felt the fear in herself and it made her lower her eyes. Schul and Laurence were squatting side by side, still studying the brooding sky.

Schul? Laurence? What sounds were these? She felt confused because her thoughts contained these sounds that she had not heard before. *Schul. Laurence* . . . She thought of the sounds and studied the man-apes. They both often looked at her with hunger in their eyes, but now were staring at the sky, which was not as it had been.

"Sky breaking!"

"And makes noise!"

The mass of dark cloud was broken up by the many lights exploding through it, the lights beaming out obliquely to form great anthill shapes, which brightly illuminated the desert floor of the plain of the gods. Those lights startled the animals and made them flee in all directions, their hooves kicking up more clouds of dust and making the air dense.

She could hear the animals crying and shared the terror that caused it, then the other sound, coming down from the sky, seemed to vibrate right through her.

Shaking, she looked up, saw the lights shredding the clouds, growing bigger and melting the darkness around them as they started descending.

The clouds had been broken up and now were over the cave-camp, widening as they silently dropped around her to form a dense mist. Those clouds also held light, trying to break through and beam down; it brightened and dimmed, over and over again, as if to the rhythm of the beating inside her heaving breast.

She shook, gibbered, and pointed as the clouds pressed down upon her, as the light, finally starting to beam through, gradually forced the clouds apart until they were swirling all around her, darkening the landscape.

The lights dimmed and brightened and repeated that rapidly, as if they were reflecting what was beating inside her breast. They were beating to a distant music, a sound fading in and out, and it gave them a life of their own, a spirit glowing and visible.

Were they lights? Or were they great birds? She could not tell for certain. They were shaped like flat stones (like the ones used to scrape the meat off bone and crack enemy skulls) but they glowed with a magical incandescence that seemed to pulsate to her heartbeat. They hovered there above the mountains, and above the great plain, and they drifted above the rocks all around the cave-camp, their magic light pulsating and fading in and out as their combined noise, which sounded like breathless growling, made the ground shake.

The floating things were dark shapes within dazzling silvery-white mist; they growled in an unbroken manner and made the earth shake, bobbed up and down like the dust when the wind did but whisper. The floating things, those flattened balls of glowing fire, cast their shadows beneath them.

Fear congealed her every instinct. She shook, gibbered, and pointed. All her brothers and sisters, including her two man-apes, were behaving in a similar manner as they looked up in terror.

The floating fireballs dropped lower, their shadows widening to touch the man-apes, then the wind, which had been increasing in strength, turned into a storm.

She sobbed fearfully and covered her eyes, fingers outspread to give her sight, saw the others doing the same while they yelped and snorted in terror. The wind hissed and swept around them, made them blind and almost deaf, while the fireballs, still floating above them, beamed their light through the murk.

"Oh, powerful ones!"

"Mercy!"

They all retreated toward the rock hole, shuffling backward through the storm, peering up through outspread fingers, through swirling dust and blinding light, to see some of the things that looked like fireballs dropping down even lower. They squealed in terror and attacked each other, taking defense in a frenzy of violence, but soon the cooler darkness of the cave started falling about them.

"Fear is me! I am fear!"

"The gods outside!"

"I *kill* fear! I *want* . . ."

The last one to speak stared at her, his eyes as bright as the things outside, and she felt the fear breaking her in two and confusing her thoughts.

He was staring at her. That one! The one she thought of as *Schul.* Yet why did she think of that word and what did it mean? *Schul:* a hissing sound. Like a serpent creating dust. She sensed that it was a sound from some other time or place, but failed, no matter how hard she tried, to attach it to anything.

For that matter, who was *she?* Where *was* she at this moment? What was beating so hard inside her that she felt she would burst?

It was him, the possessive one. He lived in memory and imagination. She saw him, identified as *Schul,* staring at her with burning eyes.

A cloud of dust swirled through the cave, making everyone cough and shout. Their terror aroused other fierce feelings and made them hide behind violence. His nostrils flared as he grabbed her, pulled her to him, pushed her down. She yelped and the other one, the better one who also wanted her, leaped with a hoarse yelp to her rescue. There was growling and pounding, a grunt, flesh on bone; she glanced up and saw Schul's clenched fist, still blurred in swift motion, as it finished its vicious, downward arc.

The other one was still falling, sliding blood-smeared down the rock wall; he rolled over as a stone held by Schul crashed onto his head. He grunted again, then seemed to sigh and sleep, his body collapsing in a heap as Schul grabbed her again.

He threw her forward on hands and knees, held her tightly, pulled her into him; she squealed when she felt him inside her, pounding against her.

It was over very quickly. She knew it when she heard him howling. He pulled out of her and let her roll away while he waved his large fists, displaying triumph and pleasure.

That, too, was over quickly. The wind howled and filled the cave. She squealed in fear with all the others as the dust swirled about her and the other noise, the vibrating bass-song of the gods, rushed into the rock hole.

She crawled across to the one in deep-sleep, fighting against the swirling dust, reached him, heard his muffled groaning, then curled up beside him.

The vibrating bass-song ceased and the swirling dust settled down. She put her knuckles in her mouth to stop her cries and watched the others do likewise. In silence they were silent, ears curling, eyes widening, then started squealing and leaping about when the dazzling lights filled the cave.

"Help-mercy!"

"Me nothing!"

"Me the gods'! Me belong to them! Me worship them!"

The lines of light were long and sharp, cutting the darkness, crisscrossing, illuminating wide eyes, pleading lips, and hands turned up for mercy. She watched, shaking violently, fear congealing her every instinct, trying to hide behind the body of the one who was blood-smeared and moaning.

Light and darkness, noise and movement. Motes of swirling dust glinting. The thin lights beamed back and forth, up and down, in constant motion, stretching from the middle of the rock hole as if out of the air itself.

Then a greater light filled the rock hole, as if the sky had exploded, and it silhouetted the creatures who seemed to be holding lights near their bellies.

Like the others, she howled and covered her eyes with her hands, too frightened to look at the unrecognizable, only aware that the beating within her breast was making her body shake. She heard other noise, a lesser sound, a wordless communication, a rising and falling of tones that were impossibly alien.

It was a *singing*-talk. Her thoughts splintered and flew apart, then raced back and forth, and she saw steaming marshlands, the gray glint of water, green grass, and flowers of all colors, an arch of fig palms. She saw herself, very different; and Laurence and Schul, also different; then raced on until she found her mother in a cluttered room in the family home. She was perched on a stool, a cigarette smoldering beside her. Her fingers were dancing lightly along ebony and ivory; and miraculously, out of the large box above her, came the talk that was singing.

Her mother said it was *music*.

Mother? What was *mother*? She lurched between the past and future, sometimes lighting like a bird on the present before taking off again. Her splintered thoughts regrouped themselves, returning order to chaos, shrinking back into their original, narrow focus on what was happening around her.

She heard the wordless communication, the ricocheting speech singing, and looked up, over the body of the one who was just awakening, to see the silhouettes advancing into the cave, the lights beaming from what now appeared to be their upraised hands and, in their silvery motion, illuminating the fear and awe of those crouched in the dirt, all of whom were gnashing teeth and gibbering dementedly as the lights, forming a bright web in the darkness, finally dazzled her own eyes.

"Me hurting. *Him* hurt me."

Her squeal of fear drowned his words as she crouched farther back, looking up over his body at the creature looming above her to turn his searching light upon her. She grabbed a stone and threw it wildly, saw the light swinging away, heard the singing-talk ricocheting from wall to wall in that confined, light-slashed darkness.

The tall black figures moved away, retreating toward the rock hole, their lights waving back and forth, forming brilliant webs in the darkness, then suddenly winking off to leave only the greater light outside the rock hole. The tall figures stood in that light, rendered black and featureless by it. There was a sudden rush and surge of their singing-talk, then they suddenly disappeared.

The blood-smeared one sat up and stared at her, confused. Still confused, he looked at the others where they huddled together. In silence, they were silent, ears curling, eyes widening, then started squealing and leaping about when a monster roared outside.

At that moment the light in the rock hole blinked out, plung-

ing the cave back into darkness. The roaring outside grew
louder, like a monster enraged, then a fierce wind rushed into
the cave and filled it with howling dust. The noise outside increased, but then faded quickly; it abruptly stopped altogether
and the howling dust settled, then thin strands of gray, natural
afternoon light beamed obliquely into the cave's darkness to
give warmth to her face.

She looked at the blood-smeared one and wondered what had
happened to him, then she saw that the other one, the possessive one, was getting his courage back. The others were not so
brave, and in fact seemed almost crushed; they moved back and
forth in the gloom, avoiding the rock hole. They kept staring at
the rock hole, then at one another, but their feet, nervously
kicking up clouds of dust, remained deep in the cave.

"Me no fear. Me *kill* fear."

It was the possessive one who had spoken, staring around
him with hard eyes, his nostrils flaring to sniff out any challenge, large fists opening and closing.

"Me no fear. Outside go me. Me kill fear and *take* all."

He stared at each of them in turn, his eyes hard, nostrils
flaring, and receiving no hint of an argument took possession of
everyone. His eyes focused on her, tongue licking his lips in
hunger, then he clenched his fists, raised them above his head,
and walked out of the cave.

With beating heart she watched him go. She held her breath
and listened intently. For all the days of her life multiplied there
was no sound at all.

She looked at the blood-smeared one, sensing his hope without recognizing it, but when he took a step toward her, she
turned away and studied the others. They were staring at the
rock hole, trying to see what was happening outside. There was
nothing to see but the gray light; no sound but a whispering
wind.

Then the one outside howled. He was commanding them to
come out. They all glanced at one another, not understanding
what shame was, then nervously kicked up the dust and shuffled slowly outside.

She left the rock hole last, fighting fear with every step. Outside, the light temporarily blinded her, but soon sank back to
grayness. The possessive one was staring at her, eyes gleaming

with triumph, tongue licking his lips to show the hunger that was now his entitlement.

She avoided his stare but glanced around her, seeing nothing but desolation. The grazing animals had returned to the great plain of the gods, and the mountains beyond had lost their color and were dull in the gray light.

She looked at the sky. Most of the others were doing the same. A few birds with large beaks and wings of skin were flying sluggishly through thin clouds. Otherwise, as it was on the desolate earth, there was nothing to see.

She stood there, trying to define her experience, but was too stunned to do so.

She was silent in the silence.

32

"**I** all. *Am* all. *Take* all."

The aggressive one raised the challenge and again received no response, so he opened and shut his large fists, then slapped one demonstratively against his open palm. The smack was hard and loud, resounding brutally in the silence, making some of the others twitch nervously and hang low their heads.

She moved away, trying to avoid him. The sound *Schul* rang in her head. She had not thought of the sound before this day, but now it seemed to belong to him. He stared at her, watching her movement, nostrils flaring to catch her scent, then licked his lips, took a deep breath, and stared down the others.

All except one—the *good* one, who also wanted her. She heard the sound *Laurence* in her head, but didn't know what it meant. The good one was growing angry, touching the blood still on his head; he gave a hoarse growl and stared at the other, then kicked up the dust. He glanced sideways at her, his gaze forlorn, but made no move toward her.

"I all. All you *mine.*"

The other was glaring at everyone, letting them know his entitlement. He had been the first one out of the cave and that made him their leader, the one who could take what he wanted and do as he pleased. Now he concentrated on her, licking his lips, nostrils flaring, and she stepped back, feeling a dull, instinctive fear, remembering pain and not wanting it.

With the gods no longer present, the aggressive one was master of his domain. Now he fondled himself, exciting himself as

he stared at her, then took a deep breath and raised his clenched
fists to display his great strength.

She stared fearfully at him, then beyond him to the wilderness; the sun was breaking through the clouds, pouring golden
light on the mountains, making the boiling lava on the volcanic
peak glitter brightly, forming phosphorescent streams of many
colors.

"I want! I *take!*"

The aggressive one came toward her, nostrils flaring, eyes
alight, swinging his fist at those in his way, then reaching out
for her. She felt the vise of his fingers, a pain darting along her
arm, as he threw her facedown on the earth and moved in
behind her.

She turned her head, spitting dust, looking sideways and up,
saw the other one, the good one, exploding into violent action.
He hurled himself at the bad one—whose sound she knew was
Schul—and swept him to the side with his weight as she rolled
away from them.

She jumped up to rejoin the others, dodged their waving
hands, heard their chattering, then looked down at the two
males as they howled and fought each other on the ground,
making dust billow densely.

They rolled over the loose stones, arms and legs about each
other, fists rising and falling ferociously in that spiraling dust.
They grunted and yelped, sometimes howled in rage or pain,
then suddenly were back on their feet, both smeared with blood.

The good one shook his head, looking weak and confused,
while the bad took a deep breath and hurled himself forward.
His left fist was a blur, sweeping down through streaming dust,
then it hit the other's head like a stone and made his body jerk
sideways. The good one fell back, hitting the earth with a dull
thud, then the bad one leaned over and took hold of his head,
hammered it more than once against the ground, then stood up
again.

Lying on the ground, the good one quivered and groaned, so
the other one, the one whose sound was *Schul,* turned toward
her again. Erect, he came at her, breath hissing in his throat,
and was grabbing her when the one on the ground suddenly
jumped up behind him.

"*No!*" he cried. "*No touch!*"

At that moment the earth shook and a bass humming filled

the air. Frances, shocked and frightened, went winging out of
herself. Her thoughts splintered and flew apart, then raced back
and forth, and she saw steaming marshlands, the gray glint of
water, green grass and flowers of all colors, an arch of fig palms.
She then returned to the wilderness, drawn back by howls and
screaming—and suddenly realized who she was; and that what
was happening here had all happened before . . . between
Schul and Laurence in Eden, in that time that was yet to be.

Now, as the snarling Schul turned away from Frances, she
saw Laurence take hold of the thick, gnarled branch that had
been lying on the ground beside him and, with his body arched,
silhouetted by the dust bowl's light, raise the weapon high
above his head. Schul was already halfway through the air, his
greedy hands outstretched, when Laurence, with a quavering,
high-pitched wailing, brought the branch down on his skull,
making Schul career sideways and roll over on the earth with
blood already splashing from his first wound.

It was the first but not the last, since as Schul attempted to
rise again, Laurence repeatedly struck him over the head and
face.

Frances screamed at Laurence to stop, hardly believing what
she was seeing, but Laurence kept striking Schul with that
fierce, releasing rage, growing more exultant as he did so, not
aware of what guilt was. Schul's hands dropped to his sides,
revealing a head like a pomegranate, then as Frances managed
to pull Laurence away, Schul fell onto his side, tried in vain to
get up again, shuddered in a long, drawn-out spasm, fell back
and was still.

Along with the others, Frances stared at that fallen body; but
as an exhausted Laurence sank to his knees and fell over, lying
flat on his back and focusing blindly on the sky, the shaking
ground and pervasive bass humming combined to distract her.

Squinting, she looked up, at first puzzled then terrified to see
a circular, solid blackness growing steadily wider as it broke
through the clouds just above and came down upon her.

The descending blackness was bizarre, playing tricks on the
eyes, now concave, now convex; now like a flat, solid, featureless object, now like a hole cut in the sky and showing the
cosmos beyond. It grew bigger as it descended, spreading out a
great distance, then she realized that it was actually sinking into

the immense crater, which as the object roared louder was being swept by large, swirling dust clouds.

"Oh, my God!" Michael exclaimed.

They both witnessed the interaction of time and space: the past meeting the future.

Now, where Laurence had been lying, Frances saw *Michael* sitting up, shielding his eyes with one hand and staring directly above him as that blackness descended, grew even wider, then developed a wavering silvery rim. Michael stared at it trans-fixed, his body smeared with dirt, then the normal light changed to a dazzling white haze that erased his lined features.

Frances felt her body's weight, the child growing in her stom-ach, and the energy seemed to be draining out of her as she looked up again. The perfect blackness was still descending, growing enormous as it dropped lower, and she realized that it was going to slot into the windswept crater as perfectly as a cork into a bottle.

The navel of the world, she thought. *The world's navel is that great dust bowl. And that dust bowl will in time become the deep lake into which, with a dubious finality, Schul's body will sink.*

She kept looking up, unafraid, now simply fascinated, observ-ing the widening blackness as its rim became an immense, flar-ing circle, dimming the light of the sky above. The earth shook beneath her feet, the bass humming vibrated through her, then she felt her skin beginning to glow with a sublime sensual heat.

"Frances!" Michael called. *"Frances!"*

He was climbing laboriously to his feet, looking absolutely exhausted. Frances started toward him, glancing around her as she did so, and saw the other people standing there, shaking their heads, clearly dazed. Then as she froze, trying to recollect who they were, light and sound exploded around her, at once dazzling and deafening. She looked up to see that the descend-ing mass had become a great flaring globe.

Not a globe, but an immense dome of pulsating light. She found herself stepping backward, farther away from the crater's edge, while the object in the sky, that mountainous arch of luminous energy, turned the wilderness of the crater into an incandescent, mesmerizing haze.

The great cork filled the crater but cast its light on the

ground around it, swallowing the distant mountains and volcanic peak, then pouring out around Frances.

She screamed as she was blinded, fell down as Michael cried
out, shuddered and saw only the white light that had burned
through her skull. She was in the light and *was* the light, and
looked into herself, aware of other lights growing out of that
spectacle and separating like molecules.

The molecules grew into silvery discs, dark-centered and
dome-shaped, and these multiplied until there were hundreds
spread out all around her. They hovered silently in midair,
above and all around her, then spread out across the great
crater as far as the mountains.

Draining out of herself, Frances sank to the earth. Kneeling
there, she saw Michael, sleeping, curled up in the pulsating
haze. She was blinded but could see, looking through herself to
the infinite, and witnessed the future living within the past and
arched over the present.

The silvery discs covered the earth, hovering magically in the
air, taking energy from the water beneath the soil and rendering
it visible. The energy danced electrically, shooting up from the
shimmering crater, silvery lines that quivered and swayed,
coiled sinuously and crackled, forming phosphorescent bonds
between the ground and the hovering discs.

Then the discs starting changing, spreading out to touch each
other, becoming long, linear lines that formed an immense,
glowing web that contained, between its countless strands, glittering stars in black space.

Frances looked and was captured, enslaved by time and
space. The glittering stars and black depths curved around her
while she floated on shimmering light. Then the stars started
moving, up and down, to and fro, floating above, below, around
and finally through her, pulsating like the discs she had seen
previously, then making her melt.

The lights were living energy, the beating heart of the eternal
present, and as they circled her, entered her and passed on to
somewhere else, they spoke to her of God and His angels and
the portals of heaven. And as she looked at them, transported,
crossing the heavenly vaults to join them, she saw time and
space overlapping around her to give shape to a new world.

That world formed out of the ether as the darkness filled with
light, the light melting the stars and letting a golden dawn have

dominion. Time shifted back and forth, curved back upon itself, and drew out of itself the other worlds that existed within it. Jeweled domes and gilded spires, glittering bridges and gleaming highways, great cities built in mountains and by rivers that flowed out to the stars. Whether real or imagined, they made the infinite comprehensible, giving Frances something recognizable as an aid to acceptance. The light beneath her turned to sand, then the sand became grass, then trees and bushes sprouted from the grass and in turn produced plants and flowers.

A wind whispered and made the trees shiver, then a white pollen rained down.

Frances looked across the valley, the plain known as *Edinu*, to see, within the towering dome of light, the white molecules dancing. The light reached out to embrace her, surrounding her with its warmth, then the molecules filled up her senses with the speech that was singing.

She watched the molecules, entranced, their music tugging at her heart, their speech, which was singing, releasing her soul to the heavenly hosts. Then the dome of light darkened—or, rather, faded away—and then the light returned to normal above the dust-filled crater, though the mountains that had been there before could no longer be seen.

Frances thought of her child but could feel herself no longer; she was adrift on the sea of her own memories and constructing from that. Here, lemon and orange trees in a grove with an arch of fig palms; there, from the nearest edge of the crater, an immense, dust-filled plain. That plain was the world's navel; it was *Edinu*, the land of Eden. That plain was the gateway through time and space, leading through to the netherworld. That world was "here" and "now"; it was also "there" and "then." It was a bridge between the past and the future—and would become the lagoon.

The great plain was desolate, rendered more drab in normal light, but soon the dancing molecules, the pulsating white lights, had spread out from the garden around Frances to cover the crater. Once there, they grew larger, then turned into glowing discs, and the discs, hovering magically, bobbing gently up and down, suddenly flared up and drew from the barren earth rich fountains of water.

The water bubbled through the soil, pushed the dust up, then

the earth, and finally geysered into fountains that poured into
one another and exploded into more spectacular fountains of
silvery spray. The water became a pool, then a lake, then a
lagoon, and soon filled the whole crater, reaching the edge of
the garden, its surface, lightly rippling and pure, reflecting the
discs still above it.

Time moved back and forth, slipping through holes in space,
emerging from the funnel of the infinite to create its own future.
The calm lagoon rumbled, giving utterance to the earth beneath, then that earth, caught in telescoping centuries, was
pushed up in great blisters. Mounds of muddy soil surfaced,
making the water boil around them, then grew higher and
wider, letting water and mud slide off them, until they had
become fecund islets in a vast steaming marshland.

Frances knew that marshland, having seen it before. She
knew it as the world had come to know it when it settled on
Glastonbury. Frances watched it being born, saw it settle, then
studied its busy sky.

The lights were in their hundreds and pulsated above the
marshland, then they moved, changed positions, drifted sideways, up and down, finally settled again but stretched out to
one another, joining up to form that same glowing web in which
glittering stars formed. The stars flared up and faded, returned
and vanished again, moving in and out of space, controlled by
time, before being pushed elsewhere. Eventually they disappeared, leaving the great web behind, then this re-formed as
molecules, which, glowing warmly and dancing, spread out
over the garden.

Frances stared at the lagoon, trying to drink in its reality,
then turned toward the arch of fig palms and saw Michael
sleeping there.

She sighed and was content. She could not feel herself. The
glowing molecules came toward her, pulsating with life, surrounded her and bobbed up and down to fill her soul with their
singing-speech. She was soothed and reassured, then seduced
into acceptance, melting inside her own sensual heat and wanting only to give life.

The molecules merged and flared up, then became a single
light, which, though as soft as a fine mist, still pulsated rhythmically.

At first the mist was impenetrable, then dark holes made it

patchy. The dark holes grew bigger, as if being torn from fine gauze, and eventually materialized as the human shapes that Frances had seen in the cave.

The ghostly figures were like the cities whose highways reached the stars: they existed to aid her acceptance of what she thought was impossible.

Frances wanted to know who God was, what He was, where He was, but she finally understood, when she gazed at the creatures around her, that she would only find Him within herself, where the mind becomes soul.

Having taught her that, they then willed it, making her one of them.

She sighed and sank back, stretching out on the cushioning grass, listening to the music of the spheres and observing the figures above her. They were human-shaped, but too tall, and they lacked distinct features. Existing as mere molecules, as pulsating energy and thought, they had come from the double star, from the invisible companion of Sirius, adopting the vague form of human beings in order to help her.

They were shadows onto which she superimposed what it was she required.

She saw Schul and Miles Ashcombe, then Laurence and her mother, each emerging out of the other where space and time met.

Laurence was standing on a grassy mound with Stonehenge behind him, shading his eyes with his right hand as he stared at the sky. A magical radiance fell upon him. He turned his head to smile at her. She willed him to go and he dissolved—as did the circle of ancient stones—and there, where Stonehenge had been, a great pool of water, a lagoon, miraculously materialized.

Jack Schul was on the bank, staring forlornly across the water. Frances followed his gaze to see Laurence and herself on a wooden raft, pushing someone's body over the side, then watching it sink. When it had disappeared, they both glanced back at the land, but Schul—the real him, or his doppelgänger—had disappeared too.

Frances felt no guilt or fear but was touched by a new compassion; she shed tears for all the sins of the world and man's pained moral growth. Her tears fell like rain on glass, obscuring her view, distorting the real, and when her eyes had dried she saw her mother standing in the bedroom at home. She was holding the curtains open, gazing down on the back lawn, and the radiance that had illuminated Laurence now shone on her loving face.

She just stood there, silent and motionless . . . eternally present.

Frances wept again, her tears washing away her mother, then erasing the walls of the house to leave only the back lawn. Miles Ashcombe was there, no longer mad, his face serene; he was walking hopefully to and fro, the Tor of Glastonbury beyond him, then a pyramid of shimmering light dissolved him and left only starry night.

Frances slept in that starry night, a mere infant, dreaming happily; a door opened and sunlight fell across her and made her awaken. She cried out and glanced around her, still attempting to define the world, then a man with a gentle, caring smile leaned down to examine her. He was gray-haired, slightly bald, his eyes brown and abstracted—obviously not a practical man, though clearly intelligent. He smiled, creating cobwebs around his eyes, letting his face fill with warmth.

"Frances," he said. "You sweet child. Let me play you some music."

She heard his singing-talk, then a piano, a violin; and because music was the language of the spheres she understood every word.

She gurgled with delight, kicked her legs, grabbed his nose, positively writhing with the pleasure of the innocent looking up at the face of God. He was her father, her creator, the only man in the world—a world divided simply between him and the woman, her mother.

Frances wept, remembering that. She cried tears, recognizing him. Love and pain coursed through her, almost managing to divide her, but then merged into the single emotion that made her whole for the first time.

Just as those ghostly figures had surrounded her mother years ago, just as they had looked on during that singular, bloodless birth, so did they now surround Frances to observe her child's dawning.

Frances lay on God's green earth, a bridge between past and

future, and watched her father opening his mouth to blow a thin stream of smoke.

Not smoke, ectoplasm: an emanation of bodily appearance. It took the shape of a fetus, then a baby, then a child, then herself. She saw herself floating above, reflected in Eden's pure air, and she smiled, letting the tears dry on her cheeks, and lay back to give birth.

God's child, she thought. *Give me God's child. For we are all His lost children.*

A sensual heat limned her being, making her spirit writhe with pleasure, and she became a bridge between the sun and moon, to give her breath to the cosmos.

She gasped as her child emerged, breaking through her shivering lips, an ectoplasm that spread like smoke above her and then formed loops and coils. The loops became eyebrows, the coils outlined the eyes; a spiraling strand took the shape of lips and then encouraged a smile.

She gasped again—dying—leaving the old world for the new, passing from one present to another and releasing more of her secret self. It came out of her casually, parting her lips as her spirit glowed, curling into toes and fingers on invisible feet and hands, beneath the blind eyes and smiling mouth of the face not yet fully formed.

She died, entering the new world, not hearing her own final breath, but letting her eyes, which were open, stay that way to see what she had lived for.

Her final breath was her signature, completing her work of art, the ectoplasm spiraling above her face to fill in what was missing. It flowed around the toes and fingers, outlining the hands and feet, then coiled up and curved back in an arc that eventually surrounded the eyes and mouth. The eyes moved and then glowed, radiating an inner life, and that life, which was a pulsating energy, spread down to reach fingers and toes, to fill out chest and belly, to lend shape and definition and character to the child of the future.

Frances briefly lost herself, her heart stopping where time met space, then her heart started beating again and she awakened to glory—soaked in the morning dew, warmed by a new sun, holding her child to her breast in God's mysterious future.

33

MICHAEL emerged to dazzling light, to a vast, silvery sky, saw the flying saucers (or what resembled such) hovering in their hundreds above the earth as far back as the eye could see. Fear made him feel weak, but he tried to climb to his feet. He saw Frances at the far side of the clearing and desperately called to her. She stared at him as he fell back, too exhausted to stand upright, and the last thing he remembered before he slept was the hope in her shining face.

He slept and knew the darkness and emerged to a different light, perhaps dreamed that the saucers were hovering nearby, then opened his eyes again.

There was a brilliant sky above him, very blue, smudged with thin clouds, strands of gold and magenta spreading through it from a perfectly normal sun. He blinked uncomfortably, then rubbed his stinging eyes, saw the same scene, so sighed with relief and tentatively sat upright.

There were no flying saucers, but there were steaming marshlands, starting at the very edge of this forest clearing and stretching as far as the eye could see. They were marshlands, not swamps, and possessed a remarkable fecundity. The humidity, a product of plentiful rain and heat, had made everything outsized.

There were lush orange and lemon trees, thick clusters of giant figs, bananas and papayas hanging heavily from very large, bright-green palm leaves. Indeed, the foliage was exceptionally vivid, overwhelming the senses; and slightly stunned, trying to accept it, his gaze roaming over it, Michael took in the clearing and the placid lake beyond it, then followed rippling waves of tall grass to where it was slapping at Frances.

She was sitting up in the grass, still wearing the same clothes but holding a crying baby in her arms, her long hair falling over it. She looked radiant in the sunlight, at peace with herself; and as she gently rocked the baby and quietly talked to it, her conversation, like that of most new mothers, was more like music than speech.

Michael stared at her, bemused. He wasn't too sure about where he was. He remembered his dream (the wonderful light and flying saucers) and, feeling even more confused, looked around him again.

There they were: the steaming marshlands. They reminded him of Glastonbury. Recalling that place, he also remembered Miles Ashcombe, Mrs. Devereux, and Laurence, and finally his own journey here with the woman he loved. He and Frances had come a long way, traveling through time and space, to emerge in a very different world, outside past and future.

Where were they? *What* were they? Michael actually *heard* his own thoughts, his mute voice vibrating across the clearing to make Frances glance at him. Rocking her baby, she smiled contentedly, then lowered her head again while Michael stared around him—at Paradise—wondering if it was real.

He nervously touched himself, running his fingers along one arm, felt the fine hairs on his skin and realized he was normal. Returning his gaze to Frances, he studied her gurgling child, aware that that ectoplasmic creation was now a physical being.

The child, which had been born just like its mother, was the seed of this new world.

Michael pondered his changed future, then impulsively cast his mind beyond it, flying out of himself to traverse time and space, going instinctively where his curiosity led him.

He soared up from where he was, glanced back down at the Earth, passed *through* space and emerged to the double star, which was the source of his being. Disc-shaped lights bobbed and weaved, forming a bridge between the two stars, a vast arch of pulsating energy in which all became one. Michael felt it and was renewed, mind and soul fusing together, then curiosity took him back to the earth he had known before Eden.

Wanting to see his daughter, Cheryl, he caught her in sleep, tossing and turning restlessly in bed because he had left her. In her grief, she dreamed about him. He was sitting near Frances. They were in a forest clearing filled with flower-brightened foliage, both gazing out over tropical marshlands of unusual beauty. The place looked like Paradise, at once verdant and serene; and Frances, who was crooning over a baby, was limned by a golden light.

Soothed by what she had seen, Cheryl stopped tossing and turning. Still sleeping, she offered a smile to the dark, silent bedroom. Young and healthy, she would endure, find a man, bear his children, then pass on to find her father waiting for her, as he was waiting right now.

Michael knew that as he watched her, casting mind and soul over her, letting her take strength from his presence as she saw him in dreaming.

In her dream she saw her father in the Garden of Eden, turning his loving attention to Frances and her child.

A light breeze blew off the marshes, rippling the water in the lake, cooling Michael before crossing the clearing to blow around Frances. She shook her head and looked up, saw him watching her and smiled; then her head moved again, bowing toward him, acknowledging him, and in so doing stopped eclipsing the sun and let it burst out around her.

He was dazzled by the light but managed to keep his eyes open, then sat back as Frances straightened up, her smile touching his heart.

Michael wept. The tears felt cool on his warm cheeks. They flowed as they had done with Cheryl, so he let them fall freely. He had ventured here in ignorance, borne on wings of faith and hope; and in traversing time and space had made them part of him. Now he could make the past as real as the present, even as he ventured into the future to return to his source. So, in coming to Eden, he had lost nothing but gained all—and thus, in letting his tears fall to the grass, he was displaying his joy.

Still weeping, he stood up, glanced around him, saw a new world, wondered where his neighbors might be, and then touched his own cheeks. He wiped his tears off with his fingers, took a deep breath, drank the clean air, then walked very shyly across the clearing and knelt beside Frances.

"Don't ask me," she said, obviously anticipating his questions, holding her gurgling baby to her breast and rocking it gently. "I don't know, but it's all right. *We're* all right. You and I, we'll survive. We were meant to continue."

He saw his daughter, Cheryl, in the depths of her eyes, and understood that what she had said was true. He was here . . . and there also.

"Amen," he whispered.